THE QUEEN OF VEILS

Other titles in this series

The City of Veils
The Veil of Ashes
The Veil of Trust
The Queen of Veils

THE QUEEN OF VEILS

S. Usher Evans

Sun's Golden Ray
Publishing

Pensacola, FL

Version Date: 3/28/22
Copyright © 2020 S. Usher Evans
ISBN-13: 978-1945438301

All rights reserved. No portion of this publication may be reproduced, stored in a retrieval system, or transmitted by any means—electronic, mechanical, photocopying, recording, or any other—except for brief quotations in printed reviews, without the prior written permission of the publisher.

Cover Design by Jo Painter
Line Editing by Danielle Fine, By Definition Editing

Sun's Golden Ray Publishing
Pensacola, FL
www.sgr-pub.com

For ordering information, please visit
www.sgr-pub.com/orders

DEDICATION

To the girls who came back stronger

Chapter One

As my idiotic schemes went, this one might top the list.

After losing my small army of thieves and soldiers to a surprise attack by Queen Ilara of Severia, I'd returned to the city of my birth, where I'd been captured within minutes. A few moments ago, I'd woken up in the same bed I'd slept in during my months as the princess of Forcadel, face-to-face with the woman who'd taken my kingdom and destroyed my army. She'd offered me mercy and a promise that if I played nicely, she would allow me to see more sunrises.

Exactly as I'd planned.

While my army had taken a hit, and I mourned the children that had been slaughtered, I was nowhere near defeat. My army had grown larger than Ilara had suspected, and I had another hundred Forcadelian soldiers under my flag, not to mention the forces and support of neighboring countries Niemen and Kulka. After months of starts and stops, gathering alliances (and making sure those alliances stuck), we were ready to take our fight to Ilara and the city of Forcadel.

The problem was getting inside said city.

Thanks to the natural defenses of Forcadel, ours had been an impenetrable fortress until Ilara had snuck her army in under my nose. She'd come on bended knee, talking about her poor country and desperate people, all the while infiltrating the city and readying her assault. I and everyone else had been caught completely unaware. Now, I wanted to repay the favor.

Putting my full faith in my friends—Felix, Katarine, Jax—to lead my army in my absence, I ventured back home and allowed Ilara to catch me as a distraction. My only job was to make her believe she'd won until we could snatch our city back from her.

So far, so good. Katarine had been sure Ilara wouldn't put me in the dungeons, but I hadn't been so sure. Waking up in this bed was a positive sign; speaking directly with Ilara even more so. There were flowers on the small breakfast table, as well as a fresh set of clothes in the wardrobe. Someone had seen to it that my bookshelf was filled with thick tomes, too.

My ears twitched at the sound of the lock turning on the door and I closed my eyes to return to the mindset they expected me in. I pictured walking down the forest trail to the camp, small, dead bodies littering the forest floor. Tears came to my eyes, but I didn't let the grief swallow me yet. I would be grief-ridden, but I'd be damned if Ilara saw me cry for real.

"Good morning, Brynna."

It wasn't Ilara; rather a Severian woman wearing a white smock and holding a breakfast tray. Her smile was kind, but there was something about her eyes that set me on edge. She would surely try to befriend me, but she wasn't to be trusted. No one was in this castle.

"I trust you slept well," she said, walking into the room and placing the tray on the small table near the seating area. "My name is Luisa, and Her Majesty has asked that I look after you while you're our guest here."

I barked a laugh. "Until Ilara takes me to the gallows?"

"Do you believe you'd be in this tower if Her Majesty wished to kill you?" Luisa asked. "Although I would watch the way you address her. Outside these walls, you may have had a certain leeway, but it is because of Her Majesty's graciousness that you still breathe air."

A voice echoed between my ears. *"Temper your tongue."*

Perhaps I was laying the attitude on too thick. I took a moment to adjust my tone then spoke again, softer. "I suppose I'm just confused why I *am* still breathing."

"It's as I said." She poured a cup of coffee from the carafe. "Her Majesty has welcomed you as a guest. She's asked me to afford you all the luxuries of any other person of importance here in the castle. Now please, come have your breakfast before it gets cold."

Keeping confusion and mistrust on my face, I crossed the room, sitting down at the small chair. The coffee reminded me of mornings with Beata when I would've done anything to get out of this room. I let the feeling linger.

"It's all right," Luisa cooed into my silence, rising to walk to the one window in the room and sliding the glass open. "Things will be much better for you if you lose that stubborn streak. Her Majesty isn't the monster you think she is."

The hundred dead kids in the forest beg to differ.

I swallowed a gulp of coffee instead of speaking. Mistrust was a good emotion, but letting my tongue loose might get me in trouble.

The soft, Niemenian voice came back. *"Be truthful when you can."*

"The coffee is good," I said. "I missed coffee."

"Did you not have it, wherever you were?"

Her question had an innocent tone to it, but this was the first attempt at probing for the truth. I'd criss-crossed the continent these past few months, reaching the mountain capital of Niemen on foot then continuing through the farmlands of Kulka down to the marshy Neveri. From there, I'd returned to Forcadel, then spent a few weeks in a camp to the north.

But I didn't know how much Ilara knew—or how much I should reveal.

"Wait for someone to tell you what they think and play off that."

"There wasn't much time for niceties," I said simply.

She nodded, and I feared I'd said the wrong thing. "The soldiers said the forest camp was quite barren when they arrived. Barbaric, actually."

I couldn't help the flash of anger that crossed my face, and after a moment of thought, I let it remain there. "It was magnificent," I ground out. "And full of life."

"I'm sure it was." Luisa rose, clasping her hands together. "I can see it's still a sensitive subject with you. I'll leave you be."

"Until when?" I lifted my gaze to meet hers. "Ilara tires of playing host?"

"That, my dear, is entirely up to you," Luisa said, her fake smile gone. "And how well you can keep that tongue to yourself."

The door shut, and I waited a minute or two before allowing myself to slump back in my chair in relief. I hadn't said much, and yet I felt I'd given away my entire plan. This lying thing was hard.

A cool breeze hit my face from the open window. Did Ilara know that I'd once attempted an escape out that way? Or had Luisa just thought I could use some fresh air?

I blew air between my lips at my indecision. It was hard to know my next move when the other players hadn't told me the rules.

I sauntered over to the window, poking my head out to gaze at the castle below. Ilara's Severian soldiers were drilling on the green and more were patrolling the perimeter. Beyond, the city seemed quiet and empty.

Pulling my head back inside, I took stock of my supplies in the room. There was an extra pair of sheets in the wardrobe, as well as more than a few tunics. If I wanted to fashion myself an escape rope, I could easily do so.

But something tickled the back of my mind. This could've been a trap—especially as Ilara's lapdog Coyle knew exactly how I'd made my escape the first time. Felix had found me, tackled me, and after some cajoling, finally allowed me to continue my work as The Veil until my coronation.

Then, I had writhed under his grip on my wrists, furious at his meddling and insufferableness. Last night, we'd been in much the same position…

I allowed myself a quiet giggle.

Felix was still meddlesome and insufferable, but he trusted me now. They all did. Which was why I needed to think long and hard about my next move. This was a delicate operation and one wrong step could ruin everything.

Doing nothing and waiting for them to tell me something was surely an option, but it wasn't my style. And even if Luisa had opened the window as a suggestion to me, I was The Veil. Surely, I could scale the tower, sneak around, and be back before anyone noticed I was gone.

The castle below held a wealth of information about Ilara's defenses, and perhaps even some insight into why she'd decided to keep me not just alive, but as her guest. That could help inform how I interacted with Luisa and put us on more even ground. I wasn't sure what else to do with her except to sulk quietly, and sooner or later, they might realize something was up if I refused to speak. Or worse—they might tire of me and send me somewhere I couldn't leave.

My decision made, I nodded to the city beyond and hoped I wasn't making another giant mistake.

Chapter Two

Felix

Sweat dripped down my neck. The sun had just set, but hours of riding had left a burn on every piece of exposed skin. I probably should've stopped at midday, but I was already behind schedule. I'd expected to be in Neveri by now, but instead...

Instead, I'd followed my queen nearly all the way back to Forcadel, confessed my undying love, and spent the evening wrapped in her capable arms. When she'd left me, it was hard not to feel like it was for the last time, and that our stolen moments were the last gasp of a relationship never meant to be. But we'd taken what we could, and I had no regrets—not even letting her leave.

Still, old habits died hard, and I hadn't been able to resist one final act of devotion. I kept far enough away so she wouldn't notice (she probably would've run me through if she had), but my heart hadn't been able to let her take that final journey completely alone. Once she'd ducked through the small grate at the foot of the city wall, I'd pried myself away and headed back to our camp in the north.

There, my best friend Katarine and the bulk of our forces would be waiting for me. Our plan was to split them in two, with half coming with me to Neveri and the other half heading to Skorsa to meet up with the rest of the Niemenian soldiers. From there, we would devise the best way to move our respective armies into Forcadel and rescue our queen without alerting Ilara.

In some way, the task ahead of me had made it easier to leave Brynna. My efforts to help her regain her kingdom had been laughable so far. I'd donned a vigilante mask to keep the peace in the city, but all that had done was land me in jail with no benefit to Brynna. After a month in the dungeons, I'd been too weak to even mount an escape, and Katarine had been forced to save me. Now, I was ready to redeem myself to both of them, and I'd be damned if I let them down again.

In the bright moonlight, the forest where our camp had been came into view. I slowed my horse and dismounted to walk somberly through the freshly-dug graves. A part of me was grateful we were leaving this place for sunnier pastures. It was hard not to remember carrying little bodies from where they'd fallen in battle to these graves. Or how it had felt to close my young cousin's eyes for the last time. But perhaps the memories were necessary to keep us on the right path.

We had moved our camp to the open plains just north of the forest, and there I was greeted by two soldiers who saluted then took the horse's reins from me.

"Where's Katarine?" I asked.

"She and her contingent left early this morning," one said. "But she asked me to give you this letter."

Frowning, I took the parchment and opened the wax seal.

Dearest Phoenix,

My brother wanted to make haste for the east as quickly as possible, so we could wait no longer for you to return. I hope that your journey was fulfilling in every way. Please send word once you have established yourself in the west.

Yours,
Wolf

P.S. - Where did our late, mutual friend like to hang his hat?

I read the letter two or three times. Before we'd left, Katarine and I had agreed that we wouldn't tell our soldiers the truth about Brynna, in case word got back to Forcadel. But the level of coding in her letter told me she was concerned our communications could be intercepted. After the losses we'd suffered thanks to Beswick, I couldn't blame her.

"Sir?" the soldier said.

"Have we finished packing the camp?" I asked, folding the paper and sticking it in my belt for safekeeping. "I'd like to leave for Neveri as soon as possible."

"Where is Her Majesty?"

"She has left on a mission with Jax and the vigilantes," I said, telling the lie Katarine and I had agreed upon. "I hope she'll be back in the next few weeks, but until then, we have a job to do. Where is Aline?"

I found my lieutenant discussing the movement of troops with another soldier. She was still young—barely graduated from my cadets in Forcadel—but she'd proven herself capable and trustworthy. She'd been integral in helping reclaim Neveri, then had been the one to stay in the city and play vigilante when Brynna left, and she seemed willing and able to watch over the troops in my stead.

"Sir," she said, saluting me. "It's nice to see you back. Did everything get delivered?"

Aline was one of the few who knew what Brynna was up to, so I nodded. "As difficult as it was to watch it go."

Her voice quieted to a murmur. "And you still think it was the smartest move? Let our queen go into the castle? Ilara could kill her."

"I trust Brynna, and I trust Katarine's judgment." I had to, or else I'd go crazy with worry. "Have the messengers come back from Neveri yet?"

"Ammon isn't thrilled that we're coming," she said. "It might be wise to camp nearby until we can smooth things over."

"I had a feeling," I said. The Kulkan prince had a long history of saying one thing and doing another, and if we managed to get him to cough up what he'd promised when the time came, I'd consider it a miracle from the Mother herself. "If everything goes according to plan, we should be on our way to the south within a few days." I paused then turned to her. "I thought Katarine was planning to stay until I returned?"

"To be honest, we weren't sure when you'd be back," she said, the ghost of a smile on her face that I didn't appreciate. "There was some talk that you might not let her go."

"Funny."

"In reality," she said, the smile turning into a small grin, "Luard received a note from Ariadna, so they decided to leave this morning so he could return to Linden."

I nodded. I would've preferred to have strategized more with her, but time was of the essence. "Give the order to move the camp, and the two of us will ride ahead to smooth things over with Ammon."

She nodded and pointed to one of the few tents still remaining in camp. "If you want to freshen up, I left that one for you."

I thanked her and continued toward the tent she'd pointed out. But once inside, I stopped abruptly. Hanging from a peg nailed to the center post was a blue uniform. A Forcadelian uniform.

Not mine, that was back in Forcadel. Or more likely, in a refuse bin.

This uniform could only belong to Jorad.

The blue material brought fresh sadness to my chest, an ache that would never heal. Jorad had been one of my most promising cadets, and not just because he was my blood. There was a spark of leadership, of earnest loyalty to the crown and country.

That spark was gone. I'd cradled his cold body, the first to die in the massacre. Ilara's troops had spared no souls that had remained within the walls, no matter the age.

I pulled the dark blue tunic off the peg and thumbed the fabric before sliding it over my arms. It was immaculate—and I would have to take care to keep it that way. It felt good to be back in my country's colors, to wear that familiar broach at my left breast. My old one was currently hanging from Brynna's neck.

I closed my eyes, whispering another prayer that the Mother would keep watch over her and that one day, I would get to hold her again.

I smoothed the fabric and considered the cost of this war that hadn't even begun. Riya, Jorad, the young thieves in Celia's camp. Celia herself. Many more would be lost along the way, mostly innocents. Perhaps even myself.

Aline cleared her throat outside the tent. "The horses are ready, C—General."

It was hard not to laugh. Brynna had "promoted" me, but much like her own title, it was merely ceremonial for now. I reached into the bag to complete the outfit with Jorad's sword and scabbard. The familiar weight of a sword at my hip anchored me, reminding me of the man I used to be. The one my queen and soldiers needed now.

Katarine's letter sat on the table where I'd left it. Before I departed to Neveri, I needed to pen a response to her. Even if it wasn't much.

There was a small writing desk and I perched on the stool and began to write.

> DEAREST WOLF,
>
> OUR FRIEND LIKED TO HANG HIS HAT AT THE RUGGED PONY. THE EVENTS DOWN SOUTH WERE QUITE FULFILLING. THANK YOU FOR ASKING.
> I AM ON MY WAY WEST. WE MAY ENCOUNTER SOME TROUBLE OBTAINING THE PROMISED GOODS FROM THE WESTERN MERCHANT, BUT I HAVE FAITH WE WILL MAKE IT. ONCE WE ARE SETTLED, I WILL TURN MY ATTENTIONS TO THE JOINT MATTER TO WHICH WE ARE ALIGNED.
> I WILL AWAIT YOUR NEXT LETTER.
>
> WITH LOVE,
> PHOENIX
>
> PS: WHERE WAS OUR MUTUAL FRIEND'S FAVORITE HIDING SPOT?

I folded the letter and sealed it with the signet on the table—the same one Katarine had used. I slipped the small ring into my pocket so I could continue to send letters that Katarine could trust were mine.

With the envelope in hand, I strode out of the tent where Aline was waiting.

"Send this with your fastest rider to the east," I said, handing her the letter. "Communication will be key. Tell them to return to Neveri with the response as quickly as they can."

"It will still take several days," Aline said.

"And hopefully, when we speak again, we will have better news to share," I said. "But for now… Onward to Neveri."

Chapter Three

Katarine

"Are we there yet?"

I looked behind me at the small child who'd spoken. I hadn't spent enough time with them to know their names by heart, but her name might've been Paca. She was a cherubic Forcadelian child with stringy brown hair that my wife tried to braid in vain.

"Almost, my dear," Beata answered, reaching forward to brush that stubborn hair from her forehead.

When we'd started out from the camp earlier in the day, my wife had been bright-eyed and excited to leave the ghosts and grief behind. But now, the day of traveling with six children under ten was wearing on her. We'd made good time across the open plains, but once we'd entered into the misty forest, a damp chill had descended. A reminder that the mountains were close at hand.

"Shall we play another game?" Beata asked, forcing a smile onto her face.

The children groaned in unison. She might've called it a game, but it was really a lesson on numbers and letters. Most of them hadn't learned to read or write, and that had been Beata's singular focus before…

Before. That was the best way to describe it. Before the massacre, before the world had been turned over. Before our Brynna left on a half-idiotic plan to distract Ilara so we could reclaim the country.

I turned to the south, where Brynna had most assuredly been captured by now. I didn't question her bravery, but she lacked the ability to hide her emotions. Brynna's survival depended on Ilara believing herself to be the victor, and that would be impossible if Brynna couldn't temper her tongue.

I exhaled, putting that worry aside. It wasn't my focus.

I had taken charge of sixty soldiers. My second-in-command Joella led the march at the front, while I remained near the back to be close to my wife and the littles. We were headed to Skorsa, the former Forcadelian city that now belonged to the country of my birth, Niemen.

"I hope Luard reached your sister safely," Beata said, resting her head on my shoulder. Clearly, she'd given up trying to teach the children, as they'd busied themselves with a guessing game.

"I hope so, too." I wrapped my hand around hers, feeling for my wife's gold band. The night of our wedding had ended in the news that one of our own, Aline, had been kidnapped, and Brynna had put together a plan to rescue her. We'd succeeded, but when we'd returned to camp, we'd found it completely decimated, and everyone within slaughtered. The only ones who'd survived were Beata, these six children, and…

I craned my neck to the front, searching the soldiers for the crop of dark hair. "Where's Elisha?"

"Did she fall behind?" Beata asked, joining my search. "No, I think I see her up there. At the very front."

Through heavy fog, I could just make out the smaller figure marching with the taller ones where my wife was pointing.

"I swear to the Mother," I muttered as Beata chuckled beside me. "Didn't I tell her to stay in our sight?"

"She's technically still in our sight," Beata said with a smile. "You can't fault her for wanting to be in the thick of things."

"She's done more than enough," I said. "We have plenty of others who can take up the mantle."

"She's going to be a handful," Beata said. "Perhaps when we get to Skorsa, things will be better." She closed her eyes. "Do you think Felix has left for Neveri yet?"

"I don't know," I said. "I hope so."

She giggled, snuggling closer to me and dropping her voice. "The better question, I suppose, is did he let Brynna go? Or do you think he tied her up and took her with him?"

"I think he let her go, but he didn't like it," I said, resting my head on top of hers. Felix had been more open with his feelings of late; perhaps his time in the dungeon had cleared his vision. The old captain would never have danced with his queen in full view of his soldiers, let alone embraced her the way he had at our wedding.

"I don't think I would've let you go," she said, looking up at me.

I squeezed her. "One day, my wife, the world won't be on fire, and we can have our time together."

"I fear if we wait for the world to calm, we'll be dust." She chuckled, though a little darkly. "How soon after we arrive in Skorsa will we move back to Forcadel?"

"Felix will be traveling via the ocean, and so we will be moving our troops down the Vanhoja river. Jax will be scouting the river for Ilara's defenses, and once we know what we're dealing with, we can move south."

Beata frowned. "Will Ilara keep her alive that long?"

"Ssh," I said, glancing at the others to make sure they hadn't heard. "She's with Jax, remember?"

Beata's cheeks reddened. "Right, with Jax. On that mission."

She ducked her head closer. "You think they'll buy that?"

"Let's hope so," I said. "Brynna's life depends on it."

From somewhere beyond the misty forest, a cry echoed, followed by another. The soldiers around us slowed their gait and listened, reaching for their weapons and gazing into the foggy trees.

"What's going on?" Beata asked, glancing back at the littles.

"I don't know," I said, rising from my seat. "But stay here until I find out."

I hopped out of the wagon and rushed through the crowd, all of whom had pulled their weapons and were staring at the trees suspiciously. A shadow moved in the mist ahead, and I readied myself, but as it drew closer, I recognized our own colors. Two soldiers were carrying a third, an arrow sticking out of his shoulder. Right behind him, a pair of soldiers carried another soldier, but the arrow had found her heart and her head lolled sickeningly.

The sound of retreat echoed through the forest, and more shadows came running toward us. I let them pass me until my gaze found the commander at the front—Joella—helping a wounded soldier walk. Two Forcadelians ran forward to retrieve their compatriot, leaving Joella and I in the middle.

"What's going on?" I said. "Who's attacking?"

"It's hard to tell," she said, wiping her brow. "The arrows just started coming out of the trees. Hard to tell who they're coming from. Somebody said it looked like Severians."

"That would make sense," I said. "It wouldn't surprise me if Ilara had put a blockade along the river." I glanced behind me, keeping my eyes peeled for more arrows. "Are they advancing?"

Joella followed my gaze, her brow furrowing. "I was too busy running to... But it sure doesn't look like it."

"That's good news," I said, thinking of the children. "I'd hoped that we could avoid going over the foothills with all of our supplies, but it looks like we won't have a choice. Tend to the wounded, then double back until we reach the forest. There is a pass we can take from Kulka to Niemen that should be less guarded, but it's not an easy trail."

"Yes, I—"

A brown-headed blur buzzed past me, and my heart dropped into my stomach.

Joella gasped. "Was that—?"

"I'll get her," I said, grabbing my skirt and jogging after her.

"Wait, Lady Katarine—"

But I didn't hear her, dashing after the young thief and cursing her as I went.

⊳———————➤

"Elisha!" I called, trying in vain to keep my voice down. "*Elisha, get back here this instant!*"

But she kept running, flying over sticks and bushes and showing no signs of slowing down. She was growing smaller in the distance, and I cursed myself for not changing into tunic and pants before leaving the camp.

My heart stopped as an arrow sailed out of the darkness, landing mere inches from her nose. It stopped her in her tracks, giving me just enough time to grab her arm and yank her behind a tree.

"You little…you little…" I couldn't form words as I caught my breath. "You do not ignore a direct order, young lady."

"You ain't the boss of me," she snapped back. "These soldiers are the same ones who killed my friends, and if I can kill a few of 'em then that's what I'm going to do."

I straightened, sweat beading on my forehead as I stared down at the pain and anger coming off her. "And if you were to die, what then?"

"I won't die. Haven't yet."

Perhaps traditional tactics wouldn't work on this girl. I would have to be cleverer. "Very well, then." I squared my shoulders, pulling my last card. "Are you not one of Queen Brynna's subjects?"

She opened her mouth then closed it. "I am."

"And has Queen Brynna not given me authority over these forces, including yourself?"

She swallowed. "Yeah, but—"

"And did I not give you an explicit order to stay behind and let me handle this?"

"Yes, but—" She straightened. "Ssh!"

"Don't *ssh* me—"

Elisha grabbed my arm and yanked me down into the bushes a moment before two Severian soldiers walked out.

"I thought I heard voices over here," one said. "Don't see anything, though."

"They told us to stay close to the border."

"Doesn't look like it's an assault anyway. Those Forcadelians turned tail and ran pretty quickly."

"Cowards."

Their disparaging continued as they disappeared into the forest. Once their voices had ceased echoing, I chanced rising.

"See?" Elisha said. "I told you I was useful. You woulda been captured."

"And we wouldn't have been out here in the first place had you not run off," I said.

"I wasn't running off," she insisted. "I was trying to help."

"In this case, running headfirst into danger was *not* helping. The rest of the soldiers retreated, and I expected you to do the same. We aren't ready to meet Ilara's forces. We need to do it smartly, and from a position of power. And you, just now, jeopardized all of that. Do you understand?"

Her eyes flashed with anger, but she nodded.

"I know that you want to avenge your friends, and I promise that, one day, you will be able to do just that. But you'll be of no use to anyone if you get an arrow through your chest," I said. "And Brynna needs you."

Again, she nodded and muttered some semblance of an apology.

The weight on my chest lessened and I put my hand on her shoulder, turning her around. "Now, back to the wagon we go. And I'd better not hear a single peep out of you until we get to Skorsa."

Chapter Four

Luck was on my side, because a thick cover of clouds rolled in during the afternoon hours. If they stuck around after the sun set, I'd have a pitch-black night to move around in. Perfect for avoiding capture.

The heavy chair I'd used as a ballast during my first escape was on the other side of the room. Knowing exactly what would happen, I pushed the chair an inch, grinning as the feet groaned against the wooden floor.

Almost instantly, the door flew open, and two Severians came running in halfway to drawing their swords.

"What?" I asked, straightening. "If I'm going to be locked in here, I might as well do some redecorating."

"Just keep it quiet," one of them said, before motioning to her partner to follow her outside.

"Damn, I'm so good," I whispered, crouching down to push the chair. Now, any loud noises would be attributed to me getting comfortable and not plotting my escape. To avoid suspicion from Luisa, or whomever else might visit, I put the small table next to the chair.

I started with the sheets in the wardrobe, sitting on the floor with the tail of my makeshift rope hidden under the bed. After tying the sheets together, I added some of the tunics and pants to give it some more length so I could climb back up. I debated allowing myself to get caught, but that might result in some punishment—a locked window, for example—and I didn't want to chance that.

The sun began to set, and I hid all evidence of my escape, opting to sit next to the open window and watch the cloudy sky change color. As if on cue, Luisa's footsteps echoed up the stairs and I forced myself back into the mindset of a defeated, dethroned, miserable princess.

It was an odd contrast to Luisa's chipper smile. "Good afternoon, Brynna. Have you had a good day?"

"Sure," I said, turning back to the window. "It's been a great day with nothing to do."

"Nothing to do?" She scoffed as she walked into the room. "There's a stack of books here to entertain you, but I see they're untouched. Did they not teach you how to read?"

I glanced at the bookshelf; I'd barely noticed it. "I'm not interested in reading about fairy tales and romances."

"Then what are you interested in?" she asked, putting her hands into her skirt pockets. "Biographies? Art history? Legends and fables?"

"Why so curious?" I asked.

"Because you are Her Majesty's guest," Luisa said. "And she's asked me to see to it that you're taken care of."

"Then unlock the door," I said.

"My dear, a locked door has never stopped you before," Luisa said. "I wonder why it should now."

I glanced over my shoulder as she set the tray down, but didn't respond. Was it a question, a test, or a suggestion? She couldn't have known about my plan, but it was hard not to feel like she was tempting me into a mistake.

"Suit yourself," she said with a small shrug. "Knock on the door when you've finished and the guard will retrieve your tray. I will see you in the morning."

I kept my gaze on the floor until her footsteps died away. After waiting for another few breaths, I silently got to my feet and walked to the window. The castle was bathed in darkness as the moon was still obscured by clouds. Down below, the guards patrolling disappeared into the shadows—and if I couldn't see them, they couldn't see me.

I blew out all the candles as if I were going to bed. In the darkness, I found the lump of sheets and pushed them out the window. They tumbled down the tower, and I listened for guards or anyone else. When I heard nothing, I climbed onto the sill and grabbed the sheet, rappelling myself down the tower. The length was perfect and I thanked myself for adding a few pairs of pants and tunics to the mix.

My feet whispered on the roof tile, still warm from the sun. There were a ton of windows to choose from, but all of them were closed—presumably locked. I didn't have my glass cutters or any other way of getting inside, nor did I want to risk breaking glass and earning unwanted attention.

But if my knowledge of the castle was correct, Katarine's office was nearby. It was a long shot, but perhaps my Niemenian sister-in-law had left her window unlocked.

With care, I lowered myself down to hang from the rooftop. Katarine's office was visible, and from the looks of it, it hadn't been disturbed. Her Niemenian crest still sat on her desk, and one of her large hats rested on a hook near the door. With a shaking hand, I released my fingers from the roof and gripped the edge of the stone around the window. I scraped my feet against the sill until they found something to stand on. With my other hand, I pushed upward on the glass, then used my foot to finish the job. Carefully, I climbed inside the room then slid the window closed. The lock had been completely removed.

"Katarine, you magnificent bastard," I whispered.

With soft steps, I continued to the door, opening it by a crack to reveal the royal office suite hallway. Ilara's office would be at the very end, but the torches were still lit—she might still be in her office working late.

Across the hall from Katarine's office was a hidden servants' entrance. The castle had a collection of secret passageways and doorways that connected the servants to some of the most important rooms in the castle, including Ilara's room and office. They weren't exactly secret, but I might be able to move around the castle a little easier. After I made sure the coast was clear, I dashed across the hall and slid the door shut behind me.

This particular passageway led down to the kitchens, where I hoped I might overhear a servant or two. But on the fifteen-minute walk, I encountered absolutely no one. The kitchens themselves were desolate, although there was a faint smell of rotting fruit.

I waited around for a few minutes, but this was a dead end— curious in and of itself. I could usually count on at least a few servant conversations to find out what I wanted to know.

Feeling brave, I ventured out of the kitchens down a main hallway that connected to the entrance hall of the castle. A pair of guards walked by and I had to duck around a pillar, but they were silent. I gazed upward at the paintings still hanging on the wall— my ancestors. Odd that Ilara had left them up after all this time.

A twitter of laughter came down the hallway and I froze, then ducked around a pillar to hide.

"By now, the latest ship should've arrived in Aunela," Luisa said. "It should return to port in the next three weeks. Would you like me to arrange your departure?"

"Not yet," Ilara said. "I'd like a bit more progress first. We can make do with the smaller staff."

"Yes, Your Majesty."

"And how is our friend in the tower faring?"

"The guards report she reorganized the furniture," Luisa responded. "Not sure if she's up to something or merely bored out of her mind."

"Perhaps a little of both."

"She's certainly not lost any of her sharp tongue. But her behavior is still confusing."

"Indeed. I think it's time to invite her to dinner," Ilara said. "Have the servants set place settings for four tomorrow night and bring something appropriate for her to wear."

"Yes, Your Majesty," Luisa said with a nod.

I held my breath until their voices faded into the night and then smiled. Ilara was just as perplexed about my motives as I was about hers. This crazy scheme of mine might just work after all.

More importantly, Ilara was planning a trip to Aunela, a Forcadelian city near Severia. That could be a boon to us; if she was out of the city, then it might be easier for my army to infiltrate. I'd have to learn more about this at dinner tomorrow—and then figure out how to get a message to my allies.

Chapter Five

"Her Majesty has decided you've been on your best behavior and would like to ask you to join her downstairs for dinner with a few select guests." Luisa offered half a smile. "Since you are, as you say, starved for conversation."

"Oh? How kind." I made sure to lace my words with sarcasm, and perhaps overdid it, based on Luisa's glare.

"Dining with our queen is an honor," Luisa said. "I'll be back later this evening with the appropriate attire."

As promised, two servants arrived to dress me mid-afternoon, and Luisa joined to supervise. One of the servants carried a blue dress—a dress that had been made for me back when I'd been princess around here.

The realization hit me like a punch to the gut, and even more questions followed. Why would Ilara keep my dresses?

"Your corset, miss."

A groan bubbled out. "Really?"

She didn't answer, but the expectant look on her face was telling enough. I couldn't remember the last time I'd been stuffed into one of these torture devices, and I hadn't missed it. But when I caught my reflection in the mirror, I recognized the princess I used to be. The only thing missing was my gold circlet, which I'd left in Katarine's capable hands.

"I hope the dress is to your liking," Luisa said, appearing behind me. "Her Majesty said it was in your closet of things. She thought it so pretty that she kept it for you, in case you came back."

"Odd, considering she thought I was dead," I said dryly.

"Perhaps she was hopeful you'd survive," Luisa replied.

I tugged at the corset. "Why do I have to wear this thing?"

"Is it not the latest in Forcadelian fashion?" she asked, tilting her head to the side.

"I'm not keeping up with the trends," I said, turning to the mirror.

"In any case, your dresses seem to be made to wear with one, so we must make do for the time being." There was a little smirk in her eyes that bode poorly for my chances of getting new clothes. "Now, why don't you have a seat and we can do your hair?"

I rolled my eyes and ran my hands down the front of the skirt —they hit something hard. I started, shocked. Making sure neither Luisa nor the servant were paying attention, I slipped my hand inside the pocket Beata had sewn into all my dresses.

There, I found a knife.

It was small—no good for anything but parrying another knife and perhaps wounding someone at close range—but it was a weapon. Had I left it in there the last time I'd worn the dress, and no one had thought to check? I closed my eyes and thanked my past self for being so obstinate. I probably wouldn't need it tonight, but it made me feel better to have it in my possession.

"Well?" Luisa said. "We don't have time to dawdle."

I removed my hand from my pocket and sat down on the small chair. "Indeed we don't."

I kept my hands hidden in the folds of my dress, tempted to grab the knife and hold onto it for luck and comfort. As long as I kept my focus on the goal—keeping my place on Ilara's good side and perhaps finding out a little more about her plans in Aunela—I would be successful. I had become good at hiding my real emotions around Luisa in our limited interactions, this would just be a longer test.

"Brynna."

I started at the voice then narrowed my eyes at the source. "Coyle."

The captain of the guard looked as annoyed to see me as I was to see him. He'd been instrumental in putting Ilara onto my throne, betraying not only me, but also my brother, who'd been his close friend. Based on his uniform, he'd managed to remain in Ilara's good graces. I shouldn't have been surprised; it was what he was good at.

"I don't think we've really spoken since you arrived at the castle," Coyle said, his tone light.

"I can't imagine why."

"Always with a quick reply," Coyle said. "I can see why Felix fell so hard for you."

He was setting a trap, but I wasn't an idiot. "So hard he absconded to Niemen."

He quirked a smile. "Is that the story you're spinning?"

"If by spinning a story, you mean telling the truth, then yes."

He took a long sip of his wine. "You know what I think? I think he and Katarine were with you the night Celia's camp burned down."

"That's fascinating. Do you have any proof of this fantasy?" I almost hoped he did. At least it would be an answer to my questions.

"You never make mistakes," Coyle said.

"I absolutely make mistakes," I said, pointing to the Severian crest above my head. "This is a pretty big one."

"And your response was to traipse across the country, gathering allies and destroying gates," Coyle said. "Yet here you are, sitting with your hands in your lap. I wonder if there isn't a reason for it."

"Maybe I've given up."

"I don't think that's in your nature. Only death would stop you, Brynna. So I ask again, is there a reason why you're being so…" He smiled. "Well-behaved?"

"Ah, my favorite people."

Ilara walked into the room wearing what I assumed was a Severian tunic. As the corset constricted my breathing, I scowled.

"This is lovely," Ilara said. "My Luisa here from Severia and my Brynna back from the dead." Coyle shifted as she looked right past him. "Let us have a toast, to Brynna," Ilara said, raising her goblet to me. "For making herself impossible to kill."

Coyle lifted his glass but didn't meet my gaze. Luisa grinned and clinked her glass against Ilara's. Mine remained on the table.

"Brynna, you should raise your glass when someone offers a toast," Ilara said. "I promise you it isn't poisoned."

I couldn't help a quip. "Based on your past history, I wouldn't bet on it."

Ilara's eyes narrowed and she turned to Coyle, a slight snarl on her lips. "Coyle, switch glasses with Brynna. Perhaps then she'll be more sociable."

Coyle did as instructed, and I half-wished he'd keel over, just so I wouldn't have to look at him anymore. But he took a long sip and placed it down.

"See?" Ilara said. "I thought I was quite clear about that. If I'm going to kill you, I will do it in front of an audience. Killing you in private doesn't please me at all." She reached across the table to pull a small date from the bowl. "And I don't wish to kill you, so don't give me a reason."

With some effort, I drank the wine. It was pungent, and perhaps a little sour. Almost like it had been opened a few days ago and was still being used.

"I know, it's dreadful," Ilara said, clearly reading my expression. "But with this blockade, we're all having to make sacrifices." Her dark eyes landed on Coyle. "If only someone had stopped the smuggling."

"We haven't seen any activity of late," Coyle said.

"Hm." Ilara turned away from him to smile at me. "Brynna, I would love to hear about your journey. Spare no detail."

"I'm sure you know the whole of it," I said quietly.

"I'm sure I don't. Just that you destroyed my gate in Neveri, you crafty, horrible woman," Ilara said with a smile. "How did you ever come across something so vile as ond?"

She knows the Niemenians helped in Neveri. "I had help from Prince Luard of Niemen."

"And how, by chance, did you end up in Niemen?" She sat back, clasping her hands on the table. "I'm struggling to piece together the journey from when I left you for dead in Celia's forest."

"I—" I blinked. "You knew it was Celia's forest?"

"But of course," she said with a small laugh. "I like you, Brynna. We could've been friends had you not been so damned stubborn. But I needed you out of my way, not dead. So I made sure your little thief woman was nearby to nurse you back to health after I plunged my knife into you."

It was hard, but I pushed the questions about that into the back of my mind. "She did heal me then sent me on my way. I'm not a charity case."

Ilara plucked another date from the bowl. "Where did you go

from there? Did you immediately decide to go to Niemen?"

"I did." In reality, I'd returned to Forcadel, met up with Felix and Katarine, and *they'd* been the ones to send me on my way. "I'd hoped they would give me asylum. Instead, Luard convinced me to try for my kingdom back."

"He must've been *very* convincing," Ilara said, dropping her gaze away from me to Luisa. Clearly, neither of them believed me. "And Ariadna? Did you happen to speak with her?"

"Just Luard. He promised he had something that could help. The ond."

"And from there? Was it off to Neveri?"

"Kulka," I said. "To ask for their help as well." It was a stipulation of Ariadna's assistance. Convince Neshua to join forces with me and she'd provide her help.

"Mm." Ilara stroked the stem of her glass. "I, daresay, Brynna you're not a very good storyteller. There's neither tension, rhyme, nor reason to this story."

"You really think I'd be happy to tell you how far I came just to be caught?" I snapped, attempting a deflection.

"You're amongst friends." Ilara's smile was sweet and unsettling. "What is that saying? A queen isn't afraid to fail; failure is just a stepping stone to greatness?"

"Greatness?" I snorted. "I'm sure I'm going to find that locked in that tower."

"Oh, my love," Ilara said. "You don't have to stay up there, you know. I'd love to have you on my court, or as my envoy. We don't have to be enemies."

This time, the incredulousness was plain on my face. After all she'd done, I couldn't ever stomach being friends. And that she'd even offer smacked of some ulterior motive.

"Just something to think about," Ilara said, sitting back as the doors opened behind us and dinner arrived.

The chicken was rather scrawny and the vegetables seemed

wimpy and old. And the dessert was nothing more than a plate of butter cookies. Clearly, this blockade was starting to affect everyone, not just the lower class, but the queen herself. Looking at Ilara, she seemed oblivious to the change. Perhaps things were just so bad in Severia that anything was better.

When they cleared the plates, I exhaled as much of a breath as the corset would allow. The end of this evening was in sight, and I'd endured it without giving too much away. Soon, I would be back in my locked tower, free from eyes and scrutiny, and I could process the bits of information I'd gleaned tonight.

Ilara, however, had other plans. "Brynna, join me for a moonlight walk?"

"I'm sorry?" The words tumbled out before I could stop them.

"A moonlight walk," Ilara said. "I'm sure those legs of yours could use a stretch. You've been cooped up for far too long."

"In...deed I have," I said slowly. But even as I allowed her to take my arm, my guard remained high. She was up to something, and the knife in my dress was heavy.

Chapter Six

"Don't wear such a frown. You'll get wrinkles," Ilara said, nudging me with her elbow. I held my tongue. Ilara might reveal more to me if I remained silent—perhaps even about Aunela and this trip she was planning.

She led me out to the front steps of the castle, the night air brushing my face like a wet rag. Summer was certainly on the horizon again. The familiarity of the weather wrapped around me, recalling nights of dashing across rooftops and getting into all kinds of trouble with petty criminals.

"This humidity," Ilara said, running her free hand through her hair. "My hair has never looked this bad. I suppose I'm just not meant for this place."

I couldn't help the snort that came out.

"Ah, there's my girl," Ilara said with a large grin. "I do miss that uncontrolled tongue of yours. Moody and miserable Brynna is the least fun."

"Sorry to disappoint."

She grinned as we reached the bottom of the stairs. "Come, let's go to the gardens."

Though it was night, the large moon overhead illuminated the gardens, alive with the sound of crickets and flashes of light bugs. Ilara had at least kept these gardens pristine, with trimmed hedges and flowers blooming from nearly every angle. It still looked how I remembered it from when I was a little girl.

"You can excuse us," Ilara said to the two guards manning the gate.

They saluted her and walked away, resting their hands on their swords. Once they'd turned the corner, she nudged me to keep walking with her. My pulse quickened. We were alone, and there was an exit to the city through the garden wall. Ilara probably knew about it, too. My fingers itched to reach for the knife in my pocket, but I kept them by my side.

"I love this place," Ilara said. "Katarine and I would take long strolls in the mornings, when the weather was bearable. She tried to teach me the names of all the flowers, but I'm hopeless when it comes to minute details." She sighed. "I'm heartbroken that she abandoned me, but not surprised."

"You do remember that you stuck her best friend in the dungeons," I drawled.

"Instead of killing him," Ilara said. "Surely, that had to have counted for something."

I saw how you treated him. I caught myself before I spoke. "If I ever see her again, I will surely ask," I said. "But if you ask me, I believe they're both safely back in Niemen with Beata."

"You don't think Felix would've moved the world to be with you?" Ilara smiled, and it almost looked genuine. "He was absolutely devastated by your death."

"The last time I saw Felix was the day you stabbed me." I forced hardness into my voice. "Right after he chose his duty to the kingdom over me. So whatever devastation he felt was probably that he'd allowed yet another royal to be murdered on his watch."

She turned away from me, and I allowed myself a small exhalation as I looked at the sky. That had gone somewhat better than I'd anticipated, even though I felt like I'd stumbled my way through it.

"I do love it out here. It's a reminder of how beautiful a fertile land can be, and how we take it for granted," she said. "You know, there's nothing that isn't earned in Severia. Not life, not happiness. Not power. If you want something, you have to take it for yourself."

"Regardless of the cost, right?" I asked.

"You see, that's why I knew you would never be comfortable with a crown," Ilara said, turning to me. "You don't understand that helping the world means sacrificing a few."

She was right—I used to be that person.

"But that's what I love about you," Ilara continued. "You aren't a queen. You're a shadow in the night. A masked hero who's more comfortable helping anonymously than being in the spotlight. And that's why I want you by my side. I could use a capable heart like yours to help me as I take my country into a new era."

"And you're willing to overlook all I've done?" I asked. "Killing soldiers in Neveri, raising arms against you?"

"If you're willing to overlook my destroying your camp."

I stiffened then looked away.

"I didn't wish to be cruel, but you wouldn't take a hint," Ilara continued, gently stroking a dark red flower. "So drastic measures had to be taken to keep the peace. It's why I sent my army to raze yours, and why I had no choice but to send Mother Fishen to the dungeon."

"You *what?*" My voice echoed in the garden long after it left my lips.

"She obviously couldn't be trusted," Ilara said. "So I've put her in irons until she's better able to remember what happened the night Katarine and Felix escaped."

It was all I could do to hold in my fury. "She's innocent."

She shrugged. "I suppose news didn't reach you. Katarine used your uncle's dead body to smuggle Felix out of the dungeons. All my guards swear they have no idea what happened, and Mother Fishen says she was consumed by a need to fall asleep." Ilara sat back. "Now, I don't know about you, but that sounds like Fishen had a hand in allowing them to escape *and* seems to have been involved with someone who knows how to sneak around the city." She turned to me, curiosity on her face. "But perhaps if you were to tell me what you know, you could secure her release."

My insides twisted, but I couldn't help Fishen. Not now. "Do you think I'm the only person who knows how to use knockout powder?"

"I don't know, actually," Ilara said, eyeing me. "I know nothing about your Veil tricks, except that you're the only one who's ever used them."

"I'm merely the most famous. But copycats abound." I leveled my gaze at her, grateful I could be honest when I spoke next. "I had nothing to do with Katarine and Felix's escape, as I was up north running my own camp."

"Well, that's just a shame," Ilara said with a sigh. "I'd hoped you could enlighten me, so I might be able to release her. I suppose she'll just stay in there."

I shook my head. "The Mother will punish you for this."

"Oh, pshaw," she said with a shrug. "The Mother loves me. Why do you think I've been able to do so much?"

I could help myself. "I'm sorry? You think the Mother condones what you've done?"

"But of course," she said. "There is a much larger game afoot, one you know nothing about. These fits and starts will lead the way to a better future for my people. Once I have everything in place...

well…it won't matter who mounts an offensive against me." She shrugged. "The Mother's hand is strong on my shoulder."

It was all I could do to stand there and not sputter. She'd uprooted thousands from their homes. Torn this country apart. Starved my people to the point where the capital was dying. And she thought all of this had been blessed by the Mother?

"You're absolutely insane," I finally managed.

"Dear Brynna, you just can't see the forest for the trees." She sighed and leaned against the wall. "That's your problem, you know. All you see is what's in front of your face. It's why Beswick continued to be a thorn in your side, even after everyone rightfully told you to let him go. And it's why I was able to so easily fool you."

"You won't do it again," I snapped.

"But I already have." She tilted her head to the side and smiled. "You tell me you haven't seen Felix or Katarine or Beata since the day I stabbed you, but Coyle reported seeing her run away from Celia's camp with a wagon full of children."

I stopped. "Coyle was there?"

"My dear, he led the attack," she said before shrugging. "Well, I wouldn't call it leading. But it was a nice reminder of his loyalties. They're so fickle, you know."

I wasn't sure why that surprised me. Perhaps, deep down, even after all the betrayals and backstabbing, I'd thought Coyle might be salvaged. He might turn one more time, and I could use him to my advantage. But even if he offered me a path to the throne, I could never work with a man who'd slaughtered children.

"The question remains, my dear Brynna," Ilara asked, tilting her head slightly. "Why did Coyle report seeing her run away with a wagon full of children if you say she wasn't with you?"

Crap. Ilara had just caught me in a boldfaced lie, and by the smirk on her face, she knew it. My heart slammed against my ribs as she continued toward another of the vine-covered walls.

"B-Beata was there, but Felix and Katarine were not," I said, knowing it sounded like a complete lie as it came from my lips.

"I'm sure," Ilara said, with a smile that said she could read me like a book. "But I wonder why you haven't used that knife yet?"

"The...what?"

"The knife, my love, the knife!" Her smile was now almost manic. "The one that I had Luisa put in your dress pocket."

My mouth fell open before I could stop it.

"I thought someone who was so furious at the thought of children dying would have wanted to slit my throat the first chance she got," Ilara said. "And yet here you are...and here I am." She glanced around the empty garden. "Now's the chance to do it. I've even led you to the secret door so you can escape into the city. With your speed, I daresay you'd make it all the way to that little grate on the city wall before anyone was the wiser."

I had no idea what to say or do next—Ilara had trapped me in my own lies. "What in the Mother's name are you playing at?"

"Come on, Brynna," she said, walking toward me. "Kill me. I know you want to."

"I don't kill in cold blood," I stammered, the only thing I could think of that almost sounded like the truth. But I was rapidly losing the mask I'd thought was hiding everything. I couldn't hold it and be flabbergasted by her comments at the same time.

"I'm sure," she said, taking a step back. "You'll kill hundreds of your own countrymen in Neveri, but you won't kill me here? You escaped last night and yet showed up back in your bed this morning. I wonder why?"

I shook my head, scrambling to come up with something that wasn't the truth.

"Perhaps you should've prepared more," Ilara said with a wink. "Guards?" Out of nowhere, two guards appeared and took me by the arms. "Take her back to her room."

I let them drag me back, unable to tear my eyes from Ilara until

I turned the corner. One thing was for sure—this game of chess was a lot more complex than I'd thought, and I was already losing.

43

Chapter Seven

Felix

Neveri was half a days ride from our camp, a small island of civilization in the middle of the marshy Vanhoja river wetlands. It had long been the crown jewel of Forcadel's conquests, a demonstration of its ability to build where others had failed. But now it belonged to the Kulkans. For the moment.

"Do you think Brynna will ever reclaim it?" Aline asked as we rode toward the skyline.

"I don't think there's value in that, as long as Ammon keeps his end of the deal," I said. "But for now, we need to work under the assumption he will, and plan to move his five promised warships into Forcadel."

"It seems rather impossible," Aline said. "The only person who's ever successfully invaded Forcadel was Ilara, and that was because she fooled Princess Brynna..." She winced, giving me a second glance. "I mean—"

"She did fool Brynna," I said with a wry smile. "And Brynna's hoping to repay the favor. But since we can't move people and troops into the city the way Ilara did, we're going to have to figure out something else. We have the sea, so that's where we'll focus."

"The sea isn't much better," Aline said. "Not with that blockade."

"What blockade?" I turned to her.

"Last time I was there, she'd completely closed off the bay with bow-to-stern ships," Aline said. "I'd guess they're still there."

I clicked my tongue. "That certainly complicates things. We might've been able to sneak a ship or two past the towers on a moonless night." I paused. "Why would she blockade the bay?"

"She'd closed the city to new shipments," Aline said. "But Beswick was still smuggling food into the city. So she took drastic measures."

I straightened. "But if she closed the city to all shipments, how are people supposed to eat?"

"They weren't," she said darkly. "I think she was content to starve the city right out of existence."

"I know Jax was hoping to use the citizenry's discontent to our benefit, but that won't help us if they're all starving," I said. "Do you think Ignacio can find a way around it?"

"Beswick couldn't," she said. "I think that's why…why he turned to Ilara. Because he was getting desperate. The enemy of my enemy is my friend, you know?" She furrowed her brow. "But I still couldn't ever figure why Ilara thought it was a good idea to blockade the city entirely. She lives there, too. Her food was going to grow scarce eventually."

I shook my head. "Who knows what she's thinking? Half the time I thought her to be a petulant child who just wanted everyone to kneel to her." My smile faded. "But Katarine saw more there. So we shouldn't underestimate her, as we did with Beswick."

"I don't think we underestimated Beswick," Aline said, before squinting into the distance. "Didn't you tell Enos and the rest of the soldiers to remain in Neveri until you arrived?"

"I did."

"So why are they camped out on the fields?"

I followed her gaze; the telltale Forcadelian flags fluttered in the distance and I sighed. "Because Ammon clearly isn't a man of his word." I shook my head. "I expected this. C'mon, let's find out what the Kulkan prince has done this time."

As we drew closer, a cry of surprise and call to arms echoed from the camp until we reached close enough for them to recognize us. The two sentries saluted and allowed us to dismount inside the tent perimeter.

The lieutenant I'd left in charge was a burly young man, his beard aging him a few years above his actual age. To his credit, he saw my face and withered a little, but remained steadfast.

"There have been developments," he said with a slightly wavering voice.

"I can see that," I said, dismounting. "Can we speak in private?"

"Of course, Captain," he said, saluting me.

"General, now," Aline said with a look.

"Yes, congratulations, you've also been promoted," I said, following him inside a nearby tent. "What's going on? Why aren't you in the city?"

"We were, up until this morning," Enos replied dryly. "Ammon said we were causing trouble and told us to camp out in the fields until Her Majesty returned."

"And you listened?" I said, second-guessing my decision to let him stay.

"I didn't think it prudent to tangle with his soldiers," Enos said. "And I couldn't disagree that our presence was causing issues. The people in Neveri aren't too pleased to have been handed back and forth like chattel. First the Severians, then Her Majesty, and now the Kulkans. There have been riots nearly every night."

"Did you do anything to stop them?"

"We did," he said with a nod. "As best we could."

I sat back, considering this new development. "Then it's a good thing we came when we did. Ammon's clearly lost his healthy fear of Brynna, and his grip on the city is failing. We'll have to move quickly if we want him to help us." I rose to my feet. "Aline, stay here and help Enos get the camp set up. We'll remain out here for the time being. The two of you are co-command in until I get back."

"Yes sir," she said, saluting with him.

I declined a horse and traveled to Neveri on foot, so I could more easily sneak inside should the circumstances demand it. The long road from the east ended at the mouth of the city, and I wasn't surprised to find a pair of spear-clad guards waiting for me.

"Halt," one of the soldiers said. "You cannot pass, civilian."

I reached into my pocket to flash my Forcadelian symbol. "General Felix Llobrega, envoy of Her Majesty, Queen Brynna of Forcadel. Here to speak with His Majesty, Prince Ammon of Kulka."

I had no idea if that would work—and Brynna wasn't technically queen yet—but I hoped it might sway this low-level guard to let me pass. The guard eyed me for a minute, unsure if she should, but finally moved her spear.

"Take him to the barracks," she said to her partner.

The city was eerily quiet, even for the middle of the day. This hub of trading and merchant activity was normally packed with people, each eager to sell their wares. But the town square had been shut down, and the only ones milling about in the city were the soldiers patrolling.

With my soldier escort, I was allowed into the barracks, but another soldier, this time a lieutenant, led me into the building and up the stairs. She hesitated, only a moment, before rapping on the door at the end of the hall.

"What?" came the response.

"Sire, a General Llobrega is here to—"

Footsteps pounded on the other side and the door was flung open. Ammon looked a bit disheveled, his hair sticking up at odd ends as if he hadn't had time to look in the mirror lately, and patchy brown stubble peppered his cheeks.

"Brynna?" he asked, looking behind me.

"No," I said, holding back a chuckle. She must've put the fear of the Mother into him. "Can we have a chat?"

He grunted, seemingly relieved that Brynna wasn't there to blow up his soldiers, and let me pass. "Where is she?"

"Taking care of business elsewhere," I said, following him into the office. "Consider me her chosen representative." I rested my hand on the pommel of my sword. "I hope we can still count on your support. I'm concerned that you kicked my soldiers out of the city."

Ammon strode to the row of bottles sat against the wall. Kulkan liquor, if I had to guess. The best in the four continents. He didn't seem to want to offer me any.

"Does your princess still intend to kill every soldier in this city if I don't help?" He took a dainty sip of the brandy. "I didn't think she was that ruthless."

"There's a lot you don't know about her," I said. "You also didn't answer my question."

"Neveri is in chaos," he said softly. "I don't know if you could tell."

"You seem to have enough soldiers," I said lightly.

"I have as many as my father will give me," he said, a hint of bitterness entering into his voice. "He's told me that this is my city, and if I lose it, it's my fault." He took a long sip. "Your little stunt a few weeks ago didn't help things. These people want to be Forcadelian."

I didn't doubt that. They'd been used as pawns in a political game they'd wanted no part in. "I am here as your ally. I have no intention of taking Neveri back for Forcadel."

"The point is I don't have a whole lot of manpower to spare. If you take these five warships and whatever else I promised the princess—"

"Five ocean-faring ships and one hundred soldiers."

"—I will have very little to defend this city against the people."

"Then perhaps you should be a better steward of the city," I said.

Ammon made a face. "When I want your advice, Forcadelian, I will ask for it."

"Indeed." I paused to let him stew for a minute. "As it stands, Ammon, you made my queen a promise and I intend to collect. We will be moving to Forcadel soon, and I will take what is owed with or without your blessing." I walked toward the door. "I suggest you prepare your soldiers accordingly."

And with that, I shut the door behind me.

Chapter Eight

Katarine

We'd lost five soldiers in the ambush, and twenty more had wounds that needed tending to. Beata and the children gave up the wagon for the hurt soldiers. More than once, Beata commented on how we could've used a Nestori in our ranks. She'd only scratched the surface of the ancient art when Nicolasa had been struck down. The frustration was clear on her face as she wrapped wounds and attempted to stave off infections.

As for the rest of our soldiers, I ordered them to head northeast toward the mountain pass and on to Skorsa. Due to the narrow paths, I sent them in groups of twenty or thirty, warning them to watch their feet and keep their wits about them.

In the meantime, I sent a few scouts back into the forest where we'd been ambushed, but only two returned. The others had been shot before they knew what was coming.

"Whatever Ilara is trying to hide, she's taking great lengths to do it," I said to Beata. "I don't want to risk any more soldiers. Perhaps Luard can provide us with some more capable scouts."

"I'm a capable scout!"

My shadow jumped up from her spot nearby. Unlike before, when Elisha had been doing everything she could to put distance between herself and the rest of us, she was now offering herself as anything I even hinted at needing.

"I'd be in and out in an hour and I could tell you everything," she said. "I wouldn't get shot, neither."

"Either," I corrected. "And I know that you think you can go, but I'm telling you that you can't."

"Why not?"

Beata buried a smile as I exhaled through my nose slowly. "Because I said so."

She cast me a scathing look and stormed off, earning an eyebrow raise from Beata. "She's certainly a little…"

I smiled at my wife's silence. "Indeed, she is."

When the morning came, it was time for us to venture through the mountain pass, I walked the horse through the rocky pathways, grateful we didn't have to venture any further north. These were the foothills of the Niemenian mountain range, and even the small slopes were an effort.

"May I *please* get off and help?" Elisha said, practically hanging off the side of the wagon.

I glanced at my wife, who shrugged. "Fine. But stay close to the wagon."

Elisha didn't need to be told twice, jumping off the cart and dashing ahead.

"What did I…" I glanced to the sky. "Never mind."

"She's a unique soul," Beata mused, glancing back at the other children, who were huddled together for warmth. "You six don't want to get off and help, do you?"

They shook their heads and huddled together. I held back a beat to tuck in their blankets a little closer.

Our movement was slow, and when the sunlight turned a

golden hue, I ordered our small band of soldiers to set up camp for the night. Elisha, who'd been at the front of the group guiding them over the mountain, finally reappeared and went to work helping to set up tents in the dwindling sunlight. The children gathered firewood, and my wife set to cooking what meager food we had on hand.

"I didn't plan for us to be on the road this long," she said, almost by way of an apology. "I'm not sure it's going to be enough to feed everyone."

"I'll go find some more meat," Elisha said, popping up from the ground.

"Take someone with you," I called as she disappeared into the forest. Two soldiers overheard me and nodded, grabbing their crossbows and heading in the direction she left in.

"She's been awfully helpful as of late," Beata said. "Did your lecture get through to her?"

"I doubt it," I said. "She's up to something. But I'll let this newfound behavior continue until I figure out what she wants."

The soldiers and Elisha returned sometime later, after the fires were large and Beata's vegetable stew was boiling. The rabbits they'd caught were gamey, but it was still meat, and the rest of our traveling party was grateful for it. I declined a bowl myself, knowing that there would be more tomorrow in Niemen and wanting the soldiers and children to have their fill. It didn't escape my notice that my bride did as well—and so did Elisha.

"Elisha," Beata called, ladling a bowl.

"Save it for those who need it," she barked back. "I'm keeping watch."

"Here," Beata said, handing me the bowl. "See if you can get her to eat something."

Carefully balancing the bowl between my hands, I walked across the uneven ground until I came up beside her. "Beata insists."

"I'm not hungry," Elisha said. But even as she spoke, her stomach grumbled.

I settled down next to her, placing the bowl on the ground between us. "We have soldiers keeping watch. You don't need to trouble yourself with this."

"I'm a soldier, too," she said, her gaze drifting down to the bowl on the ground. "And I don't need food. Used to go days without eating at the camp."

"And so you should now?" I asked. "Seems like faulty logic."

She returned her gaze to the dark forest beyond, growing quiet for a moment.

"This pressure that you've decided to put on yourself isn't necessary," I said. "We have more than enough soldiers to divvy up the work. I don't see why you want to shoulder all this burden alone."

She stared into the forest, her young eyes growing weary. "You wouldn't understand."

"I might, if you told me."

"All my friends died defending the camp, and I shoulda been right there with them," she said quietly. "But Nicolasa, she told me to go. I don't..." She cast a scathing look at the ground. "There's no reason why she shoulda done that. I'm not special."

"I wish I knew why Nicolasa felt compelled to tell you to go," I said. "But I'm thankful she did. If you hadn't been with Beata, she might've gotten killed."

"The other kids woulda been able to help."

"They were terrified," I said. "You kept your head and saved lives."

She shrugged, picking up a stick and playing with it. "Doesn't make sense."

"Perhaps not, but the Mother's gifts rarely do in the moment," I said. "The point is: She wanted you to live, so now you need to figure out what you should do with this opportunity."

"What d'ya mean?" She made a face.

"Well, I mean…before the camp…" I cleared my throat. "What did you see yourself doing when you grew up? Surely, you had dreams of more than thievery."

"I…" She shrugged. "I thought I was gonna be a thief until Celia kicked me out. Maybe I wanted to be The Veil like Brynna." She looked down again. "But I always thought I'd see the business end of an arrow before I got too old. That's the way things work, you know?"

My heart broke a little for this poor girl, and the sort of life she'd lived. "Perhaps that's the way they used to work," I began gently. "But now, if you'd like, you can do anything you want. You can go to school, you can learn politics and art and sciences. The world is wide open to you now. We could even send you back to Linden to receive the best education in the four countries. Far away from the war and fighting. You can be a normal child."

"I don't want any of that," Elisha said, making a face. "I just want to be The Veil and help people."

"Brynna will tell you that was a hard life—"

"It's the life she wanted before she was dragged into all this finery."

That was true. "There are other ways to help those less fortunate other than getting into a fist fight. Once she's back on the throne, Brynna can use her power to make real changes for people. To stop corruption and make things fair. Just as she used to do as The Veil." A lock of hair had fallen into Elisha's face, and I resisted the urge to brush it away. "And you will have a similar opportunity when we get to Skorsa. But only if you keep your nose clean and do as I say. No more running headfirst into danger, all right?" I picked up the bowl and pushed it toward her. "Now eat up and get some rest. We have a long day in the morning."

She held the bowl in her hand, then cast me a curious look. "Why are you being so nice to me?"

"Brynna told me to look after you," I said with a smile as I rose. "And I'm not going to disobey an order from my queen."

There was something like hurt that flashed across her face, but as I walked away, she took the bowl and began to eat.

We arrived in Skorsa mid-afternoon the next day. There was still a chill in the air, but the soldiers' excitement was palpable. It was a beautiful city, perched on the edge of a large lake, and by all appearances, thriving under Niemenian rule. To the north, a gate sat open, now controlled by Niemenian forces. Beyond lay the rest of the country and the Ash river that lead to the northern glacial straits. My heart fluttered in my chest at the thought of being so close to home—to Linden.

Although it had been years since I'd been in Niemen, clearly, my presence was expected because the soldiers along the road bowed as we passed. We were greeted by the blended Forcadelian and Niemenian forces, then continued on into the cobblestone streets. Several Niemenians called out to welcome me back to my home country, and to offer their congratulations on my marriage.

"Word travels fast," Beata said with a small laugh.

"I'm sure Luard had something to do with that," I said, waving to another pair of soldiers.

"It will be nice to be in civilization again," she said. "I just hope we won't have to bunk in the barracks."

"I'll see to it that we find a suitable place," I said, and I meant it.

Our soldier escort led us to the center of town where he handed us off to Joella, who'd ridden ahead with the first soldiers. I was grateful to see her, and even more grateful to hear her report that all the other groups had arrived safely before us.

"No one encountered any more trouble on the path," she said. "But the few scouts I've sent south on the river..." She shook her head.

"That's going to be a problem, considering that's our way into Forcadel," I said.

"We will figure something out," she replied. "But first, let's get you settled."

She led us through the cobblestone streets, pointing out various inns and cafes that she promised were the best in town, but not dawdling much.

"You seem to know a lot about this town," Beata said.

"Ilara stationed me here before Luard showed up," she said with a smile. "I've grown fairly fond of this city."

"When are we moving into Forcadel?" Elisha asked.

"Soon," Joella said, sharing a look with me. "But we'll get you settled first."

"Why are we getting settled if we're not staying here long?" Elisha pressed.

I gritted my teeth and Joella ducked her head to hide a smile.

"My dear, I promise you'll be able to get in the thick of the action, just as soon as there's action to be had," Beata said, saving us from having to respond.

"Here we are," Joella said, opening the wrought-iron gate of a stately-looking townhouse painted a royal blue color.

Beata squeaked in excitement, but the rest of the gaggle seemed unimpressed. Beside me, Elisha made a face, but said nothing.

Joella used a large key to open the door, revealing a beautiful entryway. Beyond was room after room furnished with the nicest Forcadelian pieces. The carpets on the floors held a light sheen of dust, as if the doors hadn't been opened in some time.

"Mother above," Beata said, walking through the entry hall to the main living room. The children bounded up the stairs, their footsteps thundering above us as they explored their new rooms.

"This is—" I began, but stopped when my gaze fell on a painting of two men—perhaps of the owners. The man standing was much younger than the last time I'd seen him, as was his husband. This must've been commissioned when they'd first gotten married.

"Oh, it's… Lord Garwood," Beata said slowly.

"Yes, this was his summer house," Joella said. "Prince Luard thought his husband wouldn't mind letting you borrow it for now."

Perhaps Luard hadn't shared the news about the former owner. "And Lord Garwood's husband?" I asked softly, running my hand across the intricately-carved table. "Surely he's been to stay in their summer home."

"No word," Joella said. "I don't think he's in Forcadel though. When Ilara invaded, he left as soon as his husband was put in jail."

My chest ached. Garwood's death had been a convenient way to move Felix out of the dungeons, but the guilt of leaving his body behind stayed with me. I doubted the Severians gave him any honor after what we'd done. I just prayed the Mother would forgive me—and that Garwood had as well.

"It's perfect," Beata said, oblivious to my turmoil. "Rooms enough for the children and the kitchen is something magnificent. A water well out back, too."

"I'm glad you're happy, my love," I said, forcing myself out of my reverie to share in her excitement. "I suppose we should—"

A crash echoed from above and Beata's face screwed up in shock and anger. "*Children*! We are *guests* in this house." She grabbed her skirt and started up the stairs. It was hard not to laugh as the stomping ceased completely and the quiet was followed by some very stern lectures.

"Thank you, Jo," I said with a soft smile. "Will you let me know when my brother returns, or if I can do anything to assist in settling the troops?"

"Of course," she said, nodding. "I will stop by in the morning with news."

"I want to go with her."

Elisha walked out of the dining hall, her bag slung around her shoulders and her face reminiscent of Brynna's stubborn scowl.

"I'm sorry?" I asked.

"I've proven that I can handle myself," she said. "I want to be a soldier and train with the soldiers and do soldier stuff. I don't want to stay here in this fancy house. I don't belong here."

Joella shared a look with me before inching backward toward the door. "I think I'm going to excuse myself."

Elisha watched her go with a glare, then turned back to me. "Well?"

"Well, I think that's out of the question," I said, crossing my arms over my chest. "Brynna told you to stay with me. And that's what I need you to do."

"You said I'd be able to avenge my friends," she said. "How can I do that stuck in this house?"

I sighed. "I need you to be patient, Elisha. We don't know anything right now. As soon as I do, I promise you will be the first to know what we're doing to move into Forcadel. But for now, go upstairs and find a bed to sleep in."

She made a noise and rolled her eyes, but stomped up the stairs anyway, slamming the door behind her so hard the paintings rattled.

"Goodness." Beata appeared at the top of the landing. "What was that about?"

"The harbinger of a difficult few weeks to come."

Chapter Nine

Clearly, I'd made a mistake. The problem was I had no idea which mistake I'd made.

Had I been too complacent? Should I have tried to stab her with the knife? Should I have known they would've checked the pockets for weapons and been suspicious when they hadn't? Or was I just hopelessly behind Ilara in every way, shape, and form?

I had plenty of time to contemplate my mistakes, though. When I'd been returned to my room, the window was bolted shut. No matter how much I pulled at it, I couldn't make it budge. The extra sheets they'd given me were gone, as was the chair. I was now to take my meals standing up or sitting on the floor, I supposed. More importantly, I now had no means of escaping.

I tried not to dwell on that as I paced the room all night.

Ilara was clearly holding on to more information than I assumed, but at least she had no definitive proof that Katarine and Felix were with me at the camp. She'd only said Coyle had seen

Beata. I could presumably massage that truth. But what could I say to the knife, and why I hadn't used it? That was the larger question.

The next morning, Luisa was nowhere to be found. Instead, it was a young Severian man who'd clearly been threatened with bodily harm if he spoke to me, because he ran from the room after I bade him good morning.

It shouldn't have surprised me, really. My only entertainment in this room was Luisa, and if I were being punished, taking away that lifeline was expected. Still, as the days passed with only a timid maid to bring and remove meals, I began to worry that instead of being killed, I was in danger of being forgotten.

But without Luisa coming to visit, I had no way to get Ilara's attention again. I would have to try something else.

I spent a few hours banging and kicking the windows, which resulted in nothing but my sweat. The guards had presumably been told to ignore everything from inside the room. I even tried climbing the walls to kick the ceiling for loose boards, but the Forcadelian construction was sound.

Returning to the floor, I lay face-up staring at the ceiling and running through every conversation with Luisa and Ilara that I'd had so far. It made no sense for them to go through all this effort to not only keep me alive, but keep me out of the dungeons. They had to have some plan for me.

My gaze landed on the bookshelf in the corner. I hadn't really paid attention to it, except to note that all the titles were Severian.

"There's a stack of books here to entertain you, but I see they're untouched."

If Ilara wanted me to look at these books, then perhaps doing so might grant me a small reprieve. Or at the very least, get Luisa back to bringing my meals. My only hope would be if the morning or evening servant saw me reading and reported back.

And if that didn't work… I didn't want to think about it.

I picked one that seemed the most riveting and returned to my bed where I began to read. The narrative didn't take long to dive headfirst into the desolation that was life in Severia. I'd known it was hard there—after all, Ilara had come to me on bended knee pretending to be desperate for her people—but this was a new level. The plot was hard to follow between the descriptions of starving children, but within the lines, I learned more about Severian culture than I'd ever cared to know before.

When I finished that book—in record time, thanks to the hours of solitude—I perused the stacks for another. This time, I chose a history of the Severian royal family, hoping to find more information about Ilara.

The royal treasury had very little to give artisans, but they certainly gave as much as they could. Unlike here in Forcadel, where commissions were limited to just important people, the Severians paid for everything from city murals to classes for young, talented artists to hone their skills. Some of those artists became the court's official artisans, given a meager stipend in exchange for creating beautiful pieces out of clay and glass.

The boring subject and the fiery heat must've done me in, because the next thing I knew, the door was opening. I rubbed the sleep from my eyes and blearily watched the servant enter the room and place the tray on the floor. Her nervous eyes landed on the book in my lap, but she said nothing and left as quickly as she'd come.

I pushed the book off my lap and stretched the crick in my neck, whispering a prayer to the Mother that this crazy scheme might work.

"Well, look at that. I guess you can read."

It was hard not to gloat to myself when I heard Luisa's voice the next morning. Just in case it took more than a few visits to see me reading, I'd read another book cover-to-cover. I'd moved on to a history of the Severian royal family, which was full of children dying in the first few years of life. That Ilara had made it to adulthood was an anomaly.

"You wore me down," I replied, putting the book down.

She exhaled, wiping her forehead. "It's quite warm in here, don't you think?"

It wasn't enough just to look like I was ingesting the information; I had a feeling I'd be getting quizzed on it as well.

"Can't imagine why." I nodded to the boarded-up window. "What with those high-elevation breezes coming through the wood."

"Odd you haven't already put your foot through it," she said, checking the tea pot. "It's almost as if you don't want to leave at all."

"Clearly, the guards haven't been telling you about my banging," I said.

"Then tell me this: why didn't you stab Her Majesty when you had the chance?" Luisa asked.

"What good would it have done?" I asked, tilting my chin up. "Other than add another life to my tally."

"It would've allowed you the chance to reclaim your kingdom," Luisa said.

"Me and what army?" I asked with a small laugh. "I have no one except myself. And this city is crawling with your people. If I killed your queen, they'd surely kill me next. Then we'd both be dead."

"So you'll just sit here and sulk?" Luisa asked. "That doesn't seem like you."

I cracked a wry smile. "Do you know why I left Celia's camp after your queen stabbed me?" She shook her head. "She kicked me out. Had one of her goons escort me to the front gates of the city and drop me off without a gold coin to my name. If I'd my druthers, I'd still be there in her camp..." I softened, remembering the state of it now. "Yeah, I'd still be there."

"But in the intervening time, you gathered an army and took Neveri," Luisa said. "So it's clear you had *some* army. And you showing up here seems like—"

"A mistake." I shook my head, allowing myself to feel all the disgust I'd shouldered during my darkest weeks. "I'm sure… Well, now I'm sure they've found out that I'm not coming back. There was discontent in the camp already, and now…" I shook my head. "I wouldn't be surprised if they all disbanded. No one's going to risk their neck for me."

"You're their queen. And The Veil."

"And clearly, I'm a better Veil than queen." I sat back. "I've never wanted this responsibility—not when I was thirteen, and certainly not now. Maybe admitting defeat is my way of absolving myself of that completely." I looked at my hands. "All I wanted was to help people."

"Then why not escape to return to a life of vigilantism?" Luisa pressed. "You aren't helping a single person by sitting here as a captive."

I shrugged. "Maybe I'm questioning just how good a vigilante I was, too. It's hard enough to lose once. Twice…" I swallowed, thinking about the pain of the past month. "It's easier to hide my face than have to admit the truth. Maybe if I just stayed here and hid forever, people might forget what I did."

Luisa was quiet for a long time. "You know, if you're looking for something to divert yourself from these dark thoughts, you might try that red dragon book. It's one of my personal favorites."

I glanced at her. "These are your books?"

"No, they're Her Majesty's." She smiled. "And she's thrilled to know you're reading them." She nodded to the open one on the bed. "That's another one of our particular favorites. What do you think?"

"I found the romance cloying," I said with a wince. "Sorry."

She giggled. "Perhaps it's because you haven't ever been in love yourself. It is something magnificent to be swept away in a flood of emotions."

"Perhaps," I said, sensing she was still fishing for information about Felix. "You seem to know all these books by heart."

"There's not much entertainment in Severia," Luisa said. "Ilara and I would read these books together as girls and imagine a life far from our desolation."

This was the sort of information I'd been desperate for. "Girls? You grew up with her?"

"Oh, yes. I was her official playmate, then we became dear, dear friends." She smiled warmly. "I hope you and Her Majesty might find a similar camaraderie through these tales. They do bring me such joy and remind me of our childhood."

More and more to think about. "I might take another book from you, if you can promise little to no romance," I said. "Something from the archives would be nice, too."

"Let me see what I can do," Luisa said with a smile. "But no promises on the romance." She walked to the door and ducked her head out. "Guard, can you please call someone to pry this window open? We can't have our guest being cooked alive."

Chapter Ten

My open window was a start, but the door was still locked and there were no extra sheets. Still, I didn't even think about escaping. Instead, I spent the day reading another book so I'd have something to talk about that evening.

When the sun disappeared and Luisa arrived, I had the book in my lap, thumbing through pages I'd already read. She asked me which story I'd chosen, and I showed her the cover.

"I do enjoy that book," she said, nodding toward me. "What did you think?"

I'd found it horrifically boring, but I talked my way through the parts that were mildly interesting. She sat on the chair across from me, her eyes lit up. It was hard to tell if she was faking.

"I completely agree," she said. "The prose in that section was expertly written. It's as if the Mother herself gave him the inspiration." She pressed her hand to her heart. "Those are some of my favorite lines in Severian literature. Her Majesty's as well. We would have it tattooed on our bodies if we could."

And here I'd thought it was too wordy. "What book should I read next? You seem to pick out the best ones."

For the next few days, we continued in this vein. I would read a book Luisa recommended and she'd arrive at mealtimes to talk about it. The books themselves were depressingly repetitive. Dazzling heroines who defied all odds to save the day, heroes who sacrificed themselves for the greater good, and more than a few that ended with no hope in sight. Ilara seemed to have some of those same ideas about herself—although the heroines in the books never killed their way to victory. But even villains considered themselves the hero in their own stories.

"How long have you been in this castle?" I asked Luisa, after a lengthy discussion about the historical novel I'd been bored to tears reading.

"Several weeks now," Luisa said. "Her Majesty wrote to me and confessed she missed me and didn't have a friend in the castle, so I packed up my things and headed straight to Forcadel."

I frowned. "But Katarine was still here, wasn't she?"

"Of course, but...well, as we saw, she couldn't be trusted." Luisa sighed. "Ilara wanted so much to be her friend."

Was this before or after she imprisoned Felix and killed August? But even as I held my tongue, something inside me was desperate to break free, so I said, "It's hard to be friends with someone who's got your best friend in the dungeons."

Luisa turned to me, surprise flashing across her face. "Yes, I suppose it is. But your Captain Llobrega made his decision to betray the crown, and Her Majesty couldn't abide that."

"I suppose so," I said.

"It did pain her to do it," Luisa said. "She'd hoped Felix had been honest about swearing fealty to her. But clearly...well, it's as Katarine said. He suffered a mental break after your near-death."

I snorted. "Doubt it."

"You disagree?" Luisa asked. "I thought he was in love with you."

"Love is a stretch," I said, digging up that latent anger I'd held toward him. "He kissed me once, and the very next day told me to reassign him because he couldn't stand to be in the castle with me. He wanted to remain loyal to the throne, and being...well, he said being in love with me complicated that." I shook my head. "Less than a week later..."

"Surely, he knows you're alive now," Luisa said. "Ilara believes he feels regret."

I allowed myself a sardonic laugh. "When Beata showed up, I thought maybe... But I don't even know how they would've known where we were. And I doubt that Felix would've wanted to risk his neck for me after all this time. I'm not his princess and I'm not..." I sighed. "I'm not worth saving."

"So you really haven't seen him?" Luisa asked.

I shook my head. "I don't know what I'd say to him if I saw him again." I smirked. "Might punch him in the face for breaking my heart."

She laughed as she got to her feet. "Then if he knows what's best for him, he'll stay far away from you."

He won't have any problem staying away with me stuck up here. But I kept that thought to myself. I wasn't ready to ask for a reprieve from this prison. It would be better if it came from my captors.

Per my count, it had been a week since I'd been out of my room, but patience was the name of the game. As long as I kept reading the books, I would eventually get out of this room. And as long as I drew breath, my armies would continue into the city.

But patience was hard to come by when all I had to distract myself with were boring, desperate books. The characters' names were starting to run together, as were the places in a country I'd probably never see. I was growing anxious from sitting still, and had considered climbing up to the rooftop of my tower just for some exercise. But I didn't trust that my window wasn't still under surveillance, even though I could see no evidence of it.

Luisa's footsteps on the stairs were a relief after the hours-long torture, although today I couldn't find it within me to pretend to read. I'd had my fill of the history of the Severian mineral varo, an ond-like substance that was hard to find, but incredibly valuable.

"Good morning."

I quirked a brow; she carried no tray today. "Where's breakfast?"

"I've been talking with Her Majesty," Luisa said. "And we both think you've been cooped up here long enough. Would you like to take your breakfast in the garden with me?"

"Seriously?" The joy that surged through me was honest and drew a giggle from Luisa.

"Her Majesty is busy preparing for a large event in the coming weeks and is no longer able to accompany me on our daily walks. This morning, she told me to bring you instead."

Was it the same event they'd been talking about when I'd overheard them weeks ago? I wouldn't ask. "Thank you. As much as I love our time reading, I'm in desperate need of some exercise." I paused, looking behind her for the Severian maids. "Are you going to make me wear a corset again?"

"Perhaps not," Luisa said. "The tunic and pants you have on should work."

Bless you. "Yes, please."

My legs protested the staircase after being confined to a small room, but I couldn't deny I was breathing easier beyond the locked door of my room. I kept my shoulders back and gaze forward, trying not to look as if I were examining every detail of the castle.

Much as they'd been during my midnight jaunt, the halls were empty. And the servants that I did see were all Severian—there didn't seem to be a Forcadelian in the castle at all. None in the city, none in the castle. But I decided against bringing it up just yet.

The front doors to the castle were wide open, and as I stepped over the threshold, the sunlight hit my face. I inhaled deeply. The scent of the bay carried on the wind, and I could almost taste the salt in the air. No matter what happened, that always remained the same. Home.

"Well, dear Brynna, shall we?" Luisa asked, breaking me from my thoughts.

"Of course," I said. "You lead the way."

We ventured to the gardens, and I was grateful she didn't ask the guard to leave us this time. But I hadn't really expected her to, either. They had accepted my narratives—at least, for the moment —and I wasn't to be tested today.

There was a table bearing my usual breakfast in the center of the garden, and Luisa and I took our seats. The sight of the greenery was so refreshing after the staleness of my room. If I never saw those four walls again, I might be the happiest girl in the world.

"Being here again must be so odd for you," Luisa said as she peeled a small fruit. "You used to walk these gardens as a child, did you not?"

"I was kept fairly close to my nursery and school room," I said. "August was the one allowed free rein. But he was next in line, so he could get away with murder."

"I suppose you miss him."

"We didn't have much of a relationship. He was older by a few years, and I ran away at thirteen. I do remember him throwing me over his shoulder and carrying me in these gardens when I was a girl." I pointed to the small well in the corner. "And being stuck in that well. It was a nasty trick." I glanced at her, deciding to change the subject. "You said you have brothers?"

She nodded. "Most of whom I never met. They died in infancy. Her Majesty is the only sibling I consider."

I doubted Ilara felt the same. After all, she'd murdered her blood siblings to ascend the throne. Family ties didn't seem to mean that much to her.

"What?"

My curiosity got the better of me. "I was told the queen killed her family."

"Oh, Mother!" Luisa giggled. "Do you really think Her Majesty so cruel? Her siblings died of natural causes, as did her parents." She shook her head. "If you heard differently, it's just the rumor mill. Every day, Her Majesty prays that her family found peace in the arms of the Mother."

It sounded plausible, especially after what I'd read, but Kieran…well, he *was* a liar. But something in my gut told me that what I'd heard was the truth. Perhaps Luisa was the one who'd been misled. After all, my own father's death had been put down to as natural causes before August had fallen ill, too. Ilara could've poisoned her family and nobody would've been the wiser.

"My apologies," I said with a smile. "My source was unreliable, it seems."

After that, Luisa took me back inside the castle, and we walked the length of the halls. She asked me about the portraits hanging on the wall, and I knew nothing about them, so I made up some stories.

"That can't be right," Luisa said, glancing at the portrait of the woman who I said had had ten husbands and twenty children. "I believe you're making fun of me."

I couldn't help smiling. "Details have never been my strong suit. I'm sure she had a very long history and did important things for the country."

"Or, perhaps, she was merely a blood relation to the king, and therefore had the money to commission a painting," Luisa said. "I find that tends to happen a lot with your kingdom."

"And not with Severia?" I asked, as I'd just bored myself reading a plethora of historical accounts of Severian royalty.

"No, our heroes never had enough money to do anything with in the first place," she said with a knowing smile. "So if they ended up in our folklore, it's because they did something impressive."

Ilara had probably already been cemented into the folklore and stories of her people, or if she hadn't, she would certainly put herself there soon.

"I supposed we should get you back to your room," Luisa said as two guards turned the corner. "I've got plenty to work on today and I've dawdled long enough."

It hadn't been much of a conversation, but it had been something. "Thank you," I said.

"For?"

"Keeping me company," I said with a small shrug. "It's been a while since I've been able to find joy in anything. I'm honestly… well, I've started to look forward to our chats."

She smiled. "As have I. I'll see you this evening."

Chapter Eleven

My walk with Luisa had been a nice break in the monotony, but it had only lasted an hour, before I was back in my room. But the next morning, a servant arrived in Luisa's place with a corset and another dress from my collection, telling me to get ready for church.

"Church?"

"Yes, ma'am," she said, avoiding my gaze. "Her Majesty requested your presence."

Walking around in the mostly empty castle was one thing, being out in public yet another. Ilara must've been feeling confident. Even as I endured the tightening of the corset, I considered another benefit to my jaunt—I could potentially make contact with one of my people.

It had been several weeks since I'd left camp, and all parties—Katarine, Felix, Jax, even Ignacio—had their marching orders. By now, Jax should've infiltrated the city with the vigilantes we'd been training. Surely, one of them had been assigned to watch me. If I could venture into the confessional—

"Oof." I winced as the corset dug into my ribcage. It seemed I'd only get a reprieve from the torture in the castle.

"Sorry, miss."

My legs protested the stairs again. I'd probably have to do this more often if I was going to remain in any sort of shape to wage war. But perhaps that was also Ilara's strategy. Soften me through idleness. Perhaps I'd have to start exercising in my room.

"You look beautiful," Luisa said, joining me at the bottom of the stairs. She wasn't wearing a corset, having opted for a more Severian-looking garb of a loose dress. I could've argued that I could wear a tunic and pants to church, but it seemed they wanted to play this game. The only thing I could do was not look too uncomfortable.

"Isn't Ilara concerned that people might recognize me?"

"My dear, I doubt anyone in this town even remembers you," Luisa said, her gaze emotionless. "And it's *Her Majesty*. If you're going to be out of the castle, you need to use her official title."

I swallowed my disgust. "Yes, Her Majesty. Of course."

But it was hard to hide my true feelings when I saw who'd be escorting us to the sermon. Coyle always seemed to pop up just when I was feeling confident. Still, escorting Luisa and me seemed like an odd job for the captain of the guard to have, and it pleased me to see him assigned to something so menial.

When we reached the carriage, Coyle held out his hand to help Luisa inside, but I made a point of ignoring his gesture, climbing into the carriage and sitting down with a huff. He muttered something under his breath and closed the door, calling to the driver to go.

"You look troubled," Luisa said as the carriage lurched forward. "Is it Captain Coyle?"

"How could you tell?"

"You don't even look at Her Majesty with such open contempt," Luisa said with a chuckle. "Why does he vex you?"

"Because he betrayed everything he stood for to save his own skin." Might as well be honest about it. "I can perhaps forgive Ilara for exploiting my weakness. But he made a decision to betray his friends."

"Was he a friend of yours? Before Ilara arrived?"

He was Felix's, and more importantly, August's. I still maintained that Coyle's was the hand that slipped the poison into my brother's food.

"No, but… There are some things I can't forgive, I suppose," I managed to say. "But I would rather not think about them."

We rode the short distance in silence and I debated if I should adjust my attitude toward Coyle, lest it reveal something about me. But considering I'd punched Felix in the face when I thought he'd betrayed me, the emotion seemed correct for the situation. I'd just have to be careful not to let it influence my words as much as my face.

When the carriage door opened, Coyle extended his hand, meeting my gaze. I hesitated for a second then walked out of the carriage without help, pushing his hand away with my shoulder. I joined Luisa, who shook her head in dismay then took my arm.

"Forgiveness is a virtue, Brynna," she said with a soft smile.

"For some," I said. "For others, the Mother will take care of them."

I made sure Coyle overheard that.

The doors to the chapel were wide open, and the temperature dropped as we came inside. The stained glass and high ceilings brought peace to my unsettled heart, if only temporarily. Even though Fishen was gone, this place was timeless, a reminder that kings and queens come and go, but stone is forever.

I'd thought Luisa might take me up the side of the pews, but she opted for the middle path, in plain view of all those who'd gathered. I couldn't help scanning their faces, but my heart sank as most of them appeared Severian. The few Forcadelians there didn't give me a passing glance.

"I doubt anyone in this town even remembers you."

Truer words, unfortunately. But more concerning, I didn't see a single vigilante amongst them.

Luisa took me to the very front of the church where we sat in silence. The corset was wildly uncomfortable, and I fidgeted for a moment until I found a comfortable position.

Out of habit, my gaze went to the ornate chair in the corner— my father's chair. Next to it were two smaller chairs, where August and I had been forced to sit as children. It had been torturous, and I'd done whatever I could to avoid it. It was also my spot during my father and August's funerals.

The space where their caskets had lain was empty now, but my mind's eye could see them clearly. I'd gazed upon my father's gray beard and August's young, pale, dead face. I'd been mad at them for leaving me with their burden and couldn't rustle up the required sadness. Felix had chastised me for it, saying that my people expected me to be sad, and I'd chafed at the idea of hiding my emotions. How far I'd come.

"You seem lost in thought," Luisa said. "What's on your mind?"

"My father," I said, turning my gaze back to the chair. Might as well be honest. "And the day of his funeral."

"My condolences for your loss," she said.

"I didn't like him," I said. "But life was easier when he was on the throne."

She patted my knee. "And now that responsibility is on Ilara's capable shoulders. You can rest easy."

I mentally smacked myself. "I suppose you're right."

"It is quite a beautiful chapel," she said. "I know Ilara took inspiration when she designed the new church in Aunela."

My heart leapt to my throat. Aunela—I hadn't heard much about that. "What…exactly is going on there?"

Luisa just smiled enigmatically. "Her Majesty has asked that it be a surprise."

"Her Majesty, Queen Ilara Hipolita Särkkä of Severia."

The congregation rose with varying degrees of swiftness as Ilara stood at the back of the church, a vision wearing a mid-calf, light brown Severian dress that revealed her sandal-clad feet, and adorned with gold necklaces and an ornate crown. Once she was certain she was the center of attention, she began to walk toward the front of the room, nodding to the Severians who called out to her. She actually stopped in front of one older man, taking his hand and wearing a kind smile that I couldn't find any fakeness in.

Still, the entire episode felt forced. Ilara hadn't been much for church before, and inviting me here to this packed place seemed to be sending a message to me. She had been on this throne for nearly a year, and the people here had accepted her as their own.

It grated every inch of my soul to see her so triumphant. Even more so when she took the chair I'd been staring at, settling with her slim fingers on the arm rests. She nodded to a sister nearby, signaling the service could begin.

The sister ascended the dais, and I realized with a start that I wouldn't be hearing from Fishen that day. Something sad echoed in my soul, but there was nothing I could do about the priest except pray the Mother would protect her.

But as soon as the service began, it was easy to get lost in the words and ceremony. The sound of a thousand voices raised in song brought tears to my eyes as I sang to the lyrics I'd known since I was a girl. It seemed to be one blissful piece of my life that hadn't been completely ripped to shreds.

After the last hymn, the congregation rose and waited for Ilara to leave. She exited much as she'd entered, stopping to speak with her subjects and looking every bit the queen they wanted her to be.

My heart sank further as they crowded her. How was I supposed to win against this?

But just as my mood darkened, I spotted a lone Forcadelian woman sitting in the pew nearby, her head bowed in prayer.

Malka—one of my vigilantes.

Tears threatened to spring to my eyes as relief echoed through my chest. I'd been harboring the fear that I'd been abandoned, that I was enduring this torture for absolutely nothing. But Malka's presence was fuel to the tiny spark of hope that had nearly gone out.

"Brynna," Luisa said, nudging me. "I believe Her Majesty is coming over."

I broke my gaze from Malka, refocusing my brain. I was abandoned. Alone. Miserable. I buried my excitement as far beneath the surface as I could.

When Ilara reached our row, Luisa curtseyed then cast an expectant look to me—but my knees protested, refusing to bend. Finally, I had to bump my joint against the pew to make them move. When I rose, Ilara wore that same triumphant grin.

"It's nice to see you here, Brynna," Ilara said with a genuine smile. "I'm glad we've come to an understanding."

"Thank you," I said with a nod. "For allowing me to come."

"I hear you've been reading my books," Ilara said. "Perhaps the three of us should sit down over tea to discuss them. It's been so long since we've had someone to share in our joy."

"That would be wonderful." Wonderful? It would be amazing. I'd thought I'd have to endure weeks of Luisa's presence before being allowed back in Ilara's.

Luisa nudged me and something uncomfortable slid into my stomach. Ilara was waiting for me to address her—using her honorific. And perhaps even a bow.

My legs refused to bend, so I knocked the back of my knee against the pew and the rest of me dipped with it. I swallowed the bad taste in my mouth and forced myself to sound sincere.

"Your Majesty."

Looking pleased, Ilara left us, and I swallowed a sigh of relief. That had been close. Bowing before my sworn enemy in front of the Mother and the candles had almost broken me.

"Would you like to visit the sister for confession?" Luisa asked, nudging me and pointing to the chamber in the corner. It had been months—perhaps almost a year—since I'd confessed and sought guidance. But if I set foot inside that vestibule, I'd probably hear from Malka, or even Jax.

And as much as I wanted to get information from them, I'd just earned a victory from Ilara. I couldn't jeopardize that.

"No," I said, after a moment. "This was enough."

Chapter Twelve

Felix

"Excuse me?" I said to the young soldier at the perimeter of the soldiers' barracks. "Ammon said I'm not to be allowed inside?"

"No, sir, I'm very sorry." He looked genuinely so, which softened my temper. "He said to tell you that he's too busy dealing with his own problems to give you any soldiers, and that you'll just have to wait."

I scowled at him but didn't push the issue. "Very good, Lieutenant. Please remind your prince that he has a promise to uphold, and if he doesn't, there will be dire consequences."

He swallowed and nodded. "I will, sir. Absolutely, sir."

I left the poor boy, sorry that he was the one to have to deliver my message to Ammon. But the Kulkan prince would be sorrier if he thought he could stop me from getting inside.

I walked through the streets, whistling as I went. Even though it was dusk, before curfew, the soldiers watched me warily. Perhaps they were disturbed by my Forcadelian uniform, or perhaps Ammon had told them to keep an eye out for me. When one of them caught my eye, I smiled and waved, just to watch him squirm.

But all of our attention turned as loud voices echoed from a few streets over. The Kulkan soldiers jogged in that direction, and I followed behind at a distance. It wasn't my place to get involved, but the two Kulkans might need some back-up.

The source of the commotion turned out to be a group of irate citizens who had cornered a trio of Kulkan soldiers. Roughly ten other soldiers had come to their aid, but the crowd didn't look any less bloodthirsty as they advanced on the trio. Someone needed to take control of this situation, and since none of the Kulkans were doing it, I supposed it was up to me.

Bracing myself, I strolled out into the crowd, speaking with a commanding voice I'd honed when ordering my young cadets.

"Everyone return to your homes," I said, holding up my hands. "There's no need for this."

"And who in the Mother's name are you?" the one in the center, presumably the ringleader, asked. "We got grievances against these Kulkan assholes."

"I'm sure you do," I said. "But this isn't the way to resolve it. Go home, sleep it off, and in the morning, you can petition the prince like rational people."

"I'd rather just kill some Kulkans," he said, baring his teeth.

"Yeah? Then you'll have to go through me first."

All heads turned to the new voice coming from the rooftop, but only I recognized it. Aline jumped from the rooftop nearby, floating easily to the ground using the specially-designed cloak. She wore Brynna's mask and cloak, and although she looked nothing like the real Veil, the townsfolk didn't know the difference. Two of the rioters dropped their weapons and broke into wide smiles.

"I knew the Veil was here to save us!"

"I'm here to save no one. I'm here to tell you to get your asses back to your houses," she growled, stepping forward with an almost uncanny impersonation of Brynna. "And if I hear of anyone else causing trouble again, I will rip off your fingernails and feed them to your children."

The crowd hesitated, but a few backed away, causing the others' resolve to weaken. "

"This isn't over," the ringleader said.

"I'm sure it is," she said. "Scram."

Those remaining disappeared into the darkness, and it wasn't until we were completely alone that Aline's menacing stare lessened.

"That was dark," I said with a look. "Is that how you did things back in Forcadel?"

"A little," she said, pulling her mask off. "I found it easier to make people believe me if I went overboard. Nobody ever called my bluff."

"What are you doing here?" I asked. "Besides breaking up fights as The Veil."

"I was canvassing Ammon's navy, like you asked," she said. "It's easier to move on the rooftops and I'm less likely to be seen wearing this mask." The tops of her cheeks flushed. "And maybe I feel a little more like Brynna in this outfit."

I couldn't argue with that sentiment. "I never had that kind of gravitas under the mask."

"It's easy to pretend I'm her," she said. "But I'm sure Brynna never got caught. Except, of course, when she wanted to be."

"She did, actually," I said, a smile drawing onto my face. "The night we dragged her back to the castle, after August died. I brought damn near every soldier I could muster to surround her, and I caught her sleeping, but I still caught her."

Aline's grin widened. "I bet she was mad."

"Furious," I said. "Until I told her I knew who she was. Then she was both furious *and* dumbfounded. It's a nice look for her."

Aline gave me a grin that bordered on cheeky, so I cleared my throat and returned to business. "You said you were canvassing the navy?"

"Yes, sir." She plucked a crudely drawn map from her back pocket and handed it to me. "These are the ones I think we should ask Ammon for," she said, pointing to the circles on the map. "They're not the best, but they'd give us ample firepower."

"I'm starting to think we won't get very far asking for Ammon's permission," I said. "He wouldn't even see me today."

"So what are we going to do?"

I honestly had no idea. We had a hostile actor, a pressing need, and a lack of resources. "Head back to camp and see if anyone has found anything else. Maybe I'll get inspired along the way."

There was a rustle of nervous energy at the camp when we arrived, and it wasn't until I saw a new face seated near a fire that I knew why.

"Orman," Aline said. "Wasn't he in Forcadel with Jax?"

I nodded. "Let's hope he's got good news to share."

"Sir," the vigilante said, hopping to his feet and saluting. It was nice to know that even after weeks of training intensely with Jax, they still maintained their decorum. "It's good to see you. I hope everything's going well in Neveri."

I cleared my throat. "Perhaps we should discuss in private."

I led him to my tent and told Aline to keep the perimeter clear. After a few minutes, I nodded to my soldier. "Tell me what you know."

"Brynna was captured the first night," he said. "Ilara put her in a locked tower."

I couldn't help but snort in amusement. "I'm sure she's thrilled. But I'm glad she's not in the dungeon."

"She may as well be," he said. "And we have no idea what Ilara's larger plans are, either. Word has spread that she's packing up the castle to move somewhere else, perhaps to the east."

Katarine had mentioned something about the eastern side of the country getting Ilara's attention, but we hadn't been able to tell what exactly she was up to. "Have you made contact with Katarine?"

"No. We've attempted to send messengers, but they've all been rebuffed at the border. Whatever Ilara's doing, she's being extremely secretive about it. I had to venture far west before cutting north."

I nodded. "What does Jax think Ilara is doing? Don't we have Ignacio working for us? Isn't he working for Ilara, too?"

"He hasn't been able to find out, either. All he's doing is shipping supplies and people from Forcadel to Aunela," he said. "And meanwhile, most of the money in the Forcadelian coffers is gone. Apparently, she's invested it in this new city for whatever purpose."

"That's…completely ridiculous," I said. "Why in the Mother's name would she be investing in a city on the other side of the continent? It's close to Severia, but still… There's no easy way to get there from Niemen or Kulka."

He shrugged. "I don't know any more than I've told you. Jax was hoping that you'd have some good news on the troop movement."

I shook my head. "Ammon refused to speak with me today, and he's wavering on his promise. I don't want to have to resort to drastic measures, but I might just have to."

"We can't waste any more time," Orman said.

"I know," I replied, nodding decisively. "We will be on the ocean within the next week. Tell Jax to keep his eyes peeled for us."

"There is a port city a few hours from Forcadel called Mollard," Orman said. "If you get the ships, Jax advises you meet there instead of coming straight into the city."

I nodded. "We will do our best."

He saluted. "Good luck to you, sir. Hopefully, the next time we meet, we will be victorious in Forcadel."

I met Aline outside the tent as Orman set off at once for the south. All this time and neither Jax nor I had good news to share. And I was tired of it.

"What's our next move, sir?" Aline asked quietly.

"I think it's time we forego pleasantries," I said. "We have to believe that Ammon is at best going to drag his feet on this. Brynna doesn't have a lot of time to spare. We need those ships and the soldiers on them. If Ammon isn't going to give us his blessing, we'll take them without it."

"I don't think we have the numbers for that," Aline said. "We're barely at seventy as it is. And they have cannons."

"But we have ond," I said, sitting back. Katarine and I had split the bag that Beswick had wanted so badly. It was still enough to make a statement.

"Are you saying we make good on Her Majesty's threat?" Aline asked, looking a little uncomfortable.

I glanced at her, taking in the cloak around her shoulders and the mask in her hand. Brynna would've never condoned me killing soldiers, even if they were Kulkan. She would've figured out an ingenious way to get what she wanted without sacrificing a single person.

"Sir?" Aline asked.

"Perhaps it's time we all feel a little more like Brynna," I said, as an idea blossomed. "Come on, I think I have the beginnings of a plan."

Chapter Thirteen

Katarine

"Everyone seems to be eagerly awaiting our next move," Joella said, leaning over the map with me in the makeshift office I'd taken in the barracks. "You haven't received word from Captain Llobrega, have you?"

"I assume it will take a few days to get settled in Neveri, and more for the letter to travel the continent," I said. "But it should be soon. And hopefully it brings good news."

"I also hope we can share something good with him," Joella said. "Unfortunately, we don't have much. We can't go any farther south along the river without encountering a heavy enemy presence. We could move the troops by land, but that would mean —"

"Going back through the mountain pass," I said. "I agree, I'd prefer to move via the river. And we need the Niemenian ships to come with us, too." I walked to a map hanging on the wall and rested my finger on the military presence just south of us. "Has this presence always been here?"

She shook her head. "Not to my knowledge. Things changed, of course, when Luard took over the city a few weeks ago. But all accounts say this is a new element."

"Hm." I tapped my finger on my chin. "We need to know why this presence appeared and what they're protecting. Do we have any scouts in our ranks? Anyone who's well-versed in sneaking around?"

"Not here, no," Joella said. "But Jax should be sending someone soon, right? Maybe they can help us."

"Soon, I hope." Jax wasn't the sort of man who'd tell me, even if I asked. He and Elisha were the only survivors from Celia's camp. The loss of his family had hit him hard, but not hard enough for a complete personality change.

"Until he shows up, our goal should be to break up the defenses at the river," Joella said. "If there's anything I've learned from watching Her Majesty, it's that nothing is impossible if you've got enough nerve—and some Nestori magic."

"Unfortunately, we lost our only Nestori," I said. "And without Jax's people, we don't have anyone with enough skill to attempt a Veil-like assault on the gate."

"What about Elisha?" Joella asked. "She spent weeks in Forcadel helping Aline. And she's eager to help."

"Her temperament leaves much to be desired," I said.

That was an understatement. While the other children had taken to their studies with Beata like fish to water, Elisha struggled to sit still. Beata reported that she was often late to lessons and argumentative during them. If she was trying to prove herself trustworthy, she was going about it the wrong way.

"Besides that," I said, glancing at the door as if she were sitting outside, "Brynna asked me to keep her away from all this. She's still a child, and she's seen enough tragedy to last a lifetime."

"Very well," Joella said with a firm nod. "I'll identify scouts to study the security forces along the river and come up with a plan to dismantle them." She saluted and turned to leave, but stopped as her hand landed on the knob. "Do you think our fair queen is still alive?"

"Brynna could talk her way out of an executioner's noose," I said with a small laugh. "Even if everything goes to hell, she'll survive. That's what she does."

"But for how long—"

"I don't know," I said, hearing the fear in her voice. "But that's why we need to be ready to move at a moment's notice."

She saluted once more and walked out the door.

My day lasted much longer than I wanted it to. Before leaving for Linden, Luard had instructed his Niemenian lieutenants to come to me for guidance and supplies, so I spent the afternoon going over the rolls and budget for both. My brother had allotted a few thousand pounds of gold to the Forcadelian army, and for that I was thankful. We would very shortly run out of supplies otherwise.

But when I looked up and night had fallen, I knew I was in trouble. After gathering my cloak and a few papers to read later, I hurried out the door and along the emptying streets until I reached the townhouse.

"Hello?" I called, closing the door behind me. At once, the thundering of feet echoed from the floor above, and a gaggle of children between the ages of six and ten came bounding down the stairs. The girls wore ribbons and the boys' hair had been slicked back and they all wore matching tunics and shoes. Clearly, my wife had been busy making sure our new little family unit was cohesive.

"Hullo, Lady Katarine!"

"Did you bring us sweets today?"

"Your dress is so fine, can I try it on?"

"Children, children," said my wife, walking out from the back kitchen. "Give her a moment to breathe."

They dissipated quickly, some grousing that I hadn't brought them anything tonight. It was hard to keep a smile from my face.

"You're late for dinner," Beata said, some of the warmth disappearing from her eyes. "The sun set some time ago."

I should've chided her for overreacting—after all, with all the Niemenian soldiers, there was little to fear here—but she'd been scarred by what had happened in the forest. And I knew all too well that her worry could very well be founded.

"I'll do my best to mind the time." I pressed my hands to hers. "How was your day?"

She told me about the children, their studies, and the new things she'd learned about them. Paca had developed a blistery rash after eating strawberries for lunch and Ronja had provided a natural remedy she'd remembered from Nicolasa. Fletcher had been found reading a book earlier...or attempting it. Sorrell had cracked his first smile in weeks and little Gerda had spent the day glued to Beata's side.

"And what of our sullen teenager?" I asked, glancing upstairs.

"Oh, that reminds me." She walked to the staircase and rapped on the wall. "Elisha, Lady Katarine is home."

The footsteps were instantaneous, and Elisha barreled down the stairs. "A letter! A letter arrived for you this evening!"

I looked at Beata, slightly annoyed it hadn't been the first thing she mentioned, but she waved off my frustration. "Elisha wanted to be the one who told you." She kissed my cheek. "I'll have dinner waiting for you inside."

She disappeared through the door and I turned to the teenager, who was nearly bouncing up and down with excitement.

"Well?" I said. "Let's have it."

Elisha deposited the letter in my hand delicately, her chest heaving up and down as she watched. I inspected the letter closely, but to my trained eyes, it seemed fine.

"What are you doing?" Elisha asked, a little close over my shoulder.

"Looking for signs of tampering," I said. "You see here?" I pointed to the wax seal. "Sometimes when the seal has been popped off, it cracks and so you have to re-do it. But this insignia is intact, and it's one I recognize—it's Felix's."

"So it's from him?"

"Remains to be seen," I said, walking to the desk in small library. My wife had already lit a candle so I could see, and left an opener sitting atop the other papers. I ran the knife through the paper and carefully extracted the letter. The handwriting was Felix's, and when I saw the answer at the top, I smiled.

"It's from him," I said.

"What does it say?" she asked, squinting at the letter.

"Here, see for yourself," I said, handing it to her. "I've got to —"

"I can't read."

The admission came out quietly, barely a whisper. Her gaze had dropped to the floor and her lip jutted out into a pout. Clearly, it was something of a sore spot with her. Beata hadn't mentioned it at all. Perhaps that explained why Elisha had been so resistant to her studies.

"That's all right," I said after a moment. "We can—"

"My sister didn't think it was important for me to go to school, you know," she continued. "Mom was sick a lot, so we both had to work. And when Mom died, Esmerelda sent me away."

"Is she still in Forcadel?"

Elisha nodded. "When Aline and I were there, I stopped by. Didn't say nothing to her or let her know I was there. Just wanted to see, you know?" She exhaled loudly. "Same ol', same ol', you know? She got three kids, two of whom look skinny as get-out. Her husband's the same as my old man—gone a lot to sea. Just home to get her knocked up."

I cleared my throat. "Well, if you want to return there—"

"I don't."

"—you are welcome to," I said. "But if you want to stay, you can, too. We'll always have a bed for you." Yet again, my fingers itched to brush the stray hair from her forehead. "And in the meantime, perhaps if you attend your lessons with Bea, you might be able to learn to read."

She made a face and sat on a nearby chair. "I don't wanna learn with the others. I'm not a baby. Sanchia can already read, and she likes to show off." She glanced up at me. "Can you teach me?"

I shook my head. "I don't know if that's a good idea. I've got a lot to handle right now, Elisha. And Beata—"

"Please?" she said, popping right back up. "I don't want to tell anyone else. It's so embarrassing. Just an hour a day—at night. Before bed." She grabbed my wrist, her dark eyes filled with earnest pleading. "Please?"

"I suppose," I said with a sigh. "If you'll keep to your other studies with Beata."

She broke out into a smile and stepped back. "Promise. Thank you, Lady Katarine."

"Now run along," I said, nodding to the door. "I've got to pen a response."

"Can't I stay?" she asked. "Deliver the letter back to the messenger?"

I opened my mouth to argue, but then thought better of it. "Very well."

Dearest Phoenix,

Our mutual friend's favorite hiding spot was the loose stone in his bedroom, next to his window.

Things continue to move at a glacial pace here in the north. Skosa remains under our control, and the people are happy. My wife doesn't sleep, but the children are happy.

I hope this letter finds you well, and that things in the west are to your liking. I confess, this will be a difficult endeavor, not the least of which is communicating across such a distance. But I have faith that if anyone can accomplish this task, it will be us working together. I wish I had more news, but so far, my one task remains unfinished.

I look forward to your letter.

Sincerely,
Your Wolf

PS: What was the second chapter of my favorite book?

I dipped my quill back into the well and stared at the letter, reviewing my thoughts, as well as the grammar and spelling.

"Can you ask him how Aline's doing?" she asked.

I shook my head. "We must take care not to divulge too much information in these letters, at least until we're certain things are secure. I'm sure she's doing all right, though. She's safe."

"She was real tore up about getting caught," Elisha said. "I told her it was my fault, but she didn't really believe me."

"It was neither of your faults," I said. "Merely an event that occurred in the back and forth of a war. It won't be the last tactical error we make, but Mother willing, it will be the worst."

"People died, 'cause—"

"Because Beswick betrayed his country and Ilara's forces have no remorse," I said, a little harsher than I'd meant to. "We can sit around blaming ourselves until we're blue in the face, but what matters is what we do about it from here. You saved Beata, as well as the other children. Aline will find some way to redeem herself— if only in her own eyes. Felix will—"

"Felix?" Elisha perked up. "He's in love with Brynna, isn't he? I saw them dancing at your wedding."

"He is," I said with a little smile on my face. "Much to his nerves' dismay. He's a strong man and an excellent leader. I have no doubts that he'll be waiting for us in Forcadel when we get there."

"Is he the one you're sending the letter to?"

I nodded as I struck a light and lit the candle beneath the wax on the desk. Luard had let me borrow his signet ring to seal the messages, so I used it to press the red wax into the folded envelope.

"You will take this to the messenger," I said, handing her the envelope. "Don't touch the wax, and don't dawdle or take any detours. Once you've delivered the letter, come straight home. Am I understood?"

"Yes ma'am!" Elisha attempted a salute like the Forcadelian soldiers, but it was a little sloppy. Still, it made me smile to watch her run out with glorious purpose.

I sat back in my chair and toyed with the quill. I wished I could send a letter to Brynna. I would tell her to have heart, keep her tongue, and that we would be there to rescue her just as soon as we climbed this impossible mountain.

Chapter Fourteen

Bowing to Ilara had felt like taking a bath in boiling swamp water, and at first blush, it hadn't seemed to have any effect. I'd been returned to my locked tower, stripped of my corset, and allowed to stare out the window and reflect. I didn't bother to read a book, too disgusted with everything Severian to stomach more of their history.

But my disgust subsided as the day wore on, and I ventured over to the bookcase to pick something else to skim before my evening session with Luisa. This subservient behavior had worked so far, and I would keep at it until it stopped.

The sky had grown pink outside when the sound of footsteps reached my ears. But instead of Luisa, it was a young maid.

"Her Majesty has asked you to dine with her," she said. "You are to come with me."

"Do I have to wear a corset?" I asked. If so, the maid hadn't brought me anything to wear.

"N-no. Her Majesty told me to bring you as you are."

Well, that's something.

I followed the maid down the winding stairs, my hands clasped behind my back as we passed the guards. They didn't move to follow us—another oddity, as they'd been a near-constant presence when I'd left with Luisa the past two times. Perhaps my public bow to Ilara had meant more to her than I'd thought.

The maid brought me to the same room where I'd dined with Ilara the first night, but now there were only three seats, and Luisa was already in one. I actually smiled in relief.

"No Coyle tonight," Luisa said, patting the seat next to her. "Just a chat between friends."

Friends. Despite everything, I was starting to think of Luisa as something of a friend. Perhaps my loneliness was getting to me.

"Ah, my favorite girls," Ilara said, walking into the room without fanfare or announcement. Clearly, this was to be an intimate dinner. She lacked any of her usual accoutrements or royal trappings tonight and looked more at ease than I'd ever seen her.

Luisa rose and bowed, and I followed suit, albeit slower. The action stung less than it had earlier in the day, but it still set my stomach on fire.

"Oh, no need for that," Ilara said, though it was after we'd both already bowed. "Sit down and let's eat."

"How was your day, Your Majesty?" Luisa asked, spearing a fruit with her fork.

"It's been a whirlwind," Ilara said, helping herself to wine. "I'm glad you forced me to go to church today, my dear friend. It was exactly what I needed."

"You must always listen to me," Luisa said with a cheeky grin. "I do know what's best for you."

Ilara grinned back at her before turning to me. "And how did you enjoy the service, Brynna?"

"I felt the same as you," I said. "It was exactly what I needed."

"I confess, I don't like going to services. I find the Mother in action, and sitting in a long ceremony has never made me feel close to Her," Ilara said. "Don't you feel much the same?"

"I do, actually," I said with a bit of an ironic smile. "There's forgiveness in service. That's..." I licked my lips. "Well, that's what brought me back to Forcadel in the first place. When I was fifteen."

Ilara leaned onto her hands. "I don't think I've ever heard this story in its entirety. Please share."

I spoke honestly, perhaps for the first time in a long time, about how I'd accidentally killed a man in the service of Celia and how that had led to becoming The Veil. It was nice to tell a story without fearing that it would give away some secret, but I still kept a tight leash on my words.

"It sounds like you'd come into your own as a vigilante," Ilara said. "Do you still feel like a failure?"

My lips parted in surprise, and I had to remember that every word I'd said to Luisa had made its way back to Ilara, including my reasoning for remaining in the castle.

"In some ways, yes," I said. "But in others..." I had nothing else but the truth to speak. "My city's changed in my absence, and I don't...I barely recognize it. I could walk out the door, don the mask, but...I'd be starting from scratch. I can't even be sure who's an ally and who wouldn't try to sell me out to the highest bidder." I toyed with my fork. "I don't know what good I'd do out there right now. Or if any good I attempted would blow up in my face."

"I never thought you'd be so unsure of yourself," Ilara said.

"A mask covers more than a face," I said with a small shrug.

Whatever Ilara was going to say was abruptly interrupted by a hurried rap on the door. She cast Luisa an annoyed look and called for whomever was there to enter. A nervous-looking Severian guard walked inside, wringing his hands.

"Pardon me, Your Majesty, I hate to interrupt your dinner—"

"Then it had better be for a good reason."

He swallowed hard, and somehow I got the feeling what he was about to say would be worse than the interruption.

"There's been...well, there's been an incident down in the dungeons. "All the guards... Well, they just fell asleep. And the prisoners have..." He swallowed. "Escaped. Including Mother Fishen."

Ilara's fork dropped to her plate and her eyes widened. Luisa's gaze went to me, but the surprise on my face was genuine. My mind immediately jumped to Malka and the vigilantes, but I doubted they would've been so brazen. They were still soldiers, after all. And Jax, who was supposedly leading them, didn't give two craps about religion.

"It sounds awfully Veil-like," Ilara said, her gaze coming to land on me. "Do you know anything about this?"

"I can't say that I do, what with me being locked in my tower all this time," I replied dryly. It was easy to be confident in my ignorance when I was, in fact, ignorant. "I don't even know how someone would get in and out of the dungeons. There's only a front door, right?"

"There's a back entrance," Ilara said. "You didn't notice it on your castle map?"

"I...didn't." Again, I was grateful I had the truth to share. "Sneaking into the dungeons wasn't ever something I thought about doing."

"Not even when Felix was there?" she asked sweetly.

"No, he was never on my list of people to rescue," I said with a bit of a glare. "In case you forgot how he broke my heart."

"Then how do you explain this?"

"Maybe you shouldn't work your guards so hard if they're falling asleep on the job."

Ilara licked her lips, surveying me before sharing an unspoken conversation with Luisa. "Are you mocking me, Brynna?"

It was a dangerous move, but it felt right. I had nothing to hide, and although I wasn't displeased that Fishen had escaped, I also had no idea who'd done it. It could've been Jax...or any number of other people.

"You put this city's spiritual leader in the dungeons," I said. "Clearly, you had to have seen this coming."

She blinked. "I've put thousands of people in the dungeons."

"Thousands of businessmen and other laypeople." I chanced a small laugh. "But you crossed a line when you arrested Fishen. People who wouldn't have cared if their neighbor disappeared will certainly care if their lifeline to the Mother was taken away."

I waited for her to respond, rage, toss *me* in the dungeons, but she remained silent, breathing through her nose. It was more unnerving than if she'd thrown her goblet on the ground.

"I see." She flexed her fingers. "I suppose that my dealings with Beswick are now over."

I crossed my arms over my chest, hoping I looked like I had no idea what she was talking about. "Why do you say that?"

"Beswick promised he would stay out of my way as long as I provided him with ample business in the east. I've done that, and he does this to me?" She snatched her goblet off the table and took another swig. "Alliances clearly mean nothing to him."

My heart thudded. Did she know Beswick had been captured?

"What?" she asked.

"I can't say for sure that it was him, or anyone affiliated with him. Beswick's not religious," I said, hoping I sounded anything but worried. "He wouldn't care if you put his own mother in the dungeons, as long as it wasn't him. This doesn't seem like something he would do."

"So who do you think it was?" she asked, leaning forward. "A new element, perhaps? I don't know where people get this knockout powder, as you call it."

"Nestoris, usually," I said, trying to avoid pinning the blame on anyone specifically. "And Beswick isn't the only criminal in town.

There are others, too, ones that might be a hair more inclined to rescue Fishen."

"Then I will have Captain Coyle sweep the town for Nestoris," she said. "Thank you for that advice, Brynna."

"I wouldn't call it advice," I said. But this was a golden opportunity to glean some information from her. "Still, if you ever want to know anything about Beswick and how he thinks, you know where to go."

"He bested you twice."

"Because I wasn't prepared for his contingencies," I said. "Beswick does scorched earth. You burn him, he burns everything you ever loved, but leaves you alive to watch the devastation. I watched him do it to countless lives in Haymaker's Corner."

She ran her finger down the side of her mouth. "And you don't think he betrayed me?"

"This doesn't seem like his style," I said. "If he's thrown in his lot with you, he wouldn't do anything to jeopardize it unless he had something better lined up."

"I doubt that," she said. "He's been paid handsomely to complete his task."

"Then it wasn't him." Something unlocked in my stomach, and a flood of relief crashed through me. Ignacio had been keeping up his end of the bargain and Ilara was none the wiser that Beswick was no longer in charge.

"Hm." Ilara twisted her fingers around the stem of her glass. "It sounds to me like you have some idea who it was."

"No, only about who it wasn't."

"That's more than my guards do," Ilara said. "I'd rather they not waste their time turning over stones you already know will result in empty caves." She smiled in my direction and something cold slipped down my back. "Perhaps you might be able to help them find out who did this."

Based on her tone, it wasn't a request.

Chapter Fifteen

"I don't really see why we need to investigate," Coyle drawled. "I'm looking at the culprit."

I might've glared at him, except my scowl was already so pronounced, I feared my face might stick that way if it deepened. Instead of being returned to my room, giving me ample opportunity to get out of this predicament, I was escorted to the soldiers' barracks and dropped in this chair. Ilara wanted this solved quickly, and there would be no time for me to come up with something.

"You must think I'm some kind of wizard," I said, breaking my gaze to glance at the Severian crest hanging over his head. When this was Felix's office, it had been a Forcadelian one. "Because I've been under supervision every day and night since I was captured. I can't imagine how I pulled this off."

"Then one of your accomplices. Felix or Katarine—"

I snorted. "Accomplices. Right. I don't know if you've heard, but everyone abandoned me."

He rose and barked at the two guards to leave then slammed the door. "Cut the crap, Brynna. You accosted me wearing that ridiculous mask and told me to keep an eye on Felix. I know you've been in contact with them. And whatever you're planning is going to fail. I would've thought you would've known that by now, considering your history."

"Fancy words," I said, not bothering to rise in anger. "I could also tell Ilara that you withheld knowledge of my presence from her for months."

"It's your word against mine."

"And you're a proven liar," I said. "What happened to all that talk about hedging bets? You think Ilara's the biggest fish in the pond now, so you're going to keep kissing her ass?"

"I don't know, is she the biggest fish?" Coyle asked, tilting his head. "Because from where I stand, you're a prisoner in her castle. And unless you've got something truly remarkable up your sleeve, I doubt you're in any position to do anything about it."

I forced my gaze onto the crest above his head. "Is it true that you led the attack on Celia's camp?"

Out of the corner of my eye, I saw him fidget uncomfortably. "Yes."

"And you gave the order to kill children?"

"I didn't know they were children."

"But you killed Jorad."

"I—" He cleared his throat. "My queen gave me a task, and I completed it. The hows and whys aren't important."

"One hundred and twenty souls," I said. "All of them on your conscience. How do you sleep at night, Coyle? Jorad was Felix's cousin. You trained him and the other twenty soldiers who died."

"They attack me, I attack back," he said, his face turning red. "I can't help their ages. You're the one who—"

"You invaded the camp. You were there to slaughter. To

pretend otherwise is cowardly." I folded my arms over my chest. "But then again, who am I talking to?"

"*Back to the matter at hand,*" he snapped. "Clearly, Ilara—"

"Ah-ah-ah," I said, wagging my finger at him. "It's *Her Majesty.* Or don't you respect your queen?"

He snarled. "*Her Majesty* wants us to work together. She must assume you still have some sort of connection to the criminals in this town."

"I might know a couple," I said. "But perhaps I like that Fishen escaped. Perhaps I don't think it was smart of Ilara to put the last bastion of hope this city had in the dungeon, and I think this is her comeuppance. What about that?"

"Frankly, I don't care if you orchestrated the whole thing," he said. "But if I were you, I'd be looking for someone to pin this on. Because if you don't, *Her Majesty* will put your neck on the chopping block instead."

I didn't doubt she would. "Give me a few days to get my bearings. Allow me out in the city by myself—"

"Absolutely not."

"So you think that my contacts will speak to me with you there?" I scoffed. "They hate you more than me."

He got to his feet. "Then for your sake, Brynna, I hope they change their minds."

Coyle was practically breathing down my neck as we left the castle. It was just me and him, but the Severian guards seemed to be keeping an eye on us as we passed. I had to think of something —and fast.

I glanced at the rooftops, but no shadows followed us. Jax might've told them to keep their distance, or maybe they weren't trailing me at all. But if I couldn't see them, neither could Coyle, so they'd be safe.

"Where are we going?" he asked.

"To get some information," I said. "Talk to some people. Rattle cages."

I was wasting time. But he didn't need to know that. There were very few options I was comfortable with. Find the culprit, possibly find Fishen, and possibly expose my vigilantes. Or, delay and obstruct the investigation, which might arouse suspicion. Coyle seemed ready to report my every move back to Ilara, as his own position was precarious. After all, this had all happened under his nose.

I had a very small list of people who'd been in town a few months ago, and who could potentially be involved in Fishen's escape. I hoped I could waste the day talking with dead ends until night fell, and then be returned to the castle.

But when we reached Mariner's Row, where several of them lived, Coyle scoffed, stopping me. "Nobody's left in this part of the city. Everybody skipped town or went out east."

East. "Everybody, Coyle?" I asked. "Every single person?"

He made a noise then moved out of the way. "Tick-tock, Brynna."

I continued toward my destination, and feigned surprise when I came to the giant hole in the middle of the row of townhouses.

"Well." I made a face. "Looks like this one's a dead end."

"I could've told you that. Poor bastard met the business end of some ond before we stopped the flow of it into the city." Coyle's gaze bored into the back of my head.

You stopped the flow, yeah, right. It was Aline and Elisha who'd stopped it and Beswick's desperation had led him to make a devilish deal with Ilara. But I was supposed to be without allies. So I kept that information to myself.

I led Coyle to the complete opposite end of the city for another house I knew to be a dead end. Sooner or later, this ruse would stop working and I'd have to come up with a plan or a patsy. But perhaps I could buy myself another day.

We arrived at the house and I rapped on the door a few times, waiting for an answer that wouldn't come.

"Well?" Coyle asked.

"Not sure what to tell you," I said. "Maybe I can break in?"

"And do what? Find Fishen locked in her pantry?" He grabbed me by the shoulder and spun me to face him. "I can't help but feel like you're taking me on one of those wild goose chases. The first house has been decimated for weeks and this one is empty."

"It's been a while since I've been in town," I said, pushing him away roughly. "And things are different."

"Goossen's house blew up days after you spoke with me in the alley," Coyle said, tilting his head to the side. "You can't tell me you didn't hear of it. The blast sounded for miles."

"I heard the blast, but had no idea it was this house," I said. "I was focused on other things."

"What kind of other things?" Coyle said, taking a step toward me. "Getting Felix out of prison?"

"If I'd wanted him out of prison, Coyle, I would've gotten him out of prison," I said with a confident smile.

"Just like if you wanted to escape, you would've done it by now?" He shook his head. "You're a bad liar, Brynna, and you always have been. I know you're up to something."

"Then arrest me," I breathed. "If you're so confident. Ilara wouldn't need proof. She'd just take your word for it, I'm sure."

His lip curled; I'd called his bluff.

"We both need a win, Brynna," he said, his tone changing. "You need to keep whatever secrets you're hiding, and I need to prove to Ilara that she can trust me, too. So if you help me, I can help you."

As much as I wanted to, I couldn't see the lie. I surveyed him for a long time, the question I'd been dying to ask him coming to the forefront of my mind.

"Why did you betray me?"

He blanched. "What?"

"Why did you let Ilara invade my kingdom?" I asked. "If you'd told Felix Ilara was coming, we could've stopped her. It wouldn't have been hard."

"No, it wouldn't have," he admitted, straightening. "All she had was surprise."

I waited, staring into his dark eyes. "You owe me the truth. For once in your life, try to be honest. Maybe if you are, I'll think about helping you."

"You're helping yourself."

"I can lie my way out of failure here," I said, crossing my arms over my chest. "You, on the other hand, seem to have encountered a string of bad luck lately. I'm pretty sure you need me more than I need you." I tilted my chin up. "So?"

He ground his teeth for a moment then turned back to me. "When I was a boy, I started in the King's Guard as a scholarship recipient," he began softly. "Some rich merchant lost his daughter at sea and thought it might be a good idea to sponsor a kid from Haymaker's Corner to join the guard. Improve their station, as it were."

"Does Felix know that?" I asked. If he did, he'd never mentioned it to me.

"I doubt it. He was too busy palling around with the prince," he said. "But I knew if I became friends with them, I would be protected."

"And you were."

"It wasn't enough for me," he said. "They might not have known about my humble beginnings, but they always treated me differently."

I snorted. "So because you felt like an outcast, you decided to betray your friends and your country?"

"No, I betrayed them because Ilara promised me something

they never could—a real chance at making something of myself." He took a step toward me. "No matter what I did or how hard I worked, I never would've been able to make captain, and I never would've been more than Felix's underling. Now, I'm the one in charge."

"Of nothing. You are in charge of nothing," I said. "Your soldiers are Severian, and don't listen to you one whit. This city is dying thanks to Ilara's edicts. And you've murdered hundreds just to satisfy your ambition."

He leaned back, scrutiny in his gaze. "And what about you, Brynna? How many people did you kill in Neveri to regain your kingdom?"

"One hundred sixty-two," I said, without missing a beat. "Deaths I think about every single day."

"Yet here you are, lapdog to Ilara." He tilted his head in my direction. "How their sacrifices must weigh on you, knowing that they were all in vain."

Something tickled in the back of my mind. Coyle was trying to get me to talk, reveal something I hadn't already.

"I will have to square with the Mother for all I've done," I replied quietly. "But at least I regret the blood on my hands. Unlike you."

Coyle's lip curled, either from indignation or frustration that I hadn't taken his bait. "You have one more day to find someone for Ilara to hang. So I suggest you quit focusing on the past and figure out which of your little accomplices you're willing to sell out."

I stared at him for a long time, mulling over what he said. His backstory hadn't moved me much, if only because Aline had a similar tale, and she'd turned out just fine. Hers was probably worse, as her parents had been trapped in Beswick's web, whereas Coyle seemed to have had a free ride with no strings attached.

But in this instance, we both needed a scapegoat. And as much as it went against every part of my being to sacrifice an innocent to further my own gains, there was so much more to lose than my life.

"Fine," I said. "Come with me."

Chapter Sixteen

It didn't take long to find my intended victim, although I would've rather taken all night. In my years as The Veil, I'd known him to haunt several different locations, but when I arrived at the first and the telltale pot was sitting outside, my heart dropped to my stomach.

"I'm going in alone," I said to Coyle.

"Do you think I'm stupid?"

"Do you want me to answer that?"

"If you think—"

"Look, I promise someone is in there, unless you killed him, which I doubt, because he's smarter than that. If you let me go in alone, this will go a lot smoother than you showing your face. I might even get him to talk a little, which could provide your queen some information."

He stared at me for a long time then stepped back. "Mark my words. If this is a ruse—"

"It's not a ruse."

"You have five minutes."

"I need two."

I walked past him into the empty house, my heart pounding in my chest. There wasn't a sound, but he'd probably heard us talking outside and taken precautions. I stepped slowly across the floor, listening to the wood creak and echo in the empty space below. There was a nice rug in the center of the room, butting up to an even nicer table. Both were covered in a layer of dust, but the rug's dust had an odd pattern, as if it had been cleaned recently.

Or more likely, when someone had lifted the corner to reach the trap door below, the dust had fallen from it.

I knelt and lifted the edge, quietly folding it on itself. I stood to the side of the trap door and moved the latch, wincing as the metal clinked. Keeping clear of the door, I opened it.

An arrow zoomed by my ear, landing in the ceiling.

"Why are you always shooting at me, John?" I asked with a smile on my face.

"W—" The former owner of Stank's bar blinked up at me, now sporting a beard and more raggedy clothing since the last time I'd seen him. "Princess Brynna?"

"Or The Veil, take your pick. Nice to see you again." I stopped him before he straightened. "You may want to stay low. Captain Coyle is outside."

"Yeah, I heard you were living in the castle now," he said, giving me a once-over. "Got something cooking?"

"You could say that," I said. "Came here to ask you some questions."

"I may have some answers, for the right price."

"The price is I don't bring Coyle in here to run you through, eh?" I flashed him a smile. "After what you did to Felix, you owe me."

"Felix? You mean Captain Llobrega?" He shook his head.

"Can't say I recall anything about that."

"Can't or won't?" I asked with a thin smile. "Kieran said the two of you met before Beswick's attack on the city. Said *you* were the one who ferried the ond to Beswick after he brought it to you. Remember anything about that?"

"Some of it, yeah." He rubbed the back of his neck. "Desperate times and all."

"People died, John. Forcadelians died."

"Forcadelians who'd allied themselves with the queen." He cast me a long look. "Which appears to include you now."

"It may or it may not. Remains to be seen," I said. "How long have you worked for Beswick?"

"I work for whomever is paying me," he said. "But Beswick hasn't come knocking in a while. Hear he's busy out east, you know."

"And what, exactly, is happening out east?" I asked.

"You should know. You're in the castle. I'm sure you hear all about it."

"They don't really invite me to their strategy sessions, for obvious reasons," I said. "So what do you hear?"

He took a long breath. "No idea, really. Beswick's keeping this one pretty close to the vest. I know he's chartered a bunch of big ships to bring people from Haymaker's Corner to Aunela. Anyone who wanted a new life and a new job got a free ride, on behalf of Her Royal Highness."

I furrowed my brow. "Awfully nice of her. And you said Beswick's been involved? Is he still involved?" If he was, that meant Ignacio was, which meant Jax would be aware of it, too.

"I don't know." He glanced out at Coyle. "Anything else?"

I licked my lips, thinking for a moment. "There was a big jail break from the dungeons tonight. Know anything about that?"

He shook his head.

"Miracle of miracles, Mother Fishen escaped," I tilted my head toward him. "Know where she happened to escape to?"

"No idea. Any other questions, or can I go back to hiding?"

"C'mon John…" I said with a smile. "You don't know *anything* about it?"

He shrugged. "There's a new element in the city. They don't use the usual channels, and they don't seem to want to have anything to do with me. Seem awfully Veil-like, you know? And here you are, asking questions."

So it was my vigilantes. Interesting that they would take such a risk—or that Jax would let them. "I wish I could tell you who they were, but Ilara's kept me locked up in the castle these past few weeks."

"How coincidental."

I stared at him for a long time. John was guilty of a lot, but I still had my doubts about what I was about to do. I stared into his dark eyes, noticed the wrinkles around his mouth, the sparse gray at his temples. It would probably be the last time I saw him.

But I had people counting on me to keep up my charade. As much as I hated to admit it, I had a decision to make.

"That'll be all." I rose. "Thank you."

With a calm sense of knowing, I strolled outside to where Coyle was waiting. "Well? Was it a dead end?"

"He's in there," I said. "And he's your guy."

"Are you sure?"

"No. But you said to deliver you someone." I pointed inside. "There you go."

Within half an hour, the soldiers swarmed the building, finding John under the trapdoor. When he was pulled from the house, he screamed to everyone within earshot about my betrayal and how I wasn't to be trusted. Through it all, I remained emotionless, watching him leave with a sick feeling in my stomach.

"Hm," Coyle said, coming to stand next to me. "You've changed. The old Brynna would've wormed her way out of this assignment."

"The old Brynna died on the forest floor a year ago," I said. "So I suggest you quit acting like I'm a saint, and start worrying a little more for your own skin." I flashed him a smile. "You're not the only one holding onto information. Back off or you might find yourself on the wrong end of Ilara's temper."

Chapter Seventeen

Felix

It took several days to come up with something that would fit the moniker of The Veil, and a little longer to gather the supplies we needed, but on a full moon night, we set in motion our plan to take the five ships that Ammon had promised in motion.

"How many Kulkans on board?" I asked, peering through a telescope as I marked the position of each ship. They were anchored near enough to the docks that we could walk on board, but the presence of the Kulkan soldiers would make it tricky.

"Each ship holds twenty sailors," Aline said. "Maybe we should consider giving Ammon a few more days to honor his agreement."

It had been days, and so far, I'd heard nothing from the prince. Meanwhile, the riots and unrest in the city had grown worse, and it was all the prince could do to keep this stronghold under his control.

"We don't have time to wait, and I don't think Ammon's timeline will ever match with ours," I said. "We move tonight."

"Are you sure this is going to work?" Aline asked. "It seems awfully risky."

"Brynna did it," I said, climbing off the edge of the roof. "And now we see if our soldiers were successful in preparing."

We moved in the shadows, taking the long way through the city until we reached the meeting spot near the river. There, I found five soldiers, including Enos, waiting in a deserted alley. They were laden with crossbows and arrows, and a large bag sat on the ground.

"Well?" I asked.

"We got what you asked for," Enos said. "But we're not quite sure what we're doing with it."

I picked up the bag, opening it to reveal smaller bags within. Knockout powder. "And we've still got the ond, right?"

"It's secure," Enos said. "But it's here."

"Ladies and gentlemen," I began slowly. "What we're going to attempt may sound a bit impossible, but I promise you it's been done before." I walked to the edge of the alley and pointed toward the docks. "You'll note that there are six warships in port out there, as well as a few cargo vessels. If all goes according to plan, the Kulkans will hand over five of them."

They shared looks of disbelief, and I merely held out my hands.

"First things first," I said, opening the bag of knockout powder. "We need to find a decoy. So everyone grab a few bags and keep your steps light."

I led the soldiers onto the docks, motioning to them to hide as a pair of Kulkan soldiers walked by. We waited until their footsteps quieted then continued along the dock, albeit slower.

"Wait," Aline said, putting her hand on my arm. "This isn't one of the warships. This is a cargo vessel."

"I know," I said with a grin, grabbing a few bags of knockout powder and heading onboard the ship.

"Hey, what are you—" Before the soldier could say another word, Aline lobbed a bag of powder at his face and he slumped forward onto the deck.

"Take him somewhere secure and tie him up," I said. "Clear everyone off this boat and make sure to put them somewhere they won't interrupt us."

"I think I know what you're doing," Aline said, a smile curling onto her face. "But it will take a miracle to pull this off."

"Then let's pray for one, shall we?" I said.

The ship was ours in minutes, thanks to a bevy of well-placed arrows and knockout powder. There was a small dockmaster house in the center of the docks where we stashed the crew. The powder would only work so long, and even tied up, the sailors would attract attention soon enough.

Enos was the strongest swimmer, so we left him onboard our empty cargo vessel with the bag of ond.

"It will blow quickly," I said. "So take care to get away as fast as possible."

"Will do, sir," he said, saluting me. "Good luck."

Our soldiers had decamped from the open field and had been split into groups of roughly twenty—each of which would take a different warship and were told a different time to come into the city, to avoid notice.

"Twenty soldiers is still a large group," Aline muttered.

"It's fewer than a hundred," I retorted. Even still, my heart beat a little faster when each group arrived, announced by a single whistle from their leader. So far, so good.

"There's the last one," Aline said, pointing to the docks where a group appeared out of the darkness.

"Let's do this," I said, getting to my feet.

My target was the crown jewel of Ammon's naval forces, a boat that had nearly twenty cannons and room for sixty. Aline had counted anywhere from twenty to twenty-five sailors onboard, as well as three Kulkan soldiers. And I doubted they'd give up their ship without a fight.

My boots echoed on the wood as I climbed the gangplank to the warship, and I was stopped by two sword points before I even got close to the deck.

"Who are you?" one of the Kulkan soldiers asked, a shiny lieutenant's pin on her chest.

"My name is General Felix Llobrega," I said. "Of the Forcadelian army under Queen Brynna. And I'm here to take your ships to Forcadel to help our queen reclaim her throne."

A giggle echoed from the lieutenant's lips, and she was soon joined by all within earshot. Out of the corner of my eye, my soldiers shifted uncomfortably, but I remained still, waiting for the laughter to die down.

"Get off my boat, Forcadelian," she said, pointing to the crest on her chest. "Until I hear from the prince himself, we aren't taking you anywhere."

"But we have the word of Prince Ammon," I continued, unbothered. "Under pain of death, he will give us a hundred soldiers and five ships."

"Did you not hear me?" she said, stepping onto the gangplank. "I said get off my boat."

"Very well," I sighed. "I didn't want to have to do this, but…" I turned behind me to one of my soldiers and nodded. He put his hand to his mouth and whistled, which was met by another whistle, which was met by another…

"What the…"

"I'd cover your ears," I said, doing the same.

The dark bay exploded in light, followed by a deafening *boom*. A ship docked in the middle of the bay was a ball of flame, illuminating the entire river. Ash wafted down like snow around us as the bay rippled from the explosion. The ship rocked violently, sending the soldiers scrambling for nearby railings and posts.

The first soldier's wide eyes turned to me, and I lifted a small bag in my hand. "There's more where that came from. Now, unless you'd like to join your friends in meeting the Mother, you'll comply with our order. You will sail this ship to Forcadel as your prince has promised."

She hesitated, just for a moment, before dropping her sword and holding her hands up in surrender. Behind her, the rest of the soldiers who'd come to see the explosion followed her lead.

"We will leave at once," I said to her. "The ship is ready to sail now, yes?"

She nodded. "His Majesty wanted us ready to set sail at a moment's notice."

"Then this is your notice," I said. "What is your name, soldier?"

"Lieutenant Kalila, sir."

"You may disembark the ship, if you so choose," I said. "But if you stay, understand that I'm your commander now. And if I hear even a hint of disobedience, you will go overboard. Am I clear?"

She nodded and saluted, before turning to the sailors, all of whom looked shell-shocked and horrified. Her orders came out shaky, but with enough emphasis that the sailors got to work. But the sailors didn't make any bones about their feelings on being pressed into service.

"Whose ship was that?"

"I don't know. I didn't get a good look at it before it blew up."

"I thought these Forcadelians were supposed to be soft. Can't believe they just…they just did that."

"Ruthless sons of bitches."

Still, they were efficient, and within a few minutes, the steam engine purred beneath my feet. Beneath the water, the paddles on the boat began to slosh the water, pulling us backward and away from the dock.

"Well, I guess I owe you a silver," Aline murmured, coming to stand next to me.

"Wait until daylight, when we have all five ships on the ocean," I replied, gazing out at the other boats. Every one of the lieutenants

I'd put in charge had been given more or less the same script as I'd used, and I just hoped the Kulkans on the other ships were as moved as Kalila.

"*You!*"

Ammon and his soldiers had arrived, his face a reddish hue even in the dark. But they were too late; our ship had already left the dock.

"Evening," I called to him over the hum of the engine.

"You *son of a bitch!*" he bellowed, nearly falling off the dock. "You blew up one of my ships!"

"I told you," I shrugged, making sure to exaggerate the movement so he could see in the dark, "help me or suffer the consequences. Perhaps you should rethink this nasty habit you have of going back on your word."

His mouth hung open as he faded from view and I couldn't help but chuckle. One day, once we had reclaimed Forcadel and Brynna was back on the throne, I might pen a letter to Ammon and let him know that the ship I'd blown up had been an empty produce vessel, the bags I'd threatened his soldiers with merely knockout powder. But for now, I'd let him and the rest of the soldiers think I was as ruthless as Ilara.

Chapter Eighteen

Katarine

It was hard to sit and wait, but that seemed to be my plight lately.

My last letter to Felix had presumably reached its destination, and the response should've been back by now. I also should've seen something from Jax in Forcadel—a messenger, a letter, *something*.

The culprit, I suspected, was this infernal blockade to the south of us on the river. Joella had lost five soldiers already, barely getting a glimpse at the woods before getting struck down by arrows. She offered to try again, but I wasn't in the habit of sending soldiers to their slaughter.

What I might do instead, I had no idea. I had spent the better part of two days thinking about options, and had come up with nothing but a headache.

Therefore, I was grateful for the knock on the door and the distraction. "Enter," I called.

A soldier walked in, Elisha hanging from his grip with a scowl on her face. "I found her skulking around in the forest. It's a miracle she didn't have an arrow through her."

"I wasn't gonna get caught," she said, tugging her arm from his grip. "And I don't *skulk*."

"Thank you," I said to the soldier. "Leave her here with me."

He bowed and walked out, making sure to close the door behind him.

"I have two questions," I began, folding my hands on the desk. "First, why are you not at home completing your lessons with Lady Beata?"

"Cause they're boring." She rolled her eyes. "And you told me you'd help me learn to read and you haven't done that yet."

"And second," I said, speaking before I reacted to her comment, "what in the Mother's name possessed you to go to the forest?"

"Nobody knew I was there."

I gestured to the door. "Clearly, someone did."

"He snuck up on me," she said, as if that were an explanation. "Look, I wasn't doing nothing. Just watching, you know? Been doing that the past couple days."

Days? I'd have to tell Beata to keep a closer eye on her. "Why were you watching?"

"'Cause I need something to do!" She tossed her hands up in the air. "Brynna told me to help, and I ain't helping sitting in that house and learning my letters."

Swallowing whatever lecture was on the tip of my tongue, I gestured to her. "What did you see?"

"Couple of days ago, I saw a guy—a soldier—leaving town to the south," she began, switching her weight from one foot to the other. "Three hours later, he came back. Then he done it twice in the past week."

I straightened. "Was he on orders from Joella?"

"Don't think so," she said with a wry grin. "'Cause he didn't come back with an arrow in his chest."

I cleared my throat. "So you followed him?"

"Yup." She bounced on her toes again. "He was going to the border and talking with someone in a Severian uniform."

I rose to my feet. "You went to the *border?*"

"I did, but—"

"Do you have any idea how dangerous that was? People have been getting seriously hurt there. You could've been killed!"

"But—"

"I don't care why you went," I said, getting to my feet. "You should've come to me and we would've handled it."

"He's a spy!"

I exhaled slowly to prevent my anger from getting the better of me. "You will do three things: you will tell me the name of the soldier you saw. Then you will march straight home and tell Lady Beata what you've done, including that you snuck to the border."

"But—!"

"You will then go to your room and await your punishment," I said. "Am I clear?"

She jumped to her feet. "His name is Denholm Jansen. And you're a bitch."

And with that, she stormed out.

I immediately contacted Joella and had her bring the named soldier to my office, and while I waited, I considered the various infractions Elisha had committed and what I might do about them. I'd never had someone so small throw an epithet at me, and I didn't care for it one bit. But at the same time, if she hadn't come forward, irreparable damage might've been done to our cause.

I rubbed my temple; the headache had returned with a vengeance.

Luckily, Joella arrived soon enough with the spy in tow. He was a young man, Forcadelian with dark hair and eyes. But the pale, sickly color of his skin was a clear indication he knew exactly why he'd been called here.

"Have a seat," I said, offering a chair to the man.

"Am I in trouble?" he asked, glancing at Joella.

"Remains to be seen," Joella said.

"Have you been leaving your post?" I began.

"Leaving my… No!" He shook his head furiously. "Of course not. I've been here the whole time."

"Then off shift," I said. "Venturing into the forest?"

A light sheen of sweat broke out on his upper lip. Trained spy, he surely was not. "J-just to take a piss every once in a while."

"Have you met with anyone on these bathroom breaks?" I asked, leaning onto the table.

"N-No, of course not!"

"Really?" I quirked a brow. "Because if you come clean now, I'm sure we may be able to offer some leniency."

He swallowed hard, glancing at me, then to Joella, and took a deep breath in. Finally, he hung his head. "I'm sorry."

"How long have you been spying for Ilara?" I asked.

He swallowed. "After Captain Mark left, I skipped out of the camp and headed back home, ready to hang up my uniform and find an honest living. But the next thing I knew, I got pulled into this room with my family—my mom's older and my sister's pregnant. The man said that if I didn't return to the camp and spy for him…"

"What man?" I asked.

"I don't know his name. Never seen him before."

His haunted gaze seemed truthful, so I nodded to Jo to stand down. "What information have you given Ilara?"

"Not much. Just the movement of our troops to Skorsa. I didn't know they were gonna…" He shook his head. "The camp. I didn't know that was gonna happen."

"Does Ilara know about Beswick?" I asked.

"What about him?"

I shared a look with Joella and nodded. That secret was still safe. "We want to know what's going on south of here," I said. "Why is the border so full of Severian troops?"

"I have no idea," he said. "I've been here, same as you. They don't tell me anything. I don't even know if..." He swallowed. "I don't even know if my family's okay."

"You have one chance to change your luck," Joella said. "So you'd better dig deep and come up with something to save your neck."

"I..." He swallowed and shook his head. "I don't know. Honest. All I know is what I've seen here in Skorsa. We're moving into position."

"Then I suppose you're useless to us," Joella said, looking at the two guards standing at attention. "Send him back to Niemen to stand trial for his treason."

"But I'm not even Niemenian!" he cried as he was hauled to his feet.

"And unfortunately, the queen isn't here to speak on your behalf," Joella said. "So I guess you're out of luck."

He called for mercy as he was pulled out of the room, but I couldn't find it within me to be sorry for him. He'd made his choice, even if he'd been coerced into it.

"If he's telling the truth, we aren't in a bad position," Joella said, leaning on the table. "The problem is, I don't trust a word out of his mouth."

"I do," I said softly. "He was obviously put into this position unwillingly and was merely a pair of eyes for Ilara. What we need to know is how much information he shared, and what Ilara's planning to do about it."

"It's a lucky break that we caught him at all," Jo said. "How in the Mother's name did you find him?"

"Elisha saw him." I winced. "I punished her for spying."

Joella gave me a look. "Not the route I would've chosen, but you are her guardian."

"She was supposed to be home studying, not skulking around looking for spies."

"Who knows how much information he could've passed on to Ilara had she not seen him," Joella said. "We're lucky he hadn't known of any plans."

"It's not as if we had any to share," I said darkly. "Gather all the soldiers in his unit and let's question them, as well as their lieutenant. We need to keep a tighter leash on our people—and make sure everyone within our ranks needs to be there."

It was another late night for me, and I hoped my wife wouldn't be too mad. Elisha's indiscretion hung in the back of my mind all afternoon, and I had very little sense of what might get through to her. My own youth wasn't much of a template; my infractions had been petty and youthful. Elisha had seen more in her young life than I had in mine. It would be difficult to bridge the gap between our two life experiences.

"Bea?" I called, opening the door to our home.

I found my wife in the back sitting room, reading a book and drinking a cup of tea. "You're late again."

"I'm sorry," I said. "We—"

"Elisha told me," Beata said. "And she also told me you punished her."

I slumped. "I don't know what to do, Bea. She insists upon putting herself into danger and has no care for what consequences there might be."

"Kind of like another little vigilante we know," Beata said with a soft smile. "You managed her very well."

"I absolutely did not," I said with a soft laugh. "Brynna learned her lessons through getting a knife in the gut. I don't want that for

Elisha."

"Sometimes these lessons have to be learned the hard way." Beata stood on her tiptoes and kissed me on the cheek. "She's upstairs waiting for you. Just be gentle."

I ascended the stairs, thinking on my youth, my wife, Brynna, and possible punishments. Standing in front of Elisha's door, I forced a stern look on my face as I knocked.

"Elisha, may I come in?"

"Yes'm." Well, at least she sounded apologetic.

She sat on her bed, staring at her hands as if she were expecting the worst, but she seemed almost a little too contrite.

"First, I want to thank you for bringing this spy to my attention," I said. "We might've never known he was amongst our ranks if you hadn't said anything."

She lifted her gaze a little. "Really?"

"Really." I shifted on the balls of my feet. "That doesn't mean you're off the hook for going to the border."

"I wasn't in any danger, I promise," she said, "Ain't nobody saw me, and if they did, I'm just a kid—"

"A kid who now lives in my house, so a potential target," I said. "What if someone had taken you?"

"Then I would've gotten out."

Arguing with her was infuriating. I pinched the bridge of my nose as yet another headache threatened to blossom over my right temple.

"Besides that, I've been close enough to what they're guarding and I have an idea how to take the border," she said. "Since it's just people, we can use knockout powder or the nightmare powder—"

"How close did you get?" I asked, my eyes widening.

"I mean…" Her face reddened. "Kinda close?"

I rose, placing my hands on my hips as I fought against my rising fury. I decided to go with an old standby. "Your punishment will be to write me an essay on why it was incredibly reckless of you to put yourself and our entire operation in danger by going to the gate."

Her cheeks reddened. "I can't..."

"Oh, that's right," I said, guilt washing over me. Elisha could neither read nor write, and I hadn't done much to help her. "Then in the morning, after we've finished our breakfast, you'll come to my office and tell me in person. Am I clear?"

She nodded. "But what about my idea?"

"Hold onto it for now," I said. "We have Niemen's brightest minds working on this problem, but if they can't crack it, we'll ask for your input."

She scowled.

I turned to the door, then hesitated. "And while you're at my office tomorrow, maybe you can stay and help me ferry messages. Do you think you can handle that?"

Her eyes lit up. "Yes, ma'am!"

The smile on her face warmed my heart, and as I closed the door behind me, I had to smile a bit, too.

Chapter Nineteen

The justice (or whatever Ilara wanted to call it) against John had been swift. I had a clear view of the town square from my tower, and kept the curtains closed until the body was removed. During my days in the dark, I prayed for forgiveness for what I'd done. He hadn't deserved to die for his crimes, and I would carry the guilt for his life as surely as if I'd killed him myself.

But perhaps it was worth it, as I received an invite to have lunch with the queen—without Luisa. I was even allowed to wear a tunic and pants—which I checked for knives or other traps. And when I arrived, Ilara was beaming with joy.

"I'm impressed," Ilara said. "I didn't expect this outcome."

"It gave me no pleasure," I said. "John was a friend."

"The betrayal you've endured this past year is heartrending," she said, patting my hand.

I could've mentioned that she'd had a big hand in that, but I held my tongue. "Did you find Fishen?" I asked.

"Unfortunately, he took his secrets to the grave," Ilara said. "But I trust that you brought me the right man. After all, you're not the kind of person to sacrifice an innocent man just to save your own skin."

Her eyes bored into mine, almost daring me to contradict her. Luckily, the servants arrived with our meal—a limp-looking salad with brownish apples and a filleted fish—and Ilara's attention shifted.

"Well, at least we have something in abundant supply," she said, poking at the fish while making a face. "Even if I do detest the taste of it."

"Not a fan?" I asked, gently pulling the meat apart with my fork.

"I can't say it was in my diet much in the desert," she said with a bit of a chuckle. "But the local farms can't seem to keep up with the demand, so we must make do." She pushed the diced apples to the side. "But I won't eat those. I'll have to have Luisa inform the kitchen that apples are no longer on the menu."

I remained silent. In Kulka, I'd seen bushels of perfectly good apples thrown out because there was nowhere to sell them. The only reason for it sat across from me.

"You're quiet today," Ilara said. "A lot on your mind?"

"Mostly just curiosity," I replied, deftly extracting a bone from the fish. "If this is how you've been eating, why not just open the borders?"

"We will get there soon," Ilara said with a smile. "The Kulkans and Niemenians are too hostile toward each other for them to hold out much longer."

"But where will they trade?" I asked, nodding out the window. "Nobody's left in the city."

"In due time, my friend, in due time." She patted my hand. "But first, I'd like to know what you thought of *The Haberdasher's Tale*? Luisa said you read it a few days ago, and I've been dying to ask you your thoughts."

"I…uh…" Should I be honest?

"The side plot of the romance was completely unnecessary," she said, giving me a coy look. "Right?"

"Absolutely," I said with something of an exhale. I hated the entire thing, but at least it wasn't Ilara's favorite, either.

"It's one of Luisa's favorites, and she thought you might like it," Ilara said. "It will give me such joy to tell her I was right."

I had nothing to say to that, so I simply smiled.

"You at least have to read *The Tale of Theophilia Kallistrate*," she continued. "She was an epic warrior and fierce defender of her people. I'm not sure how true her story is, but it's certainly diverting."

"I find it interesting that you've stocked my room with books," I said. "Severian books, even. The rest of this castle seems untouched. There are portraits of my ancestors still hanging. And yet…" I pushed a flaky bit across the plate with my fork. "Seems somewhat intentional."

She tapped her napkin to her lips with a knowing smile. "I have been, I confess. You see, I've studied Forcadelian traditions my entire life. I know your family tree perhaps better than you do. But you know nothing of my country. And I can't help but feel like we would understand each other better if you did."

"I think we understand each other well enough."

"You still have no clue why I've done what I've done," Ilara said, sitting back. "Or what I will do. You think I just took over your throne for my own purposes. But it…" She sighed. "It was for a greater good. I told you the Mother's hand was strong on my shoulder, and I hope you now have a greater understanding of our life in Severia."

It was hard not to say what I felt, to remind her that I was neither my father nor my brother, and I would've done everything within my power to improve the lives of her people if she'd just given me a chance. But as I'd learned before, Ilara was the hero of her own story, and arguing with her or anyone else wouldn't do me one bit of good.

"I do," I said after a pause. "And I'm grateful to play my part in making it better."

The lie had rolled off my tongue with ease, earning me a beaming smile from the Severian. At least for the moment, my place at her side was still secure.

Ilara asked me to dine with her every night after that. There were no more conversations about Fishen, or John, or really anything except the Severian books I kept dutifully reading and veiled discussion about a party Ilara was throwing in a few days. I had an inkling that it had something to do with her impending trip to Aunela, but the exact details remained a mystery.

This evening, our breakfast had been interrupted by the tailor, who had been trying to get in to see Ilara for weeks now. To my eyes, the cloth reams were all the same color, but Ilara found some differences in every one.

"I think the left fabric is very pretty, don't you?" Ilara asked, glancing in my direction.

I squinted at the ream of fabric on the left, finding it perhaps slightly shinier than the right. "Sure."

"Oh, dear Brynna, you don't care about any of this, do you?" Ilara asked with a bit of a chuckle. "I daresay Katarine had her fill of you."

"Not really. I merely delegated this particular task to her," I said.

"I suppose that explains the number of dresses in your closet," she replied with a coy smile. "Delegation isn't always a smart idea, my dear. I like to retain control over every aspect of my country." She sauntered over to the reams of cloth. "It's why every military decision goes through me. Captain Maarit proved that even the most loyal people will let you down eventually."

I turned to her, curious. "You never replaced Maarit?"

"I suppose I could," she said with a sigh. "Coyle, I'm sure, would jump at the chance to lead my entire army. But the only person I trust is myself."

As much as I wanted to chew on that information, I had to stuff my excitement down and keep a passive face. "I suppose I understand that. I never liked relying on others to do my dirty work."

"You see? We are one and the same," she said, turning to the tailor. "I will take this one. I want it in my chambers by tomorrow afternoon so I can be ready in time."

Tomorrow, hm? I tried to keep my face neutral.

"Now that that's finally done," Ilara said, turning away from the tailor as he swiftly packed his things. "Will you join me for a walk, Brynna? I would like to show you something."

Any time with Ilara was welcome, so I took her arm and let her lead me out of the receiving hall. There were more maids and servants than usual bustling about carrying vases, flowers, fabric, plates—it seemed Ilara had rehired everyone she'd let go to prepare for this event.

"What are we celebrating?" I asked as we passed a window.

"Ah, dear friend, don't pry." She sighed and shook her head. "I fear if you ask, I'll tell you. I'm terrible at keeping secrets."

"Are you?" The words came out before I could stop it, and earned me an appraising look from the queen. But she said nothing about the slip of my tongue, and kept walking.

My concern grew as we made our way toward the wing of the castle where I assumed Ilara now slept. She walked to a pair of double doors and stopped, placing her hands on the knobs and casting me a look as if expecting me to recognize something. When I didn't, she pushed them open, revealing a large, empty room.

Weapons lined the wall, everything from broadswords to small knives and even a crossbow or two. A large mat had been placed in the center of the room, and the windows were wide open, letting in a cool breeze and sunlight.

"What…is this?" I asked.

"Can't you tell? It's my training room." Ilara plucked a ribbon off a rack of them and tied her hair back. "I come in here once a day to take my mind off the weight of running the kingdom. I think it's good for the soul to spar often."

Once a day. And I'd been sitting on my ass all this time. "You train daily? With whom?"

"Coyle, usually, but he's just so damned honorable."She flashed a grin at me. "I'd like to try my luck with someone who fights dirty."

I took a knife off the wall. It had recently been sharpened. "I'm not sure it's smart to train with real weapons like this."

"Isn't that how you trained in Celia's camp?" she asked.

I turned to her, narrowing my eyes. "How did you know that?"

She shrugged and didn't answer. "So what do you think? Ready to go a round or two?"

"I don't think that's a good idea," I said with a shake of my head. "I'm rusty."

"Then perhaps we'll train with blunted edges," she said, walking to a trunk in the corner and pulling a pair of wooden knives similar in length to those I'd carried. I had a sinking suspicion that she'd had them made just for me. "If that will ease your mind."

"I suppose one bout couldn't hurt." I fidgeted with the knives, learning their weight. I shouldn't push this too far, not when I'd just gained her trust. Ilara wouldn't take too kindly to me defeating her.

She easily deflected my first parry. "You can do better than that. Come on, Brynna, *fight me.*"

I gave it more effort, and she met my blade, so I tried harder. She matched me move for move, even as I started to sweat a little behind the neck. She, too, was breathless, but the smile on her face was almost manic.

The urge to move faster, to sweep my leg and knock her on her ass, was strong, but I resisted. Just when I thought I might burst, I allowed her to stick me with the wooden tip of her sword—right along the scar she'd left me.

"And I win the match," she said, stepping back. "Again."

"Hooray," I replied, feigning annoyance.

She just laughed and leaned on the sword. "You see? Life is so much more fun when we're friends. I don't want us to be enemies, Brynna."

I gazed into her eyes, searching for any sign that she was lying to me. It was hard to square this version of Ilara with the one who'd gleefully taken my kingdom then stabbed me.

"I don't know if I can be friends with you," I said slowly. "Not after what you did to Celia's camp."

"Why not?" She smiled. "I forgave you after what you did in Neveri."

"You didn't forgive Maarit."

"Well..." She released my hand and a flicker of annoyance crossed her face. "Maarit should've been able to stop you. And having so many soldiers defect... Then, of course, Felix's betrayal was a black cloud over the castle. Out of respect for poor Katarine, I let him live. But I needed to send a message to my soldiers that insubordination was not tolerated. Unfortunately, she was the juiciest target."

"So you killed Maarit to prove a point?" I asked, raising my brows. "And you still think the Mother condones that?"

"As I said, the Mother approves the larger goals I have for this nation," she said.

"What goals?" I asked, trying to rein in my temper and failing.

"Starving this city into oblivion?"

"Forcadel has long been a flourishing city, and the people here have the means to move to greener pastures, as it were," Ilara said, looking out the window. "Even now, the city's population is a quarter of what it once was."

"Yeah, the quarter too poor to leave," I said. "In Haymaker's Corner."

"They will be taken care of."

"How?"

She just smiled that enigmatic smile. "You're awfully concerned about the plight of innocents, considering you just sent an innocent man to the gallows."

Dread slipped down my back. "Why did you execute him if you thought he was innocent?"

"Why did you bring him to my door if he was innocent?"

The question hung in the air, and I had no answers that weren't the truth. But perhaps I could massage the truth and still make it out of this room alive.

"He wasn't as innocent as you think," I said. "He had crimes to pay for. So what if it was your justice instead of mine?"

She stared at me for a long time then picked up her sword again. "I know you don't trust me, but I meant it when I said I wanted us to be friends. You and I have very similar proclivities. It's why I didn't kill you."

"But you killed members of my family."

"They were brutes," she said with a wave of her hand. "They didn't care for the worst among them. All they wanted was to keep their friends rich at the expense of everyone else. But you, Brynna...you embodied service. You genuinely cared for the people you served. To a fault, really." She shrugged. "That's why I make a better queen than you. I'm willing to make the hard choices without beating myself up over them for months afterward."

"Perhaps you're right," I said, instead of arguing with her.

"I am right," Ilara said. "I promise you, what I've got planned will bring such joy to your heart." She took my hand. "Swear fealty to me and I'll take all your worries."

"I've already—"

"Swear to the Mother." Her gaze was dead serious. "Swear to Her that you will be my loyal servant and together, we can make this country even better." She squeezed my hand. "I promise you, Brynna, you won't regret it."

My pulse pounded in my ears. Swear to the Mother? That felt like a bridge too far—I wasn't sure I could force the lie from my lips. But there were people counting on me. And if Ilara believed she could find salvation by focusing on the greater good, perhaps I could follow that same path, too.

Forgive me, please. "I swear to the Mother," I swallowed hard, "that I will be your loyal servant."

Ilara broke into a smile. "I'm so glad to hear it, Brynna. Truly, I am. Because what I've got planned…oh, you'll love it." She tapped me on the nose. "I'll have Luisa begin preparing your things. I suppose you'll want her to leave the corsets here." She beamed. "I see how they chafe you."

"Sure," I said, feeling like I'd missed something. "But where are we going?"

She shook her head, the truth seeming to hang around the edges of her enigmatic smile. "I don't want to ruin the surprise, so please, don't ask me again." She swung her sword. "Shall we go again?"

Chapter Twenty

After a riveting afternoon with Ilara, where I lost every bout, I was finally allowed to return to my room. But no sooner had I arrived than a pair of servants arrived with orders to bathe and prepare me for the evening's festivities. Any shred of privacy I had was gone as they dunked me under the water and scrubbed my scalp until I was sure it was bleeding. Then they did the same to my finger- and toenails, before dragging me out and toweling me dry.

I expected another corset, but I was given a solid lavender dress with enough boning to handle my ample chest without the need for binding. After they finished fastening the dress and petticoats, they turned to my hair. Instead of a simple braid, they spent their time putting pins and bands in my hair so it stayed firm at the nape of my neck in a tight bun. And after that, it was a layer of thick cream on my face, lips, eyes, and even the tops of my breasts.

Whatever was happening that night was something special.

My guards escorted me down the stairs as the sun set, and the faint sound of music wafted through the hallways. As I drew closer to the grand hall, my pulse pounded in my throat. Who would I find in there—and would I get a chance to talk with any of them?

I passed through the threshold and my breath left my body. The room was filled with people—none of whom I recognized. They were drinking from wine goblets and laughing with one another, every one dressed in their very finest clothes.

Without guards to shadow me, I walked a perimeter of the room, scanning each face for someone familiar. There was a mix of Severian and Forcadelian, but also Kulkan and a few Niemenians. Odd, considering the queen had all but banned those countries from doing business in the city.

I stopped next to a column, pretending to be awkward while keeping my ears open for conversation.

"The things I've seen…the city is magnificent."

"And the dam! I hear she had a hand in its design."

"The world will surely tell stories of Ilara for generations to come."

I burned to interject, to question them, but I stayed put. Better to keep out of sight for the moment.

"What are you doing over here?"

I straightened in surprise, then turned slowly, shock falling across my features. "*Mark?*"

The former captain of the guard—the one who'd held the position before Felix and the man who'd shown up at my temporary camp to lead my soldiers—was dressed in a Severian uniform, holding a goblet. The last time I'd seen him, I'd unceremoniously fired him after he'd pissed me off. A move I'd regretted at the time.

And now, based on his attire and smirk, I would continue to regret it.

"What are you doing here?" I asked, mentally calculating when Mark had left and when Felix and Katarine had arrived. He hadn't gone with us to Celia's camp; my story was still safe.

"I was on my way back to Forcadel after you relieved me of my command," he said. "I ran into Captain Coyle, who offered me a job back at the castle."

You little sneak. "I see."

"After all, if you had no use for me, I thought I might find my fortunes elsewhere." He puffed out his chest. "I will be assuming command of the camp just south of Skorsa in the morning."

That wasn't the worst news. He'd be out of my hair and Ilara's sight. Whatever knowledge he might have would be kept far away from Forcadel. Now I just needed to know everything he'd already told her.

"So here we are," Mark said, swirling the wine in his glass. "I can't say I'm surprised. I told you that you were going to fail."

"Clairvoyant, are we?" I asked, but I kept my temper. Mark had a nasty habit of goading me into making mistakes, and I wasn't going to let him win this time.

"I heard about the deaths at Celia's camp," he said. "How many of my soldiers did you lose?"

"*My* soldiers, you mean?" I barked. "A hundred and twenty."

"I don't care about the thieves," he said with a wave of his hand. "But the soldiers who—"

"The soldiers who trained and died alongside each other," I said. "Thief or royal guard, they were one and the same to me and to each other." I collected myself for a moment. "And for you to gloat like this proves I was right to let you go."

"If you think I'm gloating, you are sorely mistaken," he said. "Because of your recklessness, people died."

His words shot straight to my heart. "Yes, I'm aware."

"And now you're here, playing house with the very woman who took your kingdom from you," he said, taking a sip of his wine. "Well, I suppose we must all do what we think is best."

"Says the man traveling to the east to assume command of her troops."

"Of *my* troops," Mark said, giving me an evil glare. "Her Majesty has moved a hundred Forcadelian troops out of the city and is in need of someone to command them. At least if I remain their captain, I can protect them from her."

My mind was racing. Would he be willing to reassign those soldiers to my cause? Perhaps Katarine could meet with him and change his mind when he arrived in Skorsa. "I'm surprised Coyle allowed you such a prestigious position."

"He's been given a more prestigious one by Her Majesty," he said.

"Better than his current role?" I asked.

He laughed—the same condescending laugh he'd used in camp. "You really have no idea what's going on, do you?"

"Perhaps not," I said, downing the rest of my wine. "Excuse me."

I'd reached my limit in dealing with Mark, so I needed to escape before I said something wrong. My mind was like a starving man in the desert, and every scrap of information was devoured with ravenous abandon. I circled the party to give myself time to digest the news—Mark now worked for Ilara, but his loyalties remained with his soldiers; Coyle was being given a new position somewhere; there were a hundred Forcadelian soldiers in Skorsa that might be loyal to me.

Finally, when the last bit of wine had worn off, I plucked another from a passing tray to nurse and found a column to stand by. The party was in full swing, except Ilara was nowhere to be seen so far. Even Luisa hadn't made an appearance yet.

But finally, my gaze landed someone familiar—and my knees almost buckled in relief. Ignacio, Beswick's second, stood surrounded by a pair of Kulkans and a couple Severians. His pencil mustache was the same as ever, and his sharklike eyes spoke of a man who was used to getting what he wanted by any means necessary.

I took another sip of my wine to steady myself and remind myself how furious I was with him. After all, if Ilara was to believed, Ignacio was still working for Beswick, who wasn't about to be neck deep in ice in Niemen.

Funneling all my anger into my heart, I placed my empty goblet on a passing tray and crossed the room, keeping my murderous gaze on Ignacio. Just before I reached the group, he spotted me, his eyes widening in surprise before a smile curled onto his face.

"Look who it is," Ignacio said. "A disgraced princess. Surprised you're willing to show your face around here."

"I'm just full of surprises," I said, my voice dripping with acid. "Where's your boss? This doesn't seem the kind of party he would miss."

Ignacio's lip twitched, but I couldn't tell if it was in anger or amusement. "Lord Beswick is in the east, handling some business for the queen." He smiled again. "You know that they're now partners, I assume."

"I think I heard something about it when he sent her troops to raze my camp."

"And you seem to have found yourself in the wrong place again." He laughed, and there was nothing nice in it. "Caught in the streets of the city? Weren't you trying to regain your throne?"

I pursed my lips, glaring at the cup of wine instead of responding.

"I'd like you to meet my associate, Jax."

The glass nearly slipped from my hand. I hadn't recognized him without his goatee, and perhaps his hair had been lightened. Also, he wore a fine, light blue tunic instead of the dark one. But it was him.

"I know her," Jax said, leveling a death glare so fierce, I thought I might melt from it. "And it's only because the guards took my knives that I haven't stuck one of them into that black heart of yours, Larissa."

My cheeks warmed and I found myself without anything to say.

In a flash, Jax grabbed my wrist and pulled me to him, death in his eyes. "I can't talk long," he whispered. "Eyes everywhere."

"I'm so glad to see you," I said, keeping my gaze fearful in case there were onlookers. "What's happening out east?"

"I was going to ask you the same thing," he said. "You mean you don't know? What kind of useless spy are you?"

"Nobody's telling me anything. I've only just been allowed out of my room." I swallowed. "Is Fishen—"

"Fine. Safe. Wasn't my idea, but those kids I got working for me insisted." He glanced behind me then shoved my hand away roughly. "You damned traitor." He spat at my feet. "I can't even bear to look at you."

"Seems you make friends everywhere you go," Mark said, coming to stand beside us. "I just came over to make sure everything was all right."

"It's fine," I said, rubbing my red wrist. Jax certainly played the part well. "Just a conversation between old friends. If you'll excuse me."

Chapter Twenty-One

I made a beeline for the balcony, needing some air and space so I could process my thoughts without an audience. I sighed loudly as I laid my hands on the bannister overlooking the gardens and closed my eyes, allowing emotion to flow through me.

Useless? What about Jax? He hadn't given me a single hint of what was going on outside the castle walls—and insulted me, to boot. Getting to this point had taken a lot of hard work. This wouldn't happen overnight.

I chewed on my nail, ruining all the hard work the maids had done earlier in the day. Had Jax thought I'd have some brilliant bit of information for him? Should I have? It wasn't as if Ilara had volunteered anything of interest. And every time I asked about going east...

Which was another thing—if Beswick was supposedly still shipping people out east, why didn't Ignacio know what was going on?

I turned around to march back inside and yell at Jax, but stopped short. Coyle stood in the doorway, blocking my path back in. He wore a victorious smirk, one just begging to be punched off.

"What do you want, Coyle?" I asked, turning back to the balcony so I wouldn't have to look at him any more.

"Trouble in paradise?"

"What in the Mother's name are you talking about?"

He smirked. "I know that Jax guy works for Celia."

"He did," I said, glaring at him. "Left camp when I showed up. I'm not surprised he took up with Beswick."

"You two weren't all that chummy for being friends."

"I don't know, maybe he's still pissed at me for breaking his arm last year," I drawled. "Or maybe it's because every person we knew in camp, including Celia herself, is now dead, thanks to me. Take your pick, Coyle."

He chuckled and stood next to me. "I told you you're a bad liar, Brynna."

"Or maybe you're just a bad judge of character," I said. "Then again, you brought Mark back into the fold. I'm sure that won't come back to bite you in the ass."

He shrugged, unconcerned. "Captain Mark volunteered."

"Was this before or after you slaughtered twenty of his soldiers?" I crossed my arms over my chest. "Does he know you were integral in that?"

"He was the one who taught me to follow orders," he said. "And besides that, I gave him purpose again. The Forcadelian soldiers will be glad to see him and will follow whatever he says. I fail to see how this is bad news."

"And what do you get out of it?" I asked, narrowing my eyes. "I hear you're up for a big promotion. Announcing your engagement to Ilara or something?"

"No. Unlike Felix, I'm not willing to sleep my way to the crown," he said. "All will be revealed in due time."

"I'm so sick of people telling me that," I said. "But what else should I expect from a double-tongued snake?"

"Sticks and stones, Brynna." He glanced inside at the party. "But if you want answers, I'd head back inside. Her Majesty will be making her appearance."

I was about to respond, but the trumpets at the front of the room sounded and Luisa appeared at the front doors, wearing what I assumed was a Severian formal outfit. Glass baubles hung from a belt at her waist, and sparkling crystals hung from her ears. She beamed at the crowd, waiting for the conversation to die down.

"Good evening, friends," she said, her voice loud and clear across the room. "I want to welcome you to Her Majesty's gala tonight. We are so glad you could make it, and so grateful for your partnership these past few months."

I glanced around the room, reading the reactions. Nothing but joyous anticipation.

"Without further ado, I would like to introduce Her Majesty, Queen Ilara Hipolita Särkkä of New Severia."

New Severia? I hid my confusion and politely clapped with the rest of the crowd as Ilara made her entrance. She, like Luisa, wore a long dress covered in beads and sparkling with glass. Her dress was much fuller, with a petticoat underneath, and her long black hair tumbled down her front and back. On her head was the crown my father had been wearing at his funeral. It seemed to be her favorite now.

"Good evening," Ilara called out, quieting the applause. "As Luisa said, I'm so grateful to have you here with me tonight, and even more proud of what we've accomplished together. Please, give yourselves a round of applause for your hard work."

More polite clapping; this time, I didn't join in.

"But as you know, this is just the beginning of a new era." Her gaze landed on me. "For those who don't know, this isn't a welcome party. It's a farewell party."

I glanced around the room. At least I wasn't the only one surprised by her proclamations.

She continued into the room, knowing she was the absolute center of attention. "Tonight, we are saying farewell to the old ways of doing things. I've grown tired of a continent with borders and wars. We need a new way. And I'm going to provide it.

"Many of you have been integral to the development of Aunela. Since I took this crown for myself, I've had a singular aim in mind. Finding a suitable home for Severians outside the desert. Giving them a new industry that would allow them to flourish, instead of reaching for handouts from other countries." She caught my gaze. "And we've found that in Aunela. The capital of New Severia."

Two soldiers unfurled a map behind Ilara. The countries of Severia and Forcadel had been combined into a single nation. And…the rivers that had once flowed into the city of Forcadel had been diverted to Aunela. A solid trade path from one end of the continent to the other. No other cities between.

"Stretching from sea to sea, New Severia will be the last step in the combination of our countries that began when I…well…" She grinned at me. "When I deposed our dear friend Brynna here."

At once, a hundred eyes swept toward me. Despite my burning desire to become invisible, I kept my head held high.

"Water under the bridge now, as she and I have become good friends. And she will partner with me as we take this new step." She turned away, back to the crowd. "In the morning, we will be traveling to Skorsa to watch the final preparations and official rerouting of the Ash river. Once we have water flowing into Aunela, we will begin work on the secondary river from Kulka."

Two brand new rivers. Ilara was either insane or a genius. Maybe both.

"I invite all of you to come with me. My dear friend Johann Beswick has been leading the way, moving our citizens from this city to Aunela," Ilara said. "The trip is two weeks by open ocean, but once you arrive, it will be paradise, my friends."

"Indeed it is," Ignacio said, raising his glass.

"Very soon, there will be nothing left in Forcadel," Ilara said with a smile. "Nothing except a failed kingdom and crumbling buildings. The rivers will dry up, and with it, the memories of this once great kingdom." She held up her hands. "Join me in New Severia, and help me build our new future together."

The crowd erupted in cheers and applause again, and this time, I had to join in. She turned her back to me and I caught eyes with Jax, who was scowling. I wanted more time with him—to discuss strategy, a way forward, how all this impacted our once-great plan—but before I could walk over, I felt Ilara's gaze on me. She was headed in my direction, although being stopped to receive congratulations from everyone as she walked. When I looked back at Jax, he was gone, but I had a feeling he wouldn't be far.

"Evening, Brynna," she said, making sure to announce my name. A few nearby turned their heads, and one woman did a double take. "You look magnificent."

"Thank you, Your Majesty," I said, curtseying. "For your compliment and generosity. Best of luck on your new endeavor."

She smiled, taking a moment to survey those who were paying attention. "I don't need luck, Brynna. I have the Mother on my side, as I told you. Everything works out for the best when I keep my gaze on the larger picture."

"And how long have you been planning this?" I asked. "Since before you invaded?"

"But of course," she said. "Everything has its place in my plan. Even you." She smirked. "Though you did your best to disrupt it. Now, here we are at the crossroads. Forcadel as we know it will die, and New Severia will rise from the ashes like a beautiful phoenix." She exhaled, as if the flames from the firebird were warming her as we spoke. "And the people you care so deeply about will be taken care of. The only thing left for you to do is to choose."

"Choose?"

"You've proven yourself a loyal servant to me," Ilara said. "I would be honored if you would accompany me. Help me manage this new city and bring New Severia into a golden age of trade and opportunity."

Jax was nearby, standing behind Ignacio. At least the message would get out.

"Of course," I said, nodding my head. "It would be my honor."

What I might find in that city was anybody's guess. But at least I was finally getting through to Ilara. I doubted she'd bring me along if she thought I wasn't to be trusted. And with any luck, I might continue my journey deeper into Ilara's inner circle—and my soldiers would continue to follow.

Chapter Twenty-Two

Felix

The salty sea air rustled my hair, and after a few hours on the open ocean, I was acclimated to the rocking of the waves. I'd never traveled much by water, preferring my horse and being over land, but the coastline was speeding by as we made our way around the southeastern coast of the continent.

Our Kulkan sailors kept their distance, but there were surprisingly few mishaps on our ship. It helped that the Kulkans were treated with respect, and the Forcadelian soldiers jumped in beside them to help with sails and fixing equipment. The lieutenant who'd laughed in my face, Kalila, now slept in the barracks with her soldiers, as I'd taken the captain's quarters for myself. But I didn't sleep much, poring over the map of Forcadel Bay and trying to think of a different way to crack the egg that was Forcadel's defenses.

There was a knock on the door, and Kalila walked in, followed by another sailor. "Excuse me, sir, but Penino says there's a large storm brewing. He recommends we seek shelter in a port to ride it out."

I glanced out the open window at the blue sky above. "Really?"

The other sailor nodded. "The Mother's wisdom is clear to those who'll listen."

"You're a Nestori," I said, understanding. My only experience with a Nestori was the healer back in Celia's camp, and she'd basically brought me back from the dead. "The Kulkan ships can't handle the weather?"

"Not laden with this much weaponry," Kalila said, shifting a bit and sounding as if I should've known better. "There's a Forcadelian town nearby that could offer us safe harbor until it passes."

"I don't like the idea of coming into port," I said. "Someone could pass word to Ilara."

"Would you rather sink?"

Her tone was clear—this wasn't an option. "Fine. To port we go."

Almost as soon as the five ships reached the inner harbor, the deluge began. The wind howled and lightning cracked the sky. Even in the docks, the ships rocked and creaked against the wind. I was no sailor, but I could tell that our weight would not have been in our favor out on the open ocean.

I spent a little more time with Penino the Nestori, although he mostly spoke in riddles. I was glad to know we had him in our ranks, however, although his expertise seemed to be in weather forecasting instead of healing.

Someone or something banged at my door, and before I could call to the person to enter, the door swung open and Aline stumbled in.

"You look like a drowned cat," I said.

"I feel like it," she said, wringing out her long hair and wiping the wetness from her eyes. "I'm glad you made the call to come to port."

"I don't like it, though. I don't want to give away our position."

"To whom?" She glanced out at the pounding rain outside. "We're days away from the city and the moment we came in, the rain started. I doubt anyone even knows what's going on outside."

I couldn't argue with that. "It was lucky, that's for sure. How are things on the other ships?"

"Enos let word spread that Ammon went back on his word, and that seems to have heartened them to our cause." She snorted. "Nobody likes him, apparently."

"I weep for their future," I said. "I thought Kalila might be trouble, but she seems to have fallen in line. They're good soldiers, thankfully."

"How long do you expect us to stay in port?" Aline asked.

"Just until the storm passes," I said. "The Nestori said it would be after midnight."

"Then what?" Aline asked. "We can't bring five Kulkan warships into Forcadel. We'll get blown out of the water before we reach the mouth of the bay."

I stepped away from the window. "I don't know. I haven't heard from Katarine in weeks, nor from Jax since he sent that messenger. It's hard to know what our part in this play is when I can't see the other actors."

"Maybe you can send me ahead to Forcadel," Aline said. "I can make contact with Jax and the vigilantes there."

"It would take weeks over land," I said.

"Perhaps there's someone in town who'll be headed that way," she offered. "We have some time, and the taverns look full. I bet we could barter passage for one or two people to go ahead of us."

"Good idea," I said, as a rumble of thunder echoed from outside. "Grab your cloak."

The wind whipped rain at our faces, so we ducked into the closest lit building we could near the docks. The bar was thick with people, all of whom were still soaking wet.

"I'll start with the bartender," I said, nodding to the man behind the counter. "And see where it gets us. You find an empty table and eavesdrop on some conversations."

She nodded and we split off, she making a beeline for a vacant corner, and me headed for the bar. After waiting patiently for a moment, I pushed through a pair to lean on the bar.

I waved down the bartender, who came over after speaking with a Kulkan at the other end of the bar. The Kulkan had given me a long look, which set me on edge.

"Evening," I said to the tender. "Do you know—"

He was quicker. "Your name Llobrega?"

I took a step back, startled. "What?"

"I asked if your name was Llobrega?"

"It is, but—"

"You've been offered an invitation to dine," the bartender said, nodding toward the ceiling. "Upstairs and to the right. Second door."

"By whom?"

"Someone calling himself an old friend." He shrugged. "Don't know any more than that."

I backed away from the bar and found Aline, who seemed as concerned as I was.

"We should go back to the ship," she said. "It was a mistake in being here."

"No," I said. "We need to figure out who's recognized us. And see if they're friendly."

"And if they aren't?"

I put my hand on the sword at my side. "We'll cross that bridge if we come to it."

We ascended the stairs slowly, keeping our ears open for the sound of conversation. There was a light under the door the bartender had sent us to, and I nodded to Aline, who drew the small knife at her hip.

With care, I rapped on the door. The door swung open and I couldn't help the cry of surprise.

"Kieran?"

"Captain Llobrega!" The pirate wore a warm grin and a new scar on his cheek. "It is most wonderful to see you again. I'm glad you accepted my invitation. You're looking absolutely drenched. Please come in."

Aline nudged me from behind as we walked into Kieran's room. "Who is this guy, sir?"

"He's…well, I wouldn't call him a friend—"

"And why not?" Kieran said with a bit of a pout. "I've invited you to dine with me. Surely that counts for something." He caught sight of Aline and his grin widened. "And who is this young—"

"This is my captain," I said, hoping to stop his ogling before it got started. "Aline."

"The pleasure is all mine," Kieran said. "You certainly travel in beautiful company, Captain Llobrega."

"It's General."

"Oh? Did your princess give you a promotion?"

"She did," I replied. "But we tend to call her queen now."

"Ah, Queen Veil. It suits her." He smiled. "I only suppose you're responsible for the armada of Kulkan ships that pulled into port as the storm hit."

"That's not…" But it was useless to argue with him. "I hope I can count on your discretion."

"But of course, but of course." He waved his hand dismissively. "I have no master, and it doesn't benefit me to tell anyone of your plans."

"Let's just hope no one else noticed," Aline said. "In case it *does* benefit them."

"I wouldn't worry yourselves," Kieran said as he poured the wine. "Nasty storm pops up, everyone comes into town. Great for business, locally. And considering those monstrosities are Kulkanmade, I doubt anyone will know you're on your way to destroy Forcadel."

"And what are you doing in this port city?" I asked. "Smuggling in or out?"

"Neither, actually. I'm on a legitimate run to Forcadel to bring produce," he said. "It's the only business an old salt like me can get." He wasn't even thirty, but I let him have his pity party. "Beswick and his men cut me out of their lucrative smuggling business, so I'm trying to find anyone who'll let me bring something from point A to point B. It's tough out here."

"Beswick cut you out?" I shook my head. "Must've done something pretty bad to piss him off."

"How about arriving in Forcadel with none of the ond I'd promised, instead telling Beswick that The Veil wanted to have a word with him." He winced and my gaze drew to the scar again. "I'm lucky I got out of there alive."

"What do you know about the port of Forcadel now?" I asked.

"It does change so often," Kieran said, flashing me a smile. "Easier, of course, if you have legitimate business. Much more expensive otherwise. People are more willing to look the other way if you dangle a bag of gold in front of them."

I doubted we had enough gold for all the Severian soldiers in the tower now to ignore five Kulkan warships.

"What I'd recommend is scouting ahead," Kieran said. "Your ships are heavy and slow, but mine is small and fast. And to boot— I have legitimate business in Forcadel."

"Do you?"

He shrugged. "More legitimate than you."

"What do you want in return?"

"That you'll put in a good word with our favorite princess—

excuse me, queen."

"To what end?" Aline asked, leaning on the table.

"I've always liked her," Kieran said. "And she looked awfully serious when she said the next time she saw me, she'd... what was it?" He tapped his finger to his chin. "Oh, that's right. If she ever saw my face again, it wouldn't be connected to my body for much longer."

"Seems out of character for her," I said, but couldn't hide a smile. "But then again, you did bring ond into the city."

"Well, if I'd known it would've resulted in such a mess, I wouldn't have." He rose. "What do you say, General, Captain, whatever you are? Can you let an old salt like me help repair the damage to a friendship?"

I didn't want to be indebted to the pirate any more than I already was, but he was the best option to get us inside the city.

"I suppose," I said with a nod. "But my word only goes so far. Brynna has her own opinions about whom she likes and whom she forgives. I can only promise to tell her of your assistance."

"Then I hope it will be enough to return to her good graces," he said. "Come! We depart in the morning. I promise to bring you to Forcadel quickly and return you to your armada in plenty of time to start the attack."

"Sir, can I have a word with you?" Aline said. "In private?"

"Are you sure we can trust him?" she asked, almost as soon as the door closed behind us. "He's a pirate. What's to say he doesn't just take us to Forcadel and drop us off at Ilara's door?"

There wasn't anything, really, other than his word. But his gaze had changed, and the scar on his cheek was new. He may have betrayed Brynna in the past, but something had happened after he'd returned to Beswick that had sobered him somewhat.

"As it stands," I began slowly, "he clearly knows what we're up to. So I'd feel more comfortable keeping an eye on him myself. If he tries anything in Forcadel, we'll handle it."

She pursed her lips. "I don't think you're thinking clearly, sir. If what you've said is true, he's betrayed us before. And you want to get on a ship and leave? We've barely got the Kulkans under our command. You are our leader. You can't abandon us just because you want to see Brynna again."

"What's your recommendation, then?" I asked, my voice even.

"Send me instead," she said. "I can fight, I know Forcadel like the back of my hand. And you can stay and keep command."

My cheeks warmed as I recognized the truth of what she was saying. This new phase of our plan would require more sneaking around than strategy. But at the same time, Kieran and I had developed something of a rapport. And I knew Forcadel's defenses better than anyone. If we were to move our ships into the bay, I needed to see what we were up against with my own eyes.

"I apologize if I've stepped out of line," Aline said at my silence. "But I wouldn't be doing my job as your second if I didn't at least make you think about what you're doing. These Kulkans might smell blood in the water if they see the leader has left."

"Then I'll leave a capable leader in charge," I said, smiling down at her.

"Sir?"

"Aline, you have all the makings of an excellent captain—a real one, not one half-promoted by our queen." I glanced back at the room beyond. "I need to go ahead with Kieran. You will lead our forces over the ocean behind us. His ship is quicker, and it'll give me about a week to come up with a strategy."

She sighed. "I don't know if I can handle commanding five warships."

"You handled being The Veil," I said. "And you didn't even have any training in that. You've been preparing to be a captain since your first day as my cadet. Now it's time to step up."

It was her turn to be silent, and I half-expected more arguing. But she inhaled, strengthening her resolve. "I'll do my best to make you proud, sir. I actually think Kalila's starting to warm to me anyway."

"Really?"

"No, but she will," she said with a grimace. "Please give our queen my best. We will meet you in Forcadel as quickly as we can."

Chapter Twenty-Three

Katarine

We attempted to pump our spy for more information, but he had nothing else to offer. And since we had made no headway in getting to the border, we were stuck discussing the scraps and, in my mind, wasting time.

"He said he was supposed to meet with his contact weekly," Joella said, pacing the room. "I say we set up a trap to capture his Severian counterpart. At least then we'll have some understanding of what Ilara's up to."

I nodded, turning away from the window. "Or, hopefully, he'll be able to give us insight into why Ilara's been so concerned with the border lately. I'm also not convinced our Forcadelian friend has been entirely truthful."

"I could go spy again!"

Joella and I caught each other's eyes. "Elisha, I told you to wait outside," I said.

"I been waiting all morning," she said, poking her head through the door. "Just like you said."

"Give me five minutes and we'll discuss your verbal essay," I said.

"But—"

"Elisha," I said, catching her gaze in warning.

She made a noise and fell back into the chair in the anteroom to my office, folding her arms across her chest and huffing.

"Where were we?" I asked Joella.

The lieutenant walked to the door and closed it gently. "Maybe it's not the worst idea to have Elisha keep watch. We never would've found that spy if it hadn't been for her. I can't help but feel like we're wasting her talents."

"It's not just her age," I said. "She's reckless. I can't trust that she won't get us all into more trouble because she wants to be in the thick of the action. For now, she stays behind until I feel she's better able to handle her impulses."

"Then I'm at a loss," Joella said, walking to the map on the wall. "The only way to Forcadel is to come back the way we came over land, venture back to Celia's camp, then march south."

"But that would mean leaving behind our naval forces," I said.

"Do you have any better ideas?"

Before I could respond, there was a hurried rap on the door.

"Elisha, I told you to wait."

But instead of Elisha, a Niemenian soldier walked through the door, a wide smile on his face. "Pardon the interruption, my lady, but the scouts have said there's three ships arriving from the north."

"Luard's back," I said, my heart rising in my chest.

"Not just that, but it looks like…well, it looks like one of them is bearing Her Majesty's crest," he said. "I think she's come from Linden."

"Who is it?" Elisha said, appearing behind him.

"Help," I said with a smile. "My sister has come."

I sent Elisha back home to let Beata know we'd be expecting company for dinner, and prayed my wife wouldn't worry too much about putting on airs. In our home, Ariadna wouldn't be so much a queen as my eldest sister. But Beata did have a habit of overdoing it when she thought she needed to.

As I rushed down to the docks, my heart swelled three sizes. I hadn't seen my sister since leaving Linden at thirteen—over a decade. I'd been expecting Luard to return any day now, but to have Ariadna leave the safety of Linden, especially so soon after giving birth, warmed my heart.

By the time I reached the shore, the ship had already docked and the Niemenian royal soldiers disembarked, forming a solid wall of light blue down the wooden dock. Several of them winked at me as I passed, familiar faces that I recalled from my childhood.

On the ship, I found Luard talking with Ivan. Both wore fine tunics, and Luard's was trimmed and his face smooth—different from the stubble and dirt he'd worn when we'd parted ways. His eyes lit up when he saw me, and he extended his arms out.

"Dearest Kitty Kat," he said, pulling me in and kissing both cheeks. "Married life is still treating you well, I see."

"It's only been a few weeks," I said. "And you didn't have to bring the entire entourage."

"Perhaps we did," he said, turning behind him. "After all, Ari wanted to give her congratulations in person."

My sister, the queen of Niemen, was rosy-cheeked and warm as she descended the steps from the quarterdeck. She was much older now, the lines around her eyes telling of the toll that being a sovereign and mother of six had taken. But the crown and the age couldn't hide the sparkle in her eyes.

"My lovely Kitty Kat," she said, opening her arms to me.

I rushed toward her, but stopped short. "Oh, is that..."

An infant was strapped to her back, firmly wrapped with a golden cloth. The babe was almost bald; perhaps only a few weeks old.

"We've named him August," Ariadna said softly. "I thought you would approve."

My hand came to my heart, warming at the thoughtful gesture of my sister and her husband. "I'm honored. Thank you. Brynna will be thrilled as well."

She kissed my hands. "Now, before we get bogged down by morose topics, I would love to meet your beautiful wife and the children you've taken into your home."

"I absolutely agree," Luard said, putting his arms around both of us. "Shall we?"

Luard trailed us down the cobblestone streets, pointing out interesting features on the houses we passed. I could almost forget that my sister was queen of a nation, and envelop myself in the fantasy that my family was here to celebrate my new marriage.

"It truly was the most magical of nights," Luard said. "Nils and Hagan put everyone to shame with their dancing."

"As they do," Ariadna said.

"I wore your brooch," I said. "I wish you could've been there."

"As do I." She squeezed my hand. "And I'm sorry the magic was ruined by Beswick and the events thereafter. I'm happy to say he's rotting quite unhappily in a prison."

"I saw him myself when I was there," Luard said with a nod. "He's now come to understand that he has no friends, so he's doing whatever he can to save his own neck. Unfortunately, Ilara kept him in the dark."

Ariadna nodded. "He has provided the names of those in the mountain who helped him. So far, we've nabbed twenty people, although many of them had compelling stories of being coerced into helping."

"That is his trademark," I replied. "He preys on the desperate."

"I've given him until the pass defrosts to impress me with his names," she said. "And if he doesn't, he'll be put to death."

"Brynna will be happy to hear that," I said as we came up to the front door of the house, lit up with candles in each window. Beata waited out front wearing her finest dress—one she'd made herself—and she'd curled her hair and put rouge on her lips. From the way her hands fidgeted, I could tell she was nervous, but her smile was bright.

"Your Majesty," Beata said, grabbing the sides of her fine skirt and curtseying. "It is an honor to have you in our home."

"My lovely sister-in-law," Ariadna said, sweeping into the room with open arms. "You are family now. The honor is all mine."

Beata squeaked and gave me a look, but embraced my sister, hesitantly at first, then fully. When Beata stepped back, her cheeks were ruddy, and she giggled as if she'd had a little to drink.

"And where are the littles I've heard so much about?" Ariadna said, looking around.

"I will call them," Beata said. "I wasn't sure if..." But she shook her head and walked to the staircase, looking up. "Children? Come down, please."

The thundering of feet drew a smile on Ariadna's face. Almost instantly, the children descended the stairs, all wearing matching tunics with their hair combed.

"Children," I said, "this is my sister, Queen Ariadna of Niemen."

They curtseyed and bowed, just as Beata had taught them.

"Very good, children," Ariadna said, surveying all them with a smile. She stopped at the one closest to her. "You must be Paca."

She jumped then bowed nervously. "Yes'm."

"I've brought you a gift," Ariadna said, straightening. Her lady handed her a small wrapped parcel. "Katarine said you liked to throw a ball against the wall. I've brought you a game where you can toss it for points."

She gasped and squealed, taking the gift in her hand as if she'd never received something so fine.

"After dinner, you and I can go out to the garden wall and play with it," Ariadna said. "Would you like that?"

Paca nodded emphatically.

Beata came up beside me and took my hand, placing her other one on her heart. "She didn't have to bring them gifts."

"And you must be Fletcher," she said, handing him a present. True to form, she accurately named each child based on age, and had brought them a gift that spoke to their particular interests. But when there was one gift left and no child to receive it, I finally noticed who was missing.

"Where's Elisha?" I asked.

Beata glanced at the ceiling as if praying to the Mother for strength, then walked back to the staircase, calling for her. A moment later, the door opened and Elisha came walking out, dressed in the same matching tunic as the others, but wearing a scowl on her face.

I gave her a look and she bobbed her head. "Y'r M'sty."

"I hear you're a fan of the crossbow," Ariadna said, taking the large wrapped box from the lady. "I've had one specially commissioned for you."

Her eyes lit up. "Really?"

"She can't have that," I said, releasing my wife's hand. "We're trying to keep the children out of this." Ariadna cast me a curious look and I cleared my throat. "We'll hold onto the gift for safekeeping. But these kids have gone through enough. Best not to encourage them."

Elisha's grin turned back to a scowl. But she wisely said nothing.

"If that's how you feel," Ariadna said, handing me the box.

"Very well, children, I'm sure your mother has made you a good dinner."

"I'm not quite their mother," Beata said, her cheeks growing red again. "But yes, dinner is served."

My wife outdid herself with a four-course meal that the children devoured. Ariadna declared it was the finest thing she'd ever eaten, and it was all Beata could do not to melt on the floor. When dinner was over, we escaped to the back of the house to watch the children play with their new gifts. After some cajoling, Beata gave Elisha the crossbow, which she used to fire expert shots into a target Ariadna had also brought.

"I see a lot of Brynna in that little Elisha," Ariadna said. "Confidence wrapped in insecurity wrapped in a stubborn little girl. She certainly has some talent, but she needs a firm hand to guide her."

"You couldn't be more spot on," I said. "I think she still feels guilty that she didn't die with the rest of Celia's camp. It was only through the Mother's intervention that she left with Beata, and now she's…well, she's trying to make herself useful." I put my hands on my hips. "She found a spy the other day. She sensed something was amiss, followed him, gathered evidence, and presented her case. But she also went to the border—all our soldiers who've gone there have been shot with arrows. If something happened to her, Brynna might not forgive me. But I don't know how to deal with her."

"I'm sure whatever answer you and Beata come up with will be the right one. So far, you both seem to be doing well with your new family."

I toyed with the hem of my sleeve. "This is just a temporary situation, I fear. Once the kingdom's been reclaimed, we'll see to it that these children are returned to their real parents."

Ariadna shrugged. "It appears they've found their home with you."

I swallowed, warmth spreading through my chest at the thought. It was a dream we'd had, but it seemed wrong to presume that we were anything other than their guardians. These children had arrived in our care by happenstance and keeping them as our own seemed…well, it seemed rather selfish.

But as I watched them scamper around, I couldn't deny that I'd grown fond of all them. Even the scowling teenager sitting in the corner.

Chapter Twenty-Four

Everything somehow began to make sense to me. The blockades, cutting off trade with Niemen and Kulka. All the money that had been spent from the treasury. The city emptying of people. I was once again on the receiving end of one of Ilara's grand surprises and I didn't like it any better than the last few times.

Ilara hadn't been joking about uprooting everyone the next morning, either. Before sunup, I was roused to bathe and dress myself and eat a bit of breakfast (leftover cake from the night before), then dragged down the stairwell to meet the morning sun. Luisa, more bright-eyed than I was, waited in the carriage with an excited smile on her face.

"Be happy, Brynna," she said. "Today is a monumental day."

"I will be happy," I said with a large yawn. "Just as soon as I wake up."

We arrived at the dock, and our ship was already equipped

with steam paddles designed to push against the river current. Coyle was there, barking orders to Forcadelian soldiers as they packed the ship. They paid me little attention, some of them straining under the weight of the boxes.

"Enjoy your travels," Coyle said, sneering. "I will take care of your city in your absence."

"You're the leader of a ghost town," I said. "There's no one left."

He made a face. "Doesn't matter. I'll get to sleep in your father's bed."

If he thought I would be angered by that, he was sorely mistaken. "Just be careful his ghost doesn't rouse you. I hear that spirits can be quite vengeful."

And with that, I continued toward the ship, glad I'd gotten the last word. No matter what I found at the end of this journey, at least I wouldn't have to see Coyle for a long time.

Unfortunately, I'd still be subjected to Mark—at least until we reached our destination south of Skorsa. He was already on the ship, deep in conversation with a Severian lieutenant who clearly outranked him. I made sure to glare at him

I found a spot at the front of the ship, ready to get moving. The bay was magnificent today, glittering under the early spring sun. I still hadn't gotten used to seeing so much of it without ships, but it was easier to appreciate its size.

The sun was high overhead before the royal carriage finally appeared in front of the ship. Coyle had already wrangled all the soldiers into formation, snapping at those who didn't stand straight enough for him and roughly adjusting uniforms while Mark looked on without emotion.

Ilara stepped out of the carriage wearing a tunic and pants, clearly ready to travel. She walked the length of the soldiers, her head held high.

"We will depart immediately," was all she said.

The ship hummed to life beneath my feet. The paddles at the end of the ship inched forward slowly, sloshing the water for a moment before gaining speed. We moved backward, away from the dock at first. Then the paddles changed direction to push us forward—toward the Ash river.

I turned to lean my back against the railing to watch Forcadel pass us by. My heart ached a little for what it had become, and what was yet to happen. One day, I would return victorious, but every time I left, I felt further away from that goal.

"You look concerned," Luisa said, coming to stand next to me.

"I never like leaving home," I said, glancing behind me.

"But you've done it so often lately."

"Unwillingly," I replied, squinting at the sun above. "But perhaps you're right. I should be used to it by now."

It took five days to reach Skorsa, at least the last time I'd attempted it, but how far south Ilara's camp was situated was anybody's guess. Knowing I probably wouldn't get an answer if I asked, I kept my questions to myself.

I kept my gaze on the shoreline, watching the familiar geography and thinking about what might happen when the water beneath us disappeared. Forcadel city, whoever was left there, would always have access to Kulka via the open ocean. But once the river dried up…that was it. Another casualty in Ilara's campaign to completely destroy everything Forcadel once stood for.

I couldn't believe Ilara had caught me unawares again. Clearly, she'd been planning this move to Aunela for months and neither myself, nor Katarine, nor Felix had known anything about it. My only consolation was that Jax had been present at the party, so some word could get to the others. Meanwhile, I supposed I'd continue to gather intel…whatever Ilara would allow me.

When night fell, Luisa beckoned me to the quarterdeck for the first time. There, I found Ilara with a set table for four.

"You looked quite lonely out there," Ilara said. "Come, enjoy some dinner with us."

I sat at the table, and could already predict who the fourth would be.

"Evening," Mark said, walking inside. He sniffed in my direction and sat down. "Thank you, Your Majesty, for allowing me the chance to dine with you."

"It's my pleasure," she said. "I'm sure I'll enjoy the company."

Of that, I had no doubt. I braced myself for a meal filled with barbs and underhanded comments.

And Ilara didn't disappoint. "Tell me, Mark, of your time with Brynna at the camp."

"Oh, well, clearly she was involved in other things," he said. "She sent her soldiers to wait in the plains while she did…well, we really had no idea what she was doing. Then she rode up after we received word that Maarit had been set free. I understand that she had to be forcibly removed from Forcadel."

"I had no idea you were in town," Ilara said, gazing at me over her glass. "Curious that you left that out of your discussion."

I could have *killed* Mark. "I was only in town briefly," I said.

"Oh, it's such a shame we left Coyle behind," she said. "I would have loved to ask him if he saw you while you were in Forcadel."

"Indeed."

I had; I'd threatened him with manhood severance if Felix died in the dungeons, and he'd wilted like a flower. Luckily, Mark had no knowledge of who'd been in Forcadel with me, nor did he know that Felix and Katarine had eventually rejoined my side.

"If you ask me, Your Majesty, I wouldn't trust a word out of her," he said, glaring at me over the dinner table. "She's clearly hiding something."

"Yes, my utter disdain for you," I replied with a glare.

"And what of the soldiers? Surely, they suffered under such a loose grip. A leader must be present, after all."

"It was all I could do to keep them in camp," Mark said. "It's no surprise so many left when she fired me."

Under the table, I dug my nail into my palm to keep from responding. Perhaps five soldiers had left in total.

"Oh, let it out, Brynna," Ilara said, reaching across the table to poke me. "You're not normally this quiet when someone's disparaging you. You might explode if you keep your thoughts to yourself."

"I don't see the benefit in speaking," I replied evenly. "Not when I can't find anything nice to say."

"That's certainly a first," Mark said. "She was rolling around with the soldiers, eating elbow-to-elbow with them. Had very little decorum or appreciation for her station."

"It's called getting to know your soldiers," I said. "Something your protégé, Felix, taught me."

"Felix was a damned fool," he said. "It's a shame that you managed to corrupt him—and Jorad, too."

Hearing him say Jorad's name drew fire to my chest. "Jorad was a good man."

"Was, being the operative word."

I got to my feet, unable to take the abuse. "Forgive me, Your Majesty, but I think I'm seasick. If you'll excuse me."

"But of course," Ilara said, wearing a smile that said she'd enjoyed every second of that exchange.

I walked out, taking care not to slam the door as I wanted to, and didn't stop walking until I reached the end of the ship. There I gripped the railing as hard as I could, envisioning myself ripping it off the bannisters and tossing it into the river. My anger wouldn't subside, and if I happened across another person, I couldn't be held responsible for my actions.

Jorad had been nothing but a loyal, brave servant. He'd been by my side no matter how badly I messed things up. But I couldn't help but think if he'd gone with us...if he hadn't stayed behind...

"Pardon me, miss."

I gripped the ledge again. "I swear to the Mother, if you don't back up and—" The words died on my lips when I saw who I was talking to.

Narin, one of my vigilantes, wore a Severian uniform, but his expression was completely neutral.

"What?" I said, after catching the tail end of his words.

"I need to access that rope under your feet."

I stepped out of the way and he took the rope. Before he left, he offered me a half-smile and a wink. With care, I turned back toward the river so no one would see the joy that had returned to my face.

Chapter Twenty-Five

The days passed slowly. Although I was starting to get used to Mark's near constant abuse, every mention of Jorad was like a knife to my gut. Ilara made no move to stop him, although her eyes lit up every time he landed a particularly painful blow.

During the day, I did my best to avoid Narin on the ship as well, knowing that if I saw him, I wouldn't be able to avoid that surge of hope in my chest. But I longed to know what he knew, to get more answers out of him than I had with Jax. He was probably here on Jax's orders, and perhaps had some greater task than watching over me.

Luisa offered some diversion, having brought nearly all her books from the castle in a large trunk. Ilara lounged on the quarterdeck with a book in her hand while Luisa and I sat nearby. Most of them I'd already read, but I opted for anything that might keep me from giving away Narin.

"Tell me, Brynna," Ilara asked, turning the page of her book with one finger. "What is Skorsa like?"

"Typical border town," I said, looking up from the book. "You haven't been there?"

"No, I've only heard stories." She turned another page. "What was the gate like?"

"Not as magnificent as Neveri's," I said. "Just a portcullis that went up and down, basically. Why?"

"I've become quite enamored with gate designs of late. And as I'll probably never lay eyes on Skorsa, I thought I'd ask."

I cast her a curious look but didn't inquire further. That morsel of information was all she was going to give me, it seemed, as commotion at the stairs leading to the belly of the ship drew our attention.

A gaggle of soldiers came up holding a captive in their midst. My heart leapt to my throat. Narin.

The last to emerge was Mark, holding something in his hand and looking somewhat pleased. My hatred of him soared to new heights as he walked toward us. Narin had been Felix's trainee once, so Mark had surely watched him grow as Felix had.

"Captain Mark, what is the meaning of this?" Ilara asked, closing her book with a curious smile.

"I noticed we had an extra soldier," Mark said, climbing the stairs to join her on the quarterdeck. "And I found this in his personal effects."

He revealed the item in his hand—a Forcadelian seal. *Narin, you stupid, stupid moron, how could you bring that onboard?*

"I see," Ilara said. "Do you have anything to say for yourself?"

Narin stared blankly ahead. Loyal to the very end, just as Felix had taught all his soldiers.

"Brynna." Ilara's gaze turned toward me. "Any thoughts as to why we have this stowaway?"

My pulse pounded in my ears, but I forced myself to shrug. "Your guess is as good as mine," I said. "Perhaps just someone looking for passage out of Forcadel? I can't imagine having that seal is something worth getting upset over."

"It's a Forcadelian seal," Ilara said. "I had all them melted down. So I wonder how he obtained one?"

"Could've been his father's." I turned to Narin as passively as I could. "Well?"

"I know for a fact that his father was a cobbler," Mark said. "I watched this boy grow up. He's loyal to Llobrega."

I cast Mark a dubious look. "Then perhaps he can tell us where Llobrega is, because I have no idea. I have a fist that needs connecting with his face."

"I haven't seen Captain Llobrega in months," Narin said.

"He's no longer a captain, and I don't believe you," Mark said. "I think you were sent here to cause trouble. Or perhaps rescue your would-be princess."

"Did he have any weapons on him?" I asked.

"Well, no—"

I rolled my eyes. "Then how is he planning to cause trouble? He's a stowaway, and you're paranoid. Nobody's coming to 'rescue' me and if they were, they'd know that I'm perfectly capable of doing it myself." I crossed my arms over my chest. "I'm exactly where I want to be."

"Indeed you are," Ilara said, sending a chill down my spine as she turned back to Narin. "If you aren't a soldier, that means you're a defector. Put him in the river."

My chest seized. "You don't have to kill him."

"Sweet Brynna," Ilara said with a smile. "he's a disloyal soldier, which means he isn't to be trusted. The penalty for desertion is death." She batted her eyelashes, as if she'd just ordered lunch. "But if it pains you to watch someone die, you can remove yourself from the deck. I will fetch you when it's over."

The soldiers showed no concern as they pushed Narin forward toward the edge of the ship, and my loyal soldier kept his cool. It took everything I had not to scream and cry out, to beg for mercy for him. But there was nothing to be done. The river bank was within swimming distance, and the current not so bad. Narin was young, he could fight his way to the shore and head down to Forcadel.

"Put him in," Ilara ordered.

Narin's final words were lost to the wind, but I could've sworn he said, "For Forcadel" before diving headfirst into the river.

The splash was small, and a few precious moments later, his head emerged and he began swimming for shore. I whispered a prayer that he would make it.

"Shoot him."

Shock overtook me. One of the Forcadelians brandished a crossbow and fired toward the water. A pool of red appeared in the river water before his body emerged, face-down, with the arrow sticking out of his back.

Be with the Mother. Thank you for your sacrifice.

"See, that's why you never made a good queen, Brynna," Ilara said, coming to stand next to me. "You can't make hard choices like that. The only way to deal with dissent is to show no mercy. Otherwise someone could just swoop in and take your kingdom."

It took every ounce of self-restraint not to wipe that satisfied smirk off her face.

I spent the evening on the front of the ship, too pissed off to face anyone. My heart ached for my fallen soldier, for his patriotism, and how his death felt, to me, like a waste. Even if he'd just been a stowaway, there'd been no reason to kill him. And Mark, that bastard. He spoke of being loyal and protecting his troops, but he'd allowed one of his own, a cadet he'd raised, to be slaughtered like that?

And yet, there was guilt on my conscience, mostly because I

couldn't shake the looming hopelessness his death cast upon me. I had no more allies on this ship, or anywhere else. Yet again, I was all alone.

Footsteps behind me raised my hackles, and I cast a scathing glance at whomever it was. But in the dark, the young soldier didn't get the full effect.

"I just want to say," the soldier said, coming to stand next to me. "Narin was my friend. And I appreciated what you tried to do for him."

"I didn't do anything," I said sadly. "Except perhaps delay the inevitable." Then, just in case, I added, "I wish I knew why he was here."

"We're all wondering the same thing," he said. "About you."

"Best not to wonder," I said. "I'm nobody. And if I ever was, I'm not that person anymore."

"Get back to work, soldier." Mark had appeared, his eyes wide in the darkness. "If you have time to dawdle, you have time to clean."

The soldier saluted and scurried away, leaving me alone with Mark. But since Ilara had already gone to bed, I could finally say what I'd been wanting to all day.

"You could've kept your mouth shut," I said. "He wasn't hurting anyone."

"Wasn't he?" Mark asked. "Weapons or no, he could've been a spy."

"For whom?" I asked. "Me? I'm sorry to tell you that I have two eyes and two ears myself. I don't need some dumb, young soldier spying for me." I turned back to the river and leaned over the railing. "His death is on your hands. I hope you can sleep at night."

"My responsibility is to my soldiers and my queen. How can I protect them if I allow stowaways and spies on my ship?"

"He *was* your soldier," I snapped, on the verge of losing it completely.

"He deserted his post in Neveri, and if memory served, was one of the few who stayed around while you wasted everyone's time in that camp," Mark said. "If anything, you should be thanking me for not mentioning *that* to the queen, or else you might be in the river with him."

I licked my lips, stopping myself before I said everything I wanted to. "I had no loyalty to him, nor him to me. If he did once, that was lost when I was captured. There was nothing gained by killing him, other than solidifying your place at Ilara's side."

"A worthy sacrifice."

My hands clenched on the bannister. *You son of a bitch.* "You don't deserve to be called captain."

"Luckily, *you* no longer make that call," he said with a sneer. "Keep clear of my soldiers. They're not to speak with you. Clearly, association gets one killed."

Chapter Twenty-Six

True to his word, Mark's soldiers said not one word to me. Although Mark seemed sure I'd had a hand in Narin's appearance on the ship, Ilara seemed to have forgotten the entire incident. That evening, I was back inside her quarters, quietly nibbling on dinner I had no appetite for while Ilara and Luisa talked about the latest book they were jointly reading. Mark would inject himself where appropriate, but I remained silent unless provoked.

It was a lonely time, where I spent my days thinking about Narin, Riya, Jorad, Locke, the young vigilantes, and everyone else I'd lost on this journey so far. How many more would join them? Katarine? Felix? I still had no stomach for death, nor did I want one. But without any diversions, it was hard not to replay his final moments over and over in my mind.

When my anxiety grew too much, I paused and placed my faith in the Mother. Somehow, She'd help me see this through to the end. And I prayed She'd taken Narin with open arms.

Finally, we rounded a corner and came across a sign of life in the center of the river. Even from afar, the structure rivaled Neveri's gates. But instead of metal slats, this one was solid metal, keeping the water from flowing from Niemen to Forcadel. Once the door opened, it would swing all the way to the other side, thus stopping the water flow south and sending it east. The design was simple, yet effective. It would only need to be turned once for Ilara's purpose.

And it had all been done in a matter of months.

"Well?" Luisa asked, coming to stand next to me. "What do you think?"

"Reminds me of Neveri," I said, hoping honesty would buy me some points.

"Before you got through with it, I'm sure," she said with a knowing look. "Her Majesty has taken extra precautions, knowing what happened there. This is made of a sturdier metal, sourced from Severia. Practically indestructible, unlike those flimsy gates in Neveri."

I wouldn't have called it easy. It had taken ten of us leaving bags of ond every few feet to canvass it. But if the metal here wasn't as combustable the way it was in Neveri, that meant it would be harder to destroy.

"And unlike the one in Neveri, this is designed to handle the river water for centuries to come," she continued. "Her Majesty was integral in its design. It's her crowning accomplishment."

"I can certainly tell." Really, I had no idea if Luisa was simply blowing smoke or if Ilara really spent time studying how to build a gate. Then again, knowing what I knew about the books in Severia, perhaps it was something more diverting.

Our ship sidled up to a makeshift dock which only seemed to allow one ship. Clearly, the bulk of Mark's troops had arrived before us, as they lined the banks of the river. It was the biggest collection of Forcadelian troops I'd seen in a while—a bit odd, considering. Why would Ilara trust such an important job to soldiers from Forcadel and not her own?

She barely acknowledged them as she passed, making a comment to Luisa about how she was eager to find her tent and rest for a while. I moved a bit slower until I was face to face with Mark.

"Keep an eye on her," he said to his soldiers. "She's not to be trusted here."

The two soldiers didn't give me a passing glance, which hurt a little. I'd been their sovereign once. Surely they'd have some kind of fondness for me?

"So where are you from?" I asked.

"Nowhere."

"Been there myself," I said. "It's nice."

"Quit talking and get to walking."

"I'll be sure to tell Captain Llobrega you've lost your manners," I said, testing my limits a little.

"He's a traitor. I couldn't care less what he thinks."

My hopes fell. So there were a few soldiers who'd bought the lie Ilara had sold. By the look of them, they were older than Felix or perhaps even his age. They must not have trained with him, or held him in as high esteem as the younger cadets had.

My escorts deposited me inside a tent and informed me I wasn't to leave. I opened the flap and found nothing but a bedroll —not unlike what my soldiers had slept on at the camp. I straightened, not ready to be trapped inside yet another room, and stood in front of my tent, watching the camp.

"What, no golden tent this time?" I asked Mark as he walked by. "No Kulkan wine?"

He ignored me.

<hr>

Early the next morning, I was roused and ordered to follow

two soldiers. Mist permeated the surrounding trees and gave me a chill. A reminder that Niemen was only a few hours' river ride to the north.

We had docked on the northeastern side of the river—still in Forcadel, but only barely. The swift current of the river could be heard even from my tent, a powerful rushing sound that seemed almost untamable. Whether Ilara could pull off this crazy feat was beyond me.

I was stationed behind a large wooden dais bearing the Severian crest and told to remain there until Her Majesty arrived. I'd been so used to my soldiers being fresh-faced that I forgot there'd been an entire contingent left in Forcadel that was older. Some of these soldiers had gray hair, while others seemed to have their time settled around their waists. They'd all served my father, and Captain Mark, presumably, which perhaps explained why they detested me so much.

"Good morning, Brynna," Luisa said, coming to stand next to me. Her cheeks were a little pink and her breath clouded around her face. "It's quite chilly up here, isn't it?"

I glanced to the north, where the tips of the Niemenian mountains could just be seen. "Indeed."

"Her Majesty says that once we close the gate, we should know within a day or so if we're able to continue to Aunela," Luisa said. "I hope it's sooner. I don't know if I can survive at these temperatures."

"Do you…" I hesitated to ask at all. "Do you think this is going to work?"

"I have faith in Her Majesty." She nudged me. "As should you."

I quieted, lest they think I had something up my sleeve, and together we shivered and waited for Ilara to make her grand entrance. Even Luisa began to lose her cheery veneer as the minutes ticked on and her fingers grew pale with cold, but she kept her thoughts to herself.

Finally, the trumpets blared, and Mark announced Ilara's arrival. The Forcadelian soldiers saluted with precision, breaking my heart a little. Ilara, wearing what was probably a warm fur coat and the large crown that had once belonged to my father, strolled along the line of soldiers, keeping her chin high and not acknowledging a single one. A far cry from her queen-of-the-people act back in Forcadel. Beside her was a pair of Severian women I'd never seen before, both of whom carried leather notebooks and looks of concern. The architects of this crazy scheme, perhaps?

Mark assisted her as she climbed the steps onto the dais, and Luisa and I followed, making sure to give her a wide berth. She rested her hands on her hips, gazing out onto the monstrosity she'd built with a pleased expression. The two architects fidgeted nervously, toying with the edges of their notebooks.

"Close the gate," she said to Mark, who turned and whistled into the forest.

For a while—minutes, half an hour, an hour—nothing happened. I kept glancing at Ilara's face to see if she was getting annoyed, but she remained calm. Finally, the faint sounds of metal on metal shuddered through the forest, and a burst of steam echoed from somewhere far away. The chains connecting the gate house to the gate rose from their stations and grew taut. I kept my focus on the gate, hoping a chain would break or it just wouldn't move. But the water rushing beside it began to splash up higher as if it were being pushed in an unnatural direction. The chains strained against the weight of the door, and I prayed it would snag on something and get caught. But whatever was pulling the door was stronger. The space between the door and the other side grew thinner and thinner until finally…

I swallowed as metal cracked against metal. The river water, with nowhere else to go, sloshed up onto the riverbanks before falling into the gulley where the door had been. Headed toward the east—to Severia.

"How long will it take?" Ilara asked the women behind her.

"A few days, perhaps," the one on the right said.

"But you should send a scout to confirm before you move your ship," the other replied quickly.

"We will do just that." Ilara looked at Mark, who nodded.

"Yes, Your Majesty."

"I want a full report on the river by this evening," Ilara said to the scientists. "Not one drop of water should be headed south. Am I clear?"

They nodded and scurried toward Niemen, perhaps to cross the river and check the current.

"I want you to assist my engineers with whatever they need," Ilara said to Mark. "If your soldiers need to chop trees and place them at the bottom of the river, do that. This gate is my legacy, and it will remain a symbol of my reign for centuries to come."

"Of course, Your Majesty," Mark said. "It will be my honor to keep watch over this fortress for you."

"I have high hopes that you will perform admirably," Ilara said. "Dismissed."

He bowed low as Ilara walked off the dais to join Luisa and myself. The queen gave her friend a cheeky smile. "I'm getting quite good at closing gates, aren't I? Let's just hope this one lasts longer than Neveri's."

"I believe it will," Luisa said, casting me a knowing look. "We've made all the right preparations. And I don't believe Brynna's in the business of destroying gates anymore, is she?"

"If she does," Ilara said, "there will be a bigger toll than Neveri. And considering how Brynna's been sulking since we killed that poor young man, I doubt she's got the stomach for more death."

I smiled weakly, but Ilara's calculations were correct. There were perhaps two hundred Forcadelians here. Even if we somehow found a way to destroy the gate—with ond or something else—she knew I'd never risk killing so many of my own countrymen. Even if they detested me.

"Oh, let's get off this somber subject," Luisa said. "Shall we open a bottle of wine to celebrate our new river?"

Chapter Twenty-Seven

Felix

As predicted, the storm that had sent us to port passed within a few hours, and that same evening, six ships departed from the Forcadelian port city—five Kulkan warships and Kieran's faster schooner. I was taking something of a leap of faith handing the command of my ship over to Kalila, but I had four other ships, as well as a contingent of Forcadelian soldiers onboard, to keep her in line if she tried anything funny.

Kieran promised his ship would make the trip in half the time of the heavier ones, which meant I'd have a few days to get into Forcadel and find Jax before turning back to meet the ships. I just hoped he had good news for me—and he could help us find a way to bring these soldiers and ships into the city.

By sunup on the first day, I'd lost sight of the warships behind us. The pirate and his crew were experts, tilting the sails to catch the fastest wind. I stayed toward the front of the ship, keeping my gaze focused on the horizon.

After six days on the ocean, when the sky turned purple, I

spotted the two towers guarding the mouth of the bay in the distance, and my heart beat faster at the prospect of finally returning home.

I met Kieran at the back of the ship, where he was expertly navigating the rough waters of the open ocean. He wore a look of uncertainty, but flashed me a confident grin when I approached.

"We'll see if my old tricks still work," he said, handing the wheel off to one of his shipmates. A sailor had climbed the mast and was sitting on the crossbar, holding a contraption aloft. It looked like a box of some kind to signal to land.

"They're always so finicky about this," he muttered, pulling a telescope from his pocket and pointing it at the towers. "They want it to be just so, or they'll start shooting."

"What's going on?"

"We have a flag that signals we've been given passage," he said. "Or rather, to tell the gents at the top of the tower that we have a lot of gold to give them if they let us pass." He lowered the telescope and made a face. "At least, that's the way things used to run. We may have to do a quick turnaround."

I followed his gaze to the two towers, which could sink a ship before it even reached the pass. It was one of Forcadel's most important defenses, and it pained me to hear it had been so easily usurped.

"Well?" I asked, when Kieran hadn't said anything for a while.

He put the telescope to his eye again, flitting back and forth between the two towers. His hand twitched at his side, perhaps ready to give the order to turn the ship around. Behind me, the other pirates were at the ready, waiting for...

"There it is," he said, swallowing and exhaling slightly.

I squinted at the tops of the towers—light flashed in three short bursts.

"That was a bit nerve-wracking," Kieran said with a laugh. "I haven't done the pass since..."

"Since?"

"Since I lost my second," he said. "She was usually better at watching the towers, and knew the timing."

"What happened to her?" I asked.

His gaze dropped to the ocean. "Beswick took her as payment. She was a fine sailor."

"I'm sorry."

"Don't be telling your princess that, please," Kieran said, forcing a smile onto his face. "I know how funny she gets about killing people. Don't want her to think that was anyone's fault but my own."

When we drew closer to the docks creeping out into the bay, Kieran gave me the signal to hide below deck inside a small room designed for smuggling. I kept my ears open for the sound of footsteps and voices. After half an hour, Kieran's voice echoed through the space.

"Don't worry about hiding, General," he said, opening the door. "Ain't nobody here to inspect us."

"W...what?" I climbed out from beneath the deck, guarding myself for a trap or guards or something. But all that greeted me was a beautiful Forcadelian sunset, and an open dock.

"Where...is everyone?" I asked, shaking my head. "There should've been at least ten guards here."

"Your guess is as good as mine," Kieran said. "But even still, I'd be back before the sun comes up. There's no telling what Ilara's up to now, and I don't like a city that isn't guarded."

I didn't either, but I couldn't deny it would be nice to be able to walk down the streets of Forcadel without having to worry about being discovered. I hopped off the ship, gaining my bearings and keeping the concern fresh in my mind. Why would Ilara suddenly go from lockdown to open doors?

It took nearly an hour of wandering around before I finally came across my first pair of Severian guards. They didn't seem to be in much of a hurry, nor did they look to really be monitoring anything.

Before I could take another step, cold steel pressed into my back and I immediately held my hands up.

"What are you...*Captain Llobrega?*"

I squinted into the darkness then broke into a smile. Two of my young soldiers stood behind me, both wearing the telltale masks that Beata had made them weeks ago.

"Fancy meeting you here," I said, lowering my hands. "Where's your boss?"

They shared a look of concern. "Come with us."

We hurried through the city, despite the scarcity of guards. The entire city seemed empty, and I feared for my hometown, for my people, and for what I might find when I reached Jax.

My two former cadets-turned-vigilantes took me to the bell tower—still the central place for vigilante activity. We paused at the bottom of the stairs and whistled a code. After a few moments, a whistle came back down and they beckoned me to follow them.

Jax was waiting at the top of the stairs with a scowl on his face. "It's about time one of you showed up. Tell me you have good news, because I don't."

"I will have five Kulkan warships and their crews docked about a day's ride south of here in a few days," I said. "Plus my soldiers. Why? What's going on?"

"A whole lot of terrible." He sat down on a nearby trunk, almost wearily. "In the first place, Ilara and everyone else in the city has gone."

My heart sank. "Gone? Gone where?"

"Aunela," he said. "Another thing your precious princess failed to see before it happened." I could've argued that none of us had seen it coming, but I let him grouse. "This is what Ilara's been trying to do since before she set foot in Forcadel. She wants to create a new capital city in the east, closer to Severia. And she's blasted her way through the continent to create water pathways there from Niemen and Kulka."

I heard what he was saying, but it sounded so far-fetched I couldn't believe it. "She's...moving Forcadel?"

"Forcadel and everyone in it who'd go. And some of those who wouldn't. Your buddy Coyle's has stayed behind to keep tabs on things, but as you probably saw, there's not many guards left. What remains of the Forcadelian army has been moved to guard an outpost south of Skorsa where the new river begins." He sat back on the trunk. "The Ash river is low, so I'd say she's been successful there.

"Do we have anyone with eyes on her?" I asked.

"Your princess, but she's not sending any letters anytime soon," Jax said, then his gaze grew darker. "I sent one of mine as a spy but...we found his body in the river this morning. Arrow through the heart. I've lost five spies trying to get a message to the Niemenian broad in Skorsa. Nobody's getting through that border."

Which meant the other half of our army wouldn't either. "Kat's smart. She'll figure something out, I'm sure."

"She hasn't yet," he said with a look.

"She will." She had to. "How's Brynna?"

"Trying her very best to bungle all this up," he said. "But fine. Took her a little while to get into Ilara's inner circle, and if you ask me, Ilara's playing her as much as Brynna's playing Ilara. She'd be wise to keep her head and not believe anything that came out of Ilara's mouth."

"You saw her?"

"Ignacio got me into Ilara's going-away party," he said. "I got five seconds with the idiot before we had to break it up. I'd hoped she would fill me in on Ilara's plans, but she didn't have anything.

And now she's probably halfway to Aunela, and I ain't got anyone there to tell me what's going on. It takes two weeks to get there, and two weeks to come back. So whatever they know, it's gonna be a month before I'll know it."

"Then we should move ourselves there," I said. "It doesn't make sense to stay in this city, not when our enemy is in Aunela." I glanced at him. "Do you think you can secure papers for me? Ignacio surely can pull some strings."

He made a noise. "I don't trust him."

"I didn't ask if you could trust him, I asked if he'd get you papers," I said. "I've got a ship, but it would be better if we had a legitimate reason."

"And what about your other ships?" Jax asked. "Aren't they on their way here with half our soldiers?"

I nodded. "Aline and I had plans to meet in a smaller port city west of here, as you said. But they're at least a week out, and I doubt…" I sighed. "We need to get going."

I expected more from Jax, but he nodded. "I'll see about getting Ignacio to play along, but I warn you to take everything he says with a grain of salt."

"Will do," I said. "And Jax—"

"Don't say thank you," he said with a wave of his hand. "I ain't doing this for you, or your queen. So save your pleasantries for someone who gives a shit."

Chapter Twenty-Eight

Katarine

Esteemed Queen Ariadna,

Her Majesty, Queen Ilara Hipolita Särkkä of Severia, has patience, but it is running out. She is looking to receive word of your acceptance of her as true monarch of Forcadel within the next month. This will be our final letter on this matter.

Yours,

Luisa Loäät

"This is our final letter on this matter?" I said, shaking my head. "What in the Mother's name is she on about?"

"I don't know, but it was concerning enough for me to leave two days after it arrived and find out for myself what was going on down here," Ariadna said. "I offered my help to Brynna months ago, and so far, I haven't seen any significant progress. My people are suffering, and I'm getting pressure to acquiesce to Ilara's demands. Especially after that."

Ariadna glanced behind me at the open door, and Elisha's empty desk. I'd sent her off to the barracks to check for any messages so I could speak with my siblings in peace. She'd taken to hovering around the open door and eavesdropping.

"What is your plan, dear sister?" she asked.

"Felix will be bringing the Kulkan forces via the ocean from here," I pointed to Neveri on the map then moved to Skorsa and the Ash river. "And we'll be joining him, just as soon as we can get past the blockade." I tapped the black mark where I'd noted the heavy Severian presence. "I just wish I knew why Ilara was so hell-bent on this particular spot."

"Well, I say we just lob a flaming bag of ond and see what happens," Luard said. "We certainly brought enough to take out Ilara's forces."

That, I couldn't disagree with. Two days after Ariadna's ships arrived, another contingent of very small boats, manned by three soldiers each, arrived carrying mounds of ond. Their journey had been much slower, as they had to pull ashore at night. The Niemenian ore was so explosive that they risked certain death if they so much as had a spark of electricity from their clothes.

"I want to use ond as a last resort," I said.

"But you may be at that point," Ariadna said. "You've been in Skorsa for weeks now and there's been no progress. Surely, by now, Felix has made his move out of Neveri. He can't take Forcadel on his own."

"Brynna asked me to make decisions on her behalf," I said. "That doesn't mean we turn around and start blowing things up just because she's not here."

"Whatever we do needs to ensure victory," Luard said. "I understand you want to keep things civil, but I don't know if that's going to be possible. Not if they're shooting arrows at us before we can even get a word out."

Our conversation was cut short by Elisha's telltale stomping arriving in my office. She didn't bother to knock as she burst through the door, her cheeks ruddy from the cold. Her chest heaved from the effort of running across town, but her eyes were bright with mischief and perhaps something else.

"You got a letter," she said with a smile.

"Bring it here," I said, waving her in. I took a moment to examine it, finding the seal intact and the handwriting familiar. The letter inside was short and although it lacked the answer to my question, I had no doubts it was from Felix:

DEAREST WOLF,

OUR PLAN HAS BEEN SET IN MOTION. OUR WESTERN FRIEND HASN'T BEEN PLAYING NICE, SO WE WILL TAKE WHAT WAS PROMISED BY FORCE. WE SHOULD BE HOME WITHIN THE NEXT WEEK. I WILL MAKE CONTACT WITH OUR LOCAL FRIENDS AND ENSURE A WARM WELCOME FOR YOU.

ALL MY LOVE,
PHOENIX

"This was sent a week ago," I said with a frown. "He's already in Forcadel by now."

"Then we need to get ourselves there, too," Luard said. "Brynna surely doesn't have much time to waste. Felix doesn't, either. He's counting on us to bring half the forces necessary to conquer Forcadel. And we haven't even begun to think about how we'll get past Forcadel's defenses."

The pressure in my chest was growing stronger, especially as I had no other ideas. "We should attempt something else before we move to drastic measures. There must be a way we can get through without having to destroy everyone."

"Then what about my idea?" Elisha asked.

"Which is...?" Ariadna asked, a light smile teasing the corners of her mouth.

"We have this stuff called hyblatha and it makes people hallucinate," she said. "So I say we get a bunch of it and some arrows and start firing into the forest until they all drop."

Ariadna looked at me expectantly. "You haven't tried this yet?"

"In the first place, we don't have any clue how to get this powder," I said.

"I do!" Elisha said, taking a step forward. "You get it from Nestoris."

I sighed, already knowing the answer to my question. "Do you know of any in this city, Elisha?"

"No, but—"

"Then you're on a mission to find a Nestori in this city and rustle up some hyblatha," I said. "But do *not* leave the city limits. Am I clear?"

She grinned and ran from the room. Once the door slammed behind her, I shook my head in annoyance. "Hopefully, that will keep her busy for a while."

"And you think she'll stay in the city limits?" Luard asked.

"She'd better."

"Her idea isn't half-bad," Luard said. "I've seen that powder in action. It's potent. And there's some minty antidote called tinneum, too, so we wouldn't succumb."

"We have no Nestoris here," I said. "Unless there's some lurking to the north in Niemen, it's not a road we need to go down."

Luard made a noise and looked to Ariadna, who shrugged. I rose and walked to the window, staring out across the bay, deep in thought. "How long ago did you receive that letter from Ilara?"

"Three days before I departed."

"She's left the door open for a truce," I began slowly. "I wonder if her soldiers would have a different reaction if a contingent of Niemenian royal soldiers arrived with a letter from their queen?"

"And what would this letter say?" Ariadna said.

"Perhaps that you're ready to discuss a truce, in exchange for letting a few ships past the border," I said. "Or perhaps something else. The point wouldn't be the letter, it would be that we could get Ivan and Luard's guards close enough to see what we're dealing with. And at that point, we can look at different options."

"Didn't work," Ivan said, emerging from the forest.

"Not even a little," Asdis said, being carried by Hagan and Nils. Her shoulder was red and bloody from an arrow wound. When I rushed over to her, she waved me off. "I'm fine, just need to bandage it up."

"What happened?" Luard asked.

"We got within thirty feet of the border and the arrows started," Nils said. "Couldn't even get a word in. They aren't interested in talking. Just shooting."

"Did you tell them you were there on my behalf?" Ariadna said, bending down to help Asdis.

"Several times," Ivan said. "Screamed it, actually. They just started firing."

"I think it's time we consider drastic measures," Luard said. "I don't like it any more than you do, but it appears we have no choice. Brynna needs our help."

As much as I didn't want to agree, I had to. "I suppose, if we have no other options."

"You have my full support," Ariadna said, rising. "But it will have to be from afar. I must return to Linden in the morning and deal with my own warring factions." She nodded to our brother. "Luard, you have the command of all the soldiers in town to do with as you need."

"Thank you for all your help," I said with a smile. "I hope to bring good news the next time I see you."

She smiled and took my hands. "As do I, dear sister. As do I."

Another long day stretched into the night. After sending Ariadna off, Luard and I spent the afternoon coming up with our plan. My one ace would be Elisha finding a Nestori, but I wasn't confident—especially as she hadn't reappeared at all during the day.

My wife was waiting for me in the study with a small, cold dinner, and she listened intently as I told her the events of the day. When I came to the end, and our new plan to use ond, her tight smile turned into a frown.

"What if there are Forcadelian people manning the gate? What if those people..." She shook her head. "Brynna won't like it."

"We don't have much of a choice, my love," I said. "Ariadna's getting antsy. The soldiers are, too. What good are these forces if we're stuck up here?" I rubbed her shoulders, tight from work and worry. "Sometimes, we've got to make hard decisions."

"Are you making it, or is Luard making it?"

"My queen is telling me to make it."

"Your queen is Brynna," she pointed out. "Or have your loyalties changed?"

"Forgive me," I said with a half-smile. "Slip of the tongue and exhaustion. Being with Luard and Ariadna has been a reminder of what life used to be. I'm Brynna's loyal subject, which is the source of my heartache."

She settled in beside me. "Surely, there has to be another way."

"Elisha had another idea to use Nestori magic, but I have no idea where we'd begin with that. I gave her a small task to search the city for a Nestori." I half-smiled. "Perhaps she got lucky and found one."

"You can ask her in the morning. All the children have gone to bed." She smiled, a little devilishly. "As should we."

With her guiding me, as well as the promise of a night alone with her, I left some of my worries in the office. We quietly ascended the stairs, careful not to make too much noise and wake the children. She paused on the top of the landing and pointed to the bedrooms. I waited as she cracked open each door and peered inside. As she did, my heart warmed at how much she'd grown to care for these littles, and—

"Elisha isn't in her room," Beata's voice was loud and panicked.

"What?" I said, rushing over. Beata walked around the room with the candle, poking at the empty bed and opening the closets.

She turned back to me, her eyes wide with fear. "You told her to find a Nestori."

"I also told her to stay in the city," I said, my panic rising. "Very clearly."

One of the other doors opened and Paca appeared, rubbing her eyes sleepily. Beata softened immediately. "I'm sorry I woke you up, sweetheart. Go back to bed."

She nodded and closed her door, but I honestly wished she would've stayed to protect me from Beata's ire.

"I don't understand why you're looking at me like that," I said. "I didn't tell her to leave the city."

"And you've been driving her away since she arrived here," Beata said. "Telling her what she can't do instead of what she can."

My eyes widened. "But you've been right there with me, in case you forgot. We agreed to protect the children from all this."

"How is Elisha finding a Nestori protecting her?" Beata asked. "You'd better get every available soldier looking for her. And don't

even think about coming to my bed until Elisha is back in hers."
She marched into our bedroom and slammed the door.

Chapter Twenty-Nine

"We're leaving? Already?"

It had been less than two days since the river water was re-routed, and I hadn't seen hide nor hair of the two engineers Ilara had sent ahead. The river current was swift and the idea of taking a fleet of riverboats down an unknown and untested path was a little concerning.

Luisa, on the other hand, couldn't see the problem. "Her Majesty is impatient to see her city. The river has been flowing for hours now."

"Yes, but to where?"

"Have faith, Brynna," Luisa said with a smile. "The Mother will look out for us."

Already the soldiers were repacking all of Ilara's things they'd unpacked when we'd arrived. The tent where I'd been sleeping had been disassembled before I'd had a chance to return to it, as had Luisa's.

I headed toward the riverboat, casting a watchful eye on the blue water sloshing on either side of the boat. Three anchors kept the vessel from flying away with the current, but the ropes that connected them were taut.

"This will be fun," Luisa said, coming to stand next to me. "The maiden voyage on the new Ilarian river."

"Ilarian river?" I asked. "She's renamed it?"

"From the border to Aunela, yes," she said. "I think it's fitting, don't you? She was the one who built it."

Behind me, Ilara had finished her goodbyes and gave the order to remove the plank and pull the anchors. My grip tightened on the railing in front of me as the ship twisted and turned in the rushing current. The first anchor was pulled, inching us forward. Then the second. With the third's snap, we were off at a breakneck speed.

The wind whipped hard against my face, causing my eyes to water. I struggled to hang on as the ship bobbed violently. Beneath my feet, the riverboat paddles groaned as they moved backward to slow our pace. Sailors barked orders at each other as they trimmed the sails and did what they could to assist.

I glanced at Ilara, who was standing on the quarterdeck with her captain. While the man beside her was yelling and pointing, Ilara was a mask of calm, even as she lightly held onto the railing next to her.

"Look out!"

Everything went sideways as the ship swerved, including Luisa and me. I caught myself as a large rocky outcropping nearly took my head off. It snapped a few of the riggings on the sails, and the sailors jumped into action.

"And we are sure this is a good idea?" I asked Luisa.

"There is no other option," she said. "Eventually, the river will calm."

But it never did. The ship twisted here and there, with the

paddles straining to keep it under control, and the sailors trying valiantly to keep the ship from tipping. After a while, the captain seemed to have a handle on the ship, and there were fewer sudden movements. I pried my hands off the bannister and chanced a stretch. But another sharp turn had me reaching for the railing again and I didn't remove my hands for the rest of the afternoon.

As the sun began to drift behind us, the shadows of the banks did as well, making it harder to see. The sailors showed no sign of slowing down, nor had Ilara given the word to drop anchor anywhere. When the golden sky turned pink, I left the safety of my spot on the bow and slowly made my way toward the quarterdeck.

"Ah, Brynna, so good of you to join us," Ilara said.

"We can't seriously be thinking of continuing on the river after sundown?" I said, holding onto the side of the ship as it turned. "It's entirely too dangerous."

"I think it'll be fine," Ilara said. "I have faith in our captain."

"Can he see in the dark?"

She only smiled, and I turned to the captain, hoping he might see reason. But he ignored me in favor of squinting into the darkness ahead.

"Il..." I swallowed. "Your Majesty, I must insist. We have no idea what lies ahead. If we run aground—"

"Then we won't."

I pursed my lips, exasperated, then headed back toward the front of the ship. The light was fading fast, and the ship brushed harder against the soft sand beneath the murky depths. After a few minutes, Luisa joined me, resting her hands gently on the railing.

"It is getting quite dark," Luisa said, with something of a nervous edge to her voice.

"Can you talk some sense into her?" I asked.

"I've tried but..." She glanced behind her. "She has her mind set and that's that. We will continue through the night and day until we reach Aunela," Luisa said. "Otherwise it'll take twice as long."

"We can't see in the dark," I said. "And the captain's—"

Whatever I was going to say got lost when I nearly toppled over the bannister. I grabbed Luisa before she went headfirst, too. A cry for help echoed out from the river below, as a sailor flailed in the water. But within minutes, she'd been swept around the bend—or underwater.

Behind me, groans of pain echoed as the sailors gingerly got up. One sailor lay on the ground in front of the quarterdeck, his neck twisted at an odd angle. Two of his fellow soldiers confirmed he was dead.

"What happened?" Luisa asked, her face pale.

"We ran aground," I replied. Behind us, Ilara was looking more irate than wounded as she berated the captain for not seeing the riverbank.

"What is the point of having a captain if you can't even navigate the boat correctly?" she snapped. "You are a disgrace, and you—

"Your Majesty," Luisa said, rushing up the stairs before Ilara really got going. She spoke softly to Ilara, and the monarch's eyes lost some of their fire. She nodded and shook out her shoulders, pressing her hand to Luisa's arm.

"Tend to the wounded," Ilara said, somberly. "And the dead. Then we will tend to the boat."

Other than bumps and bruises and a few broken arms, the wounds weren't that bad. I did what I could to set the bones, using my knowledge from Nicolasa. The irony of using her training to help those who'd killed her didn't escape my notice, but in my heart, I knew she'd want me to use her earth magic to help people.

"What will we do with him?" I asked Luisa, nodding to the sailor who'd fallen from the crow's nest. "And will we honor the other sailor who washed away?"

"A funeral," she said. "Honoring the best of Severia."

The sailors lowered the plank to the riverbed then carried the body off. We were still on Forcadelian soil, so the ground was grassy and dewy. They laid the sailor's body on a pile of moss and sticks and used a torch to set it on fire. In a matter of moments, the pyre lit the surrounding plain, casting a red glow on everything—even the ship that was still snugly tucked against the riverbank.

"You have light now. Find out why our ship's stuck," Ilara hissed to the captain. "I want to be on the move before this fire is out."

"Ilara."

The fire flickered in Luisa's eyes, giving them an otherworldly glow. I'd never heard her address her queen without an honorific, and based on Ilara's expression, it had been some time since she'd heard it, too.

"Very well," Ilara said, grabbing the edges of her cloak. "At first light, then."

She disappeared onto the ship, the sound of her quarter door slamming echoing across the open plain.

"What got into her?" I muttered under my breath.

"Quiet, Brynna," Luisa said, turning to the pyre. "We will give this man the burial he deserves with the respect he is owed."

I glanced at her out of the corner of my eye, but said nothing.

Luisa and I stood at attention until the pyre had been reduced to ash, and the only thing left of the Severian was a pile of red embers on the ground. The sailors who'd been standing with us returned to the ship, probably to get some rest, but Luisa stayed where she was. For some reason, I felt compelled to stay there with her.

"You saved my life today," Luisa said softly.

"It was nothing," I said. "Just instinct. Someone needed saving, so I did what I could." I nodded toward the pyre. "Sorry I couldn't save him, too."

"But that someone was me," she said. "After all we've been through, I don't think I would've blamed you if you'd let me fall into the river." She looked up at the sky. "But I'm still here."

"Don't let Ilara hear you speaking so nicely to me. She'll have your head," I said with a small smile.

"I'm given some semblance of leeway as the queen's confidante," she said, a smile threatening to form on the corners of her mouth. "And I don't doubt that she's as thankful as I am for your quick actions."

Could've fooled me. I wasn't even sure if Ilara knew Luisa had nearly fallen. "What's gotten into her anyway?"

"She's ready to reach Aunela," Luisa said. "And is impatient with all the delays. But clearly…clearly some patience is required here."

"We can't navigate an unknown river in the dark," I said. "It's hard enough in the daylight. Whatever Ilara's desires to reach Aunela, they can wait a few more days. We got lucky tonight that we only lost two sailors. We could've lost the entire ship."

Luisa sighed and looked at her hands. "Sometimes, I don't know what she's thinking. And I don't like it when she doesn't listen to me."

"Does she ever?" I crossed my arms over my chest.

"On occasion," she said. "And she will listen to me from here on out. As long as the guidance comes from me, and not you." She smirked. "I don't think she appreciated you speaking to her so plainly in front of the crew."

"It's not as if I'm trying to delay anything here. I'd just like to get to Aunela in one piece, if at all possible." I shook my head. "I was merely pointing out the obvious."

"A word to the wise, dear Brynna: Ilara's malleable, but under the right circumstances. If you want her to do something, you should use your resources." She tilted her head in my direction.

"Have a good evening."

Chapter Thirty

In the morning, it took the soldiers nearly two hours to dig the ship out of the sandy bank. When it was freed, everyone braced themselves for the release of the anchor, then we were off again in the swift current. Much like the day before, the captain did his best to manage, and although his skill had improved, there were more than a few jarring bumps. But luckily, we avoided running aground again. And blessedly, Ilara ordered the anchors dropped at sundown.

As the days passed, the only change seemed to be the terrain around us. Lush farmlands and rolling hills became patches of grass and scraggly trees. The clouds that had once hung overhead were nearly gone now, leaving us to sit in the sun all day long. The Niemenian mountains had been replaced by hills of sand in the distance. My whole body felt like a raisin, desperate for the water I received at dinner each night.

After six days of travel, Ilara's mood improved and she called for the anchor to be dropped mid-afternoon instead of at sundown. There were no signs of a town or village nearby, but she ordered the plank extended to the sandy banks of the river and climbed off.

"What are we doing?" I asked Luisa.

She pointed at a speck in the distance. "Our scouts spotted a small caravan of Severians. Her Majesty would like to stop and see them. They come here every spring to harvest a particular type of sand—varo."

"I'm familiar with it," I said, having been bored by no less than three books on the subject. "I thought Her Majesty wanted to keep moving."

"There are some things that are more important," Luisa said, offering her arm. "Why don't you come and see what Severians are truly like?"

I thought I had the measure of them already but took her arm regardless. Ilara had already left us behind, accompanied by two soldiers. She marched easily over the dunes, showing no signs of slowing down or discomfort. Another queen might've asked her soldiers to carry an umbrella, but Ilara was determined to prove she was one of the people.

"How exactly does one harvest sand?" I asked Luisa. "It doesn't grow."

"No, but this place is too harsh a climate any other time of the year," Luisa said. "It's still dangerous out here, but they come anyway. They make twice as much money as with glass, and in some cases, it's what sustains them for the entire year."

Luisa was better at balancing on the sand than I was, and after a few feet, I began to pant as the sun bore down on the back of my neck. My walking partner slowed and waited patiently for me to catch my breath, perhaps even enjoying how easily her homeland had bested me. When we finally reached the camp, my legs burned with the exertion.

A small girl came running up to us, carrying a vase. She

grinned, snaggle-toothed, and offered it to us.

"We couldn't," Luisa said, before I could say anything. "Please, save it for your family."

"I mean, there is a giant freshwater river right there now," I said with a bit of a grumble as the sun dried my mouth. But I couldn't argue that these farmers were in dire straits. The only shelter as far as the eye could see was a few small tents held up by a single pole and the ends anchored with worn rocks. There were shovels stuck into the ground all around, and more sticks farther away, perhaps identifying the location of future digging sites.

The girl led us to where Ilara was seated in the shade, holding the hand of the oldest woman in the group. The queen had lost her sneer and her superiority and seemed genuinely pleased to be amongst the lowest of her people.

"We have plenty," Ilara said, her gaze soft and inviting. "And it would be my honor to dine with you. Luisa," she turned to her assistant, "have them offload my dinner. I wish to eat it here with my people and share what we have."

It took perhaps half an hour, and before long everyone in camp, perhaps twenty people, were sharing in the bounty Ilara had brought. Those who'd been out in the desert working had been shocked to find their queen amongst them, and had fallen to their knees in reverence.

"If it weren't for your varo, I wouldn't have this river flowing to the east," she said. "Our mighty Severian sand sliced through the Forcadelian rock and created a new beginning for our people."

"Just like you, my queen!"

"Well, I don't want to draw that comparison..." She covered her mouth with her hand.

After a long dinner, Ilara bade the small group farewell, but they didn't take the hint, and the entire population walked her back to the waiting ship like a protective cocoon. Luisa and I were forced to hang toward the rear, barely able to see Ilara in the moonlight.

There was something unnerving about the almost worshipful way these people gazed upon their queen. I'd had people grateful to me for saving them, but this bordered on idolatry. Ilara hadn't just cut a river through the desert and brought precious water to her people; to them, she'd been anointed by the Mother herself.

And yet, even as Ilara demurred and acted as if she wanted none of this, there were brief flashes of superiority in her smile. She not only enjoyed this, she almost expected it.

"What is it?" Luisa asked.

"I wonder if any of us know the real Ilara," I said. "She came to me on bended knee at first. Then she proudly paraded herself around as the victor. Here, she's meek and gracious and kind. It's a dizzying change from day to day."

"Her Majesty does adjust herself based on the circumstances, but so do we all," Luisa said with a soft smile. "You aren't always wielding a sword and running around in a mask, are you?"

These days, it sure felt like it. "My heart is always the same."

"As is Ilara's," Luisa said. "Everything she does is in the pursuit of making the world better for her people. When she's parading herself, as you say, she's embodying the hopes and dreams of all the Severians who look upon her. Our people have been downtrodden for so long…"

I couldn't quite trust what Luisa was saying. There was a tinge of selfishness in everything Ilara did—perhaps she *had* taken Forcadel to better her people, but there was another way, one that would've resulted in far fewer casualties and peace between our kingdoms. Even before she stabbed me, I'd been trying to find ways to improve her country's station. Even if my council had been trying to thwart me every step of the way.

Luisa gazed out into the desert. "And if she's acting meek, it's for the benefit of the people here. They've lost several people recently."

"How do you know?"

She gestured to one of the sticks pointing up from the sand. "A grave marker."

I stopped; they hadn't just lost one or two—there were hundreds littered as far as the eye could see in the moonlight. "Mother above."

"It's dangerous work out here," Luisa said. "The varo is sometimes several feet below and there's always the risk of a cave-in."

"Then why do they do it?"

"They have no choice," Luisa said. "Well, they had no choice. But now, Ilara's given them a lifeline. Some may continue the work out of respect for tradition and custom. But many of the younger folks will find work in Aunela and become more than poor miner children. And it's all thanks to Ilara."

The little girl who'd greeted us earlier was talking with Ilara, who patted her on the head before walking onto the ship and the crowd tearfully cried out to their queen. She waved to them, holding her hand to her heart as she bade them all farewell.

"This river will change lives," Luisa said. "Ships will have to pass through here to get to Aunela from Niemen and they may have to stop as we did. An entire city may spring up underneath our feet, just as they did in Forcadel."

"In order to trade with Niemen, we'd have to have a treaty with them."

"They're under pressure," Luisa said. "Any day now, I expect we will see a messenger from Kulka and Niemen, informing us that our treaty has been accepted, and that we will resume normal trading." She tilted her head in my direction. "After all, are they going to put aside hundreds of years of bad blood to trade with each other? I doubt it. Their people have been without their main trading partner for months now. They will break soon."

Worry nudged the edge of my mind. It had been months since

I'd been to see Ariadna, and King Neshua in Kulka was already on the fence about helping me anyway. Who was to say they weren't sending me troops while also acquiescing to Ilara's demands?

But what could I do when Ilara kept pulling the rug from under my feet?

"It is the start of a new era," Ilara called from onboard the ship. "And I'm grateful you are all here to witness our rebirth."

Chapter Thirty-One

The young girl's snaggle-toothed grin was imprinted in my mind, as were the sticks dotting the landscape. Reading all the Severian books in the world couldn't have prepared me for that level of desperation. And yet, there were still smiles in the camp. Humanity could endure so much and remain hopeful, it seemed. If those people could cling to some semblance of optimism, so could I.

Two days after we left the camp, the lookout above called out that he'd sighted Aunela in the distance. Ilara came to observe, resting her delicate hands on the railing as the crew worked feverishly around her.

"Excited?" Luisa asked, coming to stand next to me.

"A little," I said, shielding my eyes from the sun with my hand. "I'm curious to see what Ilara's done."

After we passed another sharp turn, a glittering bay revealed itself at the end of the river. It was green, unlike Forcadel's blue waters. But my gaze landed on the city lining the bay, rising from the sand like an oasis and crawling backward across dunes.

It was huge—bigger than Linden, bigger than Delina in Kulka, and most assuredly bigger than Forcadel. Buildings were constructed from the sandy-colored rock in plentiful supply.

"Magnificent, isn't it?" Luisa said. "Welcome to New Severia."

It was hard not to gape at the city as we drew closer. A year's worth of work, and presumably the entire Forcadelian royal treasury, had done wonders. The eastern cities had always been a lesser focus for Forcadelian trade. Unlike the west, where Kulka's rich farmlands provided much of Forcadel's food supply, Severia had nothing to offer but glass and pottery.

Now, the tables had turned.

"What is this?" I asked.

Luisa beamed. "The Ilarian Bay. Her Majesty's soldiers spent weeks carving it out from the rock."

I had to stymie an eye roll in favor of my morbid curiosity. "They dug out an entire *bay*?"

"From the sand and rock that was here before. Aunela was nothing but a small oasis of buildings when we arrived here. To turn it into a metropolis worthy of being Forcadel's replacement, we needed a large body of water to house ships and other trade vessels."

Except it was missing many of Forcadel's armaments, including the cannon towers that had been her stalwart protector. But perhaps Ilara felt confident no one would attempt a water assault from Kulka or Niemen. After all, she had a large contingent of soldiers just south of Skorsa to keep the Niemenians away, and it was two weeks from Forcadel—even further from Kulka.

It would've been good for my own forces, except for the fact that they, too, were probably still on the other side of the continent.

"The Severians were eager to help build themselves a new city,"

Luisa continued. "Many of them left their glassmaking and pottery kilns at the promise of a new life. They fabricated and laid plumbing pipes under the city then laid brick roads and constructed buildings on top of them." She beamed with pride. "They exceeded Her Majesty's every expectation."

A crowd had gathered on the docks, waving handkerchiefs and large Severian flags. They all wore light-colored smocks with sandals, some of them with flowers in their hair, each of them ecstatic to see their queen.

The ship docked quickly, and the soldiers prepared the plank for Ilara's grand exit. The crowd murmured in anticipation then erupted when she appeared wearing a crown of purple flowers. She waved graciously, beaming from ear to ear as she descended to the docks, walking amongst them as if sent from the Mother herself.

There didn't seem to be a Forcadelian amongst them, which I supposed was a good thing. I couldn't imagine my people being pleased with the woman who'd uprooted and sent them to this desert.

Ilara climbed onto a waiting, open-air carriage drawn by a horse and took off immediately, leaving Luisa and me behind. Luisa wore an amused smile as she watched Ilara go.

"I suppose it's just as well that we walk," she said. "My legs need a stretch. Don't yours, Brynna?"

And get a chance to see things up close? "Absolutely."

The city seemed to be laid out in a grid, with a large road filled with carriages and horses coming to and from the docks. Many of the buildings appeared brand new, with Severian seals still on the windows. But mixed in were more modest structures with thatched roofs. Ilara's updates hadn't been all-encompassing, leaving pockets of the previous city still visible.

A gaggle of Severian children came running out of a sweet shop, all wearing the same dark tunic with a gold patch sewn on— and each carrying a pastry. They gave us a once-over before dashing toward a large structure in the distance.

"School?" I asked.

"Yes, all children have compulsory education," Luisa said. "We've seen great strides in the numbers who can read and write. It was mostly unheard of in Severia before. Her Majesty wants an educated population."

No wonder her people were eager to accept her as their savior. She'd not spared any expense to build a paradise for every citizen. But still, something tickled at the back of my mind.

"Where are the Forcadelians?" I asked. I'd thought I'd at least see a mix of nationalities, but so far I was the only non-Severian here.

"They're around," Luisa said. "Come, let's have a pastry."

She led me into the sweet shop the children had exited, and the scent of yeast and baked goods filled my nose. The shop owner had a nice, pleasant face and was even more pleased when Luisa made her choice.

"We don't get many folks who like the old country food," he said, removing one of the glass covers to retrieve a small, flat pastry that seemed sad compared to the rest.

"I'll always take the old country food," Luisa said, paying him with a silver coin. "Keep the change."

He thanked her profusely as he deposited the coin with the rest of them, and Luisa wore a pleased smile when she turned to hand me one of the two treats she'd purchased.

"Here," she said.

"What is it?" I asked, examining the small pastry. It had a center filled with something dark and gooey.

"It's called kyushur," she said. "There's a fruit that grows on a plant native to Severia. We have to add honey and let it soak for days, but once it mellows out, it's delicious."

I took a bite and nearly gagged. It tasted vaguely poisonous, and that was the only good thing I could say about it. Bitterness and grass rounded out the flavor, and I could do nothing but swallow it.

"I'd hate to think what the flavor is when you don't mellow it out," I said, giving it a look.

"I suppose it's not that great compared to the delicacies of Forcadel," Luisa said with a bit of a huff. "But it does remind us of home."

I carried the bitter flavor on my tongue for the next half-hour, desperate for a glass of water, but not wanting to offend Luisa more. No wonder the shopkeep said no one was interested in it; I'd pick the buttery Forcadelian rolls over that garbage every time.

As we continued weaving through the city, my stomach turned more—and it wasn't due to that pastry. None of the names on the businesses were Forcadelian; none of the faces were, either. Forcadel was empty, and if Aunela was too, where had everyone gone?

"I think I've had enough walking for today," I said to Luisa. "Should we head for the castle?"

"We're almost there."

Indeed, we turned another corner and came into a town square under construction. To my left was a half-built church, one that seemed an almost exact replica of Forcadel's. And in front of me was the castle, or what would be the castle one day. The central part had been built, and the spires were under construction to about the sixth floor—equal to the floors of the main castle.

"It will be magnificent one day," Luisa said. "But for now, we must make do. Her Majesty was eager to leave Forcadel, even though it's under construction."

"Home is home," I said, looking behind me to where the church would one day stand. "I take it we won't be having services?"

"There's a church in the northeastern part of the city," she said. "But it's been vacant since we took over. All the sisters left for greener pastures, it seems. I'm sure Her Majesty will begin services just as soon as this church is completed."

Inside the castle, the smell of sawdust and mortar filled the halls, and none of the walls boasted any kind of art or painting. But unlike the castle in Forcadel, the halls were filled with people carrying all manner of things, from bricks to curtains. Again, none of them Forcadelian.

We ascended a set of stone stairs to the second floor of the castle. Here, a lush carpet lined the walls, softening the sound of our steps.

"Here's your room," Luisa said, opening an unlocked door in the middle of the hall. It was similarly sparsely decorated, but it had a four-poster bed and curtains, at least.

"It's beautiful," I said, walking past her. It didn't escape my notice that I was no longer locked in a tall tower, nor that there didn't seem to be guards posted at my door.

"I'll be down the hall, as will Her Majesty, at least until her royal suite is completed," she said. "It may take a few years, as all our builders are otherwise occupied on the rivers."

Rerouting them here. "This will do for now."

"Brynna," Luisa said softly, "things will be different here. We are no longer under Forcadelian rule, and we will conduct ourselves as Severians."

I turned to her. "What does that mean?"

"We'll be dining in the Severian tradition—together. Once in the morning and once in the evening. You'll be provided the proper attire." She walked to the curtains and opened them, revealing the afternoon sky. "Baths will happen once a week until we've completed construction of the rivers."

I nodded. "Doesn't look like there's much water to spare around here."

"And I do hope you'll take time to enjoy your new home," Luisa said. "Her Majesty has lifted the restrictions we had in

Forcadel. You're free to go wherever you wish."

Where was I going to go? We were surrounded by desert, and it took two weeks to ferry people from any kind of civilization. But it was a reprieve, at least. I could investigate the city and get the lay of the land for when Felix and Katarine arrived.

If they even arrive at all...

"I'll be back in the morning to retrieve you for breakfast," she said with a nod. "Rest well."

Chapter Thirty-Two

Felix

Jax dispatched several vigilantes into the city to search for Ignacio, but so far, the second had been hard to pin down. I didn't mind the slight delay—every day spent in Forcadel was one more that Aline had to get our forces here. But time was running out, and I didn't like the idea of skipping town before I had a chance to make sure everything was all right.

Since the bell tower was empty at night, I took to patrolling the rooftops in search of someone or something to save. But each quadrant of the city was eerily empty, and those that were still around skittered around alleys looking petrified. The entire city seemed to be waiting for something—or someone—to come for them.

As the moon lit up the city, I settled on a rooftop near the church, staring at the castle and reminiscing. Even the stone walls felt different now, like they were crying out at the changes that Ilara had wrought. One day, Brynna would lay her head on a pillow there and this city would revive. I just hoped we all had the strength to wrest the country back from Ilara *and* rebuild it.

A voice echoed from the streets below, and there was movement at the front gates of the castle. I didn't need to see the figure to know who it was.

"I told Her Majesty I'd have all them rounded up by now," he said. "If you have to break down every door in this city, do it. But I don't want a single soul left in this place."

The soldiers saluted and jogged off, leaving Coyle alone in front of the castle. They headed northwest, to Haymaker's Corner and I jumped to my feet, intent on following them—but a hand on my shoulder stopped me.

"Leave it," Jax said. "Interfering now isn't going to help anyone."

"Except those we help," I said. "Ilara's hundreds of miles away by now. What does it matter if we disrupt something here?" I nodded to Coyle, who was staring at the cobblestones with an unreadable look on his face. "Or kill him?"

"We have other things to worry about," Jax said. "And I have a feeling those soldiers are going to fetch our ride to Aunela."

"And him?" I asked, nodding at Coyle. It would've been so easy to grab a crossbow and shoot it through his heart from here. He never would've seen it coming.

"You really want to kill him like that?" Jax asked, quirking a brow.

Jax had a point; that wasn't the way Coyle deserved to go. An instant death would be too merciful after all he'd done. No, when Coyle's comeuppance came, he would be sentenced to languish in prison, kept just healthy enough to live until a ripe old age, and knowing that he would never be more than an afterthought to those he'd betrayed.

"What are you grinning about?" Jax asked. "Did you not hear a word I just said?"

"I did," I said. "I'm standing down."

"Good," he said. "Because I found Ignacio. He'll be waiting on our ship in about an hour."

Kieran wore an uncharacteristically sour expression when Jax and I arrived back on the ship. He cleared his throat and pointed at the quarterdeck.

"I didn't realize we'd be entertaining trash," he said, glaring daggers at Jax. "Why is he on my ship?"

"Because he's gonna help us," Jax said. "But just as soon as he's done, feel free to toss him in the ocean."

"With pleasure."

I led the entourage onto the quarters where Ignacio was waiting by himself. Beswick's second looked incredibly uncomfortable to be sitting all by himself in enemy territory, but I doubted Jax had let him bring any guards.

Jax scraped the chair against the floor and sat down, pulling his knife and picking at his nails. "Well?"

Ignacio tore his gaze from the sharpened blade and reached into his pocket. "A few months ago, Beswick was asked by Her Majesty—"

"Ilara," I corrected.

"Whatever you want to call her," he said with a slimy grin. "To locate citizens in Forcadel who wish to better their lives in Aunela."

"Why?" I asked.

"I'm sure I don't know," he said with an eye roll. "She made no reference to the purpose in any of our correspondence and I can't just outright ask her when I'm supposed to be working for a dead man."

"These people you relocate," I said. "What kind of people are they? Is Ilara looking for skilled merchants?"

"She hasn't given me any sort of quota. Just anyone who wants to go to Aunela."

"And how much are you getting paid for this?" Kieran asked.

"One gold piece per head, in addition to my expenses and fee."

I sat back, stunned. "And what do these travelers get?"

"A ride to Aunela, and supposedly, a job when they get there," Ignacio replied, sitting back with a surveying look. "It's all so very modern and egalitarian. She surely is a forward-thinking queen."

"Except that I just overheard Coyle sending his guards out to rip people from their homes," I said dryly. "It may have started as a volunteer effort, but now, Ilara wants this city emptied and she'll use force to do it."

"That makes absolutely no sense," Kieran said with a shake of his head. "Why not just leave the Forcadelians here? She's already moving trade to Aunela, so the people here would be left with nothing regardless."

"I don't pretend to understand her mind," Ignacio said. "All I know is what I've been ordered to do."

I rolled my eyes and turned to Jax. "We could stow away on one of those ships to get inside the city."

"I wouldn't," Jax said. "I have a feeling that whatever purpose Ilara has for these people won't include them being able to wander off on their own." He nodded to Kieran. "Better to pretend to be a crew member."

"Agreed," I said. "When's the next shipment supposed to leave?"

"Coyle is gathering my latest group tonight so they'll be ready for departure tomorrow evening. If your ship can handle twenty persons in addition to your crew..."

"It'll be tight, but I can make it work," Kieran said, still wearing his look of disgust. "Do I get a cut of this gold to fund the voyage? Perhaps something extra to put up with doing business with this bastard?"

Ignacio sniffed. "You'll get payment when the soldiers arrive as well as food and water for the voyage. I promise there'll be nothing required of you, pirate, except to get from here to Aunela unscathed."

Kieran looked ready to pounce, but I put my hand out. "We will be ready by tomorrow. Don't you dare screw us, Ignacio."

"Why would I screw you?" he asked innocently. "If your queen wins this fight, I will be in her special favor. If she doesn't, I'm already in Ilara's. Either way," he smiled, "I win."

The next evening, under the cover of a cloudy sky, a long line of wagons rolled up to the docks. Kieran gave me a dark tunic to wear instead of my uniform; I'd be sporting it for the foreseeable future. I was concerned that one of the civilian passengers might recognize me, but I doubted any of them knew what a captain of the guard was. They were from Haymaker's Corner, the slums, and looked wary of the adventure ahead of them. One by one, they climbed onboard, nodding to the sailors, including me. They appeared to be mostly families, with some younger children clinging to their parents' hands with wide eyes.

I kept myself looking busy to avoid recognition by the Severian soldier who'd accompanied Ignacio, but questions burned in the back of my mind. Something felt off about this entire operation, but unfortunately, I had no choice but to participate.

"I loathe that we have to work with him," I said to Kieran as Ignacio disappeared into the darkness. "Have the messengers come back with word from Aline?"

"Not yet," Kieran said. "Why?"

"Concerned about the Kulkans," I said. "We didn't exactly ask for permission when we took them."

"That lieutenant you left in charge seemed capable," Kieran said. "Ah, there's the rest of our crew."

Two of Jax's vigilantes—Malka and Aithne—came walking up with bags slung over their arms and their boss walking behind them. While the two vigilantes continued to the belly of the ship, Jax dropped a bag at our feet.

"What's that?" Kieran asked.

"Supplies," Jax said. "Knockout powder, some crossbows. You look in desperate need of them. And here." He reached into the bag and pulled out a folded dark cloth. "Give this to the brat if you see her."

A cloak, one of the ones Beata had specially made for the vigilante army when we'd taken Beswick. "Thanks, Jax. I know she'll appreciate it."

"I had a spare. Narin never came back from Skorsa." He snorted. "Well, he did. But not alive."

I swallowed, taking the cloak with a soft nod. "I'm sure he died with honor."

"Who gives a shit about honor? I lost my one spy in Ilara's inner circle," Jax said, but his words belied the sadness in his eyes. Despite his rough exterior, he'd grown fond of my former charges.

"Malka and Aithne are in good hands," I said.

"Whatever." He snorted and walked off the ship without another word.

"He's certainly an interesting individual," Kieran said, tilting his head. "Surprised you trust him so much."

"He's loyal to Brynna, despite what he says," I said, picking up the bag and finding it full of smaller pouches and a few extra arrows. "Deep down."

"Are we ready to depart?" Kieran asked.

I glanced to the west, giving Aline and the crew a few more seconds to appear. But we couldn't delay, not when Ilara had a head start on us. And not when she was clearly up to something with my people.

"Yeah," I said with a nod. "To Aunela we go."

Chapter Thirty-Three

Katarine

It had been a week since anyone had seen Elisha. I'd had soldiers scouring the city for her, but as the days passed, my fear grew that she'd left for good—or worse. There was no sign of her down by the border, thankfully, but when the dock master told me that two small ships had gone north for more supplies, I had a sinking suspicion our teenaged vigilante had gone with them.

My wife was beside herself with worry. She was no longer sleeping, instead standing by the window with a candle. Not that I saw much of her, as I was still banished from our bedroom. Although I swore up and down that I'd been explicitly clear about Elisha staying inside the city, Beata seemed intent on blaming me. I tried not to take it personally, but it was hard when all my dresses (made by my wife) needed a second pair of hands to tie.

"Paca?" I called, after several minutes of fruitless attempts.

"Yes, ma'am?" The girl appeared in the doorway, her eyes wide.

"Darling, can you tie the back of my dress?" I asked apologetically.

She nodded and hurried over, taking the strings in her small hands and holding them. "How do I…?"

I instructed her on how to tie the knot, and although it took her a few tries, she managed it.

"Thank you," I said, turning around. Her eyes were sad as she looked at the floor. "What is it?"

"My folks used to fight," she said. "Are you and Lady Beata gonna…"

"Most assuredly not," I said, brushing the hair out of her face. "Sometimes these things happen between people in love, especially under stress." I took her hands. "But you promise me that you have no idea where Elisha went, do you? It's all right if you do. You won't get in trouble for keeping it from us."

She shook her head. "She ain't told any of us anything."

"Hasn't told us anything," I corrected gently, squeezing her hands with a smile. "She'll turn up, I'm sure."

Beata called for Paca, and I walked her down the stairs, hoping my wife might be in a better humor this morning. But she ignored me, placing her hand on Paca's shoulder and guiding her into the schooling room.

"I'd like you to work through the next ten pages of your primer," she said gently. "I checked your work from yesterday and it was very good."

The girl beamed and bounced to join the rest of the children, who were all quietly working.

"Good mor—"

Beata shut the door in my face.

"—ning."

Luard was moving full steam ahead with the attack on the gate, even though we both had reservations about the path forward. He and Ivan were still stuck on how to get the ond itself into the defenses, especially as we still had no idea what they looked like. Their latest scheme was to send the ond with an oil-soaked rope, lit when the barge was sent down river. But so far, they hadn't been able to accurately predict how quickly the rope would burn.

"I say we overshoot it," Luard said, as yet another rope had burned too quickly. "The ond will get to them, and perhaps they'll be too stupid to notice that it's on fire."

"They know what ond is," I reminded him gently, glancing toward the north again and saying a silent prayer. "I should send scouts out again to look for Elisha. Perhaps Ariadna saw her on her way back to Linden."

"Have some faith in our little vigilante," Luard said, wincing as the second rope erupted in flames. "She's more capable than you think."

"I hate that you can be so flippant about this," I said, scowling at him.

He squinted toward the north end of the bay. "Hm. Looks like a ship's coming into port. Maybe that's her now."

"Very funny, Luard."

But as the boat drifted closer, a mop of brown hair appeared on the bow. My heart released a sigh so loud it might've shaken the mountains. But in the time it took for the ship to make its way across the bay, relief turned into fury, and it was all I could do not to march onboard and wring her neck.

"Patience, dear sister," Luard said, coming up beside me. "And see what she brought before you ground her, hm?"

"Lady Katarine," Elisha said, wearing a proud smile. "I've done what you asked. I found you a Nestori."

"I also told you not to leave the city," I said.

She made a face. "Well, there weren't any Nestoris in the city, so I had to. But I found some."

"You…" I shook my head. "You did?"

"Yeah. Hey, Jarrah!" Elisha called to the boat. "Come meet Lady Katarine!"

With a look at Luard, I walked the plank onto the boat, where

I found a gaggle of teenagers sitting on the deck, talking amongst themselves. They looked almost feral, with fur pelts around their shoulders and carrying knives that looked carved from animal bones.

When they saw me, they sent scathing looks toward Elisha.

"That ain't the girl who spared us," one of them snarled.

"I didn't say she was here," Elisha shot back, fearless. "I said she was helping her. So you guys had better can it before I throw you into the river."

"I'm sorry," I said, looking back at Elisha. "I'm lost. Can someone please fill me in on what's going on? Who are these children?"

"I think I might be able to help," Luard said, stepping forward. "You see, when Brynna was taking her journey through the mountains of Niemen, she happened upon this group who tried to kill her. Brynna spared their lives, so clearly they feel there's a debt there."

"I don't understand," I said, turning to him with a suspicious glare. "How did Elisha even know they existed? And how did she find them in the mountains..." I shook my head in realization. "*You went to the Niemenian mountains?*"

"I had a guide," Elisha said. "A lady named Brigit owed Brynna a favor. She took me into the mountains and like two days later, we found these guys. She told me to give Brynna her best and tell her the farm was doing well."

"Curious that you knew all this and thought to do it all on your own," I said, turning to my brother with fire in my eyes.

"Curious indeed," Luard said, meeting my fiery gaze with one of his own. "What a miracle it is that she found Nestoris who were willing to help us so we don't have to blow up the gate."

"You could've told me instead of letting us worry," I drawled.

"You would've worried regardless. At least now you know she's safe." Luard waved his hands. "Come, let's get our new guests settled."

"And where are they settling?" I asked.

"Your home seems large enough."

I glanced to the sky. "Beata's going to murder me."

It was a strange group walking down the streets of Skorsa. Elisha and I led the pack—literally—of feral-looking teenagers who seemed confused by everything they saw.

"Why would you lay stone over the ground? You can't feel the vibrations."

"They've been doing that the whole ride here," Elisha said with a roll of her eyes.

I glanced down at her, still nursing a bit of fury at her and my brother. "It's impressive that they followed you here."

"I think we understood each other, yanno?" she said, kicking a rock down the road. "Orphans. 'cept I had a place to come home to."

"And they listened to you when you said you were there on Brynna's behalf?"

She nodded. "It's like... It's like Nicolasa. She used to just know things. She didn't need nobody to prove nothing to her. She just asked the Mother what the truth was and She told her."

These Nestori were much wilder than Nicolasa had been, but also very clearly repaying some debt to Brynna. I couldn't fathom any other reason a group such as this would've traveled all the way down from the mountains.

Elisha snuck a glance up at me. "I know you said that you don't flog people but...am I gonna get flogged?"

"Remains to be seen," I said. "You seem to have this nasty habit of disobeying my rules, and clearly the other methods haven't worked very well on you."

"Luard told me to go!"

"And whose house do you reside in?" I asked, ignoring Luard's dirty look to my left. "Luard will suffer his own punishments, but when it comes to who you mind, Beata and I take precedence as long as you are under our roof."

She looked at the ground. "I thought I was doing good. That's gotta count for something, doesn't it?"

"Elisha, you were gone for a week," I said, staring down at her. "We didn't have any clue where you were. Do you know how much we worried about you?" I took a breath and rested my hand on her shoulder. "But I'm grateful that you're back. I don't think I slept once while you were gone."

"Ahem."

Beata, who'd clearly been watching, met us at the front door, her face a cross between fury and amusement. "Well, well, well. Look who decided to come home."

"I was on a mission," Elisha said. "It was Luard's idea!"

"Hey!"

"And who..." Beata's eyes widened. "Who in the Mother's name are all these people?"

"It's kind of a long story," I said, sheepishly. "But do you think we might have room for them at the dinner table?"

She stared down at me, and I half expected her to storm back inside and slam the door. But she stepped aside and held out her arm.

"Get inside, all of you. Wipe your feet and mind the carpet. Dinner will be ready in about an hour. Until then, you can wash and warm up by the fire."

Beata's presence was enough to cow them, and they murmured their thanks as they walked past her, Elisha leading the way. They took off their leathery shoes and left them by the door. When the last wolf was over the threshold, Beata turned her attention to Luard.

"Luard's idea, hm?" Beata said. "Care to share?"

"I would, except I have to tend to some urgent matters back at the barracks," he said, inching his way down the street. "I'm sure your lovely wife will be more than happy to fill you in on everything I did and accept punishment on my behalf."

And with that, he scampered down the road.

"Coward," I muttered.

"Well?" Beata stepped down the stairs slowly, stopping at the step above me so she was eye level with me. "How long am I to feed and house these wildlings?"

"I don't know," I said. "Until they help us take the gate."

"Does this mean you won't be destroying the gate?"

"I..." I blinked. "I suppose not, if they can help us. That's why Luard sent Elisha. I had no clue, or else I would've stopped it. But..." I closed my eyes. "I'm grateful they're here."

She took my hands, kissing them. "If it means we can take the gate bloodlessly then perhaps I can forgive Luard's treachery." She twisted the gold band on my finger. "And...perhaps you can forgive my temper."

I nodded. "Always."

"Come inside and warm yourself by the fire," she said, smiling. "It's been rather chilly here without you."

"Indeed." I threaded my fingers through hers and let her lead me inside.

Chapter Thirty-Four

I had every intention of testing the boundaries of my new rules in Aunela, but I laid my head on the pillow for one second and the next thing I knew, the door was opening and morning light was streaming in. Two Severian servants came in, each carrying two buckets of water that they poured into a small tub. I didn't see any sign of fire, so I girded myself for what was probably going to be a very cold bath.

I wasn't disappointed, my teeth chattering as my nails were scrubbed. Afterward, my hair was merely braided and left to hang down my back. They dressed me in a loose shirt and fitted me with sandals. Thank the Mother there didn't seem to be a corset in sight.

They led me out of my room, down the main hall, to a large room with a long table in the center, and benches lining either side. The center of the table bore steaming bowls of stew and baskets of bread, as well as some selected fruits that seemed fresher than anything back in Forcadel.

"Good morning," Luisa said, walking in a few moments after I did. "I trust you slept well."

We took spots near to the ornate chair in the front—clearly Ilara's. More Severians filtered in, some of whom I recognized from the party. They chatted with Luisa and took no notice of me, which suited me fine. I was more eager to listen than anything else.

Three were merchants, half-Severian by birth and grateful to have a spot at the table. They fawned over Luisa and spoke of her good health and Ilara's magnificence and gave me nothing of value. One was in charge of moving varo from the sands of Severia. His skin was a dark brown from spending days out in the sun, and his voice was deep and joyful. His wife, in contrast, seemed sickly and smiled weakly whenever he mentioned her.

More arrived—a lawyer, a healer, and even a few artists sat at the table, all in deep conversation about the future of the mural in the center of town. They all agreed it should bear the likeness of their savior queen, but no one could settle on what it should look like.

"I feel it should show her feeding the hungry and leading us to paradise."

"It should show her building this city brick by brick."

"It should show her smiting the Forcadelians," said one of the artisans, grinning until he caught my raised eyebrows. "My apologies, Lady…"

"Lady whom Her Majesty smote," I said with an icy glare. "Water under the bridge. Or whatever the expression is here in Severia."

Luisa chuckled and laid her hand on my arm. "Brynna is Her Majesty's special guest here in the castle, Alaqua. We're thrilled that she's here to help us build Aunela into a city worthy of the legends."

Alaqua wasn't impressed. "And we're sure she can be trusted?"

"She saved my life," Luisa said. My heart twisted a little.

"A Forcadelian? Saving a Severian? I never heard of such a thing," Alaqua said.

I forced a tight smile onto my face, but my attention was diverted by the sound of trumpets at the front of the room.

"Her Majesty Ilara Hipolita Särkkä of New Severia."

We rose from the benches, and I followed the rest of the table who bowed their heads when Ilara walked into the room. She had also had a bath, but I had a feeling hers was warm and refreshing instead of frigid.

"It's so nice to see all of you," she said, resting her hand on the back of her chair. "I trust everyone's journey was pleasant. Welcome to the first day of the era of New Severia. Please, eat to your heart's content."

I'd already endured a few minutes of the smell of the food, so I was better able to school my features than when I'd eaten the pastry before. The meat was mostly gristle and featured some herb I'd never tasted before, and I had to fight to swallow it. Luckily, the wine was sweet and delicious—a Kulkan varietal.

"Well, Brynna, what do you think?" Ilara asked, tapping her napkin to her lips.

"You've accomplished a lot," I said. "The city is thriving."

"Oh, not about that," she said with a laugh. "I heard you weren't a fan of the kyushur. Perhaps you'll need to acquire a taste for Severian cooking. Thank goodness we'll never have to see another fish again."

The table twittered with laughter, reminding me that everyone was listening to our conversation.

"If you didn't know," Ilara said, raising her voice to address the rest of the table, "my dear friend Brynna here was something of an adversary. The former princess of Forcadel, she moonlit as a vigilante before her father and brother mysteriously died."

Another round of laughter echoed across the table, and I dug my thumbnail into my palm to hold my tongue.

"She was on the throne when I arrived, and oh, poor Brynna, she was hopelessly fooled by my ruse." Ilara pouted at me, and I forced a smile onto my face. "Cough, cough, I'm so ill. I'm so weak. I almost felt bad for her. She offered me a place in her castle, and I turned around and took it from her!"

I snuck a glance at the rest of the table and found sneers and amused smiles. I had no friends here.

"Then this poor dear mounted a laughable attempt to reclaim her kingdom." She reached across the table and patted my hand. "It's all right, though. Because I'm a forgiving queen, and I find there's no better sign of victory to have those you once considered your enemies at your table. Especially one so inept at causing any real trouble." Her smile widened to a cruel grin. "I mean, who would've thought that an army of children would have any chance against the might of Severia?"

I clicked my tongue and couldn't mask my glower. Luisa looked a little uncomfortable, but didn't interfere. Alaqua raised his goblet. "To their stupidity!"

"Cheers!"

"Brynna, are you not going to raise your glass?" Ilara asked, smiling at me over her goblet. "Surely, you aren't going to be sour over a bit of fun."

I opened my mouth to ask how mocking murdered children was fun, but Luisa was faster, resting her hand on Ilara's arm. "My queen, leave her be."

"I suppose," Ilara said with a sigh. But I had a feeling this was only the beginning.

Blessedly, another merchant asked how Ilara was planning on designing the grand hall, and she launched into grand visions of drapes and paintings of Severian legends and vases made by Severian artisans, all of whom had been commissioned and paid out of the Severian treasury.

"How does Severia have any money left?" I asked.

"I'm sorry?" Ilara asked.

"Well," I put my hands in my lap, "I see a brand new bay and river, not to mention the new buildings within Aunela. You're talking about commissioning art and vases to rival those in Forcadel. And with the ban on all trade with Kulka and Niemen, you haven't been receiving tariffs…"

"Our debts are none of your concern," Ilara said, flashing me a dangerous look. "Besides that, Forcadel's coffers were flush with riches. We could've fed all Severia for ten thousand years on the money I found in there."

My cheeks warmed slightly. "I see."

"And as for our friends out west, I'm sure that once they see our might, they'll change their tune. I've already received some information from those in Ariadna's court that her strong will is breaking." She made a face. "Clearly, the stress of giving birth has been too much for her. I dread the day I'll have to do the same to continue the Severian line."

My heart thudded—Ilara had spies in Ariadna's court? Did that mean she knew about Beswick, too? She'd still had Ignacio at her party, but…

"Oh, Your Majesty, you'll make an excellent mother," Luisa said, smiling brightly. "One day."

"I shall have the child and hand it over to you to raise," Ilara said with a shake of her head. "I do not mind funding schools and housing children, but I do not want any part of the raising of them."

"The school is magnificent, Your Majesty," Alaqua said. "I hope you'll be visiting soon. I spent many hours designing pieces for the school, and it would be my honor to show you one day."

"You're in luck, then. I've requested a tour of the school today," she said, smiling warmly at those gathered. "And you are all invited to attend."

They clapped politely, Alaqua beaming with pride.

Ilara basked in their praise like a lizard in the sun. "You know, of all my crowning achievements, this school is the one I'm most proud of."

"Even more than the river?" Alaqua asked.

"Even more," she said with a somber nod. "Education is the most valuable asset a person can have. We do not have a future if we do not have an educated population. And the welfare of children has always been my top priority."

Except when it came to the children in Celia's camp.

The thought came unwelcome, and stung worse in the echo of the Severians' laughter. I exhaled slowly until the anger subsided and I regained control over my mind.

"Our nation's children were in dire straits," Ilara continued. "They had nowhere to go, and in most cases, parents who were out in the desert or had perished there. It doesn't matter their background, all children get an education in New Severia."

"Are there Forcadelian children there, too?" I asked.

A twitter of laughter echoed from the table. "My dear, the Forcadelians have had their day in the sun," Alaqua said.

"Have they, now?" I asked, an edge coming to my voice. "All of them? Including those in Haymaker's Corner?"

"Sweet Brynna," Ilara said, breaking through the confused looks. "I promise that I've taken care of everyone who wanted to be taken care of. Those who didn't, well..." She shrugged. "I can't help people who won't help themselves."

"So you're saying there aren't any Forcadelian children in the school?" I pressed. "If they aren't there, where are they?"

"They're adequately busy with things the new kingdom needs to function," Ilara said. "Don't worry about it. I promise you that everything is fine. After all, they're my people now."

I didn't like that answer, nor did I like the way every question I had about the fate of my people was deflected.

"I'm sure the Severian children are grateful to you," Alaqua said.

"All I hope for them is that they continue to thrive," she said, looking wistful. "I cannot wait to see what they've accomplished since I was last here."

I chanced a look up. "You started the school before you came to Forcadel?"

She shared a knowing look with the table. "There's much you don't know, Brynna. A whole world of events occurred outside the sheltered walls of Forcadel."

"And I'm sure I would've known about them, had I been on the throne longer than three months," I replied with a thin smile.

"I doubt it," the artisan said. "Forcadelians didn't seem to care about anything beyond their borders."

"Aunela was part of Forcadel," I shot back. "So yes, I was concerned about our borders."

"As it stands, you no longer have to concern yourself with it," Ilara said, something of a warning in her voice. "All you should worry about now is making Aunela the best possible city it can be. That's why you came with us, isn't it?"

I felt the eyes of the table on me. I'd let my anger get the better of me again and Ilara's eyes warned that I was dangerously close to ruining her good time.

So I forced a tight smile onto my face and pushed my head to bob a short bow. "Yes, Your Majesty."

"Excellent." She turned to the crowd. "Now hurry up and finish your meal. The students at my school are waiting."

Chapter Thirty-Five

With the large procession, it took upwards of an hour to reach the school, situated close to the water. A salty breeze fought valiantly against the dry air blowing from the desert, but the scent was a reminder of home. The bay before us—the Ilarian Bay, how ridiculous—was yet again filled with activity.

The schoolhouse was an older building that had been put to new use—the royal customs building, or so Ilara told us.

"I thought it fitting to use such a hated reminder from the Forcadelians as a place for learning," Ilara said to the crowd.

"Hated reminder?" I murmured, but clearly my words carried, at least to Alaqua.

"You may not remember this, Forcadelian," he said with a sneer. "But the tariffs that were levied inside that building meant our merchants had to go hungry."

I was sure they did, so I merely nodded.

"But now," Ilara said, catching my eye, "it is made new. Come.

Let's see the future of New Severia."

We walked through a pair of large, open doors, still bearing the Forcadelian crest, and came into a room with a mural-covered dome overhead. Although most of the art was Forcadelian, the scaffolding and lines of white paint said this was yet another place Ilara would be planting her flag. To my eyes, there was as much Severian influence here as Forcadelian, but they were doing their best to stamp out anything from the latter.

"Good morning, Your Majesty." The headmistress was a short woman with kind eyes and a bright smile. "It is my honor to welcome you here to our school."

"The honor is mine," Ilara said. "You've certainly done much since the last time I was here." She looked around the room. "There seems to be no trace of the customs department."

"We were sure to erase any sign of them," she said, holding out her arm to beckon us forward. "We've repurposed the desks for the students, and have used up all the papers and ink we found in them." She cast a wary look at Ilara. "I do hope more will be arriving soon?"

"Very soon," she replied with a smile. "And the children? How are they enjoying their studies?"

"Enjoying may not be the word for some of them, but they're eager to prove themselves," she said with a kind look. She went into boring detail about the lesson plans, which unsurprisingly included a heavy emphasis on art and design. Ilara would be churning out students with an education that rivaled the richest children's in Forcadel. It was an admirable accomplishment, if it had extended beyond the Severian children.

"Before we visit the classrooms," the headmistress said, sounding almost giddy, "we'd like to share something with you."

She led us out into a courtyard in the middle of the complex, complete with a fountain and brightly tiled floor. In the center was a large object covered with a blanket. I craned my neck to look up into the windows where hundreds of tiny faces were looking down at us.

Two older children dressed in their finest tunics were waiting behind the blanketed object, their hands held behind their back. When the headmistress gave the signal, they walked forward in unison and gripped the edges of the blanket, pulling it off and revealing a bronze statue.

Of Ilara. It was all I could do not to roll my eyes.

"We have decided to name the school the Ilara Hipolita Särkkä School for Excellence."

"Oh… Oh my!" Ilara walked forward, her hand covering her mouth. "This is…wholly unexpected."

Was it? This from the girl who'd named an entire bay after herself.

"Your likeness will look after every student in these walls," she said. "We are honored that such a gifted queen lived in our time."

"I am…" Was she actually crying? "I'm speechless. This statue is more than I ever could have wanted, or even needed!" She pressed her hand over her heart. "I did not commission and design this school to be honored, but to offer for our people the sort of life that brings them joy. This was not for me, but for us. For New Severia and everyone born under her flag."

Her speech sounded awfully rehearsed and self-serving for someone who'd been taken by surprise.

"Education is the most valuable asset a person can have," she continued, and I fought hard against my desire to scoff as she repeated the same speech from this morning. "And the welfare of children has always been my top priority."

"Who would've thought that an army of children would have any chance against the might of Severia?"

I shook her words from my mind, but the anger lingered.

"You look displeased," Luisa said, catching my gaze. "Is everything all right?"

"I suppose I'm just tired," I said, forcing a smile onto my face that even I didn't believe. I did my best to bury my annoyance and follow the crowd.

The headmistress took us back inside, and I prayed to the Mother that the rest of the day would go quickly. Instead, we were led to one of the small classrooms. Inside, around twenty children sat at identical desks. They were no older than ten, sitting with their hands folded in their laps and nary a hair out of place.

"Children," the teacher began, "please welcome our queen."

Together, they pushed their chairs back and rose. Each one bowed from the hips, their noses almost touching the wood of their desks. Then back up again, and back to their seats.

A hair too fast. You were a hair too slow.

Jorad's voice floated through my mind and I did my best to bat it away, but the back of my neck warmed.

The students showed off their skills, from their pronunciation of the cities in Severia to a few reading off the chalkboard. They were endearingly innocent, but they did little to dispel my annoyance.

Once Her Majesty had had her fill of worship, we continued to the next classroom where we found much of the same. Three more classrooms of the same exercise later, and I was starting to get bored. I didn't dare ask to be excused to explore the city on my own. Ilara wanted me present for every second of this celebration of her, if the expression on her face was any indication.

But as we approached the last room, my pulse quickened. It looked like a training arena, albeit with wooden swords and weapons. Something about it reminded me of Celia's camp, and the faces of dead children flashed across my mind.

"You look pale, Brynna," Luisa said. "Are you all right?"

"Yes." There was no reason I should've been more affected by this room than the others. But perhaps the day was catching up with me.

"All our students are learning the fine art of hand-to-hand combat," the headmistress said. "Some of them may join your ranks as soldiers one day, and we want them to be as ready for battle as any."

Planning on going to battle any time soon? I bit my tongue.

The children gathered for a demonstration, pairing off with wooden swords. They were sloppy, undisciplined, and rather weak.

Perhaps my disdain was on my face, because Ilara called my name. "What do you think of them? Are they ready for battle?"

"They look fine."

"Would they have stood a chance against the children in Celia's camp?" she asked, her eyes glittering with malice.

Go to hell. It was hard to keep the fury off my face, and I struggled against the rising tide. The children in camp would've wiped the floor with the Severians. They didn't need to win to eat; they didn't need to win to survive. If an army of soldiers came into this city, these children would cry and run, not walk headfirst into danger with Jorad. But that had gotten my soldiers slaughtered. Perhaps if they'd been a little less eager to win the day, and a little more selfish, more of them might be alive today.

Take the babies and run.

Thank the Mother for Nicolasa's firm words. Beata might never have been able to make it to safety.

And perhaps if I'd been a little more—

"Brynna?" Ilara said, amusement clear on her face. "I asked you a question. Do you think my students here would've been able to fight those children in Celia's camp?"

"Brynna?" Luisa said, concern in her eyes.

The heat in the room was now unbearable and I had to get out before I grabbed one of these weapons and jammed it through Ilara's heart. "Excuse me."

I stepped just outside into the empty hall and took a long breath to calm myself. It had been quite a while since I'd let my mask slip so far, but Ilara had clearly decided to hit harder now that she thought her victory secure.

I covered my eyes, but then all I saw were dead children in a forest. Forcing my lids open, I stared into the open hallway and banished the image from my mind. Now was not the time for grief to rear its ugly head, but perhaps that was what Ilara was after. It wasn't enough to humiliate me here—I had to be reminded what a monster she was.

More than that, I was the only one who saw her that way. The Severians didn't care what had happened to their conquered enemies.

Footsteps drew my attention, and a woman dressed plainly—perhaps a servant or maid—came shuffling into view.

She was Forcadelian.

With my gasp, she looked up, fearful, then ducked her head again. "Pardon me, missus."

"Wait!" I took two steps toward her. "Wait, what's your name?"

"I shouldn't be talking with the people," she murmured, playing with her white apron. "I'll get in trouble."

"Nonsense," I said, shaking my head. "I'm Forcadelian, like you."

She finally looked up and some of the fear left her eyes. "Are you not a servant?"

"No, I'm here… Never mind why I'm here." I waved her off. "Where are all the Forcadelians?"

"Don't know." She rubbed her hands on her apron.

"Then how did you get here?"

"Few weeks ago, a man came to my door and asked me if I had

a job. I told him I didn't, 'cause the dressmaker I worked for left town once...once Her Majesty arrived." She cleared her throat. "Next thing I knew, they'd stuck me on a boat and put me here."

"And you aren't allowed to talk to anyone?" I asked.

"Not the young misters and misses, no." She chewed her lip. "They told me I'd only have to work a year to pay off the debt for my travel, but just the other day, they told me that I was also being charged for my room and board, so now—"

"Now it's a perpetual servitude," I said with a knowing sigh. "Did a man named Johann Beswick bring you here?"

"I don't know who it was, really," she said. "He told me to show up on the docks on a certain day then..." She played with the hem of her dress. "You been to Forcadel recently?"

"More or less," I said.

"How are things back there?" She asked, her eyes filling with hope. "I left my folks there. Thought I could send them some money, but I...well, I haven't been paid, so."

My gut twisted. "I promise that things will improve. Just keep your head up."

"You look sorta familiar," she said, turning her head.

"Perhaps you saw me around the city," I replied, as a Severian turned the corner. I raised my voice so she could hear. "Thank you for the directions, maid. I think I have it from here."

The girl bowed and scurried away as Ilara and the rest of the group exited the room. I waited for Ilara to say something, but she didn't, merely wearing a satisfied smile as they continued the tour.

As the sun tilted into the west, the children's classes came to a close, as did our day spent with them. They bade their queen farewell as some of them ventured out into the streets, and yet others bounded upstairs. Orphans who had nowhere else to go, I supposed. Ilara had been told they housed some of them here.

The gaggle of artisans and merchants who'd been with us since breakfast remained steadfastly attached to Ilara's side, and I couldn't hide my annoyance on my face when Ilara invited them all to dine with her for dinner. I was now keenly interested in the Forcadelian woman I'd met in the hall. The fear in her eyes was so familiar, as was the story of her arrival here. This had Beswick written all over it. I wanted out of this crowd so I could investigate.

"You don't look pleased, dear friend," Ilara said, coming to walk next to me. "I hope my comment earlier didn't upset you."

"No, just tired from the trip, I'm sure. Perhaps I'll return to my room and rest for the afternoon."

"I don't think I've ever seen you fatigued," she said. "I do hope you'll be in a good humor for dinner."

I exhaled. "And if I'm not, may I be excused to my room for the evening?"

"Of course not," she said. "What fun is it if my favorite person doesn't join me?"

I clenched my jaw, forcing myself not to respond, but thankfully Luisa stepped up. "It has been a long day for all of us, Your Majesty. Perhaps you could allow her a small reprieve?"

Luisa's charm worked, and Ilara waved her hand. "I suppose. But rest up, dear friend, because tomorrow is a brand new day."

The gaggle left me standing in the center of the hall, and I remained there for a few minutes. In the absence of the sycophantic cloud surrounding Ilara, I breathed a little easier, the fog of anger that had followed me around all day clearing. I was completely alone in this hall, too—not a guard in sight.

You are free to go wherever you wish.

I cracked a smile. I hoped that included rooftops.

Chapter Thirty-Six

I could've probably walked out the front door, but I didn't exactly want Ilara knowing I'd snuck out. So I returned to my room and opened the window overlooking a small courtyard. There wasn't a guard below, and the stone of the castle was uneven enough for me to climb. Still, I paused at every window ledge to make sure I hadn't been seen.

When I reached the top of the castle, I hoisted myself up and kept low as I crossed toward the front. Down below, the two guards were at attention, watching the dark streets for signs of trouble.

Without my cloak, I had no way of jumping six stories to the ground, so I had to find an alternate route. A decorative brick corner on the east side of the castle did the trick, and thanks to the absence of light, the guards didn't notice me.

My boots kicked up dust on the road as I strolled down the main drag, taking my time to study the businesses and names on the windows. A few were those who'd attended Ilara's dinner. Their shops were fine, many of them holding beautiful pieces of art. I quelled the urge to light them on fire.

For tonight, I had a question to answer: where in the Mother's name had Ilara put all my people? The school could've housed maybe fifty or a hundred servants, but there'd been a mass exodus from the city these past few months. They should've been on every corner, mixing with the Severians on the street like one big happy family. That I'd only seen two—and one of them had been in the mirror—meant there was something terribly wrong.

Before I got too far, I stopped in front of a fabric store, catching my reflection in the glass. Inside, the moonlight draped across the fabrics laid out in the store—mostly white cotton as was the fashion, but I might get lucky.

Reaching into my braid, I plucked out a pair of pins and walked to the front door, crouching to work the tumblers on the lock. It opened with little effort and I pushed the door, wincing at the small tinkling of a bell above.

I walked silently, keeping to the shadows as I scoured the space for something I could use. Not as if anyone was wearing black in the hot desert sun, but maybe something…

"Ah!" I breathed, spotting something dark at the bottom of a stack of folded white fabric. Carefully moving them onto another station, I revealed a folded ream of what looked like dark green fabric. Unraveling just a little, I sliced a long, thin strip off the larger ream and cut two eyeholes in it before placing the fabric over my eyes.

Wearing the mask was like coming home. I had no illusions about my disguise—if I was seen at all, it would all be over. But there was something delicious about wearing it in Ilara's city.

As I patrolled the rooftops, making sure to avoid the one-story, thatched roofs that surely wouldn't hold my weight, I began to worry less about the Severian patrols, as I hadn't seen one in the city. Either Ilara's army was stretched pretty thin, or she was taking quite the gamble.

I took my time learning the rooftops, finding that I could walk a path, as long as I zigzagged a little. When I reached the edge of the city, I listened to the sounds of the bay. Ships creaked and groaned as the water rippled beneath them, knocking against their moorings every so often. The sound brought emotion to my throat, as I hadn't heard it in Forcadel in months.

I drew my fingers up to my necklace, toying with the coins there and thinking about home. If I closed my eyes, I could still be back on the docks, listening to the sound of—

"Get on with it! We don't have all night."

My eyes snapped open. A ship had arrived, and a swarm of sailors were moving on deck. No, not sailors—civilians. It was hard to tell in the scant moonlight, but I could've sworn they were Forcadelians.

When they came into the torchlight, my hunch was confirmed. Some were old, some young, all windblown and weary from what I could only assume was several weeks at sea. The younger children held onto their parents' hands as they swayed on the dock. Several looked sick—whether from malnutrition or from the sea, I couldn't tell. There were perhaps sixty in this group.

"Go on, get!" A Severian man forced the remaining people onto the dock and called for his partner to move them forward. The crowd shifted slowly, especially with the young children and the narrow dock.

On the street, there were several large covered wagons waiting for them, each drawn by four horses. The guards counted them off —twenty apiece—then ordered them inside the carriages. My heart seized when they split up a family of four—leaving two young children behind. Another woman took their hand and called to their parents that she would look after them.

"You're all going to the same place," the guard said. "Don't worry."

That was all I needed to hear. I jumped off the roof and landed on the street in front of the carriage. I had nothing but my fists and my wits, but the clouds had moved over the moon overhead, bathing the streets in darkness. My shadow was enough to halt the horses, who reared back.

"W—Get out of the way, you stupid girl!" the Severian called to me.

"Make me," I said, cracking my knuckles.

The soldiers hadn't been expecting this and well-trained, they were not. I probably shouldn't have taken my anger at Ilara out on them, but did it anyway. They lay on the ground, mangled and bruised when I walked back to the wagon and opened the flap.

"Evening, folks," I said.

The gaggle shrank back into the darkness, but one brave soul asked, "W-who are you? What do you want? We don't have any coin!"

"It's all right," I said, holding up my hands. "I'm not going to hurt you. I'm a friend."

"Are you The Veil?" A young girl crawled out, her eyes wide with wonder.

"I am," I said with a nod.

A cry of relief echoed from the wagon, followed by a tumbling of words and praises to the Mother. I did my best to shush them, lest we were overheard by a Severian guard, but it did no good. Hope had been scarce in their lives, and I had been the sign they'd been looking for.

"Tell me how you ended up here," I said, once they'd quieted

One of the older women spoke. "We weren't going to go," she said. "Ilara had sent soldiers out promising us a new life in New Severia, but we knew it wasn't true. Then a few weeks ago, that bastard Coyle and his thugs showed up at our front door and dragged us out of our homes. Next thing we knew, we were on a ship and ended up here."

"Did they tell you where you were headed?" I asked.

"They said something about the mines, or perhaps even building the river," she said. "But they weren't very forthcoming with information."

I stared at them, wishing I had something more to tell them. "I want you all to listen to me very closely," I said. "I'm going to find you a place to stay for the night, and tomorrow night, I'll find a way to get you back to Forcadel." I had no idea how I'd manage it, but I was determined. "Stay here for now, okay? And if anyone comes to ask why you're here, just tell them that your Severian master left to get his…horse or something. And stay out of sight."

Leaving them in the alley, my heart began to race. I had nowhere to put these people. There was nothing but a hostile city with hostile actors. I didn't even have a boat to send them back to Forcadel—

I felt a presence behind me and tensed.

A hand landed on my shoulder and turned me around, and I reared back to fight them, but stopped when I got a good look at their face.

"Don't punch me again, okay?"

Chapter Thirty-Seven

Felix

Brynna's mouth fell open in surprise as she took me in. "W... w..." She worked her jaw, staring at me as if she didn't recognize me. But finally, her eyes softened and filled with...tears?

"Felix?" She touched my face. "Is it really you? Am I dreaming?"

I pulled her into my arms. "I'm so glad I found you."

She wrapped her arms around me and pressed her head into my shoulder, closing her eyes. It wasn't like her to be so speechless. Clearly, she'd been through a lot since we'd last spoken.

"What are you doing here?" she asked.

"I came on the ship with these people," I said, nodding to the wagon below. "We arrived tonight and...well..."

"Yeah, I saw," she said with a glare. "Where were they taking them?"

"I have no idea," I said. "But wherever it was, it wasn't good. I was hoping to follow them, but you got to them first."

"Yeah..." She looked a little sorry. "I probably shouldn't have done that. But it's been a long day, and I needed to hit some Severians."

"Going well in the castle, then?" I asked, gently touching the mask at her face with a smile. "What happened to letting Ilara think she'd won?"

She turned away from me. "Felix, things are so far away from where they were when we last spoke. We aren't even in the same city. I don't know how we're even going to..."

"Why don't you start from the beginning, from the moment you were captured by Ilara?" I said, pulling her close again. "And tell me everything you know."

She spoke quickly, mentioning Mark, Coyle, Skorsa, and arriving here a few days prior. But her voice caught when she spoke of visiting Ilara's school.

"Felix, that maid is the first Forcadelian I've seen in this city," she said. "And now Ilara's bringing in people from Forcadel to go...well, who knows where?" She shook her head. "Something's wrong. I can feel it in my gut."

"We'll find them," I said.

"We have to get these people back to Forcadel," she said. "Or somewhere safe."

"I don't think that's possible," I said. "Kieran's ship's headed back out to sea to wait for the Kulkan warships."

She glanced. "Kieran? The pirate? I thought he was working for Beswick?"

"Clearly, your threats got through to him," I said with a smile. "He's absolutely determined to get you to like him again. Something about a pirate king?"

She rolled her eyes. "Great. So what do we do about them?"

I took her hand. "Our focus needs to be on getting to Ilara, on reclaiming this city. These people can..."

"We can't leave them alone," Brynna said. "The Severians will find them and send them to wherever—or worse."

"We'll think of something," I said. "You're The Veil."

"I'm The Veil," she mumbled, almost like a mantra. "What would The Veil do?"

"There isn't a bell tower around here, is there?" I asked, half-joking.

She shook her head then stopped, as if remembering something. "Luisa said there was a church in the northeastern part of the city. I've never seen it, though. I don't know if we want to sneak twenty people all the way up there on a whim."

"Leave it to us," a voice called from behind me. Aithne and Malka had followed.

"You brought friends," Brynna said, a little breathlessly. "Who else is here?"

"Just us," Aithne said. "Don't worry, Your Majesty. We'll keep an eye on the wagon and move it if we need to. You two head north and see about that church."

She nodded, a smile blossoming on her lips. "Will do."

We hurried northeast across rooftops. Brynna obviously had no clue where she was going, but she seemed in desperate need of good news. The last time I'd seen her so unsure of herself was the day I'd found out she was alive. I prayed that the Mother would reveal something to us tonight.

But when we came to the edge of the city, there was no church in sight. She jumped down to the street, defeat clear on her face as she shook her head.

"No sign of a church, steeple, nothing." She ran her tongue over her teeth. "Ilara must've knocked it down."

"Maybe we just missed it," I offered.

"I could see for city blocks, Felix," she said, walking to the point where the road faded into sand. "No steeple. No bell tower. Just old buildings."

"We'll find something, I—" I squinted, as the moonlight reflected off something in the distance. "Are you sure it's not out there?"

"What? In the desert?" She turned to look where I'd pointed.

I shrugged. "There's something. We should go check it out."

We stumbled over the sand that shifted under our feet with a cold wind that seemed to come out of nowhere. My legs burned, and Brynna's cheeks grew rosy with exertion, but we pressed on. The distant structure was still shrouded in darkness, and seemed to remain perpetually in the distance.

"Felix..." Brynna said with a small gasp. "I think that's a steeple."

She seemed to have found a burst of energy, dashing across the sand and leaving me behind. I followed as best I could, but she arrived before I did.

"Felix, it's not a church," she called, hope soaring through her voice. "It's a convent."

"A convent?" I squinted in the dark and could just make out the shape of it. A small chapel in the front—complete with bell tower—connected to a larger structure that stretched into the desert behind it.

After a long slog over the dunes, I eventually reached the church, where Brynna was working on the front door. I pressed my ear to the door and listened for the sound of anyone talking.

"It's empty, Felix," she whispered, her voice shaking as the tumblers turned over. "It's empty. It's perfect."

She pushed open the heavy door, and it groaned into the desert beyond. We slipped into a pitch-black space, and I stumbled around until I found a torch against the wall. Using a flint in my pocket, I lit it, illuminating the space. Dusty wooden pews sat in two columns, with a small dais at the front. The candle wall was covered in cobwebs, most of the wax used down to the glass.

Brynna walked to the wall, pressing her fingers to the small jars.

"Hello?" I called. "Is anyone here?" When no answer came, I left Brynna in the chapel and explored the convent. There were about fifty rooms with two beds each. Besides the beds, there was nothing else, although a few of the rooms displayed an engraved crest of the Mother.

When I came back to the chapel, I found Brynna with a single candle lit, her head bowed in prayer. After placing the torch on the wall, I crossed the space, coming to kneel next to her on the prayer bench. Her cheeks were wet, and as I reached to brush them away, more fell in their place.

"I'm ashamed to admit I lost a little faith along the way," she whispered, her voice thick. "I've been praying to the Mother that she would give me a sign. Something to help me..." She exhaled softly. "It's been hard to keep marching forward on blind faith alone."

There was something about the candlelight on her wet skin, the vulnerability in her eyes. I couldn't help myself as I leaned over and captured her lips. She responded in kind, turning to me and pulling herself closer. She tasted of salt and sadness, but also of adventure, and—

"Uh..."

I straightened, hearing Aithne's voice behind us. Brynna was on her feet in an instant, ready to attack whoever had followed us.

"Your Majesty," Malka said, bowing low.

"W-what are you doing here?" Brynna said, her voice an octave higher. "Was there trouble?"

"There was a Severian patrol getting a little close to the wagon," Aithne said. "And we saw you heading out into the desert, so we followed."

They moved out of the way and the twenty souls who'd accompanied me from Forcadel filtered into the space. They wore looks of relief and awe on their face, some of them dropping to their knees to thank the Mother for this gift.

"There's no food here, I'm sure," Brynna said.

"We'll take care of that," Malka said. "And we can use the bell tower to keep watch for anyone coming out of the city."

"We can also bring anyone who comes off the docks here," Aithne said.

"I...see..." Brynna said, looking to me in surprise. "Clearly you've got everything taken care of."

"They had a good teacher," I said with a smile.

"Excuse me." One of the older Forcadelians stood behind her, holding his cap in his hands. "May we light a candle?"

"Of course," Brynna said, stepping out of the way.

The man found a lighter stick from the row of candles and dipped it into the candle Brynna had lit. Then, with care, he touched the new flame to a candle.

"Dear Mother," he murmured, after putting out the stick, "please keep an eye on Queen Brynna and her soldiers. Please keep us safe here and lead us to victory."

"You...know who I am?" Brynna asked.

He grinned, sheepishly. "I lived two doors down from the butchery where you used to work. Saw you climb in and out of the window in that mask of yours. Watched this fellow drag you out one night." He nodded toward me. "When I saw your likeness on the posters, I knew immediately. A lot of us did." He smiled. "We were glad to have one of our own in power."

She smiled, her hand coming to her heart. "I promise, I'll do everything in my power to make this right."

"Brynn," I said, glancing out the window. "It's getting light. We should get you back to the castle."

"We'll be fine here, Your Majesty," he said, bowing. "And thank you."

Chapter Thirty-Eight

Katarine

Our new Nestori guests took to the house much quicker than I'd anticipated. They didn't mind taking their meal or sleeping wherever there was a flat surface, even if it was on the floor. Beata seemed pleased to have even more people to mother, and I was just glad we were back on speaking terms.

The morning after they arrived, we were awakened by the sound of giggling and noise from the kitchen below.

Beata opened one eye at me. "It's not even dawn yet."

"I'll go see what's going on," I whispered, kissing her and tossing the sheets off myself. Snatching my dressing robe from the hook near the door, I walked down the stairs, yawning and hoping it was just one or two causing trouble.

Instead, our dining room was filled with children—all wearing masks. A floral scent was in the air, but before I could even walk into the room, one of the wolves threw up her hand.

"You will succumb," she said. "Wear this."

She handed me a cloth mask and I wrapped it around my face.

"What's going on here?"

"We have brought the flowers," the wolf said. "But we need help pulverizing it and making the bags your daughter requested."

"W-what?" I shook my head in confusion. "Elisha? Where are you?"

The teenager in question appeared in the doorway, her eyes wide. "Shit."

"Language," I said, casting her a look. "Care to explain what you're doing here?"

"Well..." She looked around, as if seeking an escape. "I thought it would be good if they taught some of the kids Nestori stuff. They know a bit about knockout powders and bags, but I thought we could use the hyblatha on the gate."

I put my hands on my hips. "What is that, exactly?"

"It gives whoever inhales it a wicked nightmare," she said, her eyes crinkling as she smiled behind her mask. "Which makes it easier to tie 'em up. That way you don't have to blow up the gate." She crossed the room and picked up a small bag. "You just load this up on your crossbow and shoot it at whoever's shooting at you. Then listen for the screams."

The corners of my mouth twitched. "And you thought it a good idea to include the children in this task?"

"Why not? They used to do stuff like it at camp." She squared her chest. "And they're bored learning their letters."

"Elisha..."

Jarrah rose to her feet. "We have finished making our preparations. Where is your enemy?"

"To the south," I said. "But—"

She barked, and the rest of the wolves jumped to attention, as did the children. "Out."

"Out?" I shared a look with Beata, who'd joined us from a safe distance. "You can't go. We have soldiers for this."

"They do not know the Mother's magic," she said, shouldering the bags of hyblatha. "And we have to fulfill our end of the bargain to repay our debt to your queen."

"Then you go, but the children will stay here," I said, standing in front of the doorway. "It's too dangerous."

"It will be more dangerous if they do not come," Jarrah said, sidestepping me. The rest of the group passed around me and out the open door.

"It'll be all right," Elisha said, standing defiantly in front of me. "I'll keep an eye on them. But don't follow us into the forest. We can handle this."

I looked to Beata for help, but my resolve to argue was weakening as each child walked by with a stoic determination nearly identical to the wolves'. Perhaps Luard had been right; they hadn't been coddled in Celia's camp, and it was time we stopped coddling them. If they felt confident they could do this without us...

"You should fetch the soldiers for backup," Beata said, kissing me on the cheek. "The children will need it."

Joella scrambled her troops quickly, and a contingent of us marched toward the southern border. Beata and I joined Luard at the outskirts of the city, holding each others hands as we waited for news.

"How long do you think it'll take?" Beata asked.

We didn't wait long. A blood-curdling scream echoed out of the forest, but Luard shot out his arm to keep the two of us from moving forward.

"That's a man's scream," he said. "They're in. Joella, you might want to start passing out the tinneum."

He handed her a bag of the minty herb and she dispersed it amongst the soldiers as more screams echoed from the woods beyond. I closed my eyes and whispered to myself that it was merely hallucinations, that they were in no danger, but it still rattled my nerves. Beside me, Beata's hand gripped mine so tightly that I was beginning to lose feeling in my fingers.

Finally, there was movement in the treeline. Jarrah appeared, chewing like a cow as she walked. She was dragging something much heavier than a girl her size should've been able to carry.

"What is that?" Luard asked, squinting into the forest.

"I can't tell," I said. "But it looks like a person."

"Oh, Mother…did she kill someone?" Beata said, holding her hand to her mouth.

I released her hand and jogged forward with Luard, praying we wouldn't see something grotesque when we got there. These wolves were feral, but they also followed the Mother.

"You can move your troops in now," Jarrah called. "Make sure anyone who goes into the forest has the tinneum."

"You heard the woman," Joella called to her waiting soldiers. "We're taking prisoners only, soldiers. Move out!"

The soldiers, all chewing tinneum, sheathed their weapons and jogged toward the forest in waves, giving Jarrah, still dragging that body behind her, a wide berth.

"Is he…?" I asked, tentatively stepping closer to her. "Wait a second, *Captain Mark*?"

His face was a stark white, as if all the blood had been drained from it, and he'd wrapped himself into a ball, perhaps making him easier to drag. But his eyes, red from crying, were far away.

"Give him some tinneum," I said, panicking a little.

Jarrah gave me a look. "He's the leader of your enemy's forces."

"That can't be," I said. "He served Brynna's father. He's Felix's mentor. He couldn't have been the one…"

"He was rather put out when Brynna fired him," Beata said, coming to stand next to me. "Perhaps he landed in Ilara's employ after that."

There had to be a different explanation. There was no way he could've allied himself with Ilara, not after all she'd done. But he'd been the one firing on my soldiers, and his soldiers had fired on Luard's guards even when they wore Niemenian uniforms.

"Tie him up then give him tinneum," I said, after a moment.

My soldiers did as I asked and forced the bitter herb down the screaming captain's throat. He chewed, his tears and wild looks subsiding. As he came back to himself, his trembling ceased as well, in favor of looking around the forest.

"K-Katarine?"

"Welcome back," I said, kneeling down at his level. "I confess I'm very surprised to see you. Of all the people Ilara could've put here, a former Forcadelian captain wouldn't have been the one I picked. How did you come to such an assignment?"

He remained silent, the wheels in his mind clearly turning.

I sighed. "I'm here on behalf of Queen Brynna."

"Didn't know she coronated herself. Seemed like she was a prisoner when I saw her."

My heart leapt to my throat. "She was here?"

He clenched his jaw, looking to the side.

"Very well," I said, rising. "Perhaps your soldiers will offer more information. We've taken this forest and beyond for ourselves and for Queen Brynna. If you cooperate, perhaps she might find it within her heart to forgive you for allying yourself with the enemy."

"She allied *herself* with the enemy," Mark said. "I don't know if you're aware, but she's been kissing rings and bowing to Queen Ilara all this time. Sounds like she left you for safer pastures. If you're planning on taking over the kingdom in her name, you might find yourselves without a queen."

I merely smiled, grateful to hear Brynna had been such a good actress. "I'll surely take your advice to heart. Take him to the brig and perhaps a few days in confinement will loosen his tongue."

They carried him away, and Beata shook her head. "I can't

believe… Captain Mark. It just seems like…"

"I know," I said. "But you heard him—Ilara believes Brynna to be her loyal subject. Our plan is working. We can continue down to Forcadel."

"Erm…" Joella said, walking out of the forest. "I think you might want to reconsider that idea. You guys need to see this."

"It's…a dam."

It looked like something stronger than Niemenian ore had been placed in the river, cutting off the water to the south and routing it east. Something so massive surely should've come across my desk as Ilara's attendant, but clearly she'd been keeping this close to the vest for some time.

"Where does it go?" Beata asked.

"The soldiers that have come to said it goes to Aunela," Joella said. "And that's where Brynna and Ilara went."

I walked to the riverbank, staring down at the rushing water. Things were starting to fall into place for me, small conversations that, at the time had meant nothing, but were now coming into stark relief.

"Then we go to Aunela," I said softly. "Jo, how quickly can you get a small riverboat ready to depart?"

"Within the hour, m'lady."

"Then do that," I said. "I want a small cadre of soldiers— Forcadelian, so they don't arouse suspicion—to go ahead and scout the area for us. If you can make contact with Brynna, do. And if there's anyone else in the city we can call an ally, tell them the rest of our soldiers will be arriving as soon as they can."

"And what of the wolves?" Joella asked. Jarrah had followed us into the dam, a sneer on her face as she looked at the newly cut river. "Should we ask them to come with us?"

"We have repaid our debt," Jarrah said, ignoring us as she

poked at the riverbank. "And will be returning home as soon as you can ready a boat."

Joella looked ready to argue, but I shook my head. "Tend to the prisoners and see if you can get more information from them. Beata—"

"I'll help," she said, casting me a knowing look. "Seems like you could use some more hands."

When they were both gone, I approached the Nestori. "What's wrong?"

"This is an abomination," she said. "The Mother's magic was used to create this new scar in Her lands. It will not stand."

I nodded. "I wanted to thank you for your help. We couldn't have done this without you." I took a step forward. "If you would stay and join us in Aunela, we would gladly be in your debt."

She cracked a smile. "You do not need us. The children in your home are well-versed in the Mother's magic. You'd do well to trust them with it, especially the eldest. The Mother spared her life for a purpose, and you are wasting Her gift."

A shudder ran through me. Elisha could've told the Nestori about Celia's camp, but something told me she hadn't.

"Is it wasteful to keep her alive for another day?" I said, as Elisha appeared in the forest, her crossbow raised as she hunted down stragglers. "The Mother may have plans for her, but my queen gave me orders to keep her safe."

The wolf smiled as she rose. "The child will do what she wants, and you would do well to flow with the river, instead of trying to control what you cannot."

She left us as Elisha spotted me, jogging over with her crossbow pointed at the sky. She wore the serious look of someone who knew exactly what she was doing, and it broke my heart that someone so young knew such things already. But more than that, I'd just gotten her back, and now I was sending her away again. But with the Nestori's words, I could no longer deny what had been in front of my face. Elisha needed to play her part in this, and I needed to stay out of the way.

"I've swept the area, but I haven't seen any more. I think we're in the clear," Elisha said. She noticed my face and frowned. "What is it?"

"Elisha," I said, swallowing. "Go down to the docks and tell Captain Kinsella that you'll be going with her to Aunela on the scouting ship."

Elisha's eyes widened. "W-what?"

"The wolves won't be going with them, and we need someone well-versed in Nestori magic and vigilante arts to keep them safe." I straightened. "Can you handle this task?"

She licked her lips. "This ain't a trick, is it?"

"No," I said. "But you must promise me you'll be careful, and mind whatever Captain Kinsella says. If she wants you to mop floors, you will mop floors. And if she tells you to look out, you will look out only. Am I clear?"

Elisha nodded. "Why are you sending me away?"

"Because you're the best we have." Something tugged at my heart, and I couldn't quite articulate what I wanted to say. "And we could use all the help we can get."

She gazed into my eyes, as if expecting me to say something else, but then nodded. "I won't let you down."

Chapter Thirty-Nine

My soul was lighter than it had been in weeks—and not just because Felix's taste was on my lips. My allies were filtering into the city. If Felix was correct, the five Kulkan warships he'd commandeered would be arriving in the next week or so. And in the meantime, he and his two vigilantes would keep watch on the docks.

And more importantly, I'd saved twenty souls from being sent...wherever they were destined to go. The convent had been a gift from the Mother herself as a sign not to give up hope. Perhaps Felix was a similar gift.

Still, there were thousands of Forcadelians somewhere in the city, and more coming from Forcadel. The more we intercepted, the higher the risk that Ilara might notice and start a search. Our hope was that the Kulkan warships would get here before that happened—and my job was to delay the inevitable as long as possible.

When I arrived at the breakfast table, Luisa was listening to a young student. The child's eyes widened when she saw me, but Luisa patted her on the arm.

"Come sit, Brynna," Luisa said. "Ilmi here was just regaling me with her award-winning essay."

"I wrote it on how Her Majesty's kindness changed my life," the girl said proudly.

"It's changed many lives in this city," I said, trying to keep my tone light. *Think of the Forcadelians. Think of tonight. Keep it civil.* I forced a smile onto my face, and even found the strength to make it realistic. "Congratulations on your award. I know it was hard-earned."

"I only learned how to write a few months ago," she said. "I had my teacher help me with the grammar."

"But I'm sure the heart of the essay was yours." Luisa looked to me. "Did you sleep well, Brynna? You look a bit tired."

"Tossed and turned," I said, cringing as Alaqua walked into the room. "But grateful for the reprieve from dinner last night. I feel I'm ready to take on the world today."

She leaned in close to whisper, "One day she will get bored of playing with you like this and you will have some peace."

"I might die of old age before then."

"It is probable," Luisa said, glancing to Alaqua, who was talking very loudly to everyone within earshot. "You know, if you were looking to quiet him, you might comment on why he opted for bronze instead of another metal," she said. "It's a touchy subject with him."

I nodded, stashing that thought in my arsenal. "Any other tips to get through the morning?"

"Try not to look too happy," Luisa said. "And perhaps she'll tire of making you miserable."

"Good morning, good morning," Ilara said, arriving with her usual fanfare of glory. Her loving gaze paused on me for a moment, the corners of her mouth twitching up. "I hope to find everyone in a good mood today."

"Of course, Your Majesty."

"Excited to be here, Your Majesty."

"Brynna?" Ilara asked, walking to her seat. "Are you feeling better?"

"Well enough, I suppose." I nodded to her. "Though I believe you would've dragged me from my bed if I'd asked to sleep in."

There was a tense silence in the room as Ilara stared me down. I waited for her to ask where I'd been the night before, or to comment why I'd left the castle through my window instead of the front door. But her face broke into a smile and she laughed.

"That is certainly true, my dear friend. I can't imagine eating any meal without your presence. It doesn't seem fitting."

It had been a gamble, but it felt natural. The day before, I'd been in a funk and miserable and Ilara might suspect if I woke up on the right side of the bed. Besides, I had a feeling Ilara liked me a little more feisty.

Ilara turned to the student with a glowing smile. "My dear Ilmi." The poor child froze in a mixture of fear and adoration. "Would you be so kind as to read the essay you wrote?"

The student jumped to her feet, her face bright red. "Yes, Your Majesty."

"Quiet, all," Ilara said to the group. "I want your full attention on this rising star."

The student plucked the essay from her back pocket and read in a quiet, shaky voice. "W-why Her Majesty, Queen Ilara, is the best queen in the history of time…"

As hard as it was not to react to this poor child waxing poetic about this queen, I managed to keep my face passive. Ilara's confidence would be her downfall, and the more she pumped herself up, the more vulnerable she'd be.

The student finished her essay and was awarded with polite

applause, the loudest coming from Ilara herself. She beckoned the child over to give her a hug and spoke soft praise to her. The child beamed, Ilara beamed, and everyone at the table cooed in adoration.

"As you all know, I'm an avid supporter of the arts here in Aunela," Ilara said as Ilmi took her seat. "And to that end, I will be attending a tour in the arts district today. I welcome you all to join me to see what I and the other artisans have put together over the past few months."

It was hard to hide my displeasure. I'd been out all night and wanted to catch a few hours' rest before another evening of vigilante work.

"Don't pout, Brynna," Ilara said. "You may see some familiar faces on this tour."

"Forcadelians?" I asked, my hopes raising.

"Oh, no." She shook her head. "But we've transported the art you read about in the books back in Forcadel. So now you'll be able to understand the brushstrokes." She smiled. "You see? Her Majesty is always thinking ahead."

Great. "Indeed, she is."

The gaggle of people, twenty strong, wandered southeast from the castle on foot. The arts district was some way from the castle, but the appearance of murals and more pottery signaled we'd arrived. The buildings themselves didn't have any architectural interest, which led me to believe Ilara had merely dropped a pin on the map and chosen this.

I was the only one who was unimpressed, as the rest of the artisans walked with open mouths and craned necks. They pointed out particular murals to each other, complimenting the artist if they were amongst them. Ilara listened to all the conversations while holding the hand of the student, who seemed exceptionally pleased just to be there.

"One day," Ilara said, looking behind her at the crowd following her. "This will be the epicenter for all arts across the continent. Everything from operas to plays to pottery and paintings."

I sincerely doubted that she was including any Forcadelian art in that statement, but I held my tongue.

The first stop of the day was a rather large art gallery—to my eyes, it looked like it had been a Forcadelian textile mill in its past life. The artisans had attempted to hide the Forcadelian crest through chipping at it, covering it with art, and even just hanging a curtain over it. But it protruded from the wall, and even Ilara couldn't ignore it, her dark eyes lingering on a painting hanging at an odd angle.

Every room had been dedicated to something. One room held a series of paintings that seemed to be the same sandy dune at different times of the day. Or perhaps it was different—it was hard to tell. Another room had vases of different sizes. And yet another was filled with paintings of a white flower.

"This gallery will be one of my favorite places to visit," Ilara said to the crowd, between their oohs and aahs. "I hope to have a steady rotation of new art as my court-sponsored artisans create it. Students such as Ilmi will be able to study from the masters of Severian artistry." She beamed at the young student, who wilted under the spotlight. "And people will come from every corner of the continent to see what we have created."

I walked up to a painting of a woman holding a starving baby, the anguish on her face palpable.

"What do you think?" Luisa asked, coming beside me.

"I think I'm ready to be done looking at paintings," I said with a grimace.

"You aren't a fan of art?"

"I was a fan for the first fifteen minutes. Now I'm just bored."

Luisa laughed, taking my arm. "These tours won't last. Her Majesty is simply orientating herself with the city and making her appearances where she's needed. One day, perhaps even next week, she will be pulled into the business of governing again, and we will be free to spend our days as we wish."

The idea of Ilara getting comfortable here was unnerving, but I buried that deep. "Whatever will we do when we don't have sculptures to gaze upon?"

"Perhaps we can take a tour of all the bakeries in the city," she said with a sly grin. "I'd love to introduce you to more Severian sweets."

I made a face, and she laughed.

"I think you'll acclimate to life here," Luisa said, continuing our walk around the gallery floor. "Once Her Majesty's vision comes to fruition, this will be an incredible place to live. One day, you'll be free to find your place amongst all the splendor."

"And what of my people?" I asked, a little softer.

"What of them? They're Ilara's people now."

"Then why haven't I seen them out amongst their supposed brethren?" I asked, stopping her. "If Forcadelians are supposed to break bread beside their Severian counterparts, if we're all New Severians now, why am I the only Forcadelian I see?"

She licked her lips, the first sign that she was holding something back. "Perhaps you just haven't noticed them."

"That's bullshit and you know it." I released her arm. "Luisa, please—"

"Her Majesty has a plan for all things," Luisa said, drawing back into the walled-off person I'd met back in Forcadel. "And you would do well to have some patience. I promise that they're being taken care of in the city and finding as much prosperity as their Severian brothers."

I huffed, not buying that for one second.

The art gallery took nearly all morning, and when I thought we might be able to go back to the castle, Ilara announced we would continue to another one. It was much smaller than the other, and perhaps a bit more avant-garde in the topics. There were more paintings of starving children and their grieving parents, some of which were incredibly grotesque.

"Does this not raise your hackles?" Ilara asked, coming to stand next to me. "Or does your concern for the plight of others only extend to those under your former flag?"

"I think you know me well enough to answer that," I said, casting her a scathing look, then softened and added, "Your Majesty."

Ilara's smile widened at my use of her title. "Is that a loneliness I hear in your voice? Have you grown tired of being the only one of your kind in a group?"

I caught Luisa's gaze, and she looked away quickly. When she'd had a chance to tell Ilara I'd asked about the Forcadelians, I had no clue.

"I would like to know what you did with thousands of Forcadelians, yes," I said. "Are they in the city?"

"They're being taken care of," she said, patting me on the arm. "And that is all you need to concern yourself with." She sized up the painting once more then brightened as she turned back to the crowd. "I believe I've had enough of this place for now. Let's continue to the next gallery."

Chapter Forty

I cursed my own impatience. Of course Ilara wouldn't tell me what I wanted to know. And now, thanks to my big mouth, she would probably be even more inclined to keep her secrets, or I'd have to give something up to earn the information.

There seemed to be an art gallery on every corner, and Ilara was determined to visit all of them. She didn't seem to tire of hearing how grateful the artisans were for her patronage, nor did she dismiss any of their platitudes. But even Luisa seemed to be growing weary of hearing the worship, although she did her best to hide it.

As we left the fourth gallery of the day, the red hue on the dust-covered streets quickened my pulse. Soon, I would be out on the rooftops, wearing a mask and helping my people. Another ship was sure to come in this evening, and Felix and I would be ready.

It was hard to keep a smile off my face at the thought, along with the irony of how much I was looking forward to him shadowing me. A far cry from my first days as princess of Forcadel, when his mere presence had been sandpaper on my soul.

"What are you smiling about?" Luisa asked, coming to stand next to me.

"Thinking about when I'll get to sit down again," I said. "And have a respite from all this…art."

"I believe the time is drawing nearer for dinner," Ilara called to the group. "Shall we continue toward the theater?"

It was hard to stifle a groan. "We aren't going back to the castle?"

"Not tonight, no," Ilara said. "I've been fed on artistry and creativity today and hunger for more of it. The Severian players have been hard at work on an opera telling tales of my conquering of Forcadel. It would break my heart to miss it."

There was a lavish dinner waiting for us at the theater. We were entertained by a trio of singers who were to perform later in the evening, and even I couldn't help but be moved by the sweet harmony of their voices. But in the back of my mind, the clock was ticking as the sun set. I'd expected some obstacle to getting out of the castle, perhaps a guard in the square below my window. Being stuck in this theater with Ilara was a completely different story.

The chair was hard and uncomfortable, and the dark room tugged at my eyelids. But with Luisa next to me and the young student on the other side, I forced myself awake.

As the music began, though, my resolve faded. It was a beautiful melody, although the opening number was a musical retelling of how Ilara had plotted to kill my father and brother, which was a bit jarring. Soon, I ignored the words themselves and let the song carry me toward sleep.

I dreamed of the desert, of a river of fire that had traveled all the way from Neveri. Felix and Katarine rode fiery horses toward Aunela, carrying diamond-encrusted swords and leaving a blazing trail behind them.

"Fire! Fire!"

The heat rose around my face, threatening to burn me, but I couldn't move.

Another scream, this one clearly in the real world. I jolted myself awake, blinking in the darkness and looking for the source of the flame. But the stage was perfectly fine, and I didn't smell a hint of smoke. Still, Luisa was on her feet, and the man who'd run in was covered in ash.

"Fire! There's a fire!"

"What in the Mother's name?" Ilara said, a snarl on her lips. "How dare you interrupt—"

"The Ilarian Gallery is on fire, my queen!"

Her eyes widened. "Well, what do you want me to do about it? Put it out! Put it out!"

It was a mad dash out of the theater, and the scent of burning trees filled the air. The gallery across the street—the large one that had been Ilara's crown jewel—was blazing. But not the building, that was made of stone...

"The paintings! We have to save the paintings!" Ilara screamed, pointing at a nearby soldier. "What are you standing around for? Go! Go!"

But there was nothing to be done. The fire was so massive that even the front door was impossible to breach. Soldiers came running carrying small buckets of water, but they did little to dispel the flames. I swallowed hard, resisting the urge to look up and see a dark figure above, but I knew he was there.

"We should go," Luisa said, putting her hand on Ilara's arm. "There's nothing more we can—"

Ilara shrugged off her attempts. "I will stay until this fire is out." She caught my gaze, and her eyes narrowed. "And whoever started it will feel my wrath."

"It clearly wasn't Brynna," Luisa said, attempting to console her queen again. "She's been with us all day."

Ilara shoved her away. "Get all these people out of my sight."

Luisa stayed with her queen, but the rest of the crowd wisely dispersed. I returned to the castle, making sure I was seen by the front guards before climbing out the way I'd done the night before. I made a quick stop to the center of the city, where I'd stashed a mask and cloak Felix had given me the night before, relieved to find them exactly where I'd left them.

I promised I'd meet Felix by the docks, and although it was much later than I'd said, I still found my general crouched on the edge of the roof, staring down into the darkness of the bay beyond.

"So, can I thank you for that fire?" I asked.

He jumped, as if he wasn't expecting me, then grinned over his shoulder. "Had to get you out of there somehow."

"Those poor artisans," I said, settling down on the rooftop next to him. "There were hundreds of paintings in there."

"They can paint more."

"Some of them are dead."

"Are you really that broken up about paintings?"

I exhaled. "Not really. I was about to lose my mind from boredom."

"How did today go?"

"Besides the destroyed art gallery, fine," I said. "No one noticed I left the group, and Ilara's convinced she's infallible. She did accuse me of starting the fire, but only briefly." I snorted. "Luckily, Luisa was there to knock some sense into her."

"Exactly as I planned," he said with a smile.

"What do you mean?"

"If we're going to cause trouble, we need to make sure none of it comes back to you." He turned to smile at me. "I'm going to start hitting Ilara's pressure points. The gallery was just the start of it. I'm going to go after the school—"

"Don't you dare," I said, poking him in the chest. "Those kids are innocent."

"I'm not going to hurt them. Just destroy the building. Without them in it." He made a face. "I'm thinking about how best to do that."

"Any movement on the docks tonight?" I asked, nodding toward the black bay beyond.

"A lot," Felix said. "Aithne and Malka already took a wagon each to the convent."

"No sign that anyone's noticed?" I asked.

"Not yet," he said. "It's pretty far out of the way."

"It's a lot of people, and more will be coming." I chewed my lip.

He covered my hand with his. "And more help will arrive."

I closed my eyes, reveling in the comfort of it. He leaned over and kissed me, perhaps intending it to be a short one, but I kept him there. This was my reward for the weeks of punishment, and I'd be damned if I let him go.

Unfortunately, our romance was interrupted by the sound of a wagon arriving at the docks.

"Duty calls, I guess," I said with a sigh.

"Do you want to do the honors, or should I?" Felix asked.

I gestured to him. "After you."

Chapter Forty-One

Felix dealt with the wagon driver quickly, and instead of leaving him on the street, as we'd done previously, Felix tied him up and stuck him in the back with the terrified Forcadelians.

"So we don't leave a witness," he said. "We've got a few of them locked in a room at the convent."

"Smart," I said, climbing aboard the carriage. "Shall we?"

"Actually," he pointed to the roofs, "you're up top. Make sure the roads are clear."

I narrowed my eyes. "You're taking to this vigilante stuff a little too well."

"Or you're just rusty," he said, flashing a cheery grin.

I returned with an offensive gesture before climbing up to the roofs. The road was clear as far as I could see, so I waved at him to continue. He replied with a whistle—*Confirmed*—and another pleased smirk before cracking the reins and goading the horse forward.

Our pace was slow, as I had to move ahead to ensure the coast was clear. Luckily, the horse's hooves on the sandy road made little sound, and except for the occasional squeak of the wheel and groan of the carriage, there were no other signs that we were on the move. Every so often, I whistled back to Felix to stop as a patrol crossed the street. And as we inched closer to the outer rim of the city, the Severian patrols dwindled to zero.

I glanced back at the red-rimmed sky behind me. Losing all that art would be a blow to Ilara, but no one had died, so I should've been happy about it. Especially as the distraction helped us get these Forcadelians out of harm's way.

Felix stopped the carriage as we reached the edge of the packed sand road, and I hurried over to help the Forcadelians out the back. There were more kids than the first time we'd done this, and I had no illusions that Ilara would take care of them as well as the Severian children.

"Do you see that collection of stars that look like a misshapen box?" I said, as I walked the final person to the edge of the city. A few of them squinted in the distance and nodded. "Walk in that direction for roughly half an hour until you find it. There's food and water and beds for all you."

"At least food and water," Felix said. "And you should go with them."

"I will, as soon as I help you dispose of this carriage," I replied, walking back to him. "We can't just leave it here."

"I'll take care of it," Felix said. "We've got a couple of them stashed around the city in case we need them. Nowhere close to here, though."

"Good thinking," I said.

"You seem continually surprised that I have good ideas lately," he said, taking the horse by the reins and leading it in a large circle to head back to the city. "I can't tell if I should be insulted by that."

"Just go," I said with a smile. "And be careful."

My group of Forcadelians hadn't gotten very far, so I hurried to the front to lead them. A young mother had two children with her, so I took one of the younger kids on my back. It made the walk over the sand that much more difficult, but I didn't mind.

A cry of joy echoed from behind me when the convent came into view. When we reached the front door, the sentries opened both doors, bowing to me.

"Welcome back, Your Majesty," one said. "And welcome, brothers and sisters."

The church was still as magnificent as ever, except now it was absolutely filled with people. They sat in pews and on the floor, many of them eating small pieces of fruit or bread. Felix's quip about them having food but not beds made a lot more sense.

"Her Majesty has arrived!" called a young boy, jumping to his feet.

A hush descended over the room as every eye turned on me, drinking me in as if I were the most amazing thing they'd ever seen.

"My queen."

"Your Majesty."

One by one, they rose and bowed their heads to me, some of them hinging at the hip to bow fully. Two ladies curtseyed with their makeshift skirts.

"I'm glad you've all found your way here," I said, smiling. "We'll keep adding to your numbers, so I thank everyone for being patient with us. I wish that we were having this greeting back in Forcadel, but I'm thankful to see all you just the same."

"What can we do to help?" one of the ladies asked.

"Right now, the most helpful thing is to stay here, out of sight," I said. "We're undertaking a delicate operation to move even more soldiers into the city, and the last thing we need is for Ilara to find out about it." I smiled at a young girl, who was staring up at me with wide eyes. "Take care of each other, and listen to General Llobrega and his soldiers." I nodded. "We will survive this, and we will see our homeland again."

They cheered, and I winced at the sound, hoping that it didn't travel.

"You really have taken to this queen role."

I looked up at the familiar voice, finding Kieran leaning against the wall, something like pride on his face. He had a large scar on his cheek that was new, but his eyes were as mischievous as ever.

"I heard you brought Felix here," I said. "Where's the rest of your crew?"

"Anchored near the mouth of the bay to receive the Kulkan warships when they arrive," he said. "I've just come ashore to provide an update to your dear General Llobrega, as he asked, and to grab some supplies for my ship." He tilted his head in my direction. "My crew send their love."

"I'm sure Sarala isn't counted in that number."

He winced and averted his gaze for a moment before resuming his cavalier mask.

I nodded to the mark on his cheek. "Nice scar."

"A mooring hit me the wrong way."

"You're usually pretty good at ducking."

"I was distracted." He smiled tightly. "Would it be too bold to ask for forgiveness? I did deliver your general and his vigilantes safe and sound."

"Tell me what happened to Sarala," I said softly.

"She decided she'd had enough of my nonsense."

"Kieran," I said with a look. "What did he do to her?"

He exhaled, looking at the floor. "Drowned her, slowly." He swallowed hard. "Made me watch."

My heart seized in my chest, and I balled my fist in fury. "He'll suffer a similar fate if he hasn't already. I'm sorry that—"

"We all accepted the choices that we made," he said. "Sarala actually respected you."

"No, she didn't. She called me a war-mongering princess," I said. "Took me a long time to shake that from my mind."

"Perhaps she saw the error of her ways, especially as Ilara's hooks sank deeper and deeper into the city. We wouldn't be here if we didn't believe in what you were trying to do."

"I'm sorry she was caught up in this," I said softly. "Even if she did have a change of heart."

"I doubt she'll be the last." He straightened. "It's getting late. Perhaps it's time to get you back to the castle." He cracked a grin as he nodded over my shoulder. "I'd take you myself, but then your general wouldn't have the pleasure of giving you that goodnight kiss he's so looking forward to."

I turned to find Felix standing there, scrutinizing Kieran with something like jealousy. But he merely cleared his throat and held out his hand. "It's getting late, Brynn. I don't want Ilara noticing you're gone."

Felix and I headed out immediately, walking the now-familiar path back to the old part of the city before taking to the rooftops. My short nap earlier had been barely enough to stave off the exhaustion, and staying out all night was starting to catch up with me.

But even as sleep threatened to overtake me, I couldn't help but ask Felix to sit on a roof with me and watch the stars. Our moments together had been so few and far between, and if I could have just a breath with him, it would be enough to sweeten my dreams for the next decade.

"Five minutes," he said, wagging his finger at me. "Then you're back to bed."

"If only you could go with me," I said, smiling up at him. "Unfair."

He plopped down on the rooftop and tugged me down next to him. I curled up under his chin, inhaling his scent and taking this moment to be truly happy. The gallery fire was still visible from here, a reminder of the mood I'd find at the breakfast table. I just prayed Ilara didn't take it out on an innocent.

"I hope we hear news from Katarine soon," he whispered, rubbing my back. "Or from Jax."

"We should keep up the pressure in the meantime," I said. "Which means...I may not be able to come out tomorrow night. More ships seem to be arriving every night, and sooner or later, Ilara's guards are going to notice people aren't showing up where they need to be. She's going to cast blame on me, and I need to have a solid alibi, like I did tonight with that fire."

"Then it's a good thing we have more hands to cause trouble with," he replied. "Where should we start?"

"The art gallery was a nice target, but we should vary our efforts." I told him of all the different merchants who'd been in attendance for dinner the past few nights, and gave him some ideas of how he might disrupt their operations.

He nodded, listening intently. "I'll try to do you proud." He cracked a smile. "I never did tell you how I got Ammon to cough up those ships, did I?"

"He didn't adhere to the terms of our bargain?" I feigned surprise. "I'm aghast."

"We had some knockout powder, took over one of the ships, and moved it out into the open bay. Then we took another, empty cargo ship and put it in its place. Then..."

"You set it on fire," I said with a shake of my head. "Felix Llobrega, that's my move."

"And I made sure to give you all the credit." He flashed a grin and it was hard to resist the urge to kiss it off him.

But the feeling was fleeting as I turned back out to the open bay. "Even with the Forcadelian soldiers onboard, how can we be sure the Kulkans won't mutiny and turn around?"

"I left Aline in charge," he said. "And I have faith in her. Just like I have faith in you. And in us."

My gaze dropped to our joined hands, then back up, a smile teasing the corners of my lips. "Faith in us, huh?"

"In you, mostly," he said, leaning toward me. "And the rest of us will simply follow your lead."

"Nice to be followed again, I suppose."

"What can I say? I like the view."

He moved to kiss me, but I was faster, wrapping my hand around the base of his skull and curling my fingers in his short hair. Warmth shot from my mouth to every inch of my body, and I pulled his body close to mine, taking this moment and thanking the Mother for it.

Chapter Forty-Two

Felix

"If we move too quickly, Brynna thinks Ilara will take drastic measures to stop it," I said to Malka and Aithne as we convened on a roof near the docks as dawn broke over the bay. "We need to focus on trouble that's easily explainable, and most importantly, Brynna won't be held responsible."

"We'll need to move in the day, then," Aithne said.

"I say we snag a few carriages," Malka said. "The more food we can send up to the Forcadelians at the convent, the better."

"I don't know if that's going to be big enough," I said. "It could take a few days for Ilara to notice that one wagon is missing —or two. We need to move a little quicker."

They shared a look. "Then let us handle the wagons," Aithne said. "And you can find some other way to cause trouble. This morning, we had precious little bread to feed those who were there, and if more people arrive tonight…"

I nodded. "Make it happen. And be careful you aren't seen."

They saluted and climbed off the rooftop. I turned my

attention to the open bay beyond, squinting to look for Kieran's ship bobbling off the coast, even though it was too far away to be spotted. The food would soon be the least of our problems; we'd run out of space if things kept up at this pace. I prayed to the Mother that Aline would hurry.

I headed toward the arts district, as that seemed the perfect way to inflict damage without hurting anyone. But it was teeming with Severian guards, and they were quick to notice a Forcadelian amongst them.

"Are you lost?" a Severian guard said, stopping me.

"I don't think so," I replied. "Why?"

"Normally all you Forcadelians have somewhere to go when you get off the boat," he said.

"I'm just a sailor," I said, holding up my hands. "Taking a tour before we leave for Forcadel."

"Ain't nothing to see here," he said, taking a step toward me. "Now get lost."

I made like I was heading back to the docks, but instead did a loop through an alley and took a different street. But I was stopped three more times by Severian guards, all of whom bought my story about being a sailor. After the last guard asked if I needed an escort back to the docks, I took to the rooftops. As I came onto the main drag, I spotted the large building situated on the bay that might just do. Brynna had said Ilara had spoken highly of the school (but then again, she'd spoken highly of everything else, too). It would be tricky; the children inside were innocent and Brynna had been clear that nothing should happen to them.

The four-story building was definitely a Forcadelian structure in its former life, but the Severians had made sure to hide any sign of it. Inside the glass windows, uniformed children sat in classrooms, blissfully unaware of any impending trouble.

Taking care to avoid notice, I hopped to the next roof, then the next one, keeping the building in my view as I searched for a way to cause trouble without inflicting damage to the people inside.

The statue of Ilara in the courtyard…that might work. As would the small pouch of ond on my belt.

The explosion was quick and contained, and it took mere minutes for word to spread in the school, and perhaps half an hour before Ilara arrived in a carriage. My heart pounded at the sight of Ilara, fire in my veins. She looked much the same as when I'd bowed to her, except for the twisted snarl on her lips. She was livid, and it gave me immense pleasure to know I'd been the cause of it.

The queen spoke in low tones to the headmistress while her gaggle slowly joined her, having walked on foot instead of the carriage. Brynna was amongst them, her hands were balled at her side and her face completely passive. But beneath her calm veneer, there was the slightest hint of amusement. Her gaze shot to the rooftop for the briefest of moments before returning to the Severian woman beside her.

"It just…spontaneously combusted," the headmistress said, her voice carrying to my perch in a nearby building. "I don't know any more than that."

Ilara's gaze went to the rooftops, fire in her eyes. "I want to know who did this. Who do we have available, Luisa?"

The Severian woman with whom Brynna'd been speaking with stepped forward. "Most of our soldiers are investigating the arts district, as per your instructions."

"Then pull one or two of them off it and have them investigate this instead," Ilara said, her tone clipped. "And find out who in the Mother's name is causing trouble in the city." As she spoke, her gaze landed on Brynna. "Make them pay for what they've done."

"I couldn't agree more," Brynna replied with her usual sarcastic air. "You've clearly got someone out to destroy art in your city. It must be your top priority."

My chest seized at her tone—we were supposed to keep Ilara from suspecting Brynna—but the queen said nothing about it, barking orders to the headmistress and the Severian woman before marching back to her carriage.

Brynna wisely didn't make an appearance in the city that night. I still loitered around our meeting spot, just in case. The Severian guards had become more plentiful during the day, and now, at night, they seemed to be on every street.

A whistle echoed behind me, and I turned as two figures shimmied up to the rooftop.

"How'd it go today?" I asked Malka and Aithne.

"We couldn't find a wagon," Aithne said. "And even if we could, we wouldn't have been able to snatch it. The soldiers are too thick in the city. We'd better hope no Forcadelians arrive tonight."

"But the ones we have need food," I said, turning back to the castle. "What we have left isn't enough to feed them tomorrow."

They shared a look. "When are the Kulkans supposed to arrive?" Aithne asked.

"Any day now," I said, anxiety twisting in my chest. I couldn't do anything about Aline and the Kulkan ships, but perhaps I could do something about feeding the convent. "Brynna says Ilara has a grand spread every morning and evening for her guests—nearly twenty at the table. If we can find where she's storing her food, we may be able to take some of it."

With my two shadows following me, we descended to the street and began a wide circle around the castle grounds. It was clearly still under construction, so it made sense that some of the more ancillary needs would be kept in nearby buildings. My guess was, Ilara's food stores were as well.

Ilara clearly wasn't concerned about security, because besides a smattering of guards patrolling the perimeter and two at the front door, the castle was largely undefended. Based on the numbers of soldiers in the city, perhaps she'd thought her own castle wouldn't be much of a target. Her complacency would be her downfall.

"What are we looking for?" Aithne asked.

"Food was kept near the castle in Forcadel," I said, peering into the dark window of a nearby building. "Close to the kitchen door, for obvious reasons. They had drying meat, fruit, flour—all of it. I'm sure Ilara's got something similar. She couldn't be pulling together these massive dinners otherwise."

"Where's the food coming from?" Malka asked, rubbing a window to remove some of the dust before looking through it.

"Forcadel, probably," I said. "She hasn't gotten anything from Neshua, and she won't, as far as I know."

Though that might've changed since we took the Kulkan ships without his permission, but that was a concern for another day. Kulka was at least a month's journey from here over a treacherous ocean.

"Sir," Aithne called, waving me over as she peered through a window. "There are a lot of crates in here. This might be what we're looking for."

Malka picked the lock on the large doors while Aithne and I kept watch for Severian guards. When Malka cracked open the door, the three of us slipped inside. The faint scent of overripe fruit hung in the air, and I smiled at my two vigilantes.

"Malka, find us something to transport this," I said. "We'll leave it in the crates; it won't be as obvious inside the city."

"And we're just going to drive a carriage through the city while it's swarming with guards?" Aithne asked.

"General, I have to agree with Aithne," Malka said, apologetically. "It's one thing for the three of us to sneak around, but the soldiers will definitely hear a wagon. The last thing we want is for them to see where we're going."

"Then we'll just have to cause another distraction," I said.

"And how will we keep Ilara from finding out we've taken her food?"

I smiled, glancing at the bag of flour on the floor. "Empty this place. Take everything we can fit on the wagon and send it up to the convent. We're going to hit Ilara where she hurts tonight." I grinned. "And burn this place to the ground."

Chapter Forty-Three

Katarine

After so many weeks of sitting around and waiting, the gears of war were finally beginning to move for us. A small cadre of soldiers had left days ago and probably reached the city. I prayed Elisha would find Felix and impart all the information we'd gleaned so far.

Letting her go had seemed right in the context of the wolf and the look on the young girl's face, but as the days passed, I began to second-guess myself. True, Brynna had asked me to keep her out of things, even though the child was dead set on inserting herself. But even my wife had seemed at peace with this decision.

"She will be fine," Beata said, holding me tight as I confessed my fears to her. "Jarrah said the Mother would look after her."

Luard and I readied a plan of attack to move our forces. We'd had precious few defections from Mark's soldiers at the gate, but Luard was confident that with enough time, they'd see reason and join us. The problem was, we didn't have that much time to spare.

Even still, our forces numbered over one hundred Forcadelians and about as many of Niemenian soldiers. Ariadna had provided riverboats laden with weapons and supplies, as well as several smaller boats that could be used to ferry people back and forth under cover of darkness. But based on what our scouts had said as they walked the length of the river, it would be a treacherous journey for the largest ships.

"We don't have a choice," Luard said. "We could move the dam to flow the river back toward Forcadel, but that's a week on the Ash river, then another two weeks on the open ocean. If we go on the river, we're looking at maybe two weeks at most."

"We're already far behind schedule," I replied, shaking my head. "We should've been in position weeks ago." I put my hands on my hips, looking out onto the bay. "We'll move in phases. Send the smaller ships first. They'll be better able to infiltrate the city and bring back valuable information."

"You?" Luard sat up.

I nodded. "I can hide myself well enough, but I want eyes on the city before the rest of our forces arrive."

"You don't trust Joella?"

"Of course I trust Joella, but—"

"But you just want to see your precious Elisha again." The teasing smile on his lips did little to assuage my annoyance. "She's fine. Based on the speed of the river, I'm sure they've already made it."

"Hence my concern," I muttered.

"If I know Elisha, she'll be able to slip through the crowds and find someone of interest to bring back before anyone notices she's missing."

"I don't like not knowing," I said, gazing out the window to where the soldiers were packing the river boats. "I'll go with the first ship."

"I hate to break it to you, my dear sister, but anyone with eyes could name you as a daughter of our country. Even though I know your heart feels otherwise." He sat back. "Plus, your wife might have something to say about this."

I narrowed my eyes at him, seeing through his attempts at making me feel guilty. "Beata knows my role is important and what I must do. She didn't say one word about Elisha leaving with Joella."

"And what did she say when you told her your plan?"

I cleared my throat. "I haven't told her yet."

"Lying to your wife is a nasty habit, dear sister," Luard said. "I wouldn't recommend it."

"I'm not lying, I just…haven't had a chance." My cheeks warmed, and I turned away from him so he wouldn't notice and chastise me more. "Tell the soldiers to prepare to leave at first light. We've wasted enough time in Skorsa, and our queen needs us."

I took the long route home, just to avoid the inevitable. But before I knew it, I was standing in front of our home, and could delay it no longer. I ascended the steps and pushed open the door, hearing the children in the kitchen. I followed the sound, grabbing a mask from the entry table and wrapping it around my mouth. Our dining room had been transformed into an assembly of sorts, with the younger children filling bags as quickly as the other children could pulverize the flowers and Sorrell and Beata could sew. Yet again, I hoped Lord Garwood's husband would forgive the mess we'd made in their summer home.

"They've already come by to take three crates today," Beata said, her cheeks ruddy beneath her mask. Her brown eyes were lit up with excitement and pride. "They're working so hard."

"They are, indeed." I slipped my hand through hers. "Can I have a moment with you?"

She followed me to my makeshift office where we both pulled our masks off. Beata ran a hand along her sweaty forehead, huffing.

"I'm grateful to have that thing off. It's hot."

"Bea—"

"You're leaving in the morning for Aunela," she said, a smile teasing at the corners of her mouth. "I know."

"How?" I hadn't mentioned it yet, other than to indicate that the soldiers were preparing.

"Because you're my wife, and I know you." Beata took my hands in hers. "You've barely slept a wink since Elisha left, and I know you won't rest easy until you've got your hand on her shoulder again."

I blew air between my lips. "I suppose I'm a little easy to read these days."

"I'm worried about her, too," Beata said. "And thankful none of the other children seem inspired by the same desire to run head first into danger."

"You will stay here, won't you?" I asked quietly, hoping she wasn't planning on going with me.

"We'll have our hands full getting this hyblatha ready. Luard's asked me to make sure there's a full crate with every ship. I'm not sure what he's planning to do once you're in Aunela, but—"

"Neither of us know what to expect." I shook my head. "And I will stay out of the fighting, as much as I can."

"You'll be right where Elisha is," Beata said. "Which will be in the middle of things."

I snorted, shaking my head. "How has this child caused me to lose all my wits so suddenly? She is clearly capable, and yet..."

"Because you care very much for her," Beata said. "Like it or not, we've...well, we've become a little family here. And it's hard to let any of our children do anything remotely dangerous."

"They will have to go back to their parents," I said softly.

"They have no parents to go back to," Beata replied, sitting next to me. "And we can give them a life that they never could've dreamed of. I know you want them to stay."

I nodded. "I doubt Elisha feels the same way."

"She came home, didn't she?" Beata asked. "I think she might surprise you. But first, I think she's waiting for you to tell her it's okay." She nudged me. "Your heart is still a fortress sometimes, my love."

I covered her hand with mine and kissed her cheek. "Then it's a good thing I have you to remind me to open it from time to time."

At first light, Beata and the children accompanied me down to the docks. My wife's hand was firm in mine as we walked, giving me the impression she might not let me go when the moment came. Her eyes misted with unshed tears and her voice was thick when she spoke to the children. But she kept herself together, especially as we neared the docks. Most of the Forcadelian soldiers were already onboard, the final few stragglers carrying bags of supplies.

"Children," she said. "You each have things to give to Lady Katarine."

One by one, they approached with a trinket or item. Sorrell gave me a small metal figurine that looked more like a disfigured screw, but she told me it was her favorite horse, and it had been good luck. Ronja and Hershel each gave me a bag of tinneum and told me to chew it when I felt scared or sad. Paca handed me a compass, one that she said she'd made herself. And little Gerda handed me a small fistful of flowers.

"Thank you," I said, beaming down at them. "I will treasure all of these."

"Hope you have goodies for your Uncle Luard, too." My brother stomped down the dock, holding a soldier's bag on his shoulder which he dropped unceremoniously. "Or else I'm going to get my feelings hurt."

"I didn't think you'd be going with her," Beata said, looking at me curiously.

"He's not," I said. "We agreed you would stay behind and lead the rest of the troops."

"Ivan has graciously accepted that role," he said. "And Ari's favorite general is on his way down. I'm sure they'll have plenty of help moving the soldiers down this treacherous river."

"What happened to all that talk about being instantly recognizable as Niemen's child?" I asked, tilting my head to the side.

"I'm just here to make sure *you* aren't recognized," he said, flashing a grin as he held a small bag. "You'll still be the palest person in hundreds of miles, but at least your hair won't stand out."

"Your Highness, Lady Katarine." A Forcadelian soldier appeared on the edge of the dock. "We're ready to depart."

Luard reached down and picked up his bag—perhaps the first time I'd ever seen him carry his own things. But he wore a cheery smile, introducing himself to all onboard as he hopped onto the ship.

"I suppose this is it," Beata whispered, a tear leaking down her cheek. "You promise you'll—"

"I will," I said, leaning down to kiss her. "And I will see the seven of you in a few weeks."

"I'm counting the days," she said, taking a step back to put her hand on two of the children's shoulders. "Be careful."

I continued onto the ship, handing my bag to a nearby soldier before joining Luard at the helm. He was conferring with the captain, who was expressing concern about the river's speed and unknown terrain.

"Then we will go slowly," Luard said. "Right, sister?"

"Right," I said, finding my wife and the children on the docks again. "Pull anchor."

Chapter Forty-Four

It was a curious thing to be a witness to trouble instead of causing it. But as I'd been in Ilara's sights during the days and evenings, she had no evidence to convict me of the statue destruction, though she surely tried. Luisa, thankfully, kept a level head, and reminded the queen that I couldn't possibly be in two places at once. But it did little to dispel Ilara's anger.

But I made no move to leave the night before, not when Ilara's suspicions were already raised. And when I came to the breakfast table, I kept myself as morose and defeated as everyone else at the table.

"Such a shame," I said to Luisa. "The statue—"

"Don't look too pleased, Brynna," she replied, but there was a half-smile on her lips. "Ilara's in another mood this morning."

"Oh? What happened?"

She shook her head. "Another one of our food stores caught fire last night. Everything...weeks' worth of food shipments...

reduced to ash."

My mouth fell open. "What?"

"I can't imagine who would've done such a thing," she said with a sigh. "Just please keep your thoughts to yourself, if you have any."

When the queen arrived, she seemed the epitome of calm—which concerned me even more. She took her seat at the front of the table and lorded over conversations, not giving me a second glance. Even Luisa seemed to notice the change of attitude, but she silently sliced off the mold on her berry and pushed it to the other side of the plate.

"Hopefully, we'll be receiving another shipment from Forcadel," she said, gazing sadly at what was left of the fruit. "I can't believe they destroyed an entire room full of food. What a waste."

"It must be vandals," I said.

"But who would want to hurt this beautiful place?" Luisa said. "Severians are happy to be here in Aunela. Life is much better than it was in the desert. Why would anyone want to upend what we've done?"

The obvious answer was that not everyone was pleased with their new lives, but that would put the blame squarely on the shoulders of the Forcadelians. And considering I *still* hadn't seen hide nor hair of my countryman, save those I'd taken from the ships, I didn't want to attract any focus to them until I did.

"Dear Brynna," Ilara said, catching my attention for the first time during the meal. "Would you mind?"

"Mind...?" I shared a glance with Luisa, who also clearly hadn't been listening.

"I was just telling Hellis that I've been too wrapped up in dealing with these recent bouts of destruction in my city," she said, nodding to the Severian captain next to her. "And I could use an hour or two in the sparring ring."

I had a bad feeling that Ilara had been keeping up with her training during our time here, and I had not. But despite my reservations, I nodded. "It would be my honor."

Ilara's sparring room was similar to the one back in Forcadel, and based on the weapons lying around, she'd already made good use of it. Unfortunately, the room was also big enough for the gaggle of artisans and merchants to join us. I had to keep this light and let her win. That was what she wanted, after all.

Ilara met me in the center of the room, testing the weight of her sword. "You've had bags under your eyes recently," she said, tying her hair back. "Burning the midnight oil?"

"Training," I said, plucking a pair of wooden knives from the weapons trunk. "Since I don't want you to embarrass me again."

She came for me first, and I easily blocked it. But my reaction was a hair slower than usual, and my arms weaker than they'd been the last time we sparred. I only hoped hers were as well.

"Oh, this won't do," she said with a soft tut. "I need a challenge today, Brynna. I do hope you'll be up to the task. I've had a terrible few days and need a workout."

I narrowed my eyes at her, stepping back to adjust the knives in my hand. "I'm sorry about your gallery," I said. "And the other art that's been destroyed lately."

"I'm sure you are."

She swept her leg out and knocked me over, and I only just barely rolled out of the way of her sword tip, leaving one of my knives behind. The other I gripped in my right hand, crouching and glaring at her.

"You're trying to distract me from your weakness," she said, smiling. "It won't work. I can tell your strength has faded while you've been eating from my table and enjoying the spoils of war."

I couldn't argue with her there. "So? Why not get on with

defeating me?"

"I told you," she said, lowering her sword, "I'm in need of swordplay, and you're the only person halfway decent in this city." Her eyes lit up as she smiled at me. "What if we have a little wager on the fight? Something to goad you to actually fight me instead of playing around." She turned to the group, who'd been watching patiently. "After all, we have an audience."

I licked my lips, praying for guidance from the Mother. I certainly didn't feel up to giving it my all, nor was I sure I would win if I did. But there was one thing I needed from the queen.

"Fine," I said. "If I win, I want you to take me to where you've stashed all the Forcadelians you've moved out of my city."

In the corner, Luisa stiffened, but Ilara simply smiled as she walked to a different weapons trunk and opened the latch. "I had a feeling you'd ask about that. Very well, if you win this bout, I'll take you to see your brethren."

"And if I don't?"

"Then you'll agree to pay attention to every taunt, every insult, and every reminder of your epic failures at every meal until you die." She batted her eyes and smiled as she tossed a pair of knives at my feet. "Which I hope isn't for a long, *long* time."

I stared at the weapons—they were mine. I'd been wearing them the day I'd been captured. They'd been sharpened and cleaned, the handles oiled with care. Ilara had been preparing for this fight for some time—she wanted to defeat me with my own weapons.

But I wasn't going to let that happen.

"Deal."

I ran for her, drawing from every single lesson Celia's trainers had taught me. No longer tired or weak, I swung the knives in my hand and went for her—for real this time. I was nearly faster than her, but she caught me just in time.

"This is the woman I've been desperate to fight," Ilara said, struggling against me. "I want you to fully submit to me."

Instead of responding, I slashed, drawing blood from her cheek. "Do you ever shut up?"

She gasped, taking a step back and clutching her cheek. Behind her, two soldiers moved to intervene, but she held up her hand. "Let's see what you can really do."

Our blades met again, then again, and again. I couldn't find an angle to thrust my blade into her stomach—

A voice echoed in my mind, reminding me that I shouldn't win too quickly. I had a larger plan in mind, and if I showed her I could defeat her easily now, she might take that as an opportunity to kill me. I just needed to win a little.

Right, left, center. My arms were beginning to shake from the exertion, but I dug deep and found strength. But still, we were evenly matched. No matter how quickly I drew my blade to hers, she met me with the same ferocity. Had she been holding back as much as I had?

"You look tired," she whispered.

"Not even close," I said, sweat dripping from my nose. "I could do this all day."

She grinned. "You're stubborn as hell, Brynna. And I consider it an honor that I've bested you yet again."

My hand clenched around the knife. "You haven't bested me. Not even close."

I did what I could, but I was slowing down. Anger surged at my weakness, and I did my best to channel it.

But one well-placed knock of her blade against mine and my knife went flying from my hand. Before I could even blink, her sword came around to my neck, a hair's breadth from slicing through it.

"Yield?" Ilara asked, her eyes bright with triumph.

I clenched my jaw, but I could do nothing but admit defeat. "Yield."

Applause broke out from the audience, as well as some cheers for the queen. I stuffed my knives back in my belt and breathed through my anger and annoyance. There was some part of me that swore I could've won, had the situation been different. But my body ached from the effort. Ilara had been training all this time, and I'd allowed myself to become complacent. That would end tonight.

"You see, Brynna? Life is so much easier when you just do what I tell you," Ilara said, grinning at me. "And as a show of good faith, I will still take you to visit your Forcadelian brethren." Amusement flashed her eyes. "If you can't sleep, I suggest practicing your swordplay. I'll need you to be wide awake and focused at dinner when I regale the audience with your failures."

Oh, it was hard to nod my head, but I did. A bet was a bet, after all, and I was still getting what I wanted. But from the look on Ilara's face, my mealtimes were going to be nothing short of torture.

The audience politely clapped as their queen faced them, even giving them something of a bow. The sweat that stuck my shirt to my back mocked me, and I turned away to give myself a moment to collect my thoughts.

"Luisa, dear," Ilara said, taking a towel and patting her skin. "Please prepare a carriage for the three of us. We'll be visiting the varo mines today."

"Varo mines," I murmured, catching Luisa's concerned gaze. "What varo mines?"

"Your Majesty," Luisa said, keeping her voice low as she walked up to her. "I'm not sure that's the best idea. The mines are a long trip, and it's already—"

"I think I know my own lands, Luisa," Ilara said, narrowing her eyes.

Luisa shrank into herself, perhaps sensing that she'd strayed too close to the line. "Yes, Your Majesty. I will prepare the carriage at once."

She hurried from the room, and Ilara turned back to me, a bright smile on her face. "I'm sure this loss hurts, dear friend. But you will see many of your brethren today, and I hope it puts your heart at ease. Seeing your joy will help soothe my heart after the loss of our art gallery."

Dread dropped the bottom of my stomach as I looked into her merciless eyes. There was no mistaking the agony still there, or how much she wanted me to feel the same. I had a bad feeling that whatever I was going to witness, I would end the day as furious as the queen.

Chapter Forty-Five

Luisa worked quickly, because by the time Ilara and I made our way to the front of the castle, she was already waiting with a carriage. She hadn't lost the look of concern on her face, but she said nothing except to greet Ilara as the queen climbed into the coach. I followed, and Luisa made the third in what was a fairly tight squeeze. Luisa's gaze was fixed outside the window, and her unreadable expression gave nothing away.

The roads were rough, bouncing us all over the place, but Ilara didn't seem to mind. She'd brought a book with her and deftly turned the pages even as Luisa and I were jostled around.

Based on the direction of the sun overhead, we were heading due east from the castle. We'd left the inner city where buildings of all sizes were crammed next to one another. Now the desert was visible just beyond the houses along this main road, the wind whipping over the dunes and shifting them.

Neither of us said a thing, although I was dying to see if Ilara would cough up more cryptic clues about what she was bringing me to see. But she kept her thoughts to herself, even as the carriage slowed to a stop.

"My queen, we've reached the end of the road," the coachman said, opening the door. "We will have to continue on horseback."

"But isn't there only one horse?" I asked.

"Indeed, there is," Luisa said with a low sigh as she plucked an umbrella from beneath the seat.

While Luisa held aloft the shade over Ilara, the coachman unhooked the horse and readied a saddle. We were far from the ocean breezes, which at least gave some respite. When the man finished, Ilara climbed onto the horse.

"Come now," she said over her shoulder. "It will take us some time to get there."

Luisa marched forward onto the sand, and I followed suit, keeping pace with her as best I could. But as Ilara's horse moved ahead, I slowed my gait just enough for me to attempt a private conversation with Luisa.

"Can you give me some hint about where we're going?" I asked. "We can't possibly be going to that encampment in the middle of the desert."

"No, this is a mine nearer to the city, but..." She chewed her lip. "Her Majesty was clear that you were to be kept in the dark."

I blinked. "Kept in the..."

"You aren't going to like what you see, Brynna," Luisa said, a drip of sweat falling down her temple. "And you must prepare yourself for that."

"All the more reason to go," I said, worry blossoming in my chest. "I may not be their queen, but they're still my people. And if they're in trouble—"

"What would you do if they are?" Luisa asked.

"I don't know," I said. "Something."

"In some cases, it may be best to let sleeping dogs lie." She glanced at Ilara, who was now at least ten feet ahead of us. "I can't protect you from Ilara, and I would be most aggrieved if what you saw today pushed you over the edge."

"I can't imagine anything pushing me over the edge," I said, shaking my head. But the worry was growing. "Nor can I imagine that I alone can do anything to stop it."

"Girls," Ilara called, now twenty feet ahead of us. "Hurry up. I'd hate to lose you."

"I seem to recall hearing tales of the things you did as a single person," Luisa said, picking up her pace. "I wouldn't bet against you."

Luisa and I walked in silence for the rest of the way, my mind spinning with what she'd told me and clouded by exhaustion and the sun overhead. She'd said she respected me for saving her life on the river, and she'd certainly been more friendly, but that could all be a ruse. She could've been trying to get me to talk of my plans, or the plans of others. I still didn't trust her, even though I'd begun to enjoy her company.

As the sun bore down on the back of my neck, a blotch appeared on the horizon. At first, I thought it was my eyes playing tricks on me, but as we headed steadily in that direction, the dark spot turned into a smokestack and scaffolding. There was a scent in the air—metallic, acrid, burning. It made my stomach churn uncomfortably.

I'd hoped there would be some respite from the harsh sun when we arrived, but there was none. A cadre of Severian soldiers were waiting with tight smiles on their faces.

"Your Majesty," the lieutenant said, bowing at the hip. "It's an honor to have you here."

"I'm glad to be here," she said. "Show me what you've done."

I wasn't sure what to expect, but it didn't look like a mine. It reminded me of the Severian farmers we'd come across while we'd been on the river, although the holes out across the desert seemed much deeper than the ones the Severians had dug. Every so often, figures would emerge from below with buckets held on sticks that sat on their shoulders, and trudge through the desert to the main area, where they'd dump the mined varo into a large container on the ground.

From there, the container seemed to be transported via a rope from the ground to the scaffolding overhead. Then it was moved to another pole sticking out of the ground, then another, then another until it disappeared over a dune to the south.

"How much output are you getting per day?" Ilara asked.

"We've found a very productive vein over there," the lieutenant replied. "Nearly a whole wagonful by sundown." He pointed to the distance, where more towers could be seen. "We've got ten more of these under construction."

"They were under construction two weeks ago," Ilara said with a dangerous tone. "Why are they not completed?"

The soldier swallowed. "I was going to ask Her Majesty if she could spare more workers."

"More?" Ilara blanched. "What happened to the hundreds that have been pouring into the city?"

Shit. I forced myself to watch the conversation, as if I knew nothing about it.

"We haven't seen a new shipment of workers in some time," he said.

"Huh," Ilara said. "Luisa—"

"I will ask," she said, stepping forward. "It's possible they were sent somewhere else by mistake."

"Where could they have gone?" I asked. "Surely there isn't a closer varo mine."

"No, this is the only one," Ilara said, her gaze boring into me. "But we are, of course, constructing the new river to connect

Aunela to Kulka. It's possible that someone's been sending people there. I will confer with the foreman at dinner tonight and see if he can look into it for me."

Something loud echoed from the distance, and I would've thanked the Mother for the distraction, except for the pit of dread in my stomach.

"What was that?" Ilara asked.

"Mine collapse, probably," the soldier said.

"Wait—Collapse?" I took a step forward. "Like the ones we saw out in the desert? Like those collapses? The ones that kill people?"

"Which is why I've asked Her Majesty to provide us with more people. We're losing two or three per day—"

"You're losing two or three people per day?" I asked, my heart seizing.

"No," he cast me a bored look as a wail of anguish echoed in the distance, "mines."

I shook my head, glancing toward the source of the sound. None of the soldiers had moved from their positions guarding their mines. The Forcadelians, though, had stopped to look for the source, as I had. But they couldn't do anything to help, not with their guards standing watch.

I, however, had no guard.

Ignoring Luisa's call, I ran as fast as I could manage over the sand. The shrieking hadn't ceased at all, a beacon to guide me through what appeared to be hundreds of these mines—all of which had at least ten Forcadelians working them. If they were losing two to three mines per day...

Finally, I reached the screaming woman. She was on her knees, staring at the dusty cloud where a mine had been. Her lips were chapped and bleeding, but her gaze seemed to be far away. I gently knelt next to her, taking her face and bringing her gaze to mine.

"I'm here to help," I whispered. "What happened?"

She looked at me, shock on her face, then turned back to the dip in the sand. "It was a cave-in. They're all in there. All of them."

"All who?" I asked.

Her eyes filled with tears. "My husband, my son. My daughter. They're..."

"How far down were they?" I asked.

"Thirty feet, at least," she said, leaning into my chest. "There's no..." She dissolved into sobs and I held her, stroking her dusty hair and offering whatever comfort I could. Behind me, the sound of footsteps approaching boiled my blood.

"Ah, well," Ilara said. "Is there any way we can prevent this? Surely there has to be something. I fear we won't have unlimited mines, and if we spend all our time redigging the same hole—"

"Have some damn empathy," I snapped, sending a searing glare over my shoulder. "She just lost her entire family."

"Their deaths will not be in vain," Ilara said, plastering a fake smile onto her face.

"I think it's time to go," Luisa said, capturing me with her gaze. In it was a warning that if I lost my temper now, Ilara's wrath would be much worse. "The sun is getting low, and soon it will be cold."

"Indeed," Ilara said. "Carry on, Lieutenant. I'll see about finding your missing workers."

The lieutenant bowed. "Yes, Your Majesty."

"Brynna," Luisa said. "Time to go."

I looked down at the woman, her tears streaking the dust down her face. There was no one here to take her from me. I refused to leave her in the hands of the Severian guards.

"Brynna."

"One minute," I snapped, looking around for another solution.

"You can do nothing more for her," Luisa said, reaching for me. "But if you keep your tongue, you may be able to help them all."

Chapter Forty-Six

My anger simmered the length of the trudge back over desert. Luisa kept pace with Ilara instead of me, and I doubted either of them would care if I fell behind. But as the sun dipped under the horizon, the temperature dropped precipitously, so I kept trudging.

I'd probably made a mistake in losing my temper, as clearly that was what she'd wanted, but I could hold back no longer. This was more than just building a new country; this was revenge. She wanted every single Forcadelian to know what it was like to be hopeless and destitute, even if they'd already been that way back in the city. I could take the abuse directed at me, the reminders of my failure, because I knew that eventually, I would make her eat every word. But those people who'd died today, there would be no coming back for them. They were gone, and she didn't care.

I could barely stand to be in the same carriage as Ilara, let alone speak to her, so I stayed quiet. Ilara pointed out the dark window to the sand that was only barely visible on the horizon.

"The river will come through here," she said. "Eventually, we'll have to shore up this road like we did on the northern side of the city."

"Agreed, Your Majesty."

Ilara sighed and sat back. "I suppose we're too late for dinner, hm?"

"You could always call a small gathering," Luisa said, but even she couldn't hide the exhaustion in her voice. "I'm sure you could find someone to dine with you."

Ilara's gaze landed on me, and it took everything I had not to turn away from the window beyond. "No, have a small meal delivered to my room tonight. We will continue in the morning with breakfast." She paused, and her gaze on me intensified. "Would that bring a smile to your face, Brynna?"

Luisa made a noise of disapproval, but I said nothing.

"Oh, bother. You were so full of words earlier today," Ilara continued. "Did I not do as I promised? You have seen where your Forcadelian brethren have been relocated."

"And you're killing them," I said, finally turning to look at her.

"People always die," she said with a wave of her hand. "I'm not so cautious with lives as you are. If the Mother wants them to live, they will survive."

It was hard to keep my temper in check. "This isn't right, Ilara. Whatever motivations you have for punishing my people like this, it isn't right."

"It's dangerous work," she said with a small shrug. "Cave-ins happen all the time."

"Work that they're being forced to do." I balled my fists. "Work they didn't know they were being brought here to do. It wasn't enough to take over the kingdom, you had to enslave my people, too?"

"Slaves?" She twittered. "Such a barbaric term. Those I've brought into the city are here of their own accord."

"Are they?" I asked. "Because when I spoke with them, they said they're stuck working until they repay their debts. And surprise, surprise—those debts keep rising."

"Spoke with whom, my dear?" Ilara asked, challenge in her voice.

"A maid at the school," I replied, grateful I had something truthful to retort with. "She said she was brought here under the pretenses of getting a job. But surprise—once she got here, her debts kept rising. It's like Beswick all over again."

"Like, but not exactly," Ilara said, examining her nails. "Because the last I heard, Beswick was neck-deep in icy water in the north of Niemen. Or about to be."

She knows about Beswick. But I couldn't think about that now. "You are supposed to be their queen."

"Forcadelians have had their day in the sun. Perhaps it will be good for them to know a hard life."

"They've had hard lives," I said.

"Have they?" Ilara asked. "Have they known what it was to die of thirst in the desert? Have they known what it was to choose between shipping product to make a few measly silvers and feeding your family?" She leaned closer. "You've read our history books. Surely, you can see that even what the lowest Forcadelians have endured is *nothing* compared to what my people have."

"That isn't a reason to turn the tables," I said. "There's always a better way."

"This is the only way, because it's the way I've chosen," she replied. "And as I'm queen, I get to make the rules."

The castle was quiet when we arrived. There were a pair of maids waiting for Ilara, asking if she wanted a bath and to have her dinner in her room. A third asked the same of Luisa, but she declined.

"I will walk Brynna to her room," she said. "And there we will share a meal."

I clenched my jaw, not caring if she saw my distaste, and I didn't take her arm either. Still, she walked silently beside me, her hands folded at her waist, and her gaze far ahead.

"I'm not hungry, nor am I in the mood to entertain," I said, staring at my closed door. "So if it's all the same to you, I'd rather just go to bed."

"Will you go to bed?" Luisa asked. "Or will you mount an attack on the mines?"

I snorted. "Yes, let me just rally my soldiers and do that. Oh, wait…"

"As I said, I wouldn't bet against you," Luisa said. "But perhaps there's a better way to get what you want."

"What I want is for your queen to show some common human decency," I snapped. "I can't imagine that's a big ask. There's no reason for the Forcadelians to be dying. If she wants vengeance, take it from me." I shook my head. "Half those people out there are probably from Haymaker's Corner. They had nothing, and now…"

"Unfortunately, Ilara has her mind made up about certain things, and there's no way to change it," Luisa said. "But there won't always be a need for varo, especially once the rivers are completed. Then, we'll have a population in need of a champion." She looked at me. "You can be that champion, if you just play along long enough."

"Do you honestly believe Ilara would ever let me have any say in what she does?" I asked. "Or are you just that naive?"

"I—"

"I've been brought here for one reason alone: to prove to the masses that Ilara has won. That she's bested me in every sense of the word." Perhaps it was the sun, but hearing Luisa speak as if I weren't already being tortured daily was grating on my nerves. "She wants me to snap. It's why she goaded me into sparring with her this morning."

"And she won."

I made a face. "I let her."

"That's not what I saw," Luisa said.

I wish I could've disagreed with her. "What's your point, Luisa?"

"Patience, Brynna, might save your people. If you ruin the relationship you have with Ilara now, you'll never be of any use to them." She took a step back. "Just something to sleep on. Have a good night."

Luisa was either goading me into a trap, or she was completely ignorant of her queen's true nature. Ilara thought of me as her plaything, and playthings were better bested in the sparring ring and not heard. Any attempts I made to improve conditions in the mines would fall on deaf ears.

Which meant the only way to save them was to take matters into my own hands. And luckily, I'd been lying about one thing: I wasn't alone.

I snuck out the usual way, but took a roundabout way to the convent, doubling back several times to make sure I hadn't been followed. I trekked across the desert, keeping the stars in my sight as I continued northwest. It was easy to get turned around out here.

I crested a dune and saw a figure headed in my direction.

"What are you doing here?" Felix called up to me. "Is everything all right?"

"No."

He made a noise and scaled the dune, coming to stand next to me. "What's happened?"

I told him everything—from the mines, to Ilara revealing she knew the Niemenians had Beswick, to the lieutenant telling his queen that he hadn't received a shipment of new workers in weeks, to Luisa's ludicrous advice that I should just be patient until Ilara was finished with her damn river, and then I could help my people.

When I was done, Felix cleared his throat. "I hate to agree with the Severian..."

"You can't be serious," I snarled. "I'm not waiting until she builds another river—"

"No, of course not. But she's right about being patient. What you saw today...it sounds horrific. But we can't do anything to help them. Not yet."

"And why not?" I said, poking him in the chest. "We have people, don't we?"

He sighed, gently pushing away. "If Ilara took you to the mines today and tomorrow there's an attack, who do you think she'll blame? She's testing you. Maybe...maybe that's what Luisa was really saying. It sounds like she expected you to do something stupid and she was warning you against it."

I fought the urge to argue with him further. He was absolutely right. Everything about today smacked of a trap, and Ilara was quite adept at luring me into well-orchestrated and complex webs. There could be no way to free those people without it falling back on me. And based on the "gracious" way Ilara had both bested me and then taken me to see the Forcadelians anyway, I had a feeling there was more to it.

"I don't care," I said, though there wasn't much heat in it. "I have to do something."

"I know this is hard," he said. "It's hard for me, too. But we must keep our focus. Ilara can't suspect you're behind any of this recent activity. You leaving the castle tonight was bad enough. I'm sure she was expecting you to."

"So what? You'll keep defacing murals until everyone's dead?" I put my hands on my hips. "And where in the Mother's name are the rest of your soldiers? They should be here by now, shouldn't they?"

He opened his mouth to say something, then shook his head. "I don't know, Brynn. I wish I could tell you."

"And what about Katarine?" I said, my pulse quickening with anger. "It's a little ridiculous that both of you were given hundreds of soldiers and none of them have shown up here. What about Jax? Ignacio? Am I the only person who even cares a little about the people dying in the desert? Did I destroy lives in Neveri for nothing? Did Jorad and the thieves in Celia's camp die for nothing? Has everyone forsaken me?"

I turned back to him, expecting a fight, but all I got was silence.

"Do you feel better?" he asked.

"No," I huffed. "I hate being in that castle. I hate that Ilara beat me in the sparring ring this morning. I hate that I can't help my people. And I hate feeling trapped."

I jumped at the touch of his hands on my shoulders, but soon melted into his embrace. "Look at this convent, Brynn," he said, his breath tickling my ear. "You've saved all their lives. A hundred fifty, at least. Some of them wouldn't have lasted a day in the varo mines."

"And how long can we possibly keep them safe?" I asked, leaning into him. "Sooner or later, we'll run out of space, out of food, out of everything."

He tilted my chin up to catch my gaze. "I promise you, the next time we speak, I will have a plan for all this. And better news." He kissed my forehead. "Now get back to the castle before anyone notices you're missing."

Chapter Forty-Seven

Felix

I walked her into the city, both of us keeping an eye on the streets and roofs for soldiers. She promised me she would hold her tongue and temper, and I believed her, but I knew her promise was contingent on me finding something to help her.

And I had nothing.

Once Brynna was safely back at the castle, I used the dwindling night to venture down to the docks. We'd been taking turns keeping watch on what was coming and going, and today was my day. When I arrived, Malka was perched on the edge of the roof with a telescope in front of her. A new ship had arrived—the largest I'd seen so far.

"And it looks like they haven't offloaded anyone yet," she said. "I think they're waiting for something."

"That, probably," I said, nodding to the cadre of soldiers marching down the street. "Brynna said Ilara's been informed her people are missing."

"What do we do?" Malka asked.

"Wait, for now," I said. "Then we'll see what we've got to work with."

A couple of soldiers headed toward the ship, and I peered through the telescope to see who they were speaking with. "Son of a bitch. It's Coyle." I shook my head and handed the telescope to her.

"What's he doing here?"

"Probably finished clearing all the Forcadelians out of the city," I replied as the passengers filed off, two by two and were herded onto one of six waiting wagons.

"They sure don't look happy to be here," Malka said.

"Who would be?" I took the telescope back and focused it on the ship. "There's a bunch of..." My smile widened as I spotted another familiar face amongst the Forcadelians. "Well, look who decided to show up."

"Who?"

I stashed the telescope back in the bag. "We'll let the majority of the wagons go, but we need to keep an eye on one of them. I have a feeling it won't make it to its destination anyway."

The wagons filled and took off, and Malka and I followed the sixth for a few houses until there was enough separation between the wagons to make our move. Malka ran ahead and was waiting with a few well-placed arrows with knockout powder. When the soldiers were out, I sailed off the roof, holding the edges of my cloak and landing directly behind the wagon driver, clocking him on the back of the head and sending him forward.

"Whoa...whoa..." I said. Once the horses were stationary, I jumped off the top and hurried to the back, flinging open the flap.

Jax had a crossbow pointed mere inches from my head. "You know, you really should announce yourself." He lifted the crossbow. "Are you here to save us or something?"

"Sort of." I looked behind him. Four of Jax's vigilantes sat behind him, and beyond them were the rest of the terrified

Forcadelians. "Where are the rest of your vigilantes?"

"In this boat and that one," he said, sliding out of the wagon to join us. "Or spread to the four winds. I've loaned a bunch of them out, you know." He glanced up at the roof, and Malka. "Did you lose the other one?"

"She's around," I said. "What in the world is going on? How did you get here?"

Jax gestured for me to follow him further away from the wagon. "When I realized the entire city was gone, I let myself get caught." He dusted his hands off. "We were on the water for about a week when I decided I'd be a better captain, so we had a little mutiny." He grinned, devilishly. "The Severians aren't great swimmers, by the way."

"But you're still captive," I said.

"I arranged it with a couple of the other Forcadelians to take over as soon as we were in port. Some of them had been sailors in the past, so they could make it look good. I figured once we got inside the city, I'd put arrows through some people, but it seems like you've done that for me."

"Did you happen to see the Kulkan warships out there?" I asked, a little breathlessly.

"No," he said. "They haven't arrived yet?"

I exhaled, dread falling into the bottom of my stomach. "No. And they would've left weeks before you."

"Sir," Malka called from above. "We aren't out of the woods yet. There's a contingent of soldiers coming this way."

And we were sitting ducks in the center of the alley. Jax made a noise. "I just got here, and already you're making me solve all your problems, hm? Do you have a place for us to hide?"

I nodded. "A convent in the northeast. We've rescued about two hundred so far."

"That many?" Jax blinked. "And nobody's noticed yet?"

"We'll discuss that later," I said, looking up at Malka. "But for now, we need to get these people out of this wagon and to safety until we can get them up north."

"No," Jax said, shaking his head. "I got a better idea."

"I don't think we'll pass for Severian," I said, tugging at the uniform I hadn't worn in months.

"Pass for the moment," Jax said. "You asked for a solution."

Jax's grand plan had been to lure four Severian guards out looking for wagons into the alley, then steal their uniforms. It wasn't the best plan, but it was better than any I'd come up with so far.

"Shall we?" he asked, grabbing the reins.

The wagon lurched forward, and my nerves didn't like being out in the middle of the street in plain sight. The first block, I kept watch on the passersby, expecting a reaction to our presence.

"Well, if you want to draw attention to us, you're doing a great job of it," Jax said. "Quit looking like you're about to barf."

"I'm not..." I sniffed. "Fine."

"I got people up there," he said.

"What, like the Mother?"

"No, dumbass, Jansen."

As if to prove a point, Jansen whistled from up above, giving us the all clear to continue moving. The next street, we had the same. But a short whistle caused Jax to curse and slow the horses.

"Try not to cock this up, will you?"

"What—"

A Severian solder appeared in the middle of the street, coming out of nowhere. His partners flanked us as the lead held up his hand to stop the horses.

"Halt," the Severian said, holding up his hand. "Where are you going with this wagon?"

"North," Jax said. "To the mines."

"You're going east."

He squinted at the sky, which was growing lighter, then back at me. "You son of a bitch, you told me to go this way."

"It's faster," I said, thinking quickly.

"Captain Coyle gave you an approved route," he said, walking up to the wagon and throwing open the flap.

I held my breath. We'd tied up the Severian guards whose uniforms we'd swiped, and Jax had used a heavy dose of knockout powder to sedate them. In the back of the cart, they looked like they were sleeping, but I didn't know if it would fool the Severian.

But he seemed satisfied when he approached the front of the wagon again.

"Take a left here to get back on the main road," he said. "And when you've deposited your cargo, I want you to report to your superiors about this breach of conduct."

"Yes sir," Jax said, saluting perfectly. "Apologies for my idiot cohort here."

"It's all right, soldier."

We moved the cart forward, following the route that he'd given us. I was silent, watching for more guards when another short whistle came.

"Ah, excellent," Jax said with a grin. "They're making us a diversion."

"Diversion?"

A crash echoed in the distance, followed by yelling and the sound of footsteps.

"Diversion." He snapped the reins. "Now let's move!"

With all the soldiers and stops, the sun was up by the time we finally managed to reach the edge of the city. Once the civilians disembarked, I gave Malka the job of disposing of the wagon somewhere in the city.

"Put it close to the castle, so they find it quick," Jax said.

"Are you sure you want to do that?" I asked.

He glared at me. "Do as I say."

Malka nodded and hopped back on the wagon, leaving Jax and me alone. He gave me the once-over and started marching in the direction of the group.

"Good thing the wind's blowing," he said, pointing to the ground beneath him. "Anyone could see tracks here. It's like you're begging to be found out."

"We've done all right so far," I said with a bit of a frown as we walked toward the convent.

Kieran was waiting on the front steps, smoking a pipe and staring at the sky. When he saw us, he jumped to his feet and jogged over.

"Evening, General," he said. "Glad to see you again, Jax."

"Don't see a ship under you," Jax said, his gaze cold.

"That's because it's sitting out in the ocean, waiting for the Kulkan warships to arrive," Kieran replied. "You didn't happen to see any of them, did you?"

"No sign of them, but that doesn't mean anything," Jax said. "The beach is rocky and there are plenty of places to hide out. There's a chance they had to keep out of sight from all the ships coming from Forcadel."

"That's true," Kieran said. "But it still means we don't have the full breadth of your forces."

"But we have a few more than we did before," I said, searching for a bright side. "Jax is as good as Brynna. So I'm sure he'll be able to help us come up with more ways to cause unrest."

"Unrest?" he said with a look. "Aren't we trying to knock a queen off her throne? How do you plan to do that by causing 'unrest'?"

"We aren't trying to draw Ilara's attention just yet," I said. "Brynna's still living in the castle, and if Ilara even halfway thinks she's responsible for any of it, she could be in trouble."

"Forget her, *you* would be in trouble." Jax sniffed and looked around. "This place has that brat written all over it. You're the only thing out in the desert, and it'll be a miracle if no one noticed us tonight. Somebody just has to put two and two together, and you'll have Ilara's forces at your door."

"They haven't yet," I said, but I couldn't deny he'd made a good point. "And we don't really have anywhere to move them."

"You said there were two hundred in this place?"

"Civilians, not soldiers."

"There ain't a difference anymore," he said. "These people have been ripped from their homes, their livelihoods destroyed. I'm surprised they haven't already risen up against their Severian overlords." He snorted. "So yeah, we have people. Now we gotta use them."

"How?"

"There are hundreds of ships in the bay right now. Why don't we use one of those to get these people out of here?"

"Ilara isn't letting ships out of the bay once they're here," Kieran said. "Trust me, it took a few coins to bribe someone to let mine out."

"Who said they have to go anywhere?" Jax said with a shrug. "Point is, they'd be a lot safer there than here in this church. If you're too chicken to go through with it—"

"I commandeered five warships," I said, although it wasn't much of a brag when they hadn't arrived yet. "But it's a good point."

"Just leave it to me and this pirate." Jax patted Kieran on the shoulder. "We'll come up with something. You just keep… What was it?" He cracked a cruel smile. "Causing unrest. Let the adults handle the rest."

Chapter Forty-Eight

Katarine

"We have to be getting there soon," Luard said, his face bright red from sunburn.

Mine, at least, had faded to a golden brown, thanks to some aloe I'd had the foresight to bring with me. And with my newly-dyed black hair, I could pass for a very light-skinned Forcadelian if pressed. We stood on the deck, bathed in moonlight, as our sailors worked quickly to dig the ship out again. Everyone onboard had been given this particular task one night or another, and my arms still ached from having to dig the night before.

"It's hard to tell where we are on the map," I said. "But yes, it's been days."

And every single one had been agonizingly slow. Now, being so close to Aunela, my patience for finding out about Elisha was growing thin. I had plenty of time to think about what my wife had said, including how I'd seemingly closed myself off to Elisha and the other children. I had several drafts of a speech prepared in my mind, and I just hoped I would be able to use one of them.

When the lookout above called that our scouts were returning, Luard and I disembarked, walking as fast as our sea legs could carry us. The sand melted away beneath my feet, making it much harder to move as quickly as I wanted to. More concerning, the horizon was growing pink, signaling the coming sun. And with it would be its own set of troubles.

Up ahead, three figures waved at us. Two of them were our Forcadelian scouts, and the other was—

"Joella," Luard said, a smile breaking out onto his face.

"Who are... Katarine?" Joella blinked in the darkness. "What in the Mother's name did you do to your hair?"

"I figured Ilara might notice a pair of Niemenians walking around," Luard said, holding out his hand to shake hers. "Glad you made it."

"Where's Elisha?" I asked.

"She's been sent on a task into the city," Joella said. "Should be back any moment now." She looked at her fellow soldiers. "Return to the base camp and see if she's there. If so, send her to us." They saluted and left.

"You let her go alone?" I asked, incredulous. "Into an enemy city?"

"Tell us what you know," Luard said, waving me off. "Have you met with our allies? Brynna?"

"We've managed to get inside, yes," Joella said, giving me a wary look. "But there isn't a single Forcadelian within the city limits, so Elisha says. She was having trouble avoiding guards, who keep wondering if she's lost. Two tried to arrest her the other day."

"She managed to escape, right?" I said, a little breathlessly.

"She did," Joella said with a smile. "But she said it was too risky to go back during the day, so with the sun coming up, she should be back." She paused, clearing her throat. "I promise, she's been very well-behaved and listened to everything I said."

"Which won't help her if she's taken by surprise," I said.

"Why would they arrest a Forcadelian with no cause?" Luard asked. "And a child, at that?"

"Because..." Joella sighed. "Because every Forcadelian we've seen has been unwillingly employed building a new branch of the river, we think headed toward Kulka. Ilara's practically enslaved them."

I licked my lips. "That seems cruel, even for Ilara."

"I can't say what she's thinking, only what we've seen and what Elisha's been able to glean." Joella shook her head. "They've begun construction two miles northwest of the city along the river here. They've gotten about five miles in a southwesterly direction."

"Toward Kulka, I bet," Luard said. "Can you show us?"

"It's a bit of a walk," Joella said.

"We can handle it," Luard said. "Let's go, before the sun gets too hot."

Joella hadn't been kidding about the long journey. As we tumbled and slid and fell, we became more spread out, until Joella was far ahead, whereas Luard and I were dragging up the rear.

"Luard!" Joella called from up ahead. "Over here!"

"On our way," Luard grumbled, helping me stand.

"This was your idea, brother dear," I said, scowling.

The walk up the dune was difficult, and I was sure I had sand in every nook and cranny, but once we reached the top, we were gifted with a view of a vast city that stretched as far as the eye could see. It was nothing like I'd expected—I thought perhaps a few buildings and a port. But this was a vibrant metropolis rivaling Forcadel.

"This is...slightly concerning," Luard said, making a face. "The river deposits right there into the bay. Was there a bay here?"

"We don't know," Joella said.

Luard pointed the telescope toward the mouth of the river. "I see your blockade. And..." He pulled the telescope away from his eye and handed it to me. "Are those Forcadelians?"

I peered through the lens. The workers took spots at the base of the river, scooping out shovelfuls of sand and placing them on a wagon sitting on skis. Once it was full, a horse pulled the wagon away and another took its place.

"Is this how they managed to build the other river?" Luard asked. "It must've taken months—years?"

"Clearly, Ilara's been hard at work at this for a while," I said.

"They've been doing this nonstop for days," Joella said. "And based on the treatment of the workers, I'm not sure they're there voluntarily."

"I can't imagine they are," I said slowly, looking at my brother. "What do we do?"

"This could be an opportunity," Luard said. "Our ships will need to pass the security on the river, and what better place to stash our Forcadelian soldiers than down there? Swap them for these poor civilians."

"And send the civilians back on our ship?" I finished for him. "It would resolve the problem of what to do with it."

"We can send a message back to let the rest of our forces know to stay away until called," Luard said. "The last thing I want is for them to arrive to this."

"Even still, how are you planning on making the swap?" Joella asked. "These Severians watch their people like hawks. No one leaves, and the only break they get is at the end of the day. They're shuffled into small tents that are guarded as well."

"A distraction, then," Luard said. "We have ond."

"There's a chance someone could get hurt," I said. "And that big an explosion could draw unwanted attention. We're trying to move forces into position, not make things more difficult for ourselves."

"Then what do you suggest, dear sister?" Luard asked.

"You could use some Nestori tricks on them."

I jumped at the new voice, then was immediately overcome with relief. Elisha seemed pleased to have snuck up on us, but immediately drew to attention when Joella addressed her. She seemed perfectly at ease, as if this were yet another day for her.

"What's the latest?" Joella asked.

"A ton of people arrived last night," Elisha said. "But all of 'em went west instead of north. They've got them all lined up on a road leading out of the city. I couldn't get any of 'em out." She deflated. "I'm sorry."

"You did fine," Joella said with a firm nod. "Another mystery to be unraveled, I suppose."

"Our focus should remain on the problem in front of us," Luard said, nodding to the river blockade below. "You were saying something about Nestori tricks, Elisha?"

"Oh, right," she said with a nod. "If we use hyblatha, we should be able to distract the guards long enough to swap out the soldiers. And if we keep using it, the soldiers won't have to... well...work." She looked to me. "You did bring the hyblatha, didn't you?"

"Yes, but if we use hyblatha, we run the risk of poisoning our own people," I said. "And with the desert winds—"

"We put it in their food then," Elisha said.

"You can do that?" Joella asked.

She nodded. "The wolves told me about it. They said breathing in the hyblatha is good for felling large forces at once, but if stealth is the way to go, you can just sprinkle it in someone's food." She shrugged. "Same goes for knockout powder."

"So we infiltrate the guards' food supply until they've lost their minds," Luard said, nodding slowly. "How long does it take to work?"

"I don't know," Elisha said with a shrug. "Never done it before. But I can get down there and start spreading it out now."

I turned to her. "Elisha, it will be very dangerous. If they catch you—"

"They won't."

"Can't argue with that logic," Luard said with a laugh I didn't share. But he put his hand on my shoulder and smiled. "I think she's got this, dear sister."

I pursed my lips. "Very well. May I help you prepare?"

"I don't need help," Elisha said, giving me a snooty look. "But if you want to stand around and watch me, fine."

I had promised myself I wouldn't worry, but hearing about Elisha venturing into the enemy's camp set my nerves on fire. Still, I breathed through my initial instincts, hoping that some respect might help grease the wheels of our relationship.

I followed Elisha down to the belly of the ship where we'd kept the stash of hyblatha. The floral scent permeated the air, and my heart fluttered.

"Here," Elisha said, handing me a pinch of tinneum from the pouch at her hip. "Don't need you getting all scared and whatever."

I took the herb with thanks and chewed on it. "What do you need me to do?"

"Nothin'." She found a hammer on the ground and used it to crack open the crate of hyblatha with little effort. "Don't really need your help. So not sure why you're here."

I wasn't either. "Captain Kinsella says you've been very helpful," I said. "And minding her well."

"See? Told you I'd make a good soldier."

It was all I could do not to laugh. Elisha was nothing if not predictable. "When someone gives you a compliment, darling, you should tell them thank you."

"Oh." She made a face. "Thanks. I just don't see how that's a compliment."

"I suppose I didn't get a chance to tell you this before you left," I said. "But I've been thinking a lot about what the wolf said about you. That your life was a gift from the Mother."

She stopped digging in the crate and looked up at me, her brown eyes reflecting the scant light. "Jarrah said that?"

"She did," I said. "She also said that I would do well to flow with the river instead of trying to control it." I folded my hands across my lap as I took a seat on one of the crates. "But I'd still like to know that you're safe."

"Why do you care so much?" Elisha asked.

"Because I..." My cheeks warmed. "Because I suppose I care about you, Elisha. You're stubborn and headstrong, but beneath it, you've got a gentle heart. And I'd like to protect you."

"I don't need protection," she said, returning to the box. "Celia taught me how to defend myself. Same way she taught Brynna. We don't need anybody."

"Brynna certainly knows the importance of depending on others." I paused, clearing my throat. "Well, she does now. Why do you think she entrusted Felix and me with her soldiers?"

"But, like, in a fight, she doesn't need help," Elisha said, putting the bag full of powders over her shoulder. "Nor do I."

I sighed, realizing that we were yet again speaking of two different things. "I'll still worry about both of you, though." I rose and gestured toward the open door. "But I won't stop you from heading into danger. Just...be careful out there. And come back as quickly as you can."

She gave me a hesitant look then hurried out the door. As soon as she was gone, Luard appeared, chewing on an apple.

"I'd give that speech a seven out of ten," he said.

I tossed a bag of tinneum at his head.

Chapter Forty-Nine

Once I returned to my room, I tossed and turned, thinking of all the ways I could break my people free of Ilara's torture. But that small voice kept reminding me that if I was reckless, I could make things much worse. At first light, I prayed for forgiveness from the Mother, and from those who would surely perish while I waited for an opportune moment. And prepared myself for a morning of taunts, jibes, and insults.

When I walked into the dining hall, Alaqua had returned to his spot across from Luisa, but even he couldn't get a rise out of me. It was easy to ignore my own faults when there was so much more at stake.

Happily, he soon gave up, and Luisa took his seat. "You don't look like you slept."

"I don't see how you could after what we saw yesterday."

"Did you…"

"Did I what? Leave my room and mount an incredible feat of

heroism?" I laughed humorlessly. "No, I stayed put and stared at the wall. And this morning I begged the Mother for forgiveness."

"Ilara's church will be ready soon enough," Luisa said, before lowering her voice. "And with enough patience, you can ask the Mother for more than forgiveness."

Ilara arrived shortly after, greeting everyone else with an overly cheery fondness and blessedly skipping over me. I would have to temper my anger so I didn't cross the line, but I was looking forward to showing off a little. She wanted me angry, that was what she'd get.

"It appears the problem with our missing food has been solved," she said, gazing down at the fresh fruit on her place. "I'm so pleased. Our farmlands will start producing more, I hear, now that the weather's turned."

Our farmlands. My appetite disappeared.

"Brynna, dear," Ilara said, her smile cruel. "We have some new people at our table today. Perhaps you can regale us with the interesting tale of how I took your kingdom from you?"

I glanced up at her, unable to rise to anger. "Surely you can tell it better than I."

"Yes, but a bet is a bet," she said. "And I held up my end of the bargain yesterday."

Just as I thought I might explode into tears or flames, the door opened and a soldier, dusty from the desert, came walking in, a look of absolute dread on his face.

"This had better be good," Ilara said. "You're interrupting my breakfast."

"It is, my queen." He hesitated then strengthened his resolve. "The guards at the river construction, they...well, they refuse to work. And they've stopped managing our workers, so nothing's been done."

Ilara blinked, sharing a look of surprise with Luisa. "What do you mean, the guards refuse to work?"

"I can't... I wish I had another explanation. But it's as if they've... they've all completely lost their minds." He winced. "I arrived for shift change, and no one would even speak to me. They just...they just screamed."

Ilara's gaze landed on me and I was grateful it was easy to look surprised at this news. "Brynna, what do you think?"

My only option was to play along, so I shook my head. "It sounds like it could be hyblatha. But I'd have to go there to be sure."

"Do you have a cure for it?" Ilara asked.

"I have a very small bag of tinneum, which usually stops the symptoms," I said.

"Then go get it," Ilara said, throwing down her napkin. "I suppose we'll all have to go out there and see why my soldiers have decided to disobey orders." She tossed a dirty look at Luisa. "Prepare my carriage and send word to the dockmaster. I want to leave within the hour."

"You didn't..." Luisa asked as we waited for Ilara to join us in front of the castle. "You didn't do this, did you? If you did, tell me now so I can help smooth it over."

"I don't even know where the river construction is, Luisa," I said. "Or how to get there."

She didn't look convinced as Ilara arrived, walking right past us to climb inside the carriage.

"Then it behooves you to find out what's wrong and fix it before Ilara loses her temper," Luisa said, following behind.

I had absolutely no idea what was going on. The soldier had said it was only the guards who'd succumbed, so it was less likely to be hyblatha, which would've spread quickly in the winds of the desert and affected everyone. But even still, I'd pocketed my small bag of tinneum before joining the rest.

We rushed through the city in record time, and when we reached the docks, there was a sailor there to lead us onto a very small riverboat. I guessed it would hold about ten, but there were only five on it today.

"Go," Ilara snapped.

The boat pushed away from the dock and we motored toward the mouth of the Ilarian river. There were now twenty formerly Forcadelian naval ships serving as a barrier between the river and the bay. Perhaps Ilara thought the missing Forcadelians would swim to safety.

"Where are we going, again?" I asked Luisa.

"The new river that will go to Kulka will originate north of the city," Luisa said. "It'll draw from the Ilarian river and flow southwest. So they've begun construction close to it."

"I see."

There was a small dock situated at the base of a high dune covered in scaffolding and stairs, presumably so those visiting didn't have to attempt to scale the dune. When the ship docked, Ilara barely waited for the gangplank to be fully lowered before marching off and up the steps—and Luisa and I were right behind her.

I was huffing and puffing by the time I reached the top of the scaffolding, but I didn't move to continue down after Ilara. A sandy canyon—or what would eventually be this new river—stretched as far as the eye could see. Down below, shovels littered the ground, but no one was working.

"Where is everyone?" I asked.

"Come on," Luisa said, narrowing her gaze.

We reached the bottom and walked the empty canyon. Large stones had been placed along the riverbed floor but the sides of the river rose precariously around us. One wrong wind, and the sandy walls might collapse in on us. But neither Ilara nor Luisa looked concerned.

"There," Luisa said, pointing to a camp in the distance. "I see people."

As we approached, my pulse quickened. Based on the tent size, I could only assume it was a camp for the workers. But we still hadn't seen a single Severian guard. This place should've been crawling with them.

"You!" Ilara said, spotting a Forcadelian man walking out of his tent. He froze and turned toward her. "You, man! Come here this instant!"

He walked over slowly, and my heart dropped into my stomach.

He was one of my soldiers.

"Erm..." To his credit, he didn't even look in my direction. "Your Majesty."

"Where are all the guards?" Ilara said. "And why is no one working?"

"We haven't been given anything to do," he said. "And the guards are...well..." He made a face. "Come with me."

He led us across the desert to where the Severians had their covered campsite. But even before we got there, the screams became louder. When we crested the dune, we found a gathering of Severians who'd clearly been driven insane. They stumbled around in circles, screaming when their gazes landed on each other. Others just curled into balls, sobbing into their own sick.

"What the..."

"It definitely looks like hyblatha," I said with a shake of my head, walking forward. "But there's no way it could be if it's only affecting the Severians. The powder spreads too quickly, and everyone would be like this." The Severian whimpered at my feet, and I actually felt bad for him. "But maybe the tinneum will work anyway."

With effort, I pried his lips open and stuffed the herb inside, then held his jaw closed. His eyes danced everywhere but me, but their movement soon slowed and he blinked as tears gathered in his eyes.

"That's it," I cooed. "Come back to us."

I released him and he chewed the herb slowly, shaking his head. "What...what happened?"

"That's what we're hoping you'll tell us," Ilara said, gazing down at him.

He started, having not realized he was in the presence of his queen, but my gentle hand on his shoulder kept him from popping to his feet.

"Just sit here," I said. "How are you feeling?"

"Dizzy," he said, rubbing his forehead. "But no longer like my mind is running amok."

"Can you tell us what happened?" Luisa said. "Before your mind...went?"

"I don't know," he said, shaking his head. "It was just... something... Like a slow decline. I no longer trusted my own mind."

"Did anyone put any sort of powder in your face?" I asked. "Or did you smell something sweet?"

He shook his head. "Just the desert."

"Did a Forcadelian come close to you?" Ilara asked. "Stick you with something?"

"No, definitely not. We keep them far away unless they aren't moving fast enough."

My sympathy for this soldier evaporated immediately, and it was hard not to let him fall backward into the sand. "Hyblatha is a powder. Maybe someone spread it out in camp? When do you remember the madness starting?"

"While I was on my shift," he said. "I'd just arrived, but I'd been feeling ill all night. The shadows started to move a little then they grew into monsters, then..." He shuddered.

"It's not hyblatha," I said, puzzled. "That's an immediate

reaction. You get hit and the nightmares start."

"And who else could this be?" Ilara asked.

"I have absolutely no idea." I squinted toward the sun overhead. "It could be the sun, or maybe a bad piece of meat. Maybe something got into the water."

Ilara surveyed me as if she thought I was lying. And in this case, I had theories, but my knowledge was limited. I truly had no idea what had happened to these guards.

"Distribute that cure to all the guards you can," Ilara said. "And when they've come back to themselves, tell them to assemble all the Forcadelians in camp here. I want to have a little chat."

It took some time, and I didn't like depleting my bag of tinneum, but I had no choice. I was able to help around fifty guards, all of whom had the exact same story. Whatever had happened was either a divine intervention, or Felix had learned some new tricks.

Once they were back on their feet, the soldiers were instructed to round up the rest of the camp inhabitants. When the Forcadelians began emerging from the desert, my heart began to hurt for them—until I recognized one as one of my soldiers. And another. Five more. There were still some faces I didn't know, but the majority of them…they were mine.

Felix, you devious bastard.

Luckily, Ilara was too incensed to notice that what should've been a gaggle of different ages and sizes were more-or-less all young adults.

"I want it known," she said, her voice carrying across the desert, "that whomever was responsible for this poisoning will be punished. And if I have to punish—or kill—all of you to clear out the rat, I *will*."

"That won't be necessary," Luisa said, finally deciding to step in. "We have plenty of soldiers and we can replace the guards here quickly. And we'll tell them to keep an eye out for anything suspicious."

She made a face. "This river's construction is our top priority. We will have it finished on time." She scowled at me. "And no one is going to stop it."

Chapter Fifty

The riverboat moved much slower on the way back to the docks, giving me plenty of time to think. I couldn't blame Ilara for suspecting me. It was a very Veil-like strategy; distract the guards using something that would incapacitate, but not kill, and replace the civilians with my soldiers—close enough to infiltrate, but out of sight. But Ilara didn't know the second part—or so I hoped.

If I wanted to keep my spot at Ilara's dinner table, I had to figure out what exactly had been done to the Severians and put a stop to it. Or try to stay low until it blew over and hope no other messengers interrupted Ilara's breakfast.

Luisa sidled up next to me, gently resting her hands on the railing. "Any thoughts, Brynna?"

"No more than I had before," I said. "I know it means nothing to you or Ilara, but I have no idea what happened out there."

"Then isn't it so lucky that Ilara has given the investigative task to someone else," Luisa said, smiling. "And we'll be sending a new crop of soldiers out there, so hopefully the problem will resolve itself."

The docks were drawing ever closer, and there was a group of Severian soldiers waiting for us. Except…

"Is that…Coyle?" I blanched. "What in the Mother's name is he doing here?"

"He arrived last night," Luisa said. "Her Majesty gave him a special task, so he was unable to join us for breakfast." She squeezed my arm. "He'll be on his best behavior toward you."

"Will he, though?"

I had ten minutes to prepare myself for his presence, but it wasn't enough. His smirk was visible even from a distance, and something about it made me feel like I was walking into a trap.

My eyes widened. If Coyle set one foot at the riverbed, he'd recognize the soldiers immediately. After all, he'd been as intimately involved in their training as Felix. It'd be even more difficult for me to convince Ilara I hadn't been involved.

I forced myself back into a normal, loathing expression and tried not to panic.

"Your Majesty," Coyle said when the ship was close enough for conversation. He bowed. "It is wonderful to see you again."

"And you, Captain," Ilara replied, walking the gangway to the dock. "You're looking well. I trust your trip was pleasant."

"Exceedingly," he said. "No problems at all. The southern ocean weather was perfect. We made it here in record time." His gaze landed on me. "And you're looking like you swallowed a rotten egg. Having a pleasant time in the desert, Brynna?"

"Until you showed up," I said, smiling sweetly. Luisa elbowed me gently, but Coyle merely sneered.

"This is fun," Ilara said, clapping her hands together. "I missed your banter. Brynna had gotten used to Alaqua and it was no fun to watch him taunt her. But you, dear Coyle, always know how to push her buttons."

"I aim to please." He bowed again.

"And I couldn't be more grateful for your arrival," Ilara said, taking his arm and walking him away from the ship. "Things have been unsettled in the city of late, and the missing workers are just the start. Someone burned my favorite gallery and a food storage building, and someone's been defacing art."

She sighed, and I waited for her to mention the incident at the riverbed with a sick feeling. Coyle would probably insist on investigating it, and then we'd all be sunk. I would have to come up with something—and fast.

Instead, she simply patted him on the arm and said, "I'm glad to have my favorite captain at my side again to put a stop to it."

I waited for the shoe to drop, but it never did. Was Ilara not going to mention what we'd just seen?

"As soon as this last set of Forcadelians have settled in their new roles, I'll be happy to look into the vandalism that has arisen." Coyle cast a scathing look back at me. "Though I daresay I know the first person to suspect, and she's right there."

"Oh, leave Brynna alone," Luisa said. "She's been nothing but helpful since she arrived."

His eyes narrowed in my direction, daring me to say something in my defense. But I had nothing to prove to him. And I didn't have to hide my loathing of him, either.

He turned back to the front. "As per your request, I've asked the latest shipment to remain at the border so you can inspect it and ensure it meets your standards."

"Excellent work, Captain Coyle," Ilara said with a smile. "I can always count on you to come through in the end, can't I?"

"Until my dying breath."

It was all I could do not to roll my eyes.

I would've rather spent the day listening to Alaqua wax poetic about the difference between painting on plaster versus canvas, but Ilara insisted that Luisa and I follow her to the edge of town. Coyle was highly confident, riding a horse and pretending he was vastly more important than he was, with Ilara seated on another mare next to him.

Luisa and I walked behind him on foot, her arm threaded through mine.

"Is Coyle going to be assigned to the riverbed?" I asked, unable to stop my curiosity.

"I don't believe so. Her Majesty already has a full plate for him." She looked toward me. "Why?"

"I just thought it odd she didn't mention it to him," I said.

"I think, perhaps, she wants to keep this a little closer to the vest. If word spread that the Severian soldiers were experiencing madness, it could cause a panic in the city. The Severians take great pride in the Ilarian river." She gave me a look. "I think it has something to do with us being a desert people."

"Makes sense."

Up ahead, five wagons sat in a line, the first one reaching the very end of the road before it dissolved into desert. The Forcadelians had been lined up beside them, a long trail of bodies that were old, young, healthy, and not. They stared blankly out onto the street, their fury at their predicament radiating as harsh as the heat on the dark road. There were over a hundred there, and none of them looked pleased to be there—nor were any of them familiar.

"Excellent work, Coyle," Ilara said, taking his arm and walking down the line of people. "And you say there's no one left in Forcadel?"

"We left no stone unturned," he said. "Nor did we allow any stragglers to remain. Most of them fought it, but two weeks on the ocean was enough to cow them."

"*Traitor!*"

I turned my head toward the sound, thinking perhaps it had been directed at me.

"Who said that?" Coyle snarled, releasing Ilara to walk the line of people with a furious expression on his face. I might've been amused at how agitated the word had made him had I not been concerned for the citizen who'd said it.

But an older man stepped forward, his fury directed at the former Forcadelian captain. "I did, you coward. You're a traitor to the throne. A nasty, disgusting—"

With a heave, Coyle shoved the man to the ground and pulled his sword. But I was faster, breaking away from Luisa to stand between Coyle and the moaning man, whose head now sported a bloody cut.

"Move," Coyle said.

"Why? He spoke the truth."

"Get out of the way," he said, brandishing his sword.

"Make me," I snarled, getting up in his face. "And if you think I can't disarm you in front of all these people, I would love to show you otherwise."

"Brynna, Coyle," Ilara snapped. "Both of you back off. This man will get his comeuppance in the mines."

Luisa's gentle hand on my arm tugged me back to my spot, but my blood boiled just the same as the Severian soldiers hoisted the man to his feet and made him stand upright. Ilara turned her back on him and kept walking.

"Truly, excellent work, Captain Coyle," Ilara said, back to her normal tone. "These workers will be a boon. We will have the river completed in…" She tilted her head. "How many Forcadelians did you say were supposed to be here?"

"A hundred twenty, by my count."

"Then why are there only a hundred?"

He stopped, and my pulse spiked.

"Hm?" Ilara asked, looking at him.

"O-one moment," he said, turning to march toward a soldier at attention. They spoke in hushed tones, and Coyle's face grew redder and redder. But my worst fears began to come true. Where could they have gone except to our convent?

"Seems Coyle doesn't have as tight a grip on the city as he thought," Luisa said to Ilara idly.

"Give him time. He's eager to please, and eager to show me I didn't make a mistake in bringing him here."

The soldier saluted and hurried into the city, and Coyle straightened and walked back to Ilara.

"Is there a problem, Captain?" Ilara asked.

"One wagon did not arrive," Coyle said, his gaze landing on me. "Clearly, someone intercepted it."

I glared right back. "I can't imagine it was me, considering I've been with Her Majesty all morning. Or is your memory that bad?"

"It happened last night."

I felt Luisa's gaze on me, but I snorted. "Coyle, if I was responsible, you'd have no wagons here. It's not in my nature to do things half-assed."

"Don't fret, dear Coyle," Ilara said, something unreadable on her face "If the ship arrived, and the wagon was loaded, but it didn't make it here, then clearly the missing Forcadelians are somewhere in the city. I'd wager to guess they're in the same location as the rest of the missing workers."

"Yes, Your Majesty," Coyle said. "I will scour this city until I find them."

"And Brynna," Ilara said, turning to me and smiling. "Since you seem to know so much about how someone might go about doing this, and since you have such concern for your people, you will join Coyle in his investigation." She narrowed her eyes. "You will begin immediately. I look forward to meeting these missing workers this evening."

"Do you want to tell me where the Forcadelians are, or are we going to pretend you're innocent again?"

I kept my mouth shut. My mind whirled with possibilities and scenarios and explanations, none of them coming to a satisfying conclusion. To make matters worse, Coyle's near-incessant questioning was a constant intrusion, preventing me from thinking clearly.

I glanced at the sky, briefly looking for a vigilante on the roof. Surely, by now, Felix was aware that Coyle had arrived. If I could last the day and sneak out after dinner, we could meet and come up with a solution.

"Perhaps it wasn't you," Coyle said. "But your accomplices."

"Who?" I turned to him. "I'm dying to know if I have allies in this city. It surely hasn't felt that way lately. You and Alaqua would've gotten along famously. I'm sure you'll meet him."

His eyes flashed. "Did I touch a nerve, Brynna?"

"You're on my last one," I replied with a sweet smile. "Now shut up and let me do what Ilara wants."

"Don't you find it odd that you've only now been tasked with this job?"

"Why would that be odd?"

"Well, when I first arrived last night, my soldiers told me about all these mysterious disappearances. Soldiers just evaporating into thin air and cargo not making it to its destination." He glanced at me. "Perhaps Ilara's trying to see if you're willing to save your own skin at the expense of someone else's, like you did with poor John."

I couldn't help the tic at John's name. "Tell me, do you prattle on to cover your insecurities, or is it just for my benefit?"

He grabbed my arm and spun me to face him. "I know you're up to something, you little bitch. You've been entirely too complacent since you arrived."

In one move, I broke his grip, twisted his arm behind his body, and cowed him. "Call me a bitch again," I breathed, twisting harder, "and I will break your arm."

"Captain!"

Coyle's soldiers, who'd been trailing us, came rushing forward and pulled me off him. They held my hands behind my back as he straightened, wringing out his arm and trying to look like he wasn't in pain.

"You'd better find me someone to bring back to Ilara," Coyle said. "Because you don't want me to find them first."

Chapter Fifty-One

The good news about pretending to start a search was that I could waste time at "the beginning." I led Coyle down to the docks, making a good show of asking every ship captain what they'd brought in and when. But that only bought me about an hour before he got impatient.

"Clearly, the missing people got off the docks," Coyle said. "I think you've canvassed this area enough."

The next stop was the shops just beyond the docks, which got me another hour. Most of the owners slept upstairs, but they didn't recall seeing any wagons at night, nor anything amiss in the past few days.

"Seems like you're wasting time."

"I'm sure it does, to an idiot."

"I'll enjoy the day when Ilara shuts you up for good," Coyle said, opening the door to the next house. "After you."

Inside, the merchant marine sitting at his desk looked up. "Can

I help you?"

"I'm here asking about a missing wagon that disembarked from the docks yesterday," I said. "Have you seen anything suspicious?"

"Oh, yeah."

"Thank you, I— What?" My eyes widened. "What did you see?"

"I was asleep, and I heard voices early this morning," the shop owner said, nodding. "Peered out my window and saw a wagon in the alley. Two men talking about something, couldn't hear. But they changed into Severian uniforms and left the alley."

"What did the men look like?" Coyle asked, leaning on the counter.

"Forcadelians, both. One had a beard." He shrugged. "It was early, and I was afraid they were bandits. They certainly looked dangerous. One even climbed up to the roof. A girl."

"To the roof, hm?" Coyle's smile widened. "Seems familiar. You didn't happen to see what the girl looked like? Did she resemble my friend here?"

The shop owner looked at me and shook his head. "No, she had curly hair."

"See?" I said to Coyle, but my stomach twisted. "Where did they go?"

"Just out into the main road," he said. "I'm sorry I can't tell you more."

We walked out of the shop, Coyle's smug smile lighting up the entire town.

"Two men, and a girl with curly hair," he said. "Sounds like accomplices."

"Sounds like the Forcadelians didn't want to end up as slaves." I turned to him. "And I can't say I blame them. I wonder how you sleep at night, knowing you've brought your own countrymen to almost certain death."

"It's not certain. If they don't step out of line, then they'll be just fine."

"I'm talking about cave-ins," I said, whirling on him. "Spending days out in the sun with no water. Old, young, healthy, frail all driven by a whip trying to dig this damn sand so Ilara can make her dreams come true. And you, traitor, pulled them out of their homes and shipped them here."

"Are you trying to convince me you had nothing to do with their disappearance? Because it's not working."

"I don't have to convince you of anything." But my nerves had gotten the better of me, and I pulled back on my anger. "If they left the alley, and went out on the main street, maybe we should start asking around there."

He stopped, narrowing his eyes at me. "As I said. Wasting time."

"Coyle, we've gone over this. Investigating takes time. You might know that if you were any good at it."

He paused, a smile curling onto his face. "Indeed, I'm quite good at it. Solved a few curious cases in my day back in Forcadel."

I didn't like his tone. "Well? If you have any bright ideas, please, by all means, share them."

"My main suspect has a history of disruption, but not so much that she causes real problems," he began, clasping his hands behind his back as he walked around me. "She has an almost pathological need to save the world, so knowing her people are being rounded up and shipped to another country would grind on her until she was moved to action."

"I wouldn't call it pathological."

"But the question remains: where would she hide hundreds of people? There haven't been any ships leaving these past few weeks, so they have to be somewhere in the city limits." He paused, smiling. "She does have a penchant for churches."

My lip twitched before I could stop it and Coyle's smile widened. "Is that it? You've found a church to stash them all?"

"The only church in town is under construction," I said. "But nice try."

"Is it the *only* church?" His smile told me he didn't believe it. "Perhaps I'll ask Her Majesty if she knows of any others."

"You can ask," I said, trying for nonchalance. "But I don't know if she'll be pleased about you coming back empty-handed. I'd prefer to continue our investigation—"

He grabbed my arm, and I wouldn't have been surprised if he'd called his guards to put me in irons. "I'm not letting you out of my sight, you wily little shit. Your goose is cooked, and no matter what you do or say, your duplicity ends tonight."

"A convent?" Ilara said, looking back at Luisa. "Well, that does seem like a perfect place to hide people, doesn't it?"

"If it's still standing," Luisa said. "I remember it from my youth."

My pulse thudded against my ribcage, and it was all I could do to keep my face neutral. Coyle had dragged me back here surrounded by his soldiers. Even if I'd wanted to run, I wouldn't have gotten far. The only thing I could do was pray that one of Felix's vigilantes had been listening, and they could empty the convent in time.

"With your permission, I'd like to take a contingent of soldiers with me to check it out," Coyle said, bowing. "When we find the Forcadelians, where would you like me to send them?"

"The mines, of course," Ilara said, surveying me with a smile on her face. "And here I thought I was asking you to find twenty. You might've found hundreds."

"If the convent is still standing," I said, clearing my throat. "Which we don't know."

"And if I'd known it was there, I would've burned it to the ground," Ilara said, looking at Luisa. "What else are you keeping from me, dear friend?"

"Nothing, I assure you. I'd forgotten all about it until it was just mentioned," she said with a smile. But when Ilara turned away from her, Luisa's gaze landed on me for an instant.

"You may take the soldiers," Ilara said. "I look forward to hearing the good news when you return."

Coyle hadn't waited for permission, as a horde of fifty Severian soldiers was standing at attention in front of the castle, and two horses were saddled and waiting for riders—the second one's reins tied to the first.

"I can ride a horse," I said dryly. "And I don't think I'm necessary. Though it will be fun to watch you embarrass yourself."

"Defiant until the end. That's what I like about you, Brynna," Coyle said with a small chuckle. "You're looking a little pale." He climbed onto the saddle. "You'd better hope there isn't a mask and cloak in this convent."

"And you'd better hope there are people there."

The march was slow, and the sentries would be able to see the soldiers coming. But even if they managed to get out in time, they wouldn't last long in the open desert.

Or would Felix stay and fight? They were civilians, many of whom had never picked up a weapon in their lives. And even though we outnumbered them four-to-one, making a stand now would completely blow my cover. There would be no explaining why Felix and two hundred Forcadelians were here, nor why I hadn't left for his side.

"Hm, I think I see it up ahead," Coyle said, spurring his horse to walk faster, but there was no moving the animal quicker over the sand.

Still, the procession came ever closer. The convent rose from the sand, the setting sun casting a beautiful orange glow on the tower. My stomach threatened to come up as my fear overtook me.

Coyle dismounted and walked up to the convent, a man about to seize victory. He lifted his fist and rapped on the door. "Anyone home?"

"Doesn't seem like it," I replied.

"Then they won't mind if we barge in." He paused, motioning to two Severians nearby. "You two, get this open."

They dismounted and ran over to work the door. When the lock wouldn't budge, they attempted to break it down with their shoulders.

"This is stupid," Coyle said. "Brynna, get this door open."

"I don't work for you."

He snapped his fingers, and the Severians pulled me off the horse, frog-marching me over to the door.

"What do you want me to do about it?" I asked.

"Pick the damn lock or I'll have them run you through."

I rolled my eyes, pulling a pair of pins from my hair. "Amateurs."

I took my time, working the tumblers open and closed to give those inside more time to escape. But when Coyle pulled his sword and pressed it to my neck, I finally turned them open.

"There," I said, opening the door a sliver. "Happy?"

"Put her in irons," Coyle snapped as he sheathed his sword and yanked the door open.

I half-expected to see arrows firing, but Coyle and the soldiers marched inside, swords drawn, with no resistance. They poured in two by two, and I listened for the sound of struggle, or cries of anguish. But…there was nothing.

Finally, Coyle reemerged, fury etched on his face. "Where are they?"

My hopes dared to lift. "Who?"

"You stupid bitch," he snarled and yanked me inside, where I found a completely empty space. "*Where are they?*"

"I have no idea," I said—honestly. The last time I'd been here, every nook and cranny had been filled with people. "I didn't know this place was even here."

"That's bullshit and you know it," he said, leaning closer. "I see footprints in the dust. Handprints on the doors. There were people in this space. And you know where they went."

"Do I?" I gestured to the empty space. "Where am I hiding these people, Coyle? My tunic isn't that big."

That set him off because his fist came for me, but of course, I was faster. I sidestepped his punch, swung my leg around, and kneed him directly in the side. He fell to the ground, coughing and gasping in pain. This time, not even his guards came to his rescue.

"I will find out where they went," Coyle whimpered. "And when I do, you will suffer."

"Having to spend another moment in your presence is suffering enough," I said. "Take me back to the castle and quit blaming me for your own epic failures."

Chapter Fifty-Two

Felix

With no sign of Aline or our Kulkan warships, I'd had no choice but to listen to Jax's ridiculous plan. The twenty Severian vessels situated in the mouth of the river were heavily guarded by soldiers and sailors alike, and I thought we were surely about to reveal ourselves to Ilara. But the vigilantes moved like shadows, and those onboard were heaps on the deck before they knew what was coming. In the silence of the night, each ship fell one by one.

Jax had wanted to throw the enemies overboard, but I intervened, reminding him that the bodies would eventually wash up. So he stashed the soldiers in the belly of the ship, locked away in a makeshift brig.

In the meantime, Aithne, Malka, and I gathered our civilians and led them in small groups out of the convent. We walked on the outskirts of the city, a journey that took much longer over the sand and with the old and young, but we managed it in one night. Kieran was waiting with a small boat he'd "borrowed" from the Severians, which took the Forcadelians to safety. By the time the sun was up this morning, every one of our saved citizens was sleeping soundly.

But as the day wore on, I couldn't rest. The ships held some supplies, but we'd run out sooner rather than later. Our Severian prisoners might eventually become a problem as well. And based on their positioning, Ilara would probably notice if these ships suddenly disappeared.

Jax was kind enough to point this out while we stood on the deck, watching the sun set.

"What's our grand plan here, *General*? Just keep saving one Forcadelian at a time? Sit on these boats until we're found out?" He nodded toward the bay to the west. "Your ships ain't coming, sorry to tell you. So we'd better figure something else out or else all this work is gonna be for nothing."

"And Katarine's army? Are we not holding out hope for them?" I asked, heat coming into my voice. "It's rather impossible to dethrone a queen without an army."

"The whole point was for us to remove Ilara from Forcadel, and she did that for us," Jax said, his tone even and unbothered. "Now we've liberated two hundred Forcadelians—on ships, no less, that could take them back home." He tilted his head at me. "All we need to do is put an arrow in that Severian bitch and we can all go home."

"Assassination could cause chaos," I said. "These people worship her—everyone from the soldiers to the civilians. We still have half of Forcadel City in the mines up north. If we kill Ilara, the Severians could retaliate and we could lose more of our people."

"Or the Severians would be a rudderless ship without their fearless leader," he replied. "Chaos is more than enough for us to get into the castle and take charge."

"With whom will we conduct this assault?"

Jax pointed the tip of his knife down. "We got fifty bodies on this ship. Hundreds more on the others. Why not them?"

"You may have faith in these civilians, but I don't," I said, lowering my voice. "Brynna—"

"If you're waiting for your soft-hearted queen's approval, we'll be here until we die of old age," he said, returning his knife point to his fingers. "She'll never agree to kill anyone in cold blood. Mark my words, if we want something done, we'll have to do it ourselves."

His words had a ring of truth to them. "I was planning to head out to the city and try to intercept Brynna. With Coyle in town, I'm sure she'll sneak out to warn us." I sighed. "I'll see what she thinks about moving these ships, or if she has any other ideas."

"You do whatever you want," Jax said, sitting back and closing his eyes. "But you know where I stand."

Jax had an annoying way of speaking the truth. We'd wasted enough time gathering and saving people; the time to act was growing near. Assassinating Ilara would surely be the swiftest way to remove her from power, but the repercussions could be worse.

I reached the building near the castle where I'd taken to watching for Brynna's appearance and crouched low. A crowd of Severian soldiers exited the castle, all of whom had something of a disgruntled look on their faces.

"Just like back in Forcadel."

"What a moron."

"If we're lucky, he'll get sent up to the mines."

I could only hope they were talking about my favorite traitor.

After an hour of waiting, I spotted movement. Brynna shimmied down the side of the castle. She craned her neck around the corner before scampering across the street. I crossed over two or three buildings, keeping her in sight and waiting on the building where she'd be climbing up.

When her head popped up, her eyes flashed with fear for a moment before she recognized me. "Mother above, Felix, you scared me."

"Sorry," I said with a smile as I reached down to help her up. "You look a mess. Have you been out in the desert?"

Her tunic had a light sheen of brown dust on it, and her hair was filthy. "Coyle found out about the convent," she said. "But when we got there...it was empty."

The breath left my lungs. "Thank the Mother we moved when we did." I shook my head. "I won't tell Jax though. His ego'll be unstoppable."

"Jax?" Brynna said. "He's here?"

I nodded. "He thought that stashing your saved citizens in a church was a little too on-the-nose for you, so he suggested we move them."

"Where are they?" she asked. "Coyle's ready to tear this city apart looking for them."

"I doubt he'll find them," I said. "Unless he wants to check the five Severian boats sitting in the mouth of the river." To her surprised look, I added, "Again, Jax's idea."

"Yeah, best not to tell him that I appreciate him," she said with a serious nod. "Ilara would surely notice his head floating above the city."

I snorted, amused at the light in her eyes. "How bad was it when you told Ilara you found an empty convent?"

"Coyle refused to allow me entry into her office," she said. "So I snuck out while he's being eviscerated." She paused then laughed. "And I bet Jax was on that missing carriage the other day, too. You guys are just causing all kinds of trouble lately, aren't you? How did you manage to get away?"

I told her the story and of how Jax managed to commandeer the ship he'd been on.

"What else did he say about Forcadel?" she asked.

"Only that it's empty," I said. "All of our people have been taken to this city. They're either in the mines—"

"Or in the river bed," she finished. "But where did you put the Kulkan warships?"

"Warships?" I shook my head. "They still haven't arrived."

She tilted her head up at me. "Then why did I see a soldier at the river construction?"

"What river construction?"

"The one that…" She licked her lips slowly, a smile growing on her face. "You weren't responsible for poisoning the Severians and replacing the Forcadelian citizens with soldiers?"

"Nah, that was me."

I jumped at the sound of a young voice. Elisha was crouched on the roof behind us, rising slowly with a catty smirk on her face. The last time I'd seen her, she was leaving with…

"Katarine," I breathed.

"I knew it," Brynna said, pushing me aside and running over to her. "The Niemenian forces are here, aren't they? Mother above, it's good to see you."

Elisha nodded. "Why were you helping the Severians? You shouldn't have given them tinneum. I had to go back and poison them again. It's a pain in the butt."

"Have to keep up appearances," Brynna said, a lightness in her voice as she cupped the teen's face. "Tell me everything that's been going on since I last saw you."

"Well, Katarine's been real annoying," Elisha said. "Keeps getting mad when I go off and do stuff. I'm not even supposed to be out here right now—she's gonna take it outta my hide, I bet."

I snorted as Brynna fought a smile. "I meant in terms of the Niemenian forces. When did you get here, how many are with you, that sort of thing."

"Oh, right." Elisha laughed. "There's not too many of us yet, but that's 'cause Luard told the Niemenian boats to wait further down the river. Doesn't want Ilara to know they're here. The Niemenians are pretty easily recognized, being so pale and all."

"That's certainly true," I said. "But Katarine and Luard are here?"

"And Joella," Elisha said, looking at me. "Who isn't as bad about letting me out of her sight."

"What did you do to the Severian soldiers?" Brynna asked.

"Hyblatha," Elisha said. "But instead of throwing it in their faces, I put it on their food."

Brynna's mouth opened. "I…never thought to do that before. And it works?"

"I mean, you saw how nutso they got," the teenager replied.

"How in the Mother's name did you think of that?"

"Wasn't me, it was the wolves."

Brynna's eyes widened and her mouth fell open, but I asked, "Wolves? As in…animals?"

"Nah, Nestoris from Niemen," Elisha said. "Apparently, they owed Brynna a life debt. Luard had me sneak out of Skorsa, on account of Katarine and Beata being way too overprotective, and find a lady named—"

"Brigit," Brynna said, her voice tight. "How is she?"

"Real good. Said to thank you again for all your help. Said her farm was nearly paid off thanks to what you did," Elisha said. "So when I asked if she'd take me to the mountains, she agreed and even helped cart the wolves back to the boat. I brought them back to Skorsa and they took the gate out."

Brynna gasped. "Tell me they didn't—"

"With hyblatha, only used like normal," Elisha said, nudging her. "We know how you get about killing people. And it was a good thing, too, 'cause it was all Forcadelian soldiers there."

"I know," Brynna said. "Captain Mark. Was he helpful at all?"

"Last I saw him, he was spitting on Katarine," Elisha said with a growl. "And Katarine sent me off with Joella to help her get inside the city. I been looking all over for you guys, but it's a big place."

"Glad you found us," I said, placing my hand on the small of Brynna's back. "Now can you take us to Katarine and Luard?"

"Course I can," Elisha said. "They'll be happy to see you."

"Not as happy as I'll be," I muttered, walking forward to follow the teenager. But Brynna hadn't moved.

"What is it?" I asked, turning.

She was staring at the bay, her eyes shining in the moonlight. There was something unreadable on her face, a mixture of emotion I couldn't pinpoint. But when she turned back to me, her smile was genuine, as was the tear falling down her cheek.

"I have to get back to the castle," she said, wiping her cheek. "It was dangerous enough to leave in the first place, and the longer I'm gone... I'm sure Coyle will want to stick a guard under my window once Ilara's finished ripping him a new one." She beamed at Elisha. "Tell Katarine that things are going according to plan, and that I look forward to seeing her when everything is finalized."

"Will do," the kid said. "But why aren't you coming?"

"I've got a job to do," she said. "And the people I left in charge have...well, they've done more than I ever could've dreamed." She took my hand. "I trust they'll keep on making me proud."

Chapter Fifty-Three

Katarine

Elisha had made quick work of the Severian guards in the riverbed, and the hyblatha had worked faster than we'd anticipated. Once the Severian soldiers were incapacitated, Joella had helped with the move of some of the Forcadelians away from the camp and onto ships. We'd sent one full ship back with the sickest, and had sent a request back to Skorsa to commission more ships.

But on the second day, we'd hit a snag—Ilara herself had come to inspect the chaos, along with Brynna. It was both gratifying to see Brynna's acting in person and worrying that we'd perhaps made things worse for her. Still, she seemed to have played it off with absolutely flawless innocence.

When dusk fell and a new crop of Severians soldiers had arrived, I sent Elisha back out. Within an hour, they, too, had succumbed. And when Ilara's messenger showed up to check on progress, we made sure he didn't get word back to his queen.

"She's going to figure out something's amiss here," Luard said as they dragged the messenger toward the rest of the Severians. "I think it might be time for Elisha to move on the castle to make contact with Brynna."

I shook my head. "She'd never make it past the front door."

"She might."

"It's too dangerous."

"Sister," Luard said, giving me a look. "Look at what that child accomplished down below and tell me she can't handle herself."

I still had reservations, but I allowed Luard to give her his task. We were truly running out of time.

As darkness and chill descended over the desert, I kept my gaze focused on the city beyond, whispering prayers to the Mother and wishing I had a row of candles. There was no telling how heavily guarded Brynna was, especially after what we'd done here, and Elisha wouldn't rest until her job was over.

When the moon was high overhead, Luard joined me on my perch, handing me a telescope and dropping an extra cloak around my shoulders. "Since you seem intent on waiting here."

"Is this what Felix feels?" I asked, peering through the telescope. "Worrying about a headstrong vigilante all day long?"

"By now, Felix has surely settled into knowing where he can help his queen and where he can let her do her thing," Luard said. "Perhaps you can follow suit."

"I hope he gets here soon," I said, scanning the edge of the city. "I—" I spotted movement at the border of the city. "Someone's coming."

"How many?" Luard asked.

"Two—three," I said, inching closer to the edge. "It's Elisha and..."

I dropped the telescope and hurried down the scaffolding, Luard calling my name. But I didn't care; I had to know if my eyes had been playing tricks on me. The wooden steps were too treacherous for my speed, and more than once the soles of my shoes slid against the worn treads, but I kept a hand on the railing to steady myself.

I slowed when I reached the bottom, walking out onto the dock and putting my hand to my lips.

"Felix?" I called, walking slowly toward the figures.

"Hey, Kat," he said, grinning up at me. "Fancy seeing you out here in the desert. What in the Mother's name did you do to your hair?"

"Thought it might help me blend in a little better." I grinned, searching for the third figure, but my heart sank. It was Jax, the vigilante. "Where's Brynna?"

"Back at the castle," Felix said, joining me up on the deck. "But she sends her love and blessing."

"Felix, my good man," Luard said, having taken the stairs much slower. "And Jax, excellent to see you. Seems like we've all made it all right."

"Not all of us," Felix said darkly. "I'm here, but Aline and my forces have yet to arrive with the Kulkan warships." He glanced at me, hope in his eyes. "Tell me the Niemenians have come through."

"And then some," Luard said, patting him on the shoulder. "Come, let's have a chat."

We gathered in the captain's quarters where Luard and I had been sleeping and strategizing. Elisha demanded to be granted access, but Jax put a stop to that immediately.

"Scram, you brat," he barked. "This ain't no place for your annoying ass."

She scowled then sulked away.

"I wish she'd listen to me that well," I said with a hopeful smile.

He cast me a look. "You're the one who took all the kids, ain't you?"

I nodded. "They're back in Skorsa with my wife, preparing more hyblatha and knockout powder before coming this way." I hesitated, worried about his reaction. "They will be out of danger."

"Thank you," he muttered, so low that only I could hear. "For giving them a home."

My cheeks warmed, but Luard called the meeting to attention before I could respond. "Felix and I have been in discussion, and we believe the time to act is now. Tomorrow." Luard unfurled a crudely drawn map of Aunela onto the table. "The ships here have already been commandeered by Felix and are full of Forcadelian civilians. We can safely move them onto the river and back to Skorsa before first light."

"Good," Jax said. "They're doing nothing but eating and whining about how they want to go home."

"The Niemenian forces can be in the bay within two hours," Luard said. "A hundred or so Forcadelian soldiers are waiting just beyond here, and can get into position quickly, as well."

"Will that be enough?" I asked. "There are hundreds of thousands of Severians, not to mention Ilara's Severian army."

"We don't have time to wait," Felix said. "Coyle's here, and he's wise to Brynna's tricks. It's only thanks to Jax that we managed to get out of the convent in time."

"Since we're talking about how brilliant I am," Jax said, leaning back in his chair, "I say we go with my plan. Kill Ilara first then worry about the aftermath." He plucked his crossbow from his belt. "One arrow. It'll be over in seconds."

Silence descended on the group, which Felix eventually broke. "The aftermath should be worried about now. What if Brynna's killed, or the Severians raze the varo mines? We still have thousands of citizens in pockets around the city."

"You don't give two shits about them," Jax said, pointing the crossbow at Felix. "You're just afraid to piss your girlfriend off."

"She's still queen," Felix said, sounding a bit miffed. "And she wouldn't want us to risk her people like that."

"I hate to agree with Jax," Luard said with an apologetic look at both of them, "but I do. Brynna's not always made the best strategic decisions. I appreciate that we're trying to limit the risk to innocents, but there's no point if we fail entirely."

"So we just assassinate Ilara and hope for the best?" Felix said. "Brynna won't go for that."

"Well, who gives a shit what she thinks?" Jax pointed at me. "Take your fancy Niemenian ore and start blowing holes. Then we all pack up and go back to Forcadel, which is absolutely empty."

"What about the Forcadelians still in the city?" Joella asked. "There are probably thousands at the riverbed construction, and more still up north."

"We send rescue boats," Jax said with a shrug. "The Niemenians seem to have a bunch of 'em."

"And in the meantime, the Severians could kill thousands," I said.

"The Severians are already killing people," Joella said.

Luard nodded, pointing at her. "Exactly. Besides that, the Niemenian soldiers can't even fathom coming into town until we've begun the assault, and they can't wait around forever."

Silence descended again. and Felix rubbed his chin, looking tortured. I, too, had reservations about this plan, especially with all the unknowns. The Severians had come to worship their queen like a goddess, and killing her would enrage them. But the longer we waited, the riskier this entire endeavor became.

"The only way to end this," Luard said gently, "is if Ilara's gone. Everything stops with her. The military will be in chaos, and we can more easily take them prisoner. It will limit casualties."

"I still say Brynna won't like the idea of killing Ilara," Felix said. "Even after all Ilara's done, Brynna would rather she just rot in jail forever."

"Yeah, well, Brynna's not here to speak for herself, is she?" Jax said. "She may be queen, but this ain't her war. All of us got a stake in this. We've all sacrificed and lost things. And some of us wouldn't shed a tear if Ilara died a slow, painful death."

"She isn't here," Felix said. "But she trusted us to make the best decision."

"And we are," Luard said. "We may just have to beg for forgiveness once she's back on the throne in Forcadel." He looked around the table. "All in favor of Jax's plan?"

"Aye," came a chorus around the table, save me and Felix.

"Sister?" Luard said.

With a heavy heart, and unable to look at Felix, I lifted my hand. "Aye."

Luard's gaze turned to the other holdout. "Felix?"

"We don't need unanimous consent," Jax grumbled.

"But I'd like it," Luard said with a tight smile. "Well?"

He leaned onto his elbows on the table. "The moment that arrow goes into Ilara, we get Brynna out of there. She's our top priority."

Luard nodded. "Of course."

"Then aye."

"She's not going to like this at all," Felix said with a heavy sigh as we stood on the deck watching the stars overhead. "She told me she trusted me, and now we're doing the opposite of what she wants."

"She'll understand once it's done," I said.

"Understand what?" Elisha jumped down from the quarterdeck, her brow furrowed. "Are we ready to make a move?"

"Getting there," I said with a gentle smile.

"What won't Brynna like?"

"I'm sorry?" I said.

"You said Brynna won't like what you're doing. So what is it?

What's the plan?"

I held my tongue, but Felix seemed more willing to tell her the truth. "We'll remove Ilara then take the city. Once we have the soldiers under our control, we'll start putting everything back the way it was."

"You're gonna kill Ilara?"

I nodded. "Yes."

"You're right, Brynna won't like that," Elisha said, looking away. "Are you gonna tell her before you do it?"

"No," Felix said. "We need to move swiftly."

"But you gotta tell her. She's the queen."

"Elisha, there are things at work that you don't understand," I said.

"I understand plenty," she said. "I understand that you're taking advantage of the fact that Brynna ain't here. I understand that you think she's weak or whatever because she doesn't want to kill Ilara. But that's strength. That's the way The Veil became so strong. There's always a way."

"Not in this case," I said.

"In every case. You just aren't trying hard enough." She took a step toward me, but I held my ground. "You just want to take the easy way, like back in Skorsa. You would've blown up that gate before you even *tried* another option."

"That absolutely isn't true," I said. "We sent you—"

"You didn't send me, Luard did," she said. "And your queen sister gave me a ride, too. You're the only one who—"

The bag hit her face, and she blinked once, twice, then slumped into Jax's waiting arms. He cradled her as he straightened, shaking his head.

"What are you doing?" I asked Jax.

"Mitigating some risk," he said. "She's too much like Brynna for her own good."

Chapter Fifty-Four

"The wolves said they owed you a life debt."

I lay awake as the early morning sun streamed through my window, unable to shake Elisha's words from my memory. I'd completely forgotten about my trip through the Niemenian mountains, or the young Nestoris who'd nearly gotten the better of me. But they hadn't, and had come to help my forces get through an impassable barrier.

Jax had been responsible for getting my people to safety on Severian warships. Jax, who butted heads with me more often than not over my penchant for protecting people, had given thought to and executed a plan to help others. He could tell me one day that it was a strategic decision, but I knew better.

Elisha was taking Felix to meet with Katarine and Luard, who had an entire army waiting to help me reclaim my kingdom, courtesy of Queen Ariadna. The only people missing were the Kulkans and the rest of my forces, and after all I'd seen the night before, I couldn't imagine the Mother would keep them from me.

It felt like the small seeds I'd been planting all these months were finally starting to sprout, mostly in unexpected, but welcome, ways. For all my fears that my soldiers and forces had abandoned me, they'd been keeping to the spirit of The Veil all along. Save as many as possible, cause a little trouble, and get the bad guy.

I sat on the edge of the bed, filled with more hope than I'd had in months. The only thing I had to do now was be ready for whatever my trusted forces came up with.

When the servants came to fetch me, I was already dressed and ready. Knowing that Ilara would sense my happiness from miles away, I stuffed everything down low and kept myself neutral. I was, however, hoping to pump Luisa for information on how badly Ilara had eviscerated Coyle.

Unfortunately, the man himself was at breakfast—a bad sign.

"I trust you slept well," Coyle said, tilting his head up at me with a smile.

"Like a lamb," I replied, taking a seat. "Surprised you're able to sit after the ass-chewing you got."

His lip twitched, but I wasn't sure why. "Her Majesty's capacity for forgiveness is incredible. She's offered me a second chance to find the missing Forcadelians."

"Well, if you need any help," I said, smiling sweetly, "ask someone else."

Still, for all his confidence, Ilara barely acknowledged him. Today, Luisa arrived with her, and they appeared to be in deep conversation until they walked through the door. I doubted Luisa would give me any indication of what they'd spoken about, but I might be able to get something out of her.

"Dearest Brynna," Ilara said, once breakfast had gotten underway, "I'm sorry Coyle dragged you into the desert late into the night. You must be exhausted."

"I slept exceedingly well," I said with a nod. "Does Her

Majesty wish for me to continue working to find the missing Forcadelians?"

"I have confidence in Captain Coyle," she said, casting him an unfriendly look. Clearly, her capacity for forgiveness had limits. I fought a smile.

"They must've gone somewhere," Luisa said. "There aren't many places in the city. Perhaps they found a ship to take them up to Skorsa?"

"Even if they did, Captain Mark has orders to send them right back," Ilara said, spearing a potato with her fork. "Do not trouble your mind, dear Luisa. Captain Coyle will find them." She cleared her throat. "Today."

"I have a plan to smoke them out," he said. "And I will not fail you."

"See that you don't." Her glare left no doubt in my mind; if Coyle did, he'd find himself at the bottom of the bay by nightfall. And perhaps sensing his own fate was drawing nearer, Coyle excused himself from the breakfast table with his food only half-eaten.

"Quit looking so pleased with yourself," Luisa whispered.

"It's hard not to be when Coyle made a colossal ass of himself," I replied. "You can't blame me."

She pursed her lips and shook her head, but there was a little mirth in her eyes.

One of the other Severian merchants who'd been sitting nearby cleared his throat. "Your Majesty, I hope this new development doesn't preclude you from visiting the arts district today. We've made great strides these past few days to clean and rebuild, and it would mean a lot to our Severian workers to see their queen amongst them."

She smiled. "Nothing would make me happier."

After breakfast, Ilara yet again invited the gaggle of artisans and merchants to join her for the day, and Luisa and I were included in that number. I was fine with the distraction, as it told me Ilara thought nothing amiss in her city. So far, so good.

Luisa dropped back from the crowd to join me. "Pleasant day today, isn't it?"

"It's always a pleasant day when Coyle is in trouble." I cast her a sideways look. "Give me some indication of how badly Ilara tore into him."

"I shall not," she said then cleared her throat. "It wasn't that bad, actually. But her patience with him is growing thin. It's only due to his loyalty so far that she's even allowed him to retain his captain's badge. He did manage to clear Forcadel, but with so many missing…"

"With his own neck on the line, I'm sure he'll do his best to make her proud," I said. "That seems to be the only thing that motivates him, after all."

"Yes." She tilted her head up to the clear blue sky. "You know, it's funny. When we first arrived here in Aunela, I distinctly remember telling you about the convent in the northeast."

I nearly stumbled over my feet. "You did?"

"Mm."

"I must've forgotten."

"So you did." She cast me a knowing look. "It doesn't matter anyway. Coyle found nothing there, did he?"

"Indeed, he didn't."

The tension in my chest loosened, but I didn't say anything further, my mind spinning with the potential dangers all around. If Luisa knew, presumably Ilara did as well. Perhaps there was a larger target on me than anticipated. I would have to let—

"*Fire!*"

Luisa stopped short, looking behind us. "Another one?"

A soldier came running around the corner, his face pale as he blew past us toward the front of the group. "Your Majesty, come quick. The school—"

My heart dropped to my stomach before I took off toward the southeast. It wasn't long before I had a group behind me, led by the queen herself, screaming at every soldier she saw to fetch water and more soldiers. But my pace was faster than hers, and I broke ahead, running through the dusty streets as fast as I could.

A column of smoke twisted toward the sky, and I prayed that my people had nothing to do with this. Or if they had, that they'd evacuated the school first. There were hundreds of innocent children in there, none of whom had anything to do with Ilara's invasion.

"Please don't have done this," I whispered, as the scent of burning wood filled the air. "Please, oh, please."

I skidded around the corner and came onto the burning building, orange flames shooting out the windows. Out front, the children were watching with eyes wide open. The headmistress was standing in the street, her hands covering her mouth.

"How many are left?" I asked.

She shook her head. "The upper levels. I don't know—we don't have any of our older kids."

A child screamed from inside, and a small head poked out of the third-story window, waving her hands for help.

"What in the Mother's name…?" Ilara said, finally arriving. "Someone…someone do something!"

I balled my fists, breathing out through my nose and searching the rooftops. The bottom floor looked impassable, but the second story might work. A nearby building would be a jump, but I'd made longer before.

I turned and walked away, but Ilara grabbed my arm. "Where are you going?" she snarled.

"To help," I said, pushing her arm off gently.

I ran to the nearest building and climbed to the second story, finding enough room to get a running start. Exhaling, I took off as fast as I could, leaping toward the building. Down below, the street passed beneath my body, and the wind whispered through my hair. The window came closer and I braced myself, flying through the open window and landing in a heap on the floor.

"Wow."

I looked up to see ten children and their terrified teacher. The child who'd spoken offered me a small smile.

"We have to get you out of here," I said. "The building is going to collapse soon."

"How?" she said. "The stairwells are all on fire."

I swallowed and looked at the curtains on the windows. "Grab the curtains, anything you have that we can tie together. We're going to climb down."

"They're just children," the teacher said.

"I've seen younger do more," I snapped as a loud banging echoed from outside. "And we don't have time to argue, so make it happen."

With the children working together, they created the makeshift rope and I tied it to the teacher's desk and tossed the other end out the window.

"Go," I said to the first kid. "Just walk down the side of the building."

"I'm afraid of heights," he said.

Something crashed in the distance and we both ducked. "You're going to be more afraid of what's coming if you don't get a move on." But I softened, seeing real fear in his eyes. "It's okay. You won't fall. Just keep a tight grip on the curtains."

One by one, they descended, down into the waiting arms of the soldiers—who weren't exactly rushing forward to help. I didn't wait too long before sending the next student down, until there was only the teacher and me.

"I don't know who you are, but you're a saint," she said.

"Is there anyone else up here?" I asked.

"I don't know."

"Then you go. I'll keep looking."

I checked every room on this floor, then the one above, but they were empty. The fire was starting to rage, and there wouldn't be much more time before the building collapsed. So I climbed out the window and landed on the ground, rushing across the street to Ilara, who was holding onto one of the children I'd saved.

A cup of water was pushed into my hand and I looked down at a young Severian girl. "Thank you for saving my brother."

"You're welcome," I said with a half-smile as I took the cup and washed away the smoke in my lungs. "Is that everyone?"

The headmistress nodded. "You…you…"

"It's what I do," I said, looking up at the building and exhaling. Felix and I would have to have a little talk, but at least everyone was safe.

"Ilara, say something," Luisa said, pushing her queen forward with a smile.

The Severian queen, her face pale with fear and a light sheen of sweat on her forehead, looked torn between disgust and relief.

"You don't have to say a thing," I said, waving her off.

Ilara turned toward the building, folding her arms across her chest. "I suppose I can't blame you for this, can I?"

"I'm not in the habit of running into fires I started, no," I said, coughing up more smoke. "But I'd be happy to find out who did it."

She made a face. "That won't be necessary."

"For Mother's sake, Ilara, thank Brynna for risking her life to save the children," Luisa said with a look. "It's the least you can do."

"Fine." Ilara inhaled deeply. "I'm—"

Something glinted in the sunlight, and I heard the whistling of the arrow too late.

Luisa was faster.

Chapter Fifty-Five

The arrow pierced Luisa's chest, the bloody tip protruding from her back as she stood in front of Ilara. Her eyes had gone wide, and she gasped for air as she wavered on her feet. As she tilted toward the ground, Ilara caught her.

"Luisa," she whispered, touching her face as Luisa's breath came in shorter gasps.

Something grotesque was building in my chest as I watched, equal parts horror, guilt, and dread. My body was rooted to the ground, unable to move or look away as blood seeped from the wound onto the sandy ground.

"It's all right," Luisa whispered, a trickle of blood coming from her mouth. "I will be at peace with the Mother."

"I need you here," Ilara said, thick tears dripping down her face.

"I..." Whatever she said was too faint for me to hear.

"L-Luisa," Ilara said, cradling her friend. "Please, don't..."

Luisa exhaled a sigh and she sank lower into Ilara's arms. As the queen released a bone-chilling scream, I closed my eyes and whispered a prayer to the Mother for Luisa's soul, and hoped that She would welcome the Severian with open arms.

And that she'd protect the rest of us from whatever came next.

A cadre of soldiers approached, and Ilara released an almost feral growl. "Don't touch her."

"Your Majesty, we—"

"You will do nothing," Ilara snarled, her eyes red and her cheeks blotchy. This was probably a side of her no one had ever seen. When the gallery had burned, she'd been devastated. Now, she was unhinged.

What have they done?

"Please," the soldier said, her eyes kind. "We want to help."

Finally, after a tense few minutes, Ilara allowed the soldiers to help her to her feet. Her white Severian smock was covered in blood, and some of it had smeared on her face. The soldiers had brought a wagon and loaded Luisa's body onto it, covering her face with a blanket before wheeling her away.

"When I find out who did this," she announced, her voice echoing in the street, "I won't just destroy them. I will destroy everything precious to them. They will *rue* the day they crossed me."

Luisa's body was set ablaze in the town center that evening. Ilara had ordered black flags hung from every window again, and stood draped in all black as she watched her best friend burn. There were no coffins, no hiding the sight of death and Severian mourning. I remained steadfast behind her, keeping my tears to myself. I didn't think Ilara would appreciate seeing them, but my emotion was real. Luisa had been kind to me in this unkind place.

There was no dinner, so I snuck out as soon as I was seen

returning to my room. I had almost convinced myself that there was a radical actor in town now, that Felix and Katarine couldn't have sanctioned something so reckless, but even the voice in my head was weakening. I needed to know for sure.

I traipsed across the rooftops, wandering aimlessly. The convent was cleared out, so I couldn't go there. Felix wasn't in our normal meeting spot, and I had no idea where I'd find my people. But perhaps they would find me.

I stopped on the rooftop where the assassin had made their shot. The street was empty now, and sand had been brought in to cover the bloodstain on the ground. But I could still see the scene unfolding in my mind, picturing myself as the killer. The shot was so easy from here.

"She moved."

I couldn't say I was surprised to hear Jax behind me. "I thought you didn't miss."

"In this case, someone wanted themselves dead. Can't help it."

I shook my head. "You shouldn't have done that without telling me first."

"I thought the whole point of this was that you'd delegated all these decisions to us," Jax said, coming to stand next to me.

"The others are keeping me apprised of decisions. I expect you to do the same."

"They were in on it," he said, crossing his arms. "It was by unanimous consent of your council."

"It can't be unanimous if I'm not aware of it."

He snorted. "What's up your butt?"

"Luisa was a friend," I said.

"No, she wasn't," he said. "She was the enemy. Everyone in that castle is. Did you forget that Ilara killed Celia and hundreds of children?"

"Ilara did. Luisa didn't." I glared at him. "The children in that school didn't kill anyone, either."

"They're all complicit," he said. "They give her power, and with that power, she's killed our people. That's guilt enough for me."

I crossed my arms over my chest. "Take me to wherever the group is. It's clear I need to remind them of some things."

His smile was cruel. "Why in the Mother's name do you think I'd do that?"

"Because I'm the queen," I said, turning to him.

"Not really. You ain't got a crown on your head. All you are is an annoying gnat."

My heart skipped a beat. "What the hell, Jax? Are you turning on me?"

"No, you're the one who's been turned," he said. "You're here madder that I killed a Severian than that I missed the queen. You're talking about the enemy like they're your friends." He shook his head. "Felix was right. They got in your head."

My mouth fell. "He said…what?"

"Ilara played you like she's done every step of the way," he said. "Showing you the softer side of her miserable desert life. And yet again, you fell for it like a moron." He took a step toward me. "And I don't trust that if I bring you to our troops, you won't lead the Severians to us, too."

"How *dare* you?" I snarled. "Do you have *any* idea what I've sacrificed?"

"Sitting in the castle, getting to sleep in a nice bed, I'm sure it's been rough." He made a face. "Do you know what the rest of us have been doing?"

"Dying in mines," I said. "I'm doing the job that *you* told me to do. Staying close to Ilara."

"You got too close."

"I can't believe this," I said, shaking my head. "The whole point of this is to get me back on the throne. Or has that changed in my absence?"

"Perhaps it has, with the way you've been acting. Either way, we'll do what you don't have the stomach to."

"I want to speak with Felix and Katarine," I said.

"You're welcome to find them," Jax said, turning to leave. "But if I were you, I'd get your soft heart back to your friends at the castle and wait for us to take action."

He disappeared into the alley below.

I stayed on that roof for a long time, simmering in anger and replaying Jax's words. I couldn't believe Katarine and Felix had given their blessing to something I would've been so dead-set against. They wouldn't have okayed it if they'd known Luisa would be the one who ended up dead, of that I was sure. And perhaps an assassin's arrow *was* a fitting end to a woman who'd poisoned my father and brother, murdered hundreds, and broken the entire city of Forcadel just to get her revenge.

"Felix is right. They got in your head."

Was I really so soft as to fall for Ilara's machinations? I'd seen right through the books and sob stories, knowing that the harm Ilara was doing to the Forcadelians far outweighed the consequences of taking the city back. And yet, I'd cried for Luisa. I'd cried for Ilara's pain, too. I'd never known what it was to lose a close friend, but her misery was palpable.

There were soft footsteps behind me, and I looked out of the corner of my eye to find a small body standing there.

"Elisha?" I said, turning fully. "What are you doing here?"

"I heard what Jax said to you," she said. "He's wrong. They all are. You're the queen, and they shouldn't go around killing people." She looked down. "I wanted to warn you about it, but they locked me up."

I blanched. "Katarine?"

She balled her fists. "That bitch. All she does is talk down to me." Elisha sniffed. "And Jax is the one who hit me with knockout powder and locked me up. All of them can eat rocks."

It was hard not to smile. "Clearly, Jax is no match for you."

"As if I don't got pins in my hair," she said, flashing me a smile. "I learned from the best."

I warmed at her pride, but my gloom was more powerful.

"I can't believe they'd just do this," she said. "It's not what The Veil would've done."

"Perhaps it's what needed to be done, though," I said dully.

"No, it's not," Elisha said. "Killing people, setting a school full of innocents on fire, that's not what made The Veil loved in Haymaker's Corner. You never played dirty and you still came out on top." She huffed. "You should get back to the rest and tell them they need to remember who they're working for. You *are* the queen."

Her words were heartening, but I couldn't make myself stand. "Do you know what their next move will be?"

She shook her head. "I—"

We both saw the movement in the alley below at the same time and the blood froze in my veins.

"You seem to have lost your touch."

"Elisha," I whispered. "Run."

But Coyle had surrounded us in alleys and on rooftops. They had come out of nowhere, materializing as well as any vigilante could've done. Beside me, Elisha brandished her weapons, but there was no fighting. We were outnumbered.

I slowly rose to face Coyle, whose look of glee and joy was in stark contrast to the dread in my stomach. "I don't know what you think you saw or heard—"

"Everything," Coyle said. "As did everyone else."

I chewed my tongue.

"You know, the old Brynna would never have been caught so easily," Coyle said, his boots tapping on the tile roof behind us. "Returning to the scene of the crime was rather stupid. And having a long conversation with your friend here..." He tutted. "It's almost as if you wanted to get caught."

"Let the girl go, and I'll take the blame for all of it," I said.

"And let her scamper back to the rest of your rats? Not a chance."

"She's a child," I said.

"She isn't—she's one of Celia's rats," he said. "One that got away. But I'll be sure to remedy that just as soon as Ilara's finished with you."

Chapter Fifty-Six

I was returned to my room, only this time, I was in irons. My windows had been boarded shut, leaving the room stuffy and miserable. But it wasn't as if I expected to be in there for very long. If I lived another two days, I'd be surprised.

Instead of focusing on my own impending demise, I focused my attention on Elisha. She'd been deposited in the room alongside me, and even though she wore a fierce glare in front of the guards, once the door slammed shut, she lost some of her gumption. She'd never looked more like a kid, and my chest hurt at the unfairness.

"Are we gonna die?" she asked softly.

I exhaled, knowing she was looking for the truth, and for me to save her. "We'll think of something," I said, after a breath. "It's not over until it's over."

But my words fell flat. We were surrounded, the windows boarded, my weapons gone. Ilara would probably have guards stationed every few feet beneath my window and outside our door. There was no escape. I wanted to hope that Ilara might find some mercy for Elisha, but considering her current mood, I doubted that would be the case.

"This waiting stuff sucks," Elisha said, turning back to me. "I think I'd rather they just put an arrow in me and get it over with."

I laughed, as I had to agree. We'd both been in life-threatening situations, but this was different. Then, if we fought hard enough and the Mother's will was on our side, we survived. But now...

"Don't lose hope yet," I said, instead of allowing myself to fall into despair. "The armies are still out there. Felix and Katarine won't let this happen."

"But they were talking about you like you ain't the queen."

Jax's words floated through my head, but I brushed them off. "We had disagreements, but they've worked too hard to just let us die. And they've got Jax and Aline—"

"Aline never arrived," Elisha said, looking up at me.

I forced a smile onto my face. "Don't worry. Everything will work out."

"You know, now that I'm gonna die, maybe I shoulda been nicer to Lady Katarine," Elisha said, looking at her hands. "I didn't mean what I said back there. She isn't a bitch. She was real nice to me. I just wish..." She sighed. "She just always wanted me to do stuff I didn't want to do. And she was *always* worrying about me. It's annoying."

"She does that," I said with a smile. "But that just meant she cared about you. It's the same reason Felix used to drive me crazy."

"Did he stop bugging you?"

"No," I said. "But he's less annoying about it now. And maybe I see it for what it is. It's not that he doesn't think I can do it, but...he loves me. And he can't help but worry." I turned to her. "Perhaps Katarine was feeling the same way. She and Beata had always...well, I know they had wanted to become mothers. It just arrived a little sooner than they'd expected."

Elisha pursed her lips as if she hadn't ever considered that before. "So...they wanted to be my parents?"

I nodded, then stopped, remembering we were on our last few hours. Elisha seemed to come to the same conclusion, and her eyes filled with sadness.

"Yeah...maybe I shoulda been nicer," she said after a long pause. "And maybe told them I woulda been glad to join their family."

"They'll know." I draped my arm around her as best I could with the irons and pulled her close. "There's no use thinking about the past and what you could've done differently. All we can do is move forward until we can't anymore." I pressed her head to my shoulder. "We just need to keep faith."

A tiny sliver of sunlight shone through the boarded-up windows, and I could only assume dawn had risen. Elisha had nodded off sometime in the night, and I was grateful she could find a moment's peace. I'd hoped she might fall into the little family Beata and Katarine had begun gathering when I'd left them at the camp, which was why I'd sent her with them. She was a good kid, and she deserved more than this end.

I, on the other hand... I didn't really know. I couldn't imagine a better way I could've played this game, except perhaps being more cognizant of Coyle's people. But there seemed something so inevitable about my place in this room. Even if Coyle hadn't overheard me, losing Luisa would've been enough to push Ilara over the edge. She might've ordered me arrested if I'd sneezed wrong. And considering my people had been behind her death...

My pulse sped up as soldiers approached out the door. The locks turned and the door flew open, slamming against the wall and waking Elisha, who reached for her non-existent weapons.

Ilara walked into the room, wearing a black tunic, her hair pulled back into an uncharacteristic bun. "Take the girl."

"Brynna!" Elisha cried, fighting against the guards as they dragged her out. "I'll kill you all!"

"She's the spitting image of you," Ilara said, as Elisha's screams and cries echoed down the hall. "You could be sisters."

"She's a child," I said. "And had nothing to do with this. Let her live. Luisa would—"

"Don't you *dare* speak her name," she snarled, her face growing feral once again. "You didn't deserve to even know her."

I shook my head. "You won't believe me, but I had nothing to do with her death. And I'm sorry that..." I swallowed. "I mourn her, too."

I expected that to cause another reaction, but she calmed as she surveyed me. "Your soft words don't convince me. The arrow that took Luisa was destined for me, and it was shot by your people." She shook her head. "As if a simple arrow would be enough to fell me. This entire city would die for me." Her eyes softened. "I just wish it hadn't been Luisa."

Ilara's mood was swinging so wildly, I debated speaking at all. But Elisha needed me to keep trying on her behalf. "Then kill me. Torture me. Whatever you have to do to make yourself feel better. Just leave Elisha alone. She had nothing to do with Luisa's death."

"Guilt by association is still guilt."

"Mother above." I looked to the ceiling. "You have me. You can kill me. What more do you want?"

"For every Forcadelian to disappear into the abyss," she said. "Starting with that little army you've been gathering near the Ilarian river."

My heart dropped. "What did you do?"

"Nothing, yet," she said. "But I know you swapped Forcadelian soldiers for the workers. I know there's a growing number of Niemenian soldiers camping out on the dunes just beyond the city.

I'm sure your Katarine and Felix are behind some of this, but clearly, they've underestimated my intelligence." She sighed. "Yet again."

I licked my lips. "Why didn't you say anything?"

"Dear Brynna, it's all a game, isn't it?" She paced the room, walking to the window and putting her fingertips against the wood. "You had no chance of winning, but I had to make sure I knew the breadth of your forces. Why do you think I didn't send your dear friend Coyle to the riverbed? He would've noticed right away and opened his big mouth." She rolled her eyes. "But after today, if he survives, I'll send him to work alongside his fellow citizens. I'm sure you'll find that a fitting end for him."

"If he...survives?" I said. I thought I was the only one in danger of execution.

"Oh, by now, all your little minions have surely found out that you and that adorable little girl have been taken captive, and I can only imagine they'll be moving into the city for some half-hearted rescue attempt." She smiled, almost amused. "To make things easier, I've asked my soldiers to round up all the Forcadelians under the auspices of allowing the Forcadelians to," she paused, thinking, "what did I say? To witness the death of their beloved Veil Queen. I'm sure Katarine and Felix will absolutely jump at the chance to give me a taste of my own medicine."

Her confidence unsettled my stomach. "But...?"

"But, when I have you up on the gallows, and just before the moment where you're pushed to your death and they're planning to swoop in and rescue you..." She clapped her hands together and sighed. "I will light the first bag of varo under their feet."

"You...you can't," I said, slowly shaking my head. "The explosion won't just kill the Forcadelians, it'll kill your own people, too. Any soldier in the square...it could destroy your castle."

"Not the castle, no." She shook her head. "Varo is much less volatile than your precious ond. Where ond would kill fifty, varo might kill fifteen." She turned back to me and smiled. "And I'll just rebuild what I destroyed. I've done it before."

I barked an incredulous laugh. "You'd kill hundreds of people without a second thought? Even the innocent ones?"

"I'm not soft like you," she said. "I'll do what it takes to ensure absolute victory, even if it means hurting myself in the process." She looked down at her hands. "I have lost the one person I ever loved. The only thing I have left is my kingdom. And I'll be damned if I let anyone take that from me." She snapped her fingers. "We're ready. Take her."

Four soldiers swarmed in to hoist me to my feet. But I wasn't going to argue, nor was I going to fight. She'd outplayed us, perhaps for the last time. And there was nothing I could do to stop her.

The rumbling of voices in the town square filled my stomach with dread. For once, I wished that Felix and Katarine weren't so dutiful and loyal. If only they'd left me to die and gone on with their lives.

But no, there were my soldiers, mixed in the crowd. I couldn't mask my horror at what was about to befall them. Did I tell them to run? It might cause a panic, and Ilara would simply set off the bombs sooner.

They dragged me to the gallows, forcing me onto the stool that was the only thing separating me from certain death. The soldiers looped the rope around my neck, tightening it until it could go no further. My hands shook, but not at the prospect of death. Ilara was going to win, and I'd failed my people yet again.

"This is a good look for you, Brynn," Coyle said, walking up to play with the rope. "I told you one day Ilara would shut you up for good."

"I'll be sure to come back and watch you suffer when you find out how Ilara's gonna repay your loyalty," I said, glaring at him. "I told you once that you picked the wrong queen."

"As I see it, only one of you has a noose around her neck." He tapped my nose. "I think I've chosen well."

He disappeared from my line of sight and I gazed out at those gathered. Every available space had been filled with people, most of them dusty from the desert. Some of them were sobbing, and others, my soldiers, held steadfast. I had no doubts they had weapons hidden under their cloaks, but they'd be useless against the varo.

"Good morning, beautiful Forcadelians," Ilara said, a smile on her face. "You will witness not just the death of your princess, but the death of an era. Forcadel as we know it will perish as soon as the last breath leaves her lips. And we will begin again as New Severia. Together."

"Queen," I said, looking at my people.

"I'm sorry?" Ilara looked down at me.

"I said I'm a damned queen." I lifted my gaze to hers. "I may not be perfect, and I may have made some mistakes. But these people are mine, and I will fight for them with my dying breath. Unlike you, who would rather take the easy way out instead of facing us."

"Do tell?" Ilara said, leaning on the bannister. "Do you really think your army of a hundred could've been any match for mine?"

"It was an army of Veils," I said, looking out as I received nods of support. "And given the chance, we would've crushed you."

"You had your chance, and yet here you are," Ilara said, straightening. "Coyle? Do the honors."

He kicked the stool away and the air left my lungs. Black dots sparkled in my eyes, and I could've sworn I heard Nicolasa's voice in my ear. The sky above would be the last thing I saw, and my eyes watered at the beauty of it. It would be the last thing I'd see before—

An arrow sailed over my vision, then I was falling. I collapsed to my knees, gasping for air and coughing roughly, as I looked up.

Felix stood atop the building across the way, an empty crossbow in his hand.

Chapter Fifty-Seven

Felix

The crossbow string sang in my ear. My queen's gaze was fixed on me as she held her neck and gasped for breath. Beside her, Coyle's face was growing redder.

Directly across from me, standing on her balcony, was Ilara. "You're looking good, Felix," she called over the silent crowd below. "Last time I saw you, you were rotting in my dungeon. You seem to have regained your health."

I plucked another arrow from the quiver and nocked it, turning the point toward Ilara on the balcony. "Surrender now."

She laughed, but there was no humor in it. "Your people tried that yesterday. At least today you aren't hiding like cowards." She leaned onto the balcony, as if daring me to shoot. "One person with one arrow won't be enough to impress me."

"Then how about hundreds?"

Movement rippled across those gathered in the square as my soldiers revealed themselves and pointed their weapons at the Severian queen. Along the rooftops, Jax and his vigilantes appeared with crossbows. Ilara was surrounded.

But she still didn't look concerned.

"Felix!" Brynna cried. "Get out of here!"

"It will be a joy to watch you burn," Ilara said, leaning back to speak with the soldier behind her. He struck a flint then lifted the burning arrow, pointing it toward Brynna. One of the vigilantes fired a shot, but it struck the archer too late, and his flaming arrow sailed toward the gallows.

But it overshot, landing on the ground.

"You missed," I said.

"No, I didn't," Ilara said, but after a breath, she began to look concerned and whispered something to the man behind her.

"Were you looking for an explosion?" Jax called, his crossbow still aimed at her heart. "Kinda hard to set knockout powder on fire, you know."

Ilara's face grew red. "Knock... What are you blithering on about?"

"Did you really think we'd let you blow up your own people?" Jax said. "We swapped out your varo supplies with harmless knockout powder before your soldiers knew what was happening."

Ilara seemed to consider this new scenario, as her lip curled. "Then I suppose we'll have to kill you the old-fashioned way." She turned behind her and bellowed, "*Attack!*"

At once, twenty arrows sailed toward the balcony, but they missed Ilara, striking the soldiers behind her. Ilara made her way into the darkness beyond, but she wouldn't get far.

"Malka, Aithne," I called to the vigilante to my right. "Now!"

Aithne lit one of her arrows, and Malka tossed a small bag high into the air. The moment the flaming arrow hit the bag of varo, it created a bang so loud it made my ears ring. The Niemenians, waiting just beyond the border on the river, would begin their incursion into the city now.

Down below, an unarmed Brynna faced Coyle, who had drawn

his sword and was advancing on her. I gathered the edges of my new cloak, courtesy of Beata and her children, and floated down to the ground below. I managed to kick two Severians in the head along the way, helping a pair of soldiers who thanked me before rushing off to tackle someone else.

The distance was impossibly long, and time slowed down as Coyle lifted his sword. I forced my way through a pair of fighting soldiers and jumped up on the platform.

"*Coyle*!" I called, jumping onto the gallows with my sword drawn. "Step away from her."

But before I could do anything, Brynna—hands bound and neck bruising from the noose—dropped into a crouch, swung her leg around, and knocked Coyle onto his ass. With his sword pointed up, she swiped her bound hands to free herself. Then she reared back and kicked him in the stomach for good measure, sending him over the edge of the gallows.

"I got it, thanks," she said, flashing me a grin.

"I never doubted you," I replied weakly. "Are you all right?"

"Might sound like a frog for a while," she said, rubbing her neck. "How did you know about the varo?"

"Katarine thought Ilara would be unhinged after losing Luisa, and when the Severian soldiers didn't even check ours for weapons when they rounded them up, we knew something was up. Malka was watching the northern road and saw them bringing in varo along with more Forcadelians. We put two and two together."

"Finally, someone got the better of her," she said, looking up at the balcony. "We need to take her alive. This fighting won't end unless she tells them it must."

"You think she'll want to end it?"

"I'm going to try reason," she said, staring at me through her lashes. "I suppose I should thank you for saving me."

I touched her cheek. "I wanted to fight Coyle—"

Her eyes widened and she yanked me down just as an arrow

landed inches from where our heads had been. Coyle had reappeared and found himself another weapon. He tossed the bow away and climbed on top of the dais with his sword.

"Guess you'll get your wish," she said, kissing me on the cheek. "Give him hell!"

"Wait, where are you going?" I asked, reaching for the knives at my belt. "Take a weapon!"

"No." She cracked a grin as she turned back to me. "I want mine."

Before I could stop her, she flew off the dais and ran back toward the castle.

"Always just out of your reach, isn't she, old friend?"

I turned slowly, narrowing my eyes at my enemy. "I've been waiting for this for a while. You've got a lot to pay for."

"I'm sorry I had you tortured," he said with a roll of his eyes. "It brought me only a small amount of joy to watch you wallowing in your own filth."

"If you thought that was torture, you must think me soft," I said, swinging my sword in my hand.

Our blades clashed, the metal singing as it vibrated in my hand. Coyle's arms shook as I pushed at him; his time as Ilara's lapdog had made him weaker. I, on the other hand, had been drawn into daily bouts with my soldiers—and Jax had taught me a few things too.

"You brought poison into our kingdom," I said. "You killed our friend."

"*Your* friend," he said, walking toward me. "August couldn't care less about me."

"So you admit it."

"Yes, I killed him," Coyle said. "Slipped the poison into his dinner while Katarine and her lover spent the night together." He cracked a cruel smile. "I watched him die, too, so he'd know who did it. It was slow and painful, and I enjoyed every moment."

I snarled. "What did August ever do to you to earn such hatred? We cared about you—"

"That's a lie," he said. "I was the poor boy you pitied. And now, I'm the sword that's going to kill you."

"You can certainly try."

Our match continued, and Coyle seemed to have unlocked some well of strength. There were times when he'd left himself open, and I could've pulled my knife and stuck it in his gut. But I wanted to beat him as a soldier, not as a vigilante. And I wanted him to know it.

"You've lost your touch," I said, sweat dripped down his cheek.

Coyle pushed me away finally. "It doesn't matter if you beat me or not. Ilara will always win. You've barely got a hundred here."

I glanced around at the square and the clashing soldiers. "More are coming. Brynna's made a lot of friends, and Ilara a lot of enemies. You picked the wrong side." I smiled. "It will be so nice to know you're below my feet, rotting in the dungeons back in Forcadel. Maybe I'll visit you from time to time."

"I would rather die."

I smiled. "My queen wouldn't allow it."

"Your queen is a little bitch."

I advanced toward him, anger surging. "Say that again."

"Your queen is a—" He lost his words and footing as an explosion rocked the ground around us. It felt like an earthquake except…three more followed.

"What the…" I looked out at the ocean, my hopes daring to rise. *Could it be…?*

But in the moment of my distraction, Coyle's sword came for my neck. Luckily, another blade was faster.

"I don't think so, you damned traitor," Aline snarled, pushing him back into the waiting arms of two Kulkans. "I can't wait to see a noose around *your* neck for all the shit you've done."

My jaw hung as my heart sang. "You're…alive? You're here!"

"Yeah, sorry we're late," Aline said, watching Coyle struggle in the arms of the Kulkans. "Turns out there were a bunch of Forcadelian ships on the open water, so we kept having to turn into port to hide from them. Then we hit some weather, and it was just one thing after another..." She beamed. "We arrived last night and found our welcoming party. Kieran said to wait for your signal."

"I'm glad to see you," I said, watching as more Forcadelian soldiers ran into the fray. To the north, pale Niemenians were starting to fill in the town square. It seemed the Severians were finally outnumbered.

"Where's Brynna?" Aline asked.

"Taking care of business," I said. "As should we."

Another boom echoed from the bay beyond, followed by another. "If the Severians don't put their swords down now, they're fools."

"They're fighting for more than pride," Coyle said, still struggling. "This is their home. They love their queen. You'll have to kill all of them to get them to stop fighting."

"Let's hope that's not the case," I said, nodding to the Kulkans. "Take him back to your warship and leave him there. Our queen wants him alive so he can face justice back in Forcadel."

He fought harder, but the Kulkans were stronger, dragging him backward toward a clear alley.

"If I die today," Aline said, watching him go, "at least the Mother saw fit to grant my one wish."

"You aren't going to die today," I said with a nod. "Not when we finally have the upper hand."

Chapter Fifty-Eight

Katarine

"These Severians surely have heart," Luard said, watching the fighting through a telescope. We stood atop the dune separating the city from the riverbed construction. It was the best place to keep watch on the activity. Beside him, Ivan waited with a light and mirror that he was using to communicate directions to those on the ground.

"Tell the second brigade to do a sweep on the northeast. I see some Severians trying to flank us," Luard said, turning the telescope slightly to the east.

Ivan flashed the light toward the city and a moment later, we received confirmation our message had been received by Nils down in the city. He would pass the message to another Niemenian soldier closer to the action.

"The Kulkans are making excellent work of the docks," Luard said, sweeping his lens toward the bay. "Glad they finally felt like showing up."

"I'm sure they'll have an adequate explanation," I said. "Do you see Elisha yet?"

"Not yet," he said. "But don't worry, Felix will find her. You stay right here."

It was hard to do that, what with the flashes of steel glinting in the sunlight below. Jax had insisted that he'd secured her well enough, but clearly Elisha had learned a few things recently. My stomach hadn't settled since I'd come into the small room to bring her breakfast and found her gone.

"Ivan, tell the western guards to close the hole about..." He made a noise. "Ten o'clock from the castle. They'll notice it when they see it. I don't want any Severians escaping into the desert."

"You got it, boss," Ivan said, flashing the lights. The confirmation came swiftly.

"There they go," Luard said. "Good. Now—"

"Boss," Ivan said, squinting at the flashing lights in the distance. "Looks like they're moving on the castle."

"Excellent," Luard said, putting down the telescope. "Well, dear sister, we should have this wrapped up by lunch."

"May I see?" He handed me the telescope and I peered through it. I could see pieces of the square, enough to know there was intense fighting there, but not enough to see if Brynna or Felix had made it out. But if I knew my queen, she would've laughed at Felix's suggestion she leave the battle. As would the other girl I was currently searching for.

"Ivan, ask if anyone has eyes on Elisha yet." I handed the telescope back to my brother.

Ivan passed along the message and a few minutes later, the response came back.

"Elisha's still in the castle," Ivan said, looking up at me. "And she...has told the Niemenian guard to...pound sand?"

"Mother above," I snarled, marching over to the weapons laid out on the dock and picking up a small sword.

"Sister, you can't be serious," Luard said. "I'll tell the soldier to take her by force."

"I'm not wasting any of our resources on one wayward teenager," I said. "All I'm doing is standing here. I'll retrieve this little brat and march her back here myself."

"There's a battle going on down there," Luard said.

"I've been taught how to defend myself," I said, giving him a scathing look. "You two stay here and keep watch over the city."

I took the stairs two by two, ignoring the pain in my chest and my legs. My only option to cross the bay quickly would be one of the four rowboats perched on the beach. Water sloshed over my pants as I pushed the small vessel into the water, then climbed on and grabbed the oars. It had been years, but I got the rhythm down.

The waves in the bay were high from the cannon fire, which made it difficult to move quickly. But I kept at it, my shoulders aching with the effort.

"You little shit," I muttered to myself. "You'd better appreciate what I'm doing for you."

The sound of a steam engine drew my attention. Behind me, a small ship was speeding toward me. My heart skipped a beat—was it one of Ilara's? I was a fair swimmer if they tried to sink me, but I'd be in trouble if they started firing arrows.

I kept rowing, but it caught up with me in mere minutes. My pulse throbbed against my temples as I faced the man who stood on the bow of the ship, his foot perched on the edge as he grinned down at me like a cat that had caught the canary.

"Need a ride, m'lady?"

"Who are you?" I asked.

"I'm Kieran," he said. "And the flashing lights up there told me to come give you a lift to the fighting." He brandished a knife at his waist. "And to make sure you and a wayward vigilante end up back on this shore."

"How can I trust you?" I asked.

"Am I firing at you right now?"

"Well, no, but—"

"Then come on up," he said, lowering a rope ladder. "And welcome aboard."

In the interest of time, I maneuvered the boat over to him and climbed the ladder, his crew helping me up the rest of the way. They were a mixture of different nationalities, but all of them gave off an air of danger. When none of them drew their weapons, I exhaled a sigh of relief and followed their captain to the deck.

"Thank you," I said, coming to stand next to him. "What's your role in this?"

"I'd thought I might angle for pirate king," he said as the paddles behind us began to push us toward the smoldering city. "But I think that position's been filled." He cracked a smile. "Heh."

My cheeks reddened at his insinuation. "Felix might have a problem with you talking that way about his queen."

"Who do you think brought Felix to her door?" he asked. "But I daresay the problem will be when we try to extract Brynna from this fight. She won't go willingly."

"That's not the vigilante in question," I said with a knowing look. "There's a teenager who doesn't understand the meaning of keeping herself safe."

"Says the woman walking headfirst into an epic battle with a tiny sword," Kieran said with a shake of his head.

The ship sidled up to one of the few docks that hadn't yet been decimated by the Kulkan warships, and I jumped off just as soon as I could. The pirate called for me to wait, but I didn't have time. Elisha had been in the thick of things for a while, and she could be hurt—or worse.

The streets had begun to empty as civilians took cover inside buildings to keep from getting swept away in the fight. I passed my first pair of dead Severian soldiers as I ran into the square. There, the scent of blood was thick, and the fight was intense. Severian battled valiantly against Forcadelian and Niemenian—even Kulkans had joined the fray. Finding Elisha in this mess would take a miracle.

I kept to the edge of the square, ignoring the dead eyes of those who were slumped against the wall. Closer to the castle, the fighting had intensified, but I was able to squeeze through without being seen.

Inside, the front hall was littered with more bodies. My footsteps echoed in the strangely silent hall, as I forced myself to search every face for Elisha's. Some of the soldiers were the ones we'd brought from Niemen.

"You son of a bitch!"

Jax.

I ran toward the cry and found Jax battling three Severian fighters by himself. I gripped my sword and rushed forward, but he tossed a bag into the air and shot a crossbow arrow at it. The soldiers fell back and began to scream.

"Back up," Jax growled at me. "Unless you got tinneum."

"Where's Elisha?" I asked.

"She ain't with you?"

"She ran away last night," I said. "Your locks didn't work."

"Little shit." Jax shook his head with a snarl. "I ain't got time to worry about her right now."

"I'll find her," I said, holding my breath as I ran by him.

"And tell her I'm gonna beat her ass when I see her next," Jax cried before another pair of Severian soldiers came for him.

I ran to a large room at the end of the hall. A table had been set with food, but the meal had been stomped into oblivion. Inside, I found Felix and Aline fighting against a group of soldiers.

"Kat!" Felix cried as he pushed against a blade coming dangerously near to his face. "Next room!"

I nodded, rushing away so I wouldn't distract him further.

In the adjacent room, a receiving hall, there was even more fighting, but in the center, a small figure was holding her own against a Severian twice her size. She looked exhausted, her cheek was bloody, and perhaps only her stubbornness kept her upright. Her opponent knocked her sword and she lost her grip on it. With a shove, he pushed her to the ground and raised his blade.

I waited for her to react, but she just stared at the sword, ready for the final blow. I pulled my knife from my belt and flung it at him, landing it squarely in his chest.

The Severian gasped for air before falling forward in a heap on the ground. Elisha stared open-mouthed as he fell, then her gaze landed on me.

"W-what are you doing here?"

"Saving you, apparently," I said, walking forward. "What in the *Mother's* name are you thinking, running away like that? You could've been killed just now, and it's a damned good thing I—"

She jumped to her feet and ran over to me, slamming into my midsection and burying her face in my chest.

"I'm so sorry," she whispered.

"O-oh." Shocked, I put my hand to her head and stroked her sweaty scalp. "This is—"

"I didn't mean to be rude and run away and treat you guys so bad," she said, looking up with tears in her eyes. "You been nothing but nice and you gave me a home and..." She swallowed. "I told the Mother that if I ever got to see you again, I'd tell you that."

My anger softened. "I'm just glad you're safe, Elisha. You have no idea how much I worried about you." Outside the room, someone shrieked in pain, reminding me where we were. "Now, we need to get you out of here. You've done more than enough."

Joella came running into the room, carrying a few bags on her shoulder. "Good, you're still alive. The pirate Kieran just dropped this stuff off for us to spread around town. Compliments of your wife, Katarine."

I could've cursed her and the children. "What do you want us to do with it?"

She tossed two crossbows and a quiver full of arrows she'd been carrying at our feet. "Elisha knows what to do. And hurry—the fighting's getting bad out there."

"Absolutely not," I said to her retreating back, but Elisha was already shouldering the bags.

"It's not dangerous," she said, offering a half-smile. "Just gotta put the city to sleep."

I licked my lips. "Elisha, it's time to get out of here."

"If we don't do this, more people will die," she said. "Brynna wants us to do this." She half-smiled. "Us. You and me. Can you walk on a roof? It's real easy."

"If I can carry a book on my head, I'm sure I can keep my balance," I said, taking the crossbow. "And I'm an excellent shot."

"Prove it." She ran toward the door, but stopped in the doorway. "C'mon, Mom!"

She flashed me a grin as the air left my chest in surprise. Then, taking advantage of my stupor, she dashed out the door.

I shook myself and followed her, intent on keeping the little brat I loved with all my heart safe. And if that made me her mother, then so be it.

Chapter Fifty-Nine

It was selfish, perhaps, but I knew where this battle was going to end, and I wanted my own weapons to fight it. The castle had nearly been overtaken, with soldiers fighting guards. More than a few of them were screaming in terror, so I could only assume hyblatha was being used unceremoniously. I didn't have any tinneum left, so I'd just have to avoid it.

I skidded into the training room, running toward the trunk and avoiding the skirmishes. I kicked open the top and found my beauties, sharpened and oiled. I quickly hung them around my waist, taking a moment to thank Ilara for being so petty.

There was movement behind me, and I drew my weapon just as the blade came down. It was a Severian soldier.

"You...bitch..." He spat at me. "All we wanted was peace."

"And if your queen will quit ruining everything, you can have it," I said, pushing his blade away. With a hard punch to the jaw, he fell down in a heap.

Ilara had been on the balcony on the top floor of the castle, and based on the fighting below, she was probably still there. There would be no escape for her, but I doubted she wanted to anyway. She would see this through to the very end.

I came to the top floor and ran into a wall of Severian guards. Ten of them, to be exact.

"Perfect," I said with a look to the ceiling.

The hall was narrow, making it difficult for more than two of them to attack me at once. I needed to keep them in front; if they surrounded me, they'd be able to subdue me easily. I had no tricks up my sleeve, just fury and skill.

"Well, let's do this."

The first two came for me. I bent backward, dodging their blades and slamming my hands into their wrists to make them drop their weapons, then stood upright. One got a knee to the stomach, the other an elbow to the cheek. Down they went.

The second two had smaller blades, and I parried one while sticking my knife into the other's shoulder. The first got a fist to the back of the head.

The third two were much larger, but they left a hole between them, allowing me to slip past them and slice my knife along the backs of their legs. The fourth two came right after, and I swiped with my knives, missing one but not the other. The one I'd missed joined up with the other two and ran for me, swords pointed for my neck. I dodged one, two blades, but the third nicked my neck. I pushed it away, shooting my foot out to connect with whatever stomach I could find then my elbow went to whomever was behind me. One soldier remained, and I spun to touch the edge of my knife to his neck.

"Yield," I breathed.

"Never."

"Fine." I kneed him in the stomach, then clocked him in the jaw. He fell motionless with the rest of his countrymen.

I looked behind me at the trail of Severian soldiers and nodded. "I guess I can fight off ten soldiers at once."

I heard Ilara before I saw her. She was in a large room, standing over a table and barking orders at a pair of hapless Severian soldiers. I'd never been more certain that Ilara had overly centralized her military leadership. Clearly, she'd never learned the valuable lesson of delegation.

"Do I have to do *everything?*" she hissed. "We have five ships out in the bay that are filled with artillery. Why hasn't the order been given to *fire back on those sons of bitches?*"

"We have given it, but the ships are unresponsive, my queen."

"Yeah, that's because I commandeered them," I said, leaning on the doorframe. "Sorry about that. Needed a place to stash the population you ripped from their homes."

Ilara and the others in the room swiveled toward me, the three guards pulling their blades.

I held up my hand. "I wouldn't. I just incapacitated ten of your friends outside. Might as well put down the blades and—"

They rushed for me anyway, and I took care of them swiftly, leaving me alone with Ilara. She was looking out the window, calm coming over her face as she watched the destruction of her city beyond.

"What a waste," she said, turning away from the window. "Are you here to fight me?"

"I'm here to ask you to surrender," I said. "My ships will keep firing on your city, hurting innocent people, until you do. One word from you and all this stops."

"Do you really think so?" she asked with a mirthless laugh. "Honestly, do you think my word and yours is enough to stop all the fighting? People want revenge, Brynna. Severians want revenge against the Forcadelians. Forcadelians want revenge against the

Severians. And around and around we go. It never ends."

"It ends because I say it does," I said. "The beauty of being a queen."

"I don't see a crown on your head."

"That's the thing about being a queen," I said. "You don't get power by wearing a crown. You get power because the people have given it to you." I nodded toward the open window. "And those people have chosen me to lead them to victory."

"You'll have to survive first," Ilara said, walking toward me and grabbing a sword from the desk. "And I promise that I've been holding back in our sparring sessions."

"Ah," I said with a small shrug. "So have I."

Her first strike was tentative, and I met it with perfect timing. The next strike was the same. She was feeling me out, trying to determine how much I'd been lying.

"I can't believe you condoned all this death," she said. "I can't believe you ordered Luisa's death."

"I didn't condone any of it," I replied, easily deflecting her. "My people made a strategic decision."

"Your people." She scoffed. "So you've delegated leadership to your underlings."

"Tell me," I asked over the clanging of metal, "who's leading *your* army while you fight me?"

Her eyes flashed and her next strike was quicker. The next was quicker still, until there was nothing but the sound of our blades clashing. She landed a blow I was only just able to block, crossing my knives in front of my face.

"You were bluffing," she said. "You weren't holding back at all. You're weak."

"Perhaps," I said, taking a large step to the left as someone whistled down below. "But the thing about delegation is that I don't have to do things alone anymore."

On cue, an explosion rocked the castle, taking out the wall

we'd just been standing near and half the floor. Ilara had to jump out of the way to avoid getting swept away in the collapse. Her nostrils flared as she stared out into the open city beyond.

In the distance, Elisha and someone who looked an awful lot like Katarine but with black hair (*really?*) rushed along the rooftops, arming crossbows with small bags and shooting them into the alleys below. My heart lightened at the sight of them and others doing the same. Soon the city would be blanketed, and the fighting would end.

"Who's firing on my city?" Ilara asked, her gaze on the smoldering remains of the docks.

"Kulkan warships," I said. "A few weeks late, but better late than never."

"K-Kulkan?" Her eyes widened and it was hard not to revel in *finally* getting one over on her.

"You didn't know?" I said, grinning. "See, Ariadna promised she'd help me but only if Neshua agreed to kick in some people. Neshua, on the other hand, wanted me to—"

"Take Neveri," she finished. "My, my, so much of your story I was unaware of."

"I would love to tell you every minute detail," I said, swinging my knives in my hand. "Just say the word and we can sit down and have a chat."

"I don't think so."

She turned and ran for the rubble on the edge of the building, climbing to the roof of the castle. Cursing, I sheathed my knives and ran after her. When I reached the top, I barely missed her blade coming down.

"Ilara, you can't win this," I said, pulling my knives again. "The best you can hope for is—"

She slashed and hacked and I rolled out of the way, landing in a crouch then standing. Her attack was fierce, as if the only victory she wanted today was over me. But her anger had made her sloppy, and when I saw an opening, I swept my foot under hers and sent her to her rear.

"Surrender," I said, putting my blade to her neck.

"Never." She knocked me backward with her foot, giving herself a chance to get to her feet. Back and forth we fought, moving precipitously close to the edge of the roof. But Ilara could see nothing except the two of us, and knew nothing except victory.

"There's no dishonor in admitting defeat," I tried again, but she simply slashed my cheek in response.

Another explosion rocked the castle, and we teetered. Ilara tilted backward, losing her balance and falling. I jumped for her, clamping down on her wrist and holding on for dear life. Her hand remained limp in mine, as she dangled over the ground.

"You're pathetic," she said calmly. "Always trying to play the hero."

"You don't have to die," I said, praying she would see reason.

"I refuse to go back to Severia. I refuse to go back to the life I once led."

"It doesn't have to be one or the other," I said. "We can find a way to keep Aunela and Forcadel open. We can work together instead of at odds. We can—"

Something metal flashed in her hand and before I could stop her, she flicked her blade against my arm. I cried out in pain and my hand opened.

Her hair haloed around her face, framing her peaceful expression as she closed her eyes in acceptance. Her lips moved—perhaps in prayer to the Mother—as she readied herself to meet the divine goddess.

I looked away just in time, but couldn't shut out the sound of her body hitting the ground. I exhaled a breath as my eyes watered from pain and from…well, sadness. Another senseless death.

"Brynna!"

Someone yanked me from the ground, pulling me upright so

quickly I saw spots. But Felix's brown eyes came into focus, and before I even knew what was happening, he'd pressed his lips to mine, crushing me to his body.

"I'm fine," I said, pushing him away slightly. "I'm fine." My wrist was bloody. I looked down at Ilara's body, whispering a small prayer for her soul. I didn't know what the Mother would do to her, but I prayed Ilara might find some peace.

"You tried to save her," Felix said. "It's all you could've done."

"I know," I said, leaning into his embrace. "I just don't know who's going to lead the Severians."

"You." He looked down at me. "You're their queen now."

"Are you two done cuddling up here?" Jax had appeared, carrying two large bags and two crossbows. "In case you didn't know, we have to subdue an *entire* city and we need some help doing it. Quit screwing around, grab some tinneum, and get your ass in gear."

"You heard the man," I said, coming to my feet and taking the crossbow. "Let's subdue a city."

Chapter Sixty

Our forces easily overwhelmed theirs, especially with the help of the Nestori powders. Between the knockout and hyblatha, we managed to keep casualties low. But there were still too many for my heart not to feel heavy with guilt.

Aithne was found in the square with an arrow through her chest, and Malka had died in the assault on the castle. Fifteen of Jax's vigilantes had died, all of them with multiple wounds. They'd fought well and to the bitter end, as had the Forcadelian soldiers that Katarine and Felix had led into the city, of which we'd lost thirty-two.

Luard reported twenty Niemenian casualties, but thankfully Katarine and Elisha had made it out all right. But the largest toll had been from innocents caught in the crossfire—both Forcadelian and Severian.

"That's a part of war," Luard said heavily. He and his sister had gathered in Ilara's former office to give me an update. "It was unavoidable."

"And the larger goal was achieved," Katarine added.

"And the prisoners?"

"Many of them laid down their weapons when they found out Ilara was dead," Luard said. "Those who didn't are locked up in the brig on our warships. Perhaps a hundred."

"We'll transport them back to Forcadel," I said. "But I want the rest of the ships focused on bringing Forcadelians back to the city."

"There are vastly more people than ships," Katarine said. "And it will take some time to go over the ocean."

"I know." I still hadn't figured out what to do with the river flowing from Niemen into Aunela. If we swung the gate back, sending water to Forcadel, Aunela would revert to the deserted town it had been before, and all the people living here would be in dire straits. But I also needed a water path back to Niemen, my strongest ally.

There was a knock at the door, and Felix came inside. He wore his Forcadelian uniform proudly now, and seemed glad to be in his familiar colors.

"I've implemented a curfew," he said. "And soldiers have their patrol routes within the city. If there's any unrest, we'll put a stop to it." He paused, then added, "Gently."

I snorted. "Thank you. I hope there won't be any. With the supplies coming in from Niemen, we should have enough to keep the Severians happy for a while."

"They won't remain that way," Luard said. "No matter how much you placate them, you are still the queen who took their kingdom from them. They'll always resent you."

"I know," I said. "But at least my own conscience will be clear."

"I...uh, also paid a visit to our favorite traitor," Felix said, a smile teasing at the corners of his mouth. "He looks so miserable in the bottom of the Niemenian ship behind thick bars. I told him it was a good look for him."

"Try not to gloat too much," I said with a shake of my head. "Has he begged for his life yet?"

"No, actually," Felix said. "The coward asked if we'd just go ahead and kill him."

I snorted. "I'm unsurprised. What did you tell him?"

"I told him you don't like killing," Felix said with an overly cheery grin. "He told me to, well…"

"I can fill in the blanks," I said with a laugh.

"We'll make sure to have a nice cell ready for him back in Forcadel," Felix said.

"And what of the other task I gave you?"

His eyes grew somber. "I'm not sure I agree with it, but we've gathered the Severian dead and put them in the town square. The Forcadelian and Niemenian dead have been placed on Kieran's boat, and we'll send them out to sea in the morning."

"I want to be on that ship," I said. "And I want everyone in attendance tonight."

When the sun began to set, I joined my Council and soldiers in the town square. It was filled with bodies covered with white sheets —every single Severian who'd lost their life in the battle. I walked along the line of bodies, my heart breaking at the sight of so many lives ended so abruptly. In nearby buildings, the shadows of living Severians looked down on me from above. For them, we would honor the valor of the soldiers who'd fought against us. As well as for the woman in the center of the square.

I pulled the sheet from Ilara's face, resting it on her chest. I'd told Felix to allow the Severians to prepare her body, and they'd adorned her with the same purple flowers she'd been wearing when she arrived here. Her skin had grown paler in death, and her lips blue, but she was beautiful and formidable.

"Rest in the Mother," I whispered.

After replacing the shroud, I lit the pyre. Behind me, Forcadelian soldiers did the same to the others, illuminating the square with a ghostly orange flame that reached toward the sky.

The sweet sound of music echoed from the edge of the square. A gathering of young Severians, wearing their school uniforms, were singing. I had no idea what it was, but it felt like a funeral song. A tear came to my eye as I listened to their young voices swell over the sound of the crackling fire.

"Brynna," Felix came up beside me, "we must tend to our own now."

I nodded, following him out of the Severian funeral with my head held high.

At first light the next day, I joined Felix, Luard, Katarine, and Jax onboard Kieran's ship and headed out into the ocean just beyond the bay. On the deck and in the belly of the ship, each of the soldiers we'd lost were wrapped in shrouds of their own. I made Felix and Luard tell me every name of every soldier we slipped into the water while Nils played a somber song on his lute.

"These fifteen are mine," Jax said, stepping forward. He reached into the slingbag at his back and pulled a mask that he placed gently on top of the wrapped body. To each of them, he whispered a prayer that was lost to the wind. And when the last fell into the water, he wiped away a tear and stood next to me.

"I'm tired of losing people," he said.

"Me too," I said, glancing out at the faces of those gathered. "But I'm grateful for those I have left."

Nils began to play a different song—the Niemenian royal anthem, if I were to guess. Asdis, Ivan, Hagan, and Luard escorted the Niemenian dead to the edge of the boat. With a prayer, they joined their Forcadelian brethren in the water.

We stood on the deck, listening to the sound of the water lapping against the hull between the song Nils strummed. But finally, I gave the order to return to port. We could mourn our dead no more; it was time to rule.

Immediately following the funerals, I installed a Forcadelian governor in Aunela, but I also gave him a council filled with both Severian and Forcadelian members and explicit instructions to listen to all five of them equally.

Next, I instituted a lottery system to divvy up who would get to go home first and saw the first group over the open ocean with the Kulkan warships. Lieutenant Kalila gave me her word she would safely deliver them to the port city before continuing back to Neveri.

"Please thank your prince for his help," I said, shaking her hand. "I hope that Kulka and Forcadel can rebuild their alliances."

"Let's also hope Neshua remains healthy," she said dryly.

"Your Majesty," Aline said, coming to stand next to us. She, too, was back in her Forcadelian uniform and seemed comfortable there. "I'll start the process of preparing the castle for you when I arrive."

"Thank you," I said. "But your first priority is to settle the Forcadelians peacefully." I shook her hand. "And thank you for everything you've done and will do. I'm lucky to have you in my army."

Kieran's ship would presumably get back to Forcadel long before the Kulkans. He, too, shook my hand when I climbed on board to say my goodbyes.

"Still too late for pirate king?" he asked with a charming smile.

"I believe so, yes," I said with a laugh. "But if you'll settle for friendship, I would be glad to have it."

"Can a queen be friends with a pirate?" he asked. "Seems like it would be against the rules."

"Good thing I get to make the rules now," I said with a smile. It faded slightly when I spotted Jax helping with the rigging. "Is he going with you?"

"He volunteered," Kieran said with a nod. "Seems like he's tired of being in charge. Offered himself as my second-in-command if I'd have him. I can't see much daylight between being a thief and a pirate anyway."

My heart sank but I nodded. "I'm sure you'll cause more than a little bit of trouble on your adventures."

"When those adventures send us into Forcadel," he said, taking my hand again, "I'll be sure to stop in and say hello." He kissed my knuckles. "Fare thee well, Queen Veil."

That afternoon, I boarded a Niemenian warship destined for Skorsa with Felix, Katarine, Luard, the Niemenian guards, Joella, and—

"Mother above, where's Elisha?" Katarine huffed.

"Right here!" She slid down a rope from the scaffolding above, landing on her feet in front of her mother.

Katarine pursed her lips and put her hands on her teenager's shoulders as they looked out onto the bay. "Beata's going to have words with you when we get back. Her last letter was…not very pleasant to read."

"I read what I could of it," Elisha said with a grimace.

"I'm sure your mom will put in a good word for you," Luard said, joining them on the railing. "Or perhaps the queen might."

I winked at Elisha, earning me a smile.

The journey back to Skorsa was slower, but much less terrifying than the journey to Aunela, as we were traveling against the current. But after a week had passed, the land had turned green and lush again, and the large gate keeping the water from going south became visible, along with the encampment.

As predicted, Beata was waiting on the dock, her hands balled into fists and her face red. But instead of berating them, she gathered Katarine and Elisha into her arms and held them there, sobbing openly in relief. My heart warmed at the sight of Elisha's contented smile, and of the grinning faces of all the other children who joined the group hug.

"Brings a tear to your eye," Felix said, walking me off the ship and into the city beyond where Joella was waiting for us.

"Your Majesty," she said, bowing. "We've been investigating your idea, and I think it'll work."

"What idea?" Felix asked.

"You'll see," I replied with a smile. "And what of Mark's former charges?"

"Many of them have agreed to lay down their weapons and retire," she said with a bit of a grimace. "They don't...well, they won't rise up against you, but they don't want to join your forces, either."

"That's fine," I said. "Let any go who want to. There's no need to keep them prisoner."

Felix nodded. "What about Captain Mark?"

"He won't pledge his allegiance to you," Joella said. "We've been trying to get him to for days, but he refuses. Even after hearing Ilara had died."

"Then let me talk with him," I said. "Perhaps I can make him see reason."

"Captain Mark," I said with a smile on my face. "You're looking well. Captivity suits you."

He made a dismissive noise and said nothing. He looked rather pitiful sitting there by himself, and I couldn't find it in me to hate him.

"Forcadel could use a captain such as yourself," I said. "I promise not to fire you this time."

"And yet, here you are, demonstrating ignorance," he said, looking up at me. "I served your enemy and you offer me a job."

"You did what you had to do in order to protect your soldiers," I said. "But we'll need help to put our country back together, so I can't be picky."

He sniffed and looked the other way. I waited for him to say something, but he remained silent. With a heavy heart, I knelt before him with a key, reaching for his hands. His eyebrow quirked when he looked down and when the shackles fell from his wrists.

"You can go," I said, rising. "But if I ever see you in Forcadel again, rest assured I won't be so merciful."

Later that afternoon, I—and the rest of those gathered in Skorsa—stood in front of Ilara's massive gate, which had already been decorated with small bags of varo. Luard and Ivan had inspected the gate and chosen the spots most apt to blow, and were excited to try this new exploding sand.

"In our tests, it appears to have the same effect as ond, but without the massive explosion," Luard said, rubbing his hands together. "The possibilities are limitless."

"Quit yammering and blow up the thing," Beata barked at him, her hand resting on Gerda's shoulders. "I want to go home."

"And you're sure there's enough water for Aunela and Forcadel?" I asked Joella.

She nodded. "It won't be as deep as it is now, but it should hold enough for ships to pass south and east. The longer it flows, the deeper it'll get, too."

"Good," I said, nodding to Elisha and Luard. "Will you do the honors?"

Elisha struck a match and lit an arrow Luard had nocked into a bow. Luard lifted his aim and fired, sending the arrow sailing toward the gate and landing exactly where it meant to.

The gate exploded in a fireball, smaller than Neveri's, but no less loud. Beata and Katarine cast Luard a dirty look as they checked the children, but all the Niemenian prince could do was laugh.

I reached for the coins at my neck, grateful they'd still remained with me throughout this journey. But my heart swelled as the rushing blue water overtook the remnants of the gate to flow southward once more.

"What now?" Felix asked.

"Now?" I smiled. "Now, we go home."

Chapter Sixty-One

Six Months Later

Putting Forcadel back together was a task so large I wasn't sure I could do it in my lifetime. People who'd lost their homes wanted them back, and people who'd taken them wanted compensation for it. Businesses needed start-up money to function again, and considering my treasury was nearly gone, I had very little to help them with.

But as these things do, eventually order came back to the world. Our newly negotiated agreements with Kulka and Niemen meant food was flowing freely into the trade capital once more, and thanks to the new trade route along the Ilarian river, there was now a market for varo. The Niemenians found it a more precise explosive ore for their mining purposes and paid a pretty penny for it. Extraction was dangerous, but the Severian engineers were hard at work coming up with new safety measures, with my blessing.

For now, Severia remained a part of Forcadel, but I didn't know how long that would last. We were slowly replenishing the money Ilara had spent by charging a half-silver tariff for every pound of gold made within Severian borders. One day, when Forcadel had been paid back, we might officially sever ties.

In the meantime—

"Brynna," Katarine said, walking into my office. "It's time."

I made a noise and scribbled my signature on the payment for the merchants. "I still think this is a waste of time—and money. Nobody needs this."

"We all need this," she said, leaning against the doorframe. "Now hurry up. I'm already going to have to scrub the ink off your hands as it is."

I put down my quill and sat back in my chair. "If you insist."

"I do."

Knowing she would drag me by my elbows if I resisted, I followed her out of my office, pursing my lips. She led me up the stairs to the royal suite then to my tower. I'd honestly become so used to the place that I couldn't imagine staying anywhere else, and I'd moved my official residence up there. The former royal suites would be used for something else—a decision I'd put off for as long as possible.

There, in the tower, Beata was waiting, an assortment of hair jewels by her side. The children were playing tag in the space, all of them wearing their best tunics. But with one word from their mother, they stopped their horseplay and straightened up.

"Good morning, Your Majesty," they chorused in unison.

"Has Felix been working on them?" I said, taking a seat on the pouf in front of the mirror.

"He's not the only one who knows how to bow," Beata said, brushing my hair. She'd taken to her life as a housewife and mother of seven with ease, but had agreed to style my hair today as a personal favor—and because I hadn't found another maid yet.

"Are you nervous?" she asked, deftly braiding my hair the way she used to do.

"Why would I be nervous? I've been doing the job for months

now."

She smiled, nodding to the open window. "There's quite the crowd out there."

The roar was deafening, even all the way up here. "Still, they're my people."

"You could be nervous that you'll trip and fall on your face."

"Thanks, Elisha," I said, glancing at the teenager. Unlike her brothers and sisters, she wore a white dress similar to the one I would be wearing. "I hope you don't trip and fall on your face. Figured out how to wear that dress yet?"

"I can't see why I have to wear one of these," she said, fussing with the hem. "I can bring you your crown wearing a tunic and pants."

"You most certainly cannot," Katarine said, looking around. "Where did you put the crown?"

"It's right over here."

"Don't you dare lose it."

"It's kinda hard to lose a big, honking thing."

"Don't be sassy to your mother," Beata snapped, nearly sticking me in the head with a pin. "Or else I'll throw out your tunics and make you wear dresses all day long."

"Don't tempt her, Elisha," I said, as Beata turned to apply rouge to my cheeks. "She'll do it."

After she finished my makeup, she and Katarine dressed me in a white number, a dress that had been made for me some time ago that I'd never gotten to wear. It had been adjusted to my royal "burn all the corsets" decree, but it still reminded me of that fateful day nearly two years before when I'd last worn it.

"Are we ready to go?" Katarine asked, looking at her pocket watch. "Elisha, do you—"

"Yes, *Mom*." She held up the crown that had been placed on a red pillow. "I got it."

Katarine and Beata beamed as they took us in, standing side by side, and it was hard not to grimace along with Elisha. But I simply cleared my throat and motioned to the time.

Katarine and Beata held my hands and the rest of the children carried the train of my immense dress as we carefully walked down the staircase to the bottom story. There, waiting in his finest dress uniform, was Felix.

He stepped forward, his eyes sparkling with joy. "You look beautiful."

"I look like I'm wasting money."

"Our little princess has grown up," Katarine said with a soft smile before looking behind me. "Elisha, you're going to drop that thing if you aren't careful."

"If I kiss you, will it mess up your makeup?" Felix asked, tilting his head down toward me.

"I don't think it's prudent for my general to kiss the would-be queen," I said. "And I think Beata might murder you if you smeared my rouge."

He lifted my hand and gently kissed my fingertips, reminding me of the previous night and why I'd gotten no work done. My cheeks reddened but I kept myself together, as there was an audience.

"We're ready to walk," Katarine said. "Felix, you stand with me."

As we walked into the main hall of the castle, headed toward the open doors, lining the hall were a fresh crop of Forcadelian cadets that Aline had been running ragged. Their youth made me excited for the future, and I couldn't help but feel like Jorad would approve.

The young soldiers pulled out their swords and pointed them to the sky as I walked through them. Aline was at the end, her gaze sharp on her soldiers. But as the three of us passed, she winked and gave me a small nod.

The Forcadelians crowded the square, but the soldiers at

attention—the ones who'd been by my side since Neveri—kept them at bay. There was a space every few soldiers to mark one we'd lost, and my gaze lingered on the gap at the front, where Jorad would've stood. Felix reached down to squeeze my hand as we passed.

The church had been decorated with flowers and ribbons, the doors flung wide open. The bell tower, too, no longer my secret hiding spot, was similarly adorned. A blue sky shone overhead, though only a hint of summer remained in the air.

Inside the church, Felix and Katarine fell out of step with me, but Elisha scampered in front, the crown steady on the pillow. She grinned at me, and I smiled back. As soon as the music began, she took her first steps out, and I followed.

I walked alone, accompanied by the chorus of young voices and music playing. Seated just to the right of the dais was the Niemenian delegation—Luard and their sister Erlina. Ariadna hadn't felt it right to make the trip, but she'd sent me a heartfelt letter extending her blessing for my rule. To the left of the dais were Ammon and his wife, who I'd had the pleasure of dining with the night before. She was as lovely as he was sour, and we agreed to remain in regular contact. The Kulkans had also come bearing a letter from Ammon's father, although it was much less heartfelt and much more concerned about the tariffs on Kulkan ships coming into the Forcadelian bay.

Filling the pews were business leaders, merchants, and everyday people who'd been selected from a lottery. I'd wanted the entire audience to be comprised of lottery winners, but my Council thought otherwise, considering the help certain people were giving to rebuild the city.

My gaze landed on a pair of familiar faces, and I smiled. Kieran hadn't come asking for his solid gold statue yet, and Jax hadn't come looking for his money. But I'd heard the two of them were causing trouble in the Kulkan waters, and I did my best to avoid crossing paths with them.

In front of me, Elisha waved at her fellow thief, causing the crown to bobble, and behind me, Katarine sucked in a breath. But I just snorted, especially as Elisha steadied herself and kept walking.

At the front of the church, standing on a dais, was Mother Fishen. Jax and the vigilantes had made sure she was safely ensconced in a small town to the north, and once the coast was clear, she'd returned to her ministry to cheers and cries of relief.

I walked the two stairs to the dais then knelt before her.

"Are you ready to be queen, Brynna?" she asked softly, so only I could hear. "Officially?"

And, swear to the Mother, I could honestly say that I was.

Acknowlegments

First and foremost, thank you to the reader, for going on this wild adventure to me. When we started, neither Brynna nor I imagined that we'd turn this supposed duology into a monster four-book series. Nearly half a million words has been written in pursuit of getting Brynna her throne back, and I'm so relieved to have finally put her back on top.

Thank you to Dani, my magnificent line editor, for always helping me make things better.

Thank you to my QA checker, Lisa, who always manages to find the small little details that I miss.

Thanks, as always, to my support network: Hadley, my folks, and my dogs, for reminding me when it's time to get up and go for a walk.

Special mention goes to the Northwest Florida National Novel Writing Month (also known as NWFLNaNo) for being there to sprint with me in the mornings as I pounded out thousands of words every day. Especially Amanda and Kaylyn, who are always there to listen to me whine, and Meghan, who sprinted with me nearly every day in November 2019. This book would not have been drafted on time without your support (nor edited, nor revised, nor…)

Also By the Author

THE SEOD CROÍ CHRONICLES

After her father's murder, princess Ayla is set to take the throne — but to succeed, she needs the magical stone her evil stepmother stole. Fortunately, wizard apprentice Cade and knight Ward are both eager to win Ayla's favor.

A Quest of Blood and Stone is the first book in the *Seod Croí* chronicles and is available now in eBook, paperback, and hardcover.

Lexie Carrigan Chronicles

Lexie Carrigan thought she was weird enough until her family drops a bomb on her—she's magical. Now the girl who's never made waves is blowing up her nightstand and no one seems to want to help her. That is, until a kind gentleman shows up with all the answers. But Lexie finds out being magical is the least weird thing about her.

Spells and Sorcery is the first book in the Lexie Carrigan Chronicles, and is available now in eBook, paperback, audiobook, and hardcover.

Also By the Author

THE MADION WAR TRILOGY

He's a prince, she's a pilot, they're at war. But when they are
marooned on a deserted island hundreds of miles from either
nation, they must set aside their differences and work together if
they want to survive.

The Madion War Trilogy is a fantasy romance available now in
eBook, Paperback, and Hardcover.

empath

Lauren Dailey is in break-up hell, but if you ask her she's doing
just great. She hears a mysterious voice promising an easy escape
from her problems and finds herself in a brand new world where
she has the power to feel what others are feeling. Just one problem
—there's a dragon in the mountains that happens to eat Empaths.
And it might be the source of the mysterious voice tempting her
deeper into her own darkness.

Empath is a stand-alone fantasy that is available now in eBook,
Paperback, and Hardcover.

About the Author

S. Usher Evans was born and raised in Pensacola, Florida. After a decade of fighting bureaucratic battles as an IT consultant in Washington, DC, she suffered a massive quarter-life-crisis. She decided fighting dragons was more fun than writing policy, so she moved back to Pensacola to write books full-time. She currently resides with her husband, daughter, and two dogs, Zoe and Mr. Biscuit, and frequently can be found plotting on the beach.

Visit S. Usher Evans online at:
http://www.susherevans.com/

Twitter: www.twitter.com/susherevans
Facebook: www.facebook.com/susherevans
Instagram: www.instagram.com/susherevans